DATE DUE

8/7	
10/19/07	
11-26-07	
2-11-08	
3-17-08	
24 Mar 08	
5-6-08	

GAYLORD   PRINTED IN U.S.A.

BODY OF LIES

ALSO BY DAVID IGNATIUS

Agents of Innocence

Siro

The Bank of Fear

A Firing Offense

The Sun King

BODY
OF LIES

A Novel

DAVID IGNATIUS

 W. W. NORTON & COMPANY   NEW YORK LONDON

For information about permission to reproduce selections from this book,
write to Permissions, W. W. Norton & Company, Inc., 500 Fifth Avenue,
New York, NY 10110

Manufacturing by The Haddon Craftsmen, Inc.
Book design by Lovedog Studio
Production manager: Anna Oler

Library of Congress Cataloging-in-Publication Data

Ignatius, David, 1950–
Body of lies : a novel / David Ignatius. — 1st ed.
p. cm.
ISBN-13: 978-0-393-06503-9 (hardcover)
ISBN-10: 0-393-06503-0 (hardcover)
1. Terrorists—Fiction. 2. Europe—Fiction. 3. Middle East—Fiction. I. Title.
PS3559.G54B63 2007
813æ.54—dc22   2006102362

W. W. Norton & Company, Inc.
500 Fifth Avenue, New York, N.Y. 10110
www.wwnorton.com

W. W. Norton & Company Ltd.
Castle House, 75/76 Wells Street, London W1T 3QT

1 2 3 4 5 6 7 8 9 0

FOR EVE

AUTHOR'S NOTE

THE WAR DESCRIBED IN these pages is all too real, but this book is a work of fiction. The characters, events and institutions are imaginary. I have given my Jordanian intelligence service the same name as the real one, and a bit of its panache, but the rest is invented. I am greatly indebted to friends from many countries, who share my fascination and despair about the Middle East and who, over many years, have tried to point me toward the truth. These brave people, who risk their lives to try to make things better in that part of the world, are the secret heroes of this book.

I owe special thanks to several people: to my friend of forty years, Jonathan Schiller, who generously offered me a desk at his law firm, Boies Schiller & Flexner, where I could hide out and chip away at this book over many months; to Eve Ignatius and Garrett Epps, who read early drafts of the manuscript; to my peerless literary agents, Raphael Sagayln, Bridget Wagner and Eben Gilfenbaum, who kept encouraging and pushing; to Bob Bookman at Creative Artists Agency, who offered wise advice about the book and characters; to my editor at Norton, Starling Lawrence, who teaches a master class in writing with his acidulous marginal notations; and finally to my friend and boss at the *Washington Post*, Donald Graham.

"To mystify and mislead the enemy has always been one of the cardinal principles of war. Consequently, *ruses de guerre* of one kind or another have played a part in almost every campaign ever since the episode of the Trojan horse, or perhaps even earlier. The game has been played for so long that it is not easy to think out new methods of disguising one's strengths or one's intentions. Moreover, meticulous care must be exercised in the planning and execution of the schemes. Otherwise, far from deceiving the enemy, they merely give the show away."

—*Lord Ismay, foreword to*
The Man Who Never Was, *1953*

BODY OF LIES

It took nearly a month to find the right body. Roger Ferris had very particular requirements: He wanted a man in his thirties, physically fit, preferably blond but certainly and recognizably Caucasian. He should have no obvious signs of disease or physical trauma. And no bullet wounds, either. That would make it too complicated later.

Ferris was on assignment in the Middle East most of the time, so it fell to his boss, Ed Hoffman, to manage the details. Hoffman didn't trust his colleagues to locate a body without thinking they had to notify a congressional committee or otherwise botching the job. But you could find someone in the military who was willing to do almost anything these days, so Hoffman contacted an ambitious colonel on the J-2 staff at Special Operations Command at MacDill Air Force Base in Florida who had been helpful on other matters. He explained that he needed a favor, and an odd one at that. He required a white male, approximately six feet tall, early middle age, muscular enough to be believable as a case officer, but not so muscle-bound that he looked like a trigger-puller. The ideal candidate would be uncircumcised. And he had to be dead.

The colonel found a body three weeks later in a morgue in south Florida. He had tapped a network of retired officers who were working private security and claimed they could get anything done. The dead man had drowned the previous day while windsurfing off the Gulf Coast near Naples. He was a lawyer on vacation from Chicago. He was physically fit, brown-haired, disease-free and in possession of a foreskin. His name was James Borden, and he was, or had been, thirty-six. The body was altogether suitable, except for one detail: it was due to be cremated at a funeral home in Highland Park, Illinois, in two days. That presented a challenge. Hoffman asked the colonel if he had ever staged a black-bag job, and the colonel said no, but he was game for anything. That was a sentiment Hoffman rarely heard at CIA.

They worked up the body snatcher's version of a two-card monte. One corpse went into the cargo hold of the airplane in Fort Myers, and another one came off at O'Hare. The coffin was the same, but the man inside was now a seventy-eight-year-old retired insurance executive who had died of a heart attack. The colonel sent an NCO to the funeral home in Highland Park to make sure nobody decided at the last minute on a public viewing. They had prepared a cover story in case something went wrong—about how the airline had made a terrible mistake and confused two coffins in transit, but now it was too late because the other body had been cremated in Milwaukee. But they never needed to use it.

James Borden's corpse wasn't perfect, but it was close enough. The upper body was muscular, although the tummy had begun to sag, and he had a bald spot at the crown of his head. It turned out that he had an undescended testicle. The more Hoffman thought about these imperfections, the more he liked them. They were the real, human details that would make the larger deception believable. Perfect artifice includes mistakes.

To this corpse, Hoffman now attached a legend. He became Harry Meeker, not James Borden. They rented Harry Meeker an apartment in Alexandria and got him a home phone and a cell phone. Using the picture from Borden's Illinois driver's license, they obtained a Commonwealth of Virginia license, and then a passport, and then a man in Support dummied up the right stamps and visas. For the passport photo, Hoffman's colleague Sami Azhar surfed the Web site of Borden's law firm and got a portrait of him that had been used in the firm's promotional mailings.

Harry Meeker's cover job would be with the U.S. Agency for International Development, so they got him a USAID identification card. They had business cards made up, too, with Meeker's private phone extension. It had the right prefix—712—but when you rang the number, the recording sounded hollow, not quite the voice of a real secretary but more like someone who was covering for Meeker. They gave Meeker a parking space beneath AID's headquarters in the Reagan Building on Pennsylvania Avenue, with a reminder card for his wallet in case he forgot the number of the space. This was the easy stuff; no more than the agency usually did in building integrated cover. Now they had to make Harry Meeker a real person.

Harry needed clothes. Hoffman was oblivious to fashion and wore whatever his wife picked out at Target, so he was the wrong person to go shopping. Azhar was dispatched to Nordstrom's; that seemed to have the right upwardly mobile, northern Virginia feel. Stylish, but also safe. The mental picture they had developed of Harry Meeker was of a rising CIA officer on the staff of the Counterterrorist Center at Headquarters, a midcareer guy trying to make his bones—a guy with smarts who had some Arabic and the savvy to handle a sensitive case. They didn't know yet exactly where the body would end up, but it would probably be somewhere along the northern frontier of Pakistan, where it could get cold. So Azhar bought a medium-weight blazer, a pair of pleated Dockers woolen slacks, a white shirt but no tie, a pair of rubber-soled shoes that would be suitable for trekking and city wear. He took the clothes to the cleaners several times until the sheen was gone, but the shoes were a problem. They looked too new, even when they had been deliberately scuffed. Shoes needed to feel as if real, sweaty feet had been in them. Azhar wore them for a week, with an extra pair of socks so that he wouldn't get a blister.

And what of the inner life of Harry Meeker? Ferris had already decreed that he should be divorced; that was the one biographical detail anyone would assume about a CIA officer—that he had dumped his first wife, and now he screwed around. To suggest the divorce, Azhar drafted a letter from a lawyer representing Meeker's imaginary ex-wife, "Amy," directing him to send his alimony payments to a new address and warning him not to contact Amy in person. Was Meeker a shit, or had his wife taken up with someone new? It worked either way.

Now Harry Meeker needed a girlfriend. She should be pretty; sexy, even. Everybody had seen James Bond movies, including jihadis, and people would just assume that a real American spy must be banging a hot chick. Hoffman wanted a picture of a blonde with big tits in a bikini, but Azhar said that would be too obvious, the Pamela Anderson thing. They should make her sexy, but someone who could work for the agency, too. Ferris had a clever stroke: The girlfriend should be African-American. That was just unlikely enough to be totally believable. Hoffman suggested his secretary—a cocoa-skinned beauty with a dazzling smile. He asked if she would mind posing for a picture in a low-cut blouse. Her name was Denise, which seemed about right, so when the picture was developed Hoffman asked her to write on the back, "I love you, baby. Denise," with a little heart.

Ferris wondered about a love letter, but decided that would seem phony. People didn't write love letters anymore; they sent e-mails. Harry Meeker wasn't going to be carrying a computer, but Azhar suggested text messages on Meeker's cell phone, and that seemed perfect. They sent two from "Denise's" phone. One just said, "sweet sugar." The other said, "baby come back. i miss u 2 much. xxoo. dee." Sexy, not slutty. Hoffman said Harry should have a condom in his wallet, to suggest that maybe he was getting a little on the side while he was away from home.

The cell phone was a challenge. Azhar programmed Denise's number and the headquarters number at USAID, and then added a number for an imaginary other girlfriend he called "Sheila," and one for an imaginary friend, "Rusty," whose number was actually Azhar's home phone. To throw in some raw meat, Azhar called the Meeker cell phone from several different extensions at CIA, with the recognizable 482 prefix. He put some other teasers into "Received Calls" and "Dialed Numbers"—a couple of restaurants in McLean near agency Headquarters, several Pentagon numbers, one from the U.S. Embassy in Islamabad, another from the U.S. Embassy in Tbilisi. Everyone's cell phone is a digital record of his life. You wouldn't have to spend much time with Harry Meeker's phone to suspect that this man was leading a secret existence.

They dressed the corpse one day in late fall in a cold room Hoffman had built specially for the purpose under the CIA's North Parking Lot. Harry's skin was yellowing ivory, the color of a fading neon light, ice-cold to the touch. The hair was a little shaggy, so they trimmed it almost to the scalp to give him a Bruce Willis look. Harry lay naked on the gurney, undescended testicle and all.

"Jesus, put some fucking clothes on this guy," said Hoffman. He suggested briefs, but Azhar cocked his head and said, "I think not," so they found a pair of well-washed boxers and pulled them up around his waist. They pondered for a minute whether Harry would wear an undershirt, and decided no, too prissy. Putting on the shirt and trousers was easy, but the shoes were difficult: The feet were rigid from death and the cold, and they didn't bend at the toes or ankles. Hoffman sent a secretary out to buy a portable hair dryer, which he used to warm the feet just enough to make them pliable.

Finally, they added the pocket litter—the little bits of paper in the pockets and the wallet that would make Harry Meeker convincing or give him away. They had a charge slip from Afghan Alley, a restaurant in McLean frequented by CIA officers on their lunch break, charged to Meeker's Visa card. Hoffman added a second charge from the agency's favorite expense account restaurant, Kinkead's Colvin Run Tavern in Tyson's Corner—nearly $200 for dinner for two. Maybe Harry was getting serious about Denise.

Ferris supplied the card of a jewelry store in Fairfax, with the hand-written notation, "2 carat—$5,000???" Harry was thinking about getting engaged, but worried about the money. Azhar suggested a receipt for dry cleaning at Park's Fabric Care in the McLean shopping center. People always forgot to pick up their laundry before going on a trip. And a receipt from the Exxon station on Route 123, just before the entrance to Headquarters. That was a nice touch. So was the coupon for a free car wash at a gas station in Alexandria, near Harry's apartment.

Hoffman wanted to give Harry an iPod, and they debated what sort of music their imaginary case officer would like. But then Azhar had a brainstorm—they shouldn't download music onto the iPod, but an Arabic language course. Whoever found the body would spend hours puzzling over the phrases—wondering if they were a secret code—and then realize it was just a language lab for spoken Arabic training. That was precisely what an ambitious, self-improving case officer would be carrying with him—so earnestly, annoyingly American. Hoffman had an old ticket stub from a Washington Redskins playoff game, and he put that in one of the jacket pockets, too.

They would add the finishing touches later: the documents Harry Meeker would be carrying to his contact in Al Qaeda; the photos and cables that would explode like virtual time bombs as they made their way up the network—the evidence that the enemy's cells had been turned and betrayed. What they were constructing with such care was a poison pill, one wrapped so believably and tantalizingly that the enemy would swallow it. The poison pill was Harry Meeker, and he could burst every node and capillary in the body of the enemy. But first, they had to swallow the lie.

1

FOUR DAYS AFTER THE car bomb exploded in Milan, Roger Ferris traveled to Berlin with the chief of Jordanian intelligence, Hani Salaam. The message traffic back at Amman station was a digital blizzard, with the seventh floor screaming for anything on the Milan bombers that the director could take to the president. But they were always screaming about something at Headquarters, and Ferris thought the trip with Hani was more important. In this instance, Ferris turned out to be right.

Ferris had heard stories about the prowess of the Jordanian intelligence service. CIA officers called them "the Hearts," partly because of their cryptonym, QM HEART, and partly because it fit their style of operations. But it wasn't until the Berlin trip that Ferris really saw the Hearts in action. The pitch wasn't anything very fancy. The setup had taken months of planning, but in the moment of time in which it played out, the operation was simplicity itself. It was a question that had only one answer. Ferris didn't give much thought then to the complexity that lay beyond his vision: the maze that was so perfectly constructed you didn't think to ask whether it was perhaps inside a larger maze; the exit path that was so brightly lit that you didn't think to wonder whether it was really an entrance to something else.

They made their way to an apartment building in the eastern suburbs of Berlin, a district that had been mauled by the Red Army in
1945 and never fully recovered. A pale October sun gave a faint
metallic wash to the clouds, and the cityscape was the color of dirt:
mud-brown plaster on the walls, oily puddles that filled the potholes
on the street; a rusted old Trabant parked along the curb. Down the
street, some Turkish boys were kicking a soccer ball, and there was
traffic noise from the Jakobstrasse a block away, but otherwise it was
quiet. Ahead was a grim block of flats built decades ago for workers
in the nearby factory; they were now urban ruins inhabited by immigrants and squatters and a few aging Germans who were too dazed
or demoralized to move. The smells coming from the few open windows weren't of cabbage or schnitzel but garlic and cheap olive oil.

Ferris was just under six feet, with bristly black hair and soft features. His mouth fell into an easy smile, and there was a sparkle in
his eyes that made him appear interested even when he wasn't. His
most obvious flaw was a limp, which was the result of an RPG that
had been fired at his car on a road north of Balad in Iraq six months
before. Ferris had been lucky; his leg had been raked with shrapnel,
but he had survived; the Iraqi agent driving the car had died. They
say that good intelligence officers are gray men, the people whose
faces you forget in a crowded room. By that measure, Ferris was in
the wrong profession. He was hungry and impatient, and looking for
something he didn't yet have.

Ferris followed behind Hani and his assistant, Marwan. They
stepped carefully around the trash overflowing the dumpster in the
alleyway and made their way toward the back door. The wall was
smeared with fat block letters of graffiti, written in a mix of German
and Turkish. The word next to the door looked like "Allah." Or
maybe it was "Abba," the Swedish rock group. Hani put his finger to
his lips and pointed to the windows on the third floor. Through the
stained brown curtains, you could see lights. The target was home,
but that was no surprise. Hani's men had been watching the place for
several months, and they didn't make mistakes.

• • •

HANI SALAAM was a sleek, elegantly dressed Jordanian. His hair was a lustrous black, too black for a man in his late fifties, but the mottled gray in his moustache gave his age away. He was the chief of the General Intelligence Department, as Jordan's intelligence service was known. He was a commanding, well-spoken man, and people usually addressed him by the Ottoman honorific "Hani Pasha," which they pronounced with a "B" sound so that it came out "Basha." Ferris had found him intimidating at first, but after a few weeks, he began to think of him as an Arab version of the lounge singer Dean Martin. Hani Salaam was cool, from the glistening polish of his shoes to the smoky lenses of his sunglasses. Like most successful men of the East, he had a reserved, almost diffident demeanor. His smooth manners could seem British at first, a remnant of the semester he had spent at Sandhurst long ago. But the bedrock of his character was the generous but secretive spirit of a Bedouin tribal leader. He was the sort of man who never told you everything he knew.

Hani had joked once, when he was giving Ferris his first tour of the GID in Amman, that Jordanians were so scared of him they referred to his headquarters as the Fingernail Factory. "You know, these people are very foolish," he had said with a dismissive wave of his hand. Of course he didn't allow his men to rip people's fingernails out. It didn't work; the prisoners said anything to make the pain stop. Hani didn't mind that people thought him cruel, but he hated the idea they would think him inefficient. Hani explained to Ferris at that first meeting that when he had a new Al Qaeda prisoner, he would keep the young man awake for a few days in the interrogation room the Jordanians called "the blue hotel," and then show him a picture of one of his parents or a sibling. Often that was enough. The family can do what a thousand blows from the prison guard cannot, Hani had confided. They undermine the will to die and reinforce the will to live.

People back at Langley always described Hani as a "pro." There was something condescending in that, like white people describing a well-spoken black man as "articulate." But the plaudits for Hani masked the fact that the agency had come to depend on him more than it should. As acting chief of station, Ferris was supposed to establish rapport with the head of the liaison service. So when Dean Martin himself had personally invited him two days earlier to join an operation in Germany, it was a big deal. The paper pushers in the Near East Division had objected that he should stay at his desk and answer cables about the Milan bombing. But Ed Hoffman, the division chief, had intervened. "They're idiots," he said of the subordinates who had tried to block Ferris's trip. He told Ferris to call him when the operation was over.

THE JORDANIAN eased open the back door and waved Ferris and Marwan forward. The passageway was dark; the walls smelled of mildew. Creeping on the toes of his Jermyn Street loafers, Hani ascended the concrete stairs. The only sound was the smoker's wheeze of his lungs. Marwan went next. He looked like a street tough who had been cleaned up for Ferris's benefit. He had a scar on his right cheek next to his eye, and his body was as lean and hard as a desert dog's. Ferris followed; the limp was almost imperceptible even though his leg still hurt.

Marwan was carrying an automatic pistol, its outlines visible under his jacket. As they climbed the stairs, he took the pistol out of its holster and cradled it in his hand. The three stayed close, moving in unison. Hani froze when he heard a door opening on the floor above. He motioned to Marwan, who nodded and steadied the gun against his leg. But it was just an old German woman heading out with her cart to go shopping. She passed the three men on the stairs without looking at them.

Hani continued up the stairs. All he had told Ferris back in Amman was that he had been preparing the operation for many months. "Come and watch me pull the trigger," he had said. Ferris didn't know if Hani and Marwan were actually going to shoot someone. That would be illegal, technically, but Headquarters wouldn't mind if he wrote the report the right way. They weren't so fussy about that kind of thing anymore. America was at war. In wartime, the rules are different. Or at least that was what Hoffman was always telling him.

The Jordanian motioned for them to stop when he reached the third floor. He took a cell phone from his pocket, put it to his ear and whispered something in Arabic. Then he nodded for them, and the three crept toward the door of the apartment marked "36." Hani knew that Mustafa Karami would be there that afternoon. Indeed, he knew nearly everything about him—his job, his habits, his school friends when he was a boy in Zarqa, his family back in Amman. He knew what mosque he prayed at in Berlin, what cell phone numbers he used, what *hawala* wired him funds from Dubai. Most of all, he knew when Mustafa Karami had gone to Afghanistan, when he had joined Al Qaeda, who trusted him in the organization and who communicated with him. Hani had gone to school on him, so to speak, and now it was graduation time.

Marwan raised his pistol as Hani approached the door. Ferris remained in the shadows a few yards back. He had his own pistol in a shoulder holster under his coat and now put his right hand on the pebbled metal butt. Upstairs, in another apartment, he heard the faint jangle of Arab music. Hani raised his hand to signal that he was ready. He knocked once loudly on the door, waited a moment and then rapped again.

The door opened a crack, and a voice grunted in German, *"Bitte?"* Karami had a chain on the door, but he peered warily through the opening. He tried to slam the door when he saw the strange faces, but Hani quickly wedged his foot in the way.

"Hello, Mustafa, my friend," said Hani in Arabic. "God is great. Peace be with you." Marwan poised his leg so that he could kick down the door if he had to.

"What do you want?" answered the voice inside the apartment. The chain was still bolted.

"I have someone who wants to talk to you," said Hani. "Take this phone, please. I promise you, it is only a phone. Don't be afraid." He handed the cell phone slowly through the crack in the door. Karami didn't touch it at first.

"Take the phone, my dear," said Hani softly.

"Why? Who is calling me?"

"Talk to your mother."

"What?"

"Talk to your mother. She is waiting on the telephone for you."

The young Arab put the phone to his ear. He listened to a voice he had not heard in three years. He had trouble understanding at first. She was telling him that she was so proud of him. She always knew that he would be a success, even when he was a boy in Zarqa. And now he was doing great things. He had sent her money, and a refrigerator, and now even a new television set. With the money, she would be able to find a new apartment, where she could sit in her chair and watch the sun set over the hills. She was so proud of him, now that he was a success. He was a great son, thanks be to God. He was a mother's dream. He was God's blessing. She was crying. When she said good-bye, Mustafa was crying, too. From the joy of hearing his mother, certainly, but also from the torment of knowing that he was caught.

"You are your mother's dream," said Hani.

"What have you done to her?" Mustafa brushed the tears from his eyes. "I did none of the things she said. You tricked her."

"Let me come in, so we can talk."

Mustafa waited, as if trying to imagine some means of escape, but already he was in Hani's power. He unbolted the chain and opened the door. The three men entered the room. It was eerily empty of furniture or decoration, with only a mattress against the wall and a prayer rug angled toward Mecca. Mustafa's gaunt body was slack and crumpled, like a discarded suit. "What do you want?" he asked. His hands were shaking.

"I have helped your mother," said Hani. He loomed over the younger man. He did not have to state the obvious corollary—that he could hurt her, just as he had helped her.

"You tricked her," repeated Mustafa. He trembled slightly as he said it.

"No, we have helped her. We have given her many gifts, and we have told her that these gifts come from her son, who she loves. This is a *hasanna* that we have done, a good deed." Hani let the words hang in the air.

"Is she in prison?" asked Mustafa. His hands were still shaking. Hani handed him a cigarette and lit it.

"Of course not. Did she sound like she was in prison? She is happy. And I would like her to remain so, all her days."

Ferris watched, wide-eyed, from the corner. He didn't move a muscle, for fear he would break Hani's rhythm. His employers had paid for this show, in a manner of speaking, but he was just a member of the audience.

The silence stretched for many seconds, as Mustafa contemplated his predicament. They had his mother. They had made him a hero. They could destroy him, and his mother, if they chose. These were facts.

"What do you want me to do?" Mustafa asked at last. Ferris strained to hear the Arabic, to make sure he caught every word. He had a feeling that he was watching the onetime performance of a masterpiece. Hani had not touched his target or threatened him openly, or even pitched him, really. That was the beauty of the operation. Hani had built a sluice down which his prey was being carried involuntarily, inexorably.

"We would like you to help us," Hani said. "And it is very simple, what you must do. We want you to continue your life, as before. We do not want you to be a traitor, or a bad Muslim, or to do anything that is *haram*. We only want you to be a friend. And a good son."

"You want me to be your agent."

"No, no. You misunderstand. We will talk about all this later. But first, I would like to give you a special phone, so that you can contact me." Hani handed him a small wireless phone. Mustafa stared at it warily, as if it were a grenade that would detonate.

"I will meet you tomorrow, in a safe place, so that we can talk," Hani continued. He passed him an index card, with an address in a Berlin suburb. "Please memorize that address, and then give me back the card."

Mustafa looked away, wanting somehow to escape the net that was closing around him. "What if I say no?" he asked. There was a tremor in his voice.

"Your mother would be unhappy. She is proud of you. You are God's blessing for an old woman. That is why I know you will not refuse."

The words were gentle, but the look in Hani's eyes was not. Mustafa could see there was no escape. He turned back to the index card and studied the address for ten seconds, then closed his eyes.

"Give me back the card, if you are ready," said Hani. The younger man scanned it one last time and returned it.

"Good boy." Hani gave him a smile of reassurance. "So it is agreed, we will meet at 114 Handelstrasse tomorrow at four. You should knock on the door of Room 507 and ask if Abdul-Aziz is there. I will answer by asking if you are Mohsen, and you will say yes. That is the recognition code. I will be Abdul-Aziz, and you will be Mohsen. If you cannot come tomorrow afternoon, go to the same address at ten the next morning. Use the same names. Do you understand?"

Mustafa nodded.

"If you try to trick us and run away, we will follow you. If you try to contact your friends, we will know. We are watching you day and night. If you do anything stupid, you will hurt yourself and those you love. Do not be stupid. Do you understand me?"

The young man gave a second nod of acceptance.

"Repeat the names, times and the address."

"Abdul-Aziz and Mohsen. Four tomorrow afternoon, or if I cannot come, then ten the day after. The address is 114 Handelstrasse, Room 507."

The Jordanian intelligence chief took Mustafa's hand and pulled him close. Mustafa obediently kissed the older man on both cheeks. "May God protect you," said Hani.

"Thanks be to God," said the younger man, so softly that you could barely hear him.

THAT NIGHT, at a quiet table in a nearly deserted restaurant off the Kurfurstendamm, Ferris asked Hani a question. Part of him didn't want to say a word, and just savor the last notes the maestro had played in the silence after the music stopped. But he had to ask.

"Is your guy going to help us with Milan?" That was the only thing the NE desk officers would care about.

"Well, I certainly hope so. And if not this Milan, then the next one, or the one after. This is a long war. There will be many attacks. We have a new piece of the thread in our hand now. We will follow it. And when we see where it leads, perhaps we will understand all the Milans. Don't you think so?"

Ferris nodded. That wasn't really an answer, at least not one the NE drones would understand. They would ask why Ferris had accompanied the Jordanian all the way to Berlin, if he hadn't learned anything. And it would be a reasonable question.

"Why did you invite me along, anyway?" ventured Ferris. "I was just baggage."

"Because I like you, Roger. You are smarter than the people Ed Hoffman usually sends to Amman. I wanted you to see how we operate so that you would not make mistakes like the others. I do not want you to be arrogant. That is the American disease, isn't it? I do not want you to die from it."

Hani was veiled in the filmy blue smoke of his cigarette. Ferris looked at him. The worm was turning. A month before the Milan bombing, there had been one in Rotterdam. They were using car bombs regularly in Europe now. These attacks should have made the members of the network easier to catch, but they had become more elusive. The enemy had changed its order of battle. There was a new intensity in its operational planning—the hand of someone new. Ferris was sure that Hani saw it—that was the thread, wasn't it? That was what had brought them to Berlin that day.

"Who are you going after?" asked Ferris quietly.

Hani smiled through the tendrils of smoke. "I cannot tell you, my dear."

But Ferris thought he knew. Hani was chasing the same man Ferris was—the man whose presence Ferris had first sensed months ago, in a safe house north of Balad, a few days before his left leg was ripped by shrapnel. When Ferris closed his eyes, he could see a flickering image in his retinal camera—of the man who was sending the bombers into the capitals of what people still wanted to believe was the civilized world. There wasn't a photo; there wasn't a location; there wasn't even any certainty he existed. There was only a name, and when Ferris's Iraqi agent had spoken it that day near Balad, his voice had been a furtive whisper. "Suleiman," the Iraq agent had said. He had almost swallowed the word, as if it would kill him if it became audible. Suleiman. This was the name of terror.

2

A MMAN SEEMED PRICKLY AND anxious when Ferris returned the next day, but most places had the jitters these days. America had kicked over a hornet's nest in Iraq, and they were buzzing into every souk and mosque in the Arab world—and soon, into every mall and shopping center in the West. The analysts back at Langley called this proliferation of Iraqi terrorism "bleed out." On the Royal Jordanian flight back from Berlin, Ferris overheard two well-dressed Arabs in the row ahead of him in Crown Class talking knowingly about the Milan bombing. The car bomb was just like the one in Rotterdam; no, it was bigger, and there were propane cylinders in the car to enhance the blast. It was the work of Al Qaeda; no, it was the Shiites, pretending to be Al Qaeda; no, it was a new group, more terrifying than any of the others. They had no certainty about anything, except that it was America's fault.

Even the flight attendant seemed skittish. She was dressed in a red skirt that hugged her ass, a fitted red jacket and a red pillbox hat, the kind you never saw anymore except on flight attendants. That was the endearing thing about Royal Jordanian: Like Jordan itself, it was caught in a time warp. But she hadn't responded when Ferris tried to chat her up, and she had looked away with a slight grimace when she served him his meal. Her manner said: This is your fault, you Americans.

Ferris could feel the hostile stares as he went through passport control in Amman. The flight from Tel Aviv arrived at the same time, and the Jordanians were glowering at anyone who looked Israeli or American. The Jews. The Crusaders. For the Arabs, they had become interchangeable. Ferris wanted to get to work, to do something useful that might keep all these angry people from wreaking even more havoc. It was late afternoon, and most people at the embassy would still be at work. He could call Hoffman, look at the message log, answer the cables that had come in, think about how he was going to answer when people asked him what he, Roger Ferris, was doing to stop the car bombers before they arrived in Peoria and Petaluma.

THE AIRPORT highway into Amman was lined with billboards that might trick you into thinking that the world was still on the upswing: advertisements for competing cell-phone networks, for beachfront real estate in Dubai, for Citibank and the Four Seasons Hotel and the whole cornucopia of services that the global market had arrayed across these dry hills in the Arabian desert. It was only when you saw the giant roadside posters of the young king—looking faintly comic in Arab tribal clothes he would never have worn in real life, or embracing his late father in photographs that had become national amulets to pretend the old man was still alive—it was only then that you realized how nervous everyone was. This was still the land of lies and secrets, where survival was the only true aim of politics.

Ferris liked Amman, for all that. Its chalky white buildings gave the city a monastic look, that dizzying, arid purity of the desert that, every millennium or so, drives people so crazy they invent religions. Even at high noon in midsummer, Amman felt like a bracing sauna, as opposed to the wilting steam bath Ferris remembered from Yemen, or the pitiless furnace of Balad. And it retained many of the quaint folk-ways of the Arab world; even here on the airport road, young boys at makeshift stands were hawking fruit and vegetables and dispensing fragrant, bitter Arab coffee in tiny cups. Herds of sheep wandered onto the highways, attended by shepherds in flowing cloaks, as if they had fallen out of a time capsule. However much it tried to look like the West, Jordan was still the East. Hidden away in its markets were spice merchants and fortune-tellers and arms dealers—a whole secret life that was wired into a different set of circuits from those of McWorld.

Living well might not be the best revenge, but it was the only one currently available for the Palestinians who were now a majority of the population. They came back from Doha and Riyadh with small fortunes, which they used to build huge villas in Amman where they could entertain each other, hatch business deals and show off their wives, Western-style. Cosmetic surgery had become a leading industry in the new Amman; a woman hadn't arrived until she'd had her nose fixed or her breasts done. It was like Los Angeles, without the ocean. Amman even had a magazine called *Living Well*, with ads that told young Arab women where to shop for bikinis and *Sex and the City* DVDs and retro furniture. The recent Iraqi refugees had added their own acrid flavor to the mix; they were bidding up local real estate and providing work for thousands of thugs to protect them from the other thugs.

The young king seemed to understand that cupidity was Jordan's national glue. Under his reign, the nation had graduated from the petty corruption of the old days to a baroque, Lebanese-style corruption—where even some of the army generals had their own bagmen. The leading operatives were so well known that their identities were an open secret, gossiped about around town but never published. Hypocrisy was mother's milk here.

And Jordan had Islam, the secret inspiration and torment of every Arab country. That was the Amman station's biggest concern, other than ministering to the young king. The Jordanians were Sunnis, and the state-run network of mosques here was as ossified as the Church of England. The big pink-and-white-striped Husseini Mosque in the old downtown was nearly empty on Fridays. Religious people went to little mosques in the slums and refugee camps outside of town—or to Zarqa, the big industrial city just north of Amman that was the prime recruiting ground for the underground. Sometimes it seemed the fundamentalist sheiks were the only people who told the truth in this society; they mocked the corruption and decadence of the new elite—voicing the anger everyone felt when they saw the Mercedes-Benzes and BMWs driving by, but could never express openly. The young king might be hosting the titans of the World Economic Forum down at the fancy resort hotels on the Dead Sea, but in the back alleys of Zarqa, they were selling carpets bearing the image of Osama bin Laden and listening to cassettes of his declaration of war on America.

Ferris had called it the "Pipeline" in a cable to Hoffman that he sent a few weeks after he arrived. There was a jihadist network that passed through Zarqa, carrying people in and out of Iraq, slipping them into the lymph nodes of the Arab world and then into the global bloodstream. Ferris was looking for a network that had a name—the name he had bought at such a high price in Iraq, and which he had been tracking since he arrived in Amman two months before. He knew the location of the safe house in Amman where his Iraqi agent had been recruited; he knew the names of a few people who traveled between Zarqa and Ramadi. Those shards of information had nearly cost him his life, but they were a starting point.

From his first day in Amman, Ferris had been brandishing these few facts as a chisel that might break into the underground cavern. He had established fixed surveillance at the safe house in Amman. The NSA was listening to all the phones and computer links of anyone who had ever been near the house. Overheard reconnaissance tracked cars that left the villa. Ferris didn't tell Hani who he was targeting, but he suspected he didn't have to. In Berlin, he had become certain that they were chasing the same man.

THE AMERICAN Embassy sat like a gaudy fortress in the neighborhood of Abdoun, outside the city center. It was a façade of white marble that opened in the middle to a crescent-shaped courtyard decorated in salmon-pink stone. It was pleasing to the eye, but forbidding. Jordanian armored personnel carriers were parked out front, manned by hawk-nosed members of the Jordanian special forces in their blue camouflage uniforms. It looked like the embassy of a nation under siege, which was about right. The embassy car took Ferris into the compound, and he made his way upstairs to the top floor and the secret precincts of the CIA station. Most people were still at their desks when he arrived. Perhaps they wanted to impress him, but to Ferris it was a sign they had nothing better to do than sit in the embassy.

Ferris closed his office door and called Hoffman on the secure phone. He'd sent a cable from Berlin, but he hadn't had a chance to talk directly to his division chief. He had learned over the past several years that it was a mistake to assume you knew what Hoffman wanted. Like the agency itself, he was a series of compartments. You could be in one box, thinking you understood the big picture, and then suddenly discover that what really interested Hoffman was in another compartment, which you might or might not have known about. Ferris had learned to call the watch officer when he wanted to reach his boss. The folks at NE Division often seemed to have trouble tracking him down—although it wasn't clear whether they were being deliberately unhelpful or really didn't know. The watch officer put Ferris through.

"I've been waiting," said Hoffman. "Where the hell have you been?"

"On a plane. Then in a car. But I'm here now." Ferris had expected that he would have to give Hoffman an oral summary of the Berlin operation, but from Hoffman's abrupt tone, that evidently wasn't necessary.

"What's Hani after? That's what I want to know. Is this Berlin thing going to get us inside the tent?"

"I'm not sure yet. Hani won't tell me much. You know him better than I do, but my sense is that he moves at his own speed. He doesn't like to be rushed."

"Hani has two speeds, slow and reverse. But that isn't going to work now. This slowly, slowly shit has got to stop. We have to move him into a different gear. The Milan bombing has everybody spooked. The president is screaming at the director, asking why we can't stop these guys, and the director is screaming at us. Or at me, to be more precise. We have to break this network. Now. You tell Hani that."

"He's not back yet. He's still in Berlin."

"Great! That means he's working his new boy without us. That's not going to fly. Who does he think is paying the bills?"

Ferris debated a moment, and then decided to share his suspicion with Hoffman. "I think he's after my guy. I can't be sure, but I think that's what his Berlin op is about."

"Suleiman?"

"Yes, sir. Otherwise, I can't figure why he would work so hard to set it up. Or why he would invite me along. It's got to be the Suleiman network he's trying to penetrate."

"That settles it," said Hoffman. "I'm coming out to see you. We've got to own this one. Otherwise the president is going to have my ass. And yours, too, not that anyone would care. I'll send you some goodies for Hani, to show we love him. Try to soften him up when he gets back. Big Daddy will be out soon to finish the job."

"Are you sure that makes sense?" Ferris had a sinking feeling, partly that he would be losing his handle on the Berlin operation and partly something else that he couldn't put in words, even to himself. That wasn't how things worked in this part of the world. You couldn't kick someone's ass and then assume they would cooperate. This wasn't the KGB. Arabs helped you because they trusted you. They would do everything for a friend and nothing for a stranger; and less than nothing for someone who treated them with disrespect. He was going to try to talk Hoffman out of the trip when he heard a click on the other end of the line and realized that his boss had hung up.

3

W HEN FERRIS HAD FIRST HEARD the name Suleiman, he was beginning what was supposed to be a one-year assignment at the CIA's base in Balad, Iraq. Hoffman had resisted giving him the Iraq job at first, wanting to keep Ferris as his executive officer, but Ferris had insisted. If anyone should go to Iraq, it should be him: He spoke the language and understood the culture. He had been tracking this target, one way or another, for a decade—ever since he had become interested in Islamic radicals while he was a student at Columbia.

"Iraq is fucked up," Hoffman had said.

"So what," Ferris had answered. "That's what makes it interesting."

Ferris wasn't interested in policy. That was for the State Department, or people on TV talk shows. He was the one person in America who didn't want to talk about what a disaster Iraq was. He wanted to be there. Working for Hoffman, he had helped devise the tradecraft that was keeping young officers alive. The Arab headdress and robes, the darkened moustache; the cheap shoes; the rickety cars with Islamic beads hanging from the mirrors, Arab music blaring from the stereo cassette player. For a certain kind of person, it was the only job that was interesting. Hoffman knew he couldn't stop his protégé, so he arranged an assignment that could actually make a difference.

"Your job is to feed the machine," Hoffman told Ferris before sending him off. Ferris hadn't understood what that meant until the day he arrived at the Balad air base about fifty miles north of Baghdad. The agency's small fleet of Predators was based there, and most members of the CIA base spent their days watching what they liked to call "Pred Porn." These were the real-time images from the cameras on board the three unmanned aerial vehicles that were cruising lazily over Iraq. Ferris got his introduction from the base chief. He escorted Ferris into the operations room and pointed to a giant screen that loomed over them.

"My star agents," said the base chief. Displayed in military block letters below the screen were three names: "CHILI," "SPECK" and "NITRATE." They sounded like the names of pets or cartoon characters, but these were the code designators of three Predators operating out of Balad. On a smaller screen were images from the three drones stationed in Afghanistan—"PACMAN," "SKYBIRD" and "ROULETTE." The pictures were riveting, even when you didn't know what you were looking at. Ferris gazed up at the Iraq screen and saw a dark car poking along a two-lane road and then slipping onto a side road heading toward the desert. The Predator puttered along behind it, a thousand feet above, silent and invisible. Ferris asked what they were looking at.

"Western Iraq, near the Syrian border," answered the base chief. "We think the car is picking up a high-value target." They stood together watching the car for perhaps ten minutes and then the picture went dark. The base chief spoke to one of the operators and then advised Ferris, "Dry hole." Meaning that the target, of whatever value, wasn't in the car after all. That was the moment Ferris began to understand the problem.

The base chief was summoned for a videoconference with Langley, and he left Ferris sitting in his chair in the command platform at the center of the ops room floor. There was a low buzz in room, with people peering at the banks of flat-screen monitors, doing the rote work of planning and targeting and assessing. The watch officer seated near Ferris was monitoring a half dozen separate online chat groups that carried the latest raw intelligence from all the birds and bugs around the world. It was the dull hum of intelligence work, until there was a sudden whirr of attention and everyone was looking at the Afghanistan screen.

"Check out PACMAN," murmured an Air Force NCO at the desk next to Ferris. That particular afternoon, PACMAN was lingering over Waziristan in northwestern Pakistan, looking for one of Al Qaeda's elusive chieftains. The drone was almost motionless, above a cave high in the trackless mountains—waiting for its prey to emerge, hovering, searching, lazily looping over the craggy slopes and the snowy summits. "I think something's moving in the cave!" said one of the watch officers, and nobody spoke in the big dark room.

The people controlling PACMAN were back at Langley, in a building in the parking lot. They were studying the sensors, waiting to launch a Hellfire missile if they saw a tall, gaunt man in the shadows of the cave. Ferris could see more movement in the shadows, and then something broke into the light, and Ferris thought: This is it.

But it turned out to be a yak that had broken out of the cave's deep shadows into sunlight. There were groans around the room. PACMAN had once again led them to a treasure trove of bats and vermin and animal dung. Still Ferris lingered, as PACMAN moved on toward another set of coordinates and the camera captured the slow efface-ment of the Hindu Kush, the ravines and escarpments and roaring rivers. He found himself transfixed by images that normally could be seen only by a hawk or a falcon. Here was the genius of American intelligence—that it could fly its mechanical bird of prey over the world's most hostile terrain. The folly was that most of the time it didn't know what it was looking for down below. A bird with per-fect eyesight and no brain.

Feed the machine. Now Ferris understood what Hoffman had been talking about when he made the assignment: Bring in real intel-ligence, so that the controllers will know where to send the drone; so they will know who is in the sedan meandering along the Syrian border, know which ramshackle bus is carrying the latest group of jihadis from the Damascus airport to the safe house in the Baghdad suburbs, know which battered GMC belongs to the operations planner. If Ferris could gather that information, then the Predator could watch each stop the target made, each accomplice who helped along the highway, every place they stopped to eat or sleep or take a shit. But someone had to feed the machine.

"You're perfect for the job, you poor bastard," Hoffman had said, and it was true. Ferris spoke Level Four Arabic; he had the dark hair and complexion that would allow him to pass as an Arab in his robes and kaffiyeh, and he had that essential hunger, which he thought he could satisfy by taking risks.

ON HIS way in, Ferris spent a week with the ops chief in Baghdad. He was a burly Irishman named Jack, but when he dyed his red hair and moustache and put on a loose galabia, he could pass for a Sunni sheik. Jack gave Ferris a tour of the agency's hideaways in the Green Zone: the body shop where they repainted cars overnight; the hundreds of dummy license plates; the back entrances the agency used to slip its operatives out of the zone and into real life; the dozens of beat-up agency cars parked on the other side in the Red Zone, each raunchier than the last; the locations of safe houses across central Iraq, where Ferris would be operating. They drank and joked, to keep away the fear.

"Don't get captured," Jack said on the last day, before Ferris went north. "That's the main rule here. If they capture you, they're going to kill you eventually, but first they'll make you spill your guts. So don't get captured. That's all. If you see a roadblock and you think they're going to try to stop you, start shooting, and keep shooting until you're out of there or you're dead."

"My Arabic is pretty good," said Ferris.

Jack shook his head. "I'll say it again. Don't get captured. You're not going to talk your way out of a fucking thing with these people. Shoot first. That's what they respect. Don't try to be smart. If you shoot enough of them, it won't matter whether your Arabic is good or bad."

ON THE DAY Ferris got lucky, he had been in Iraq for almost three months. He was scared almost every day he was there, and this one was no different. The base was mortared early in the morning while he was showering, and he had to scramble bare-assed from the latrine near his trailer, with a towel barely covering his privates, and duck under the concrete barrier that served as a shelter. Two mortar rounds landed, one of them a quarter mile away. They didn't bother to sound an all-clear anymore, because it was never all clear. Ferris went back and finished his shower, but he thought—wrongly, as it turned out—that starting the day this way was a bad omen.

He was heading back that morning into what his colleagues called "the shit," which meant anything outside the walls of the compound. His practice was to spend a week outside, then a week back in. Hoffman hadn't liked that—the most dangerous part of the job was transiting back and forth—and he wanted Ferris to meet his agents inside the perimeter. The NE Division chief was genuinely afraid that he might lose Ferris in Iraq, a fight he wasn't sure was worth it. But Ferris knew that caution was useless. Better not to have any agents than to rely on ones who made their way back and forth to an American compound. That was the point about Iraq: There was no way to be half in.

Ferris put on his sweat-stained robe and his checkered kaffiyeh. He had grown the required moustache in Iraq and a stubbly beard, never quite shaven or unshaven. With his coloring, he could easily pass for an Arab. Not an Iraqi, perhaps, but an Egyptian, which was his cover identity. He had in fact first learned his Arabic in Cairo, during a semester abroad when he was at Columbia, and he still spoke with the soft "G" of the Egyptian dialect. Ferris wondered what his wife Gretchen would say if she could see him. She always imagined his spy life as a version of James Bond, with nice suits and martinis. If she saw him now, she would tell him to go change. Gretchen liked everything about Ferris except his real life.

Ferris left the compound with the other Arab workers when the night shift ended and the day shift came on base. He knew they wouldn't talk to him; Iraqis who worked at American bases didn't talk to anyone. They were risking their lives for the extra money they could bring home. If the insurgents found them, they were dead men. So they scattered as soon as they were outside the gate, and Ferris scattered with them.

An Iraqi car was waiting for him on the outside. It was a beat-up Mercedes from the mid-1970s, purchased back when Iraq was flush with money. The driver was one of Ferris's agents—a young man named Bassam Samarai. He had been living in the Iraqi community in Dearborn, Michigan, and had been dumb enough to believe the American rhetoric back in 2003 and head for Iraq with a fat stipend from the CIA. His family was from this area; they had protected him, and pretended to believe his story about coming home to start a new business importing satellite dishes and decoders. One day he would end up with a bullet in his head, Ferris knew. But there was nothing he could do about it.

"Ya Bassam! Marhaba," Ferris greeted his agent. He slumped into the front seat and rolled up the window. The Iraqi was wearing a cheap leather jacket, and he had his hair slicked back with gel.

"How are you, man?" said Bassam. "Are you cool?" He liked American street talk, even though Ferris told him it was insecure. It reminded him of home, in Dearborn. But it wasn't just that. Bassam had a twinkle in his eye today, as if he were dying to tell Ferris something.

"I'm okay," said Ferris. "It's good to be out of there. I get sick of Balad. Too many crazy Americans. I'm ready for some crazy Iraqis."

"Well, boss, I have someone very crazy for you today. This one you are not going to believe. Really, man. He's too much." Bassam was sounding like a DJ in his excitement.

"What have you got?" said Ferris.

"The real thing, man. An Al Qaeda guy, from up near Tikrit. I knew him when I was a kid, before I left. His name is Nizar. He wanted to come to America but he couldn't get the papers, so he worked in Saddam's Moukhabarat. He got all messed up in the head after liberation, you know, like a lot of those Tikritis, and he started working with Zarqawi. At least that's what he says. He's scared shit-less now, man."

Ferris's eyes were alight. He pulled the kaffiyeh a little tighter, so people in nearby cars couldn't see his face. This was what he had been waiting for these past three months, if it was true. "How did you find this guy, Bassam?"

"He found me, man. He's terrified the bad guys are going to kill him. He was supposed to do a martyrdom operation, but he got scared. He knows a lot of shit. He wants us to help him—you know, get him out of here."

"Oh, fuck." Ferris shook his head. "You didn't tell him you're working for Uncle Sugar, did you?"

"No way, man. I'm not dumb. No, he came to me just because I used to live in the States, that's all. He thinks I can fix shit for him. I told him I'd see what I could do. He's up at my uncle's house, between here and Tikrit. I told him we'd come see him today."

Ferris looked at his hip-hop Iraqi agent. "You are the real deal, Bassam. You know that? I'm proud of you."

THEY DROVE with the morning traffic up Highway 1, the main route north that followed the banks of the Tigris toward Tikrit. U.S. supply convoys rumbled past, and like all the Iraqis, Bassam slowed down to let the trigger-happy American soldiers pass. That would be the worst, thought Ferris, to get blown away by some reserve NCO from Nebraska who was riding shotgun for an armed convoy bringing steaks and soda pop to the troops up north. Bassam was playing Radio Sawa, an American station that mixed American and Arab music and was the one real propaganda success the United States had achieved. He was rapping along with an Eminem song when Ferris broke in.

"We have to be careful, Bassam. If this guy is as good as you say, they are going to kill him as soon as they find he's on the lam. You have to get real serious about tradecraft now, brother. You hear me?"

"Yes, boss. I'm cool."

"No, you are not cool. You're going to get us killed, along with your pal Nizar. So pay attention. We have to move around, starting tonight. I can't stay in the same place twice this week, and neither can you. If your man Nizar checks out, he's solid gold. We're not going to get him killed with sloppy shit. We don't get chances like this very often, and I'm not going to blow it. You hear me? Huh? You fucking hear me?"

"Yes, boss," Bassam said again. But Ferris knew that he understood.

BASSAM'S UNCLE lived down a long dirt road near Ad-Dawr, a few miles south of Tikrit. It had once been a farm; you could still see the irrigation equipment, but now the fields were a mess of tangled weeds and derelict equipment. Ferris told Bassam to park the car behind the main house so it couldn't be seen from the road. A smaller house stood under a eucalyptus tree about fifty yards from the main villa. Bassam said it was empty. Ferris told him to bring Nizar over to the smaller house, and not mention to his uncle or anyone else that Ferris was here. Bassam gave him a wink, trying to look cocky, but Ferris could tell that he was scared.

Ferris let himself in the little house. It stank of shit, animal or human he couldn't tell. It was a coarse fact of Iraqi life that people took a dump in almost any space that was unoccupied. He opened the windows to air the place out, set up the chairs so he could talk to Nizar without being seen. And then he sat and waited.

Bassam arrived ten minutes later with Nizar in tow, talking an

Arabic version of the singsong patois he adopted in English. Nizar was a short man, built like a fireplug, with a big moustache that drooped over his lips. Ferris didn't understand all the Iraqi slang, but he could tell that Nizar was nervous. There was a tremor in his voice, even talking to Bassam, and his eyes darted back and forth, scanning the horizon for the danger he knew was out there. When he entered the little house, he peered at Ferris, trying to make out his face in the shadows.

"This is my Egyptian friend," said Bassam, pointing to Ferris. "Maybe he can help you."

They exchanged Islamic pleasantries. Peace be with you; God grant you health. Bassam had brought a bottle of water with him from his uncle's house, and he poured it out ceremoniously into three dirty glasses. It took a while to get started, but it was always a mistake to rush anything in this part of the world.

"I can help you, my friend," said Ferris in his Egyptian-accented Arabic.

"Thanks God," said Nizar.

"But why do you need help? What are you afraid of?"

"I know too many things, sir. I have traveled with Abu Musab. I know his secrets. They trusted me. They were going to send me outside Iraq. They prepared me. But then a few days ago they said sorry, they needed me for a martyrdom operation in Baghdad. I think they did not trust me anymore. I don't know why. Rumors, maybe. They hear that I know Bassam, maybe. That was when I ran away. They have too many martyrs. I don't want to die. I want to go to America."

"I can help," repeated Ferris. "I know people who can get you to the United States. Money, a visa, a green card. Everything. But you know the Americans. They are greedy. You must give them something, or they will never help you. So what can you give them? You tell me, and then I will know if I can help you."

Nizar shook his head. "It is too dangerous," he said. "I will tell only the Americans. I cannot trust the Arabs. They will betray me."

Ferris thought a moment. Everything the man had said so far

sounded rational. And he was right to think that he could not trust Arabs. The pitch would have to come from an American. Ferris knew that revealing himself as an American this early was a violation of his ops plan, but he couldn't think of any other way to make it work. He leaned forward in his chair so that his face was in the full sunlight, and took off his kaffiyeh so that Nizar could see his features

"I am an American, Nizar. I work for the National Security Council," Ferris said in English, and then he repeated it in Arabic. "I can help you to get to America, but you must tell me what you know. Then we can make a good plan."

Nizar studied Ferris's face, trying to make up his mind. Then he did the one thing Ferris didn't expect. He fell to the floor and kissed Ferris's hand. There were tears in his eyes. That's how scared he was that Zarqawi's people were going to kill him.

"Tell me what you know," said Ferris, slowly and evenly. "Then I can help you. Tell me the thing that will make my big boss back in Washington, the president, most happy."

Nizar closed his eyes. He knew what it was. This was the only card he had to play. Ferris reached out his hand and touched the Iraqi man on the forehead, as if he were healing him. He'd never done that before with anyone in his life, but in the moment, it felt right.

"They wanted me to leave Iraq," said Nizar.

"Yes," said Ferris. "You told me that. Why did they want you to leave Iraq?"

"Because of my training, with the Moukhabarat. I know how to make bombs. I know how to run operations. I have all the training. They said they needed it, for the operations in Europe. The car bombs. That is their plan, for car bombs in Europe, just like Baghdad. But they do not have enough people. They needed me." He stopped, frightened to continue.

"Who needed you?" Ferris looked him in the eyes and then repeated it. "Who needed you, Nizar? Tell me, or I will leave now."

"The man who runs Al Qaeda's new network. The one who is

planning the bombings in Europe. The one who frightens the Americans the most. The people here are in touch with him. They wanted to send me to him."

"And who is that?"

Nizar fell silent again. He sat there, shaking his head—terrified and uncertain what to do.

Ferris sensed he might lose him if he didn't act quickly. He rose from his chair, as if ready to walk out. "Come on, Bassam," he said. "We're leaving."

Nizar said a word, but his voice was barely audible.

"Speak up," said Ferris.

"Suleiman," he whispered. "That is not his real name, but that is the name they give him. Suleiman the Magnificent. He is the planner."

Oh my God, thought Ferris. *This is it.* How are we going to keep this guy alive?

4

FERRIS CALLED ED HOFFMAN ON his satellite phone from the derelict house near the Tigris. It would be four in the morning back in Washington, but that didn't matter. Hoffman would be furious if he hadn't been awakened, when he found out what Ferris had. He routed the call through the NE Division ops center. The watch officer sounded peeved, as if he had been interrupted from the solitaire game on his computer. But he put the call through to Hoffman at home.

"What the fuck?" were Hoffman's first words. And then: "What time is it?"

"Sorry to wake you up," said Ferris. "But I think we may have found the real thing out here in Dodge City."

"Oh yeah?" said Hoffman, now fully awake. "What have you got?"

"I am debriefing an Iraqi walk-in. He's a Sunni from Samara who used to work for Saddam's intelligence service. He's part of Al Qaeda in Iraq now, or at least he was until a few days ago when they told him they needed him for car-bomb duty. Now he's on the run. He just told me something pretty interesting."

"Yeah? Okay. I'm waiting."

"He said that Al Queda was going to send him outside, to connect up with the man planning their operations in Europe. They're building a network to do car bombings in Europe. At least he says they are. He had a name for the planner. He called him Suleiman."

"You're right. That is pretty damn interesting." Hoffman let out a low growl of excitement. "What else did he say?"

"Shit. Isn't that enough? I want to get him out, Ed. We need to debrief him carefully."

"Sorry, I didn't catch that."

"I said I want to get him out. If he stays here, he's a dead man. I told him I would get him out if he gave me the goodies."

"No fucking way. This guy is gold. Milk him now. But you've got to leave him in place for a while so we can see his network. Put one of the Preds on him. We can watch everyone he talks to and then nail them."

"But they'll kill him. I told you that. He's on the run."

"Tough shit. If they kill him, then we can at least see who's pulling the trigger."

Ferris looked through the window at Nizar, who was standing outside in the sun. There was a hint of a smile on his face. He thought he was going to be delivered into the protection of the Americans.

"I don't feel good about this, Ed. I feel we're doing this thing wrong. It's my case. Let me develop it."

"Sorry. No can do. Debrief him now. Get everything you can, in case he does get nailed. But cut him loose today when you're done. We'll watch him for a while and then bring him in. I hate to be a prick, but that's the way we're going to run it."

"Christ." Ferris put the phone aside for a moment. There was no point arguing the case, not with Hoffman. "Can I promise him money and resettlement, at least?"

"Sure. No problem. Whatever you like." Hoffman didn't even ask how much Ferris would be offering. He knew he would never have to pay it off.

• • •

FERRIS SAT Nizar down in the house again and said he had a few more questions. The Iraqi was in a good mood now, relaxing, decompressing, imagining that his part of the nightmare would be over soon. Ferris had a little digital tape recorder going now, to capture the debrief. He asked Nizar for the names of his contacts in Al Qaeda in Iraq. He asked for the locations where he met with the members of his cell. He asked how he had been recruited, and the Iraqi explained that it had been in Amman—at a safe house near Jebel Al-Akhthar, on the southern edge of the city. He recited the address and Ferris wrote it down carefully in his notebook. If they could monitor the Amman safe house, maybe they could take down an entire network. Ferris asked for the SIM card of his cell phone, and Nizar handed that over, too.

The little Iraqi talked on for several hours. Ferris sent Bassam out to get some food, and he came back with some kebabs and Heineken beer brewed in Egypt, which Nizar devoured. It was midafternoon before they finished. Ferris was getting nervous that they had been at Bassam's uncle's house for so long. People in the neighborhood would know and tell others. When night fell, it would be dangerous for them here.

When Ferris had finished all of his questions, Nizar looked at him attentively.

"We are ready to go to Green Zone now, sir?" he asked.

"Not yet, Nizar." Immediately the Iraqi's hopeful smile dissolved. "It will take my friends a little while to arrange your departure from Iraq. In the meantime, you should go about your business. Be careful. Don't panic. Everything will be okay."

"But sir, they will kill me. I tell you that when we first talk."

"They won't kill you. We will be watching you and protecting you. We have big eyes and ears."

Nizar was shaking his head. "Sir, I am sorry, but you cannot protect anyone. Not even yourselves. How you protect me?"

"We will take care of you. Your friend Bassam will be close. But he cannot stay with you. Neither can I. Until we come to take you out, you have to take care of yourself."

The Iraqi made a low moan. He had given everything and gotten nothing. Ferris couldn't leave him like that. In his depression, he would wander into a trap and be dead before sundown.

"I am going to open a bank account for you now in America. Is that all right?

Nizar's eyes brightened slightly. "Yes, sir. How much please?"

"At first, a hundred thousand dollars. Plus we will resettle you and your wife and kids in America."

Now the Iraqi was really perking up. "One million, please. I do not have a wife."

Jesus, thought Ferris. A moment ago he was a goner, and now he's dickering over money. "We'll see about the million dollars. Right now I want to talk about how you're going to stay safe." He called over Bassam, and they talked through the security procedures Nizar would adopt over the next week. Ferris gave him a new cell phone to use in emergencies. The Iraqi took it greedily, as if it were a first down payment on the million dollars.

"I want to live in Los Angeles," he said. "I want a house on the beach. Just like on *Baywatch*."

"Sure," said Ferris. "No problem." He shook hands with the Iraqi, who slipped out the door and trundled across the dusty yard to his black BMW, thinking about girls in bikinis. He waved goodbye in their direction and drove off. That was the last time Ferris ever saw him.

BASSAM PICKED up word through one of his subagents that Nizar had been killed the following morning. Nizar had been taking his breakfast in a café off the main road in Samara, a place where people knew him. That was stupid—the opposite of what Ferris had told him to do. When he left the café, two cars had followed him. The only good news was that he hadn't been captured. He had his own gun and managed to fire enough shots at his pursuers that they had to kill him, which meant they hadn't been able to question him.

Ferris waited until late in the evening to call Hoffman. He hid out in a villa behind the police station. It wasn't just that he was angry, it was that he knew what Hoffman would say and he didn't want to hear it. When it was nearly midnight Iraq time, he picked up the satellite phone and dialed Langley. The watch officer put him through to Hoffman.

"He's dead," said Ferris. "The kid I recruited. They nailed him this morning."

"Already? Shit. That didn't take long. Did they interrogate him before they killed him?"

"Not from what we heard. But we weren't there when he took the bullet. I have it secondhand, from one of my guys."

"Fuck." Hoffman groaned. "What did you get out of him, before they got him?"

"Good stuff. He talked for a couple of hours before I let him go. How he was recruited in Amman. The address of the safe house. Who's in his network here. I have it all on tape. He couldn't stop talking, he was so excited. The poor fucker."

Even Hoffman could tell that Ferris felt guilty. "Sorry, Roger, but shit happens. I could apologize, but what's the point? He was going to get killed no matter what he did. Because he talked to you, maybe it will save some lives."

"Maybe," said Ferris. "Like you said, shit happens."

"The point is, now you've got to get out. We have to assume you're blown, whether this guy talked or not. I want you back to Balad. Then we'll see about getting you reassigned. You're too valuable to waste."

"I'm not leaving. There's a war on. I have other agents here. I'm not abandoning them just because we fucked up. That's our problem around here, if you hadn't noticed."

"Don't be sentimental, Roger. It's not safe. I am not losing my best young officer because he feels so guilty about a dead Iraqi that he decides to commit suicide. Sorry, no goddamn way."

"I'm not leaving," Ferris repeated.

Hoffman's voice went cold. He spoke slowly, with barely suppressed anger at the fact that Ferris was challenging him.

"I want you back in Balad tomorrow, Ferris. That is an order. If you don't obey it, you can find another job. Assuming they don't send you home in a bag. Is that understood?"

Ferris didn't know how to respond, so he broke the connection. When Hoffman called back, he didn't answer. That alone was enough to get him fired, but in that moment, Ferris didn't care. He tried to sleep, and when he couldn't, he read the dog-eared Charles Dickens novel he had brought along for moments like this.

BASSAM COLLECTED Ferris the next morning outside his little villa. Ferris was wearing his robe and kaffiyeh—at a quick glance, he was just another scruffy Iraqi man in his early thirties. Bassam had his hair gelled, as usual, but it was obvious he hadn't slept much, either. He looked hollow-eyed and nervous—no color left in his cheeks. Stoicism in the face of danger was a code of honor for Iraqi men, so he did his best to sound buoyant.

"Hey, boss-man," he said when Ferris got in the car. "Everything's cool."

Ferris answered in Arabic. "No English today, Bassam. It's too dangerous." He looked in the side mirror. A BMW with three Iraqis had pulled up behind them. "Pull over, let the car behind pass," said Ferris. Bassam obeyed silently, no chatter now. The BMW idled, and Ferris was about to tell Bassam to gun it and make a run, but at the last moment the Iraqi driver pulled out and passed them. One of the men in the BMW stared at Ferris full in the face. Shit, he thought. They know. They've made me.

"Head south," said Ferris. "Go to the house Nizar told us about, the one he said is the local headquarters for his cell. If there's anyone there, I want to call in the Predator and take some pictures. See who's coming and going."

"You sure?" asked Bassam. He was nervous, Ferris could tell. He thought the American was pushing his luck. He was right, but Ferris didn't care. In that moment, he was determined to finish the job. He was still angry about Nizar, the little fireplug Iraqi who had trusted Ferris and now was dead. They headed south along the banks of the Tigris, a big ugly river that seemed more mud than water.

Bassam knew the directions—knew the house, even. In these parts, every family knew where every other family lived. Every space on the checkerboard was covered with something. They turned off the main road, past a grove of olive trees and toward a half-finished villa a mile distant. It was spooky—dead quiet in the stillness of the morning, no cars on the road, no birds in the air, even. Ferris got out his satellite phone and checked the GPS coordinates, so he could be sure of the location when he contacted Balad to call in the Predator.

Ferris saw a little cloud of dust rise next to the villa when they were about a quarter mile off. It was a car coming or going, he couldn't tell which, but it was motion.

"Slow down," he told Bassam. He got on the phone to his base chief in Balad and asked him to dispatch CHILI, SPECK, or NITRATE. He gave the GPS coordinates and told the chief to hurry. This was a live target; the operating base of a confirmed terrorist cell.

Bassam had slowed the Mercedes to fifteen miles an hour. "Should I turn around now?" he asked.

"Why?" said Ferris. "We're almost there. Let's check it out."

"But sir, they are coming at us." There was a tremor in the Iraqi's voice Ferris had never heard before.

Ferris studied the dust cloud in the distance. It was getting bigger, and you could make out the car now. Bassam was right. Whoever was in the car was heading their way. Ferris couldn't know whether they were coming in pursuit, but he had to make an instant decision.

"Turn around," said Ferris, adding in English: "Gun it." Bassam threw the wheel over, swerved into a quick 180-degree turn and put the pedal to the floor. Bassam's Mercedes kicked up a plume of dust of its own, obscuring the view of the car behind.

As they neared the main highway, Ferris realized they were in deep trouble. The chase car was still behind them, but another car, a faded yellow Chevrolet, lay in wait on the shoulder of the paved road. Ferris popped the glove compartment of the Mercedes, where Bassam kept his gun. He hefted it in his hand. It was a small-caliber automatic pistol, almost useless. They were nearing the intersection.

"What you want, boss?" said Bassam.

"Turn south," said Ferris. "Toward Balad."

Bassam surged into the curve, barely missing an oncoming dump truck. The yellow Chevy parked on the shoulder roared to life and took off after them, followed by the car that had been pursuing them on the dirt road. Ferris got back on the satellite phone to Balad.

"You got that bird up? We have a problem out on Highway One."

"Roger that, sir," answered the duty officer. "SPECK is on the way to the coordinates you gave us. A few minutes away."

"Listen, we are in some serious fucking trouble here. I think some bad guys have made me and one of my agents. We are in an old red Mercedes south of Samara, coming down Highway One. We are being pursued by two cars. The lead car is a yellow Chevy. If you can get a gunship in the air you may save a couple of lives."

"Roger that," repeated the duty officer. "Stay on the line. We're calling down to the flight line for choppers. We'll see what we can do."

Ferris looked back toward the yellow car. He saw a man leaning out from the back-seat window on the driver's side. He had something big in his hands. It looked almost like a television camera and then Ferris realized: Fuck no, it's an RPG.

"Faster," he said to Bassam. "As fast as it will go." Bassam revved it all the way, pushing the needle past eighty, then ninety, but there were cars up ahead and he had to slow so that he wouldn't rear end them.

And then in an instant Ferris's world nearly flickered out for good. He didn't hear the roar of the RPG as it left the muzzle of the launcher. He saw a sudden burst of light to his left, just beyond Bassam, and then the shattering sound of the grenade exploding at the front wheel base, and then everything was white, and things went into slow motion. The car rocked up off its wheels from the concussion of the explosion, swaying once, twice and then settling back down on its tires. He heard a piercing scream in Arabic from Bassam, and saw that he was spurting blood from wounds across his chest. Oh, shit, thought Ferris, and he reached out his arm in a strobe-lit motion and then pulled back in horror. Where Bassam's stomach had been was a mess of blood and intestines. The shrapnel had carved into his gut like a surgeon's knife. Bassam was screaming, but somehow his hands were still on the steering wheel and his foot was on the gas pedal. Ferris felt a sharp sting, like he had been bitten by wasps up and down his leg, and only then did he see that the shrapnel of the grenade had hit him, too. His left leg was blood and bone, from midthigh down toward his calf. He put his hand to his balls to make sure they were still there.

"Can you drive?" shouted Ferris. All he heard back was the screaming, but Bassam managed to steer around the cars that had stopped up ahead because of the explosion and was accelerating into open highway. "Can you drive?" asked Ferris again, but the car was already weaving and he could see the life going out of Bassam's eyes and in a moment his body slumped over.

Ferris grabbed the wheel and managed to steady the car, but he couldn't move his left leg past Bassam's to reach the gas. The car began to slow. This is how I am going to die, thought Ferris. He thought of his mother, his dead father. He did not think of his wife. The car was slowing and the pursuers were coming faster. He heard a loud noise, but he was too dizzy to know what it was. The noise was louder still, and then there was an explosive roar, like another missile coming at him, but his vision was dimming and he could no longer process the signals. This is it, he thought. I did it. That was the last thought he had before everything went black: I did it.

· · ·

THE NOISE Ferris heard was a helicopter gunship that had been dispatched from Balad when his call to the duty officer had come in. The Apache took out the yellow Chevy in an instant, and then destroyed the second chase car behind. Two more helicopters landed and formed a perimeter by the highway. They put Ferris on a stretcher, and were going to do the same with Bassam until they saw that he was dead, so they put him in a bag. Ferris was back inside the Balad perimeter a few minutes later—safely across the line that separated life from death—and he was in the emergency room of the Balad field hospital twenty minutes after that, where the doctors struggled to save his leg.

The first call Ferris received when he woke up was from Hoffman, and he said pretty much the same thing Ferris had said to himself: You did it. It sounded like an ending, but that was really the beginning of their story.

5

WASHINGTON

F ERRIS WAS LUCKY: They put his leg back together, got him out of Iraq and found him a private room at Walter Reed. Most of the soldiers in the nearby ward hadn't been as fortunate. They had lost arms, legs, parts of their faces, pieces of their skulls. Ferris was embarrassed by his good luck. He had come out of Iraq on a C-130 with the remains of a dead soldier—Private Morales, someone said—who had died from a mortar round at a forward operating base south of Baghdad. The box that contained what was left of him wasn't really a coffin; more like a metal locker, but it had an American flag draped around it. They received the body in Kuwait with a solemn ceremony, they called it the "Patriot Drill," but after they had saluted the dead soldier's remains, the honor guard hoisted the metal locker and shoved it into what looked like a meat truck. The soldiers fell out and the truck drove it away.

The director himself paid a call at Walter Reed soon after Ferris was airlifted home. He looked as sleek and sly as a Venetian aristocrat. Accompanying him was Ed Hoffman, big stomach and spiky crew cut, walking with a stiff-legged strut like a football coach from the 1950s. Ferris was still heavily sedated, and when he awoke, he realized that the director was holding his hand.

"How are you, son?" asked the director.

Ferris groaned, and the director squeezed his hand.

"We're proud of you. You hear me?" There was no response from Ferris, so the director continued. "I brought you something. It's a medal for bravery in action. Rarely given. Precious." Ferris felt something heavy land on his chest. He tried to say thank you, but the words didn't come out very clearly. The director was speaking again. He was talking about silent warriors. Ferris was trying to compose a reply when the director said perhaps he should be going so the patient could get some rest. He said the last bit in a jaunty voice: Get some rest, old boy. Ferris managed to say, "Thank you," and then closed his eyes. Before he fell back into his drugged sleep, he saw in his mind the faces of the two dead agents he had left behind in Iraq.

Hoffman came back a few days later. Ferris was feeling better now. The sedatives were wearing off, which meant his leg hurt more but his mind wasn't so dull.

"You did good," the Near East Division chief said. "Your father would be proud of you."

Ferris pulled himself up in bed so that he could see Hoffman better. "My dad hated the CIA," he answered.

"I know. That's why he would have been proud of you. You got some dignity back."

And it was true. Tom Ferris had worked in the agency's Science & Technology Division, laboring on the communications links for several generations of spy satellites—and he had disliked almost every minute of it. After he got fired in the Stan Turner housecleaning of the late 1970s, he had worked for the Washington office of an aerospace company, but he was drinking heavily and screaming at Ferris's mother late at night. Ferris knew that his father regarded himself as a failure, a once-talented engineer who had wasted his life in the agency's deadening secret bureaucracy. He would mutter about the CIA when he was drinking. "Mediocrity," he would say. "Mendacity." His words would slur. He was spared by an early heart attack from the knowledge that his only son had joined the enemy.

Maybe Ferris's father would be happy to know his boy had gotten a medal out of the people who had tormented him, but he doubted it.

"I want to go back to Iraq," said Ferris.

"No way," answered Hoffman quickly. "Out of the question. You're burned. The bad guys know who you are. So forget it."

"Then I quit. Send me back in or I'm looking for another job."

"Don't be an asshole, Roger. And don't threaten me. It won't work. Anyway, I have another idea for you. How would you like to do something for me here that is a little, shall we say, unconventional?"

"At Headquarters? Absolutely not. If you try to make me, I won't just quit. I'll defect."

"It's not Headquarters, exactly. It's not even on the organization chart. Like I said, it's unconventional. You'd like it, I promise. It's made for a troublemaker like you."

"What is it?"

"I can't tell you unless you're in."

"Then forget it. I want back to Iraq. Like I said, it's that or I'm out."

"Stop it. And grow up. I told you Iraq is impossible. You're making a mistake turning down my proposal, but that's your problem. If you insist on going back in the field, I'm prepared to offer you the next best thing to Baghdad, which is Amman. It's better, actually, because you can do real operations—as opposed to being hunkered down hoping you don't get your ass shot off. I'm willing to send you in as deputy chief of station, which is unheard of at your age. So shut up. Actually, don't shut up. Say, 'Thanks, Ed. Amman is a plum. I really appreciate your confidence in me.'"

Ferris scratched his prickly beard. "When do I leave? If I agree to take Amman, that is."

"As soon as you can walk without falling over, which they tell me will be in about a month."

Ferris looked out the window, across the lawn and down toward the clog of traffic on 16th Street: Pizza Hut delivery boys and FedEx drivers and commuters racing home to catch their favorite shows on television. America was so normal. The bloody mess in Iraq might as well be on another planet. He turned back toward Hoffman, who was obviously waiting for an answer. Despite the Bear Bryant act, Hoffman was like anyone else. He wanted people to tell him good news. Ferris wasn't in the mood. His leg hurt too much.

"We're losing this war, Ed. You realize that, don't you?"

"Of course I do, assuming you mean the little war in Iraq. But we're not losing the big war, at least not yet. The one that could take down everything from Los Angeles to Bangor, Maine, and make ordinary folks so scared they will be crapping in their pants. In that war, we are still holding our own. Barely. That's why I want you in Amman. You came up with the real thing in Iraq, before you got your leg blown apart. The Suleiman network is for real. We've gotten collateral the past few days from other sources. We have to take him down. *Have to.* So stop feeling sorry for yourself and get mended. Do your physical therapy. I'm shipping you out as soon as I can—to Amman. Do we understand each other?"

Ferris offered a wan smile. "Do I have a choice?"

"Nope." Hoffman stood up to go, and then reconsidered and sat back down in his chair. He wanted Ferris to understand. This wasn't a consolation prize. He squinted one eye, as if he were trying to focus on something far away. "Remember the first time you showed up in my office, right after you got out of The Farm?"

"Sure. You terrified me."

"You flatter me. But here's the thing: From that first meeting, I knew I wanted you working for me. You know why? You had done well in training, obviously. They sent me a report. You aced everything."

Ferris nodded. He had met with Hoffman a few days after graduating from the training facility known as The Farm, perhaps the least-secret covert facility in the world. It was a vast, fenced tract of land in the swampy Tidewater area near Williamsburg, full of snakes and vermin and burned-out case officers who were assigned there as instructors when their covers got blown. Ferris had found it a kind of glorified scout camp, with training in map reading, high-speed driving, marksmanship, even parachute jumping—elaborately disguising the fact that most graduates were destined to spend their time going to embassy receptions. Ferris had excelled in his courses. He was a good athlete, which gave him an advantage in the brawny activities like hand-to-hand combat, and his tradecraft instructor said he was a "born recruiter."

"You were a star," continued Hoffman. "But that wasn't it. A lot of people who do well at The Farm are disasters as case officers. It's like high school. There's a sort of inverse relationship between early success and the real thing later on. No, it was something else that caught my eye. Something so rare, I worried it had disappeared in our line of work."

"Okay. I give up. What was it?"

"You were a natural. That's the only way I can put it. You hadn't even started yet, but you already knew what you were doing. You knew there were some scary people out there who wanted to kill Americans. You had studied them. You spoke their language. You knew they were coming at us, which was more than ninety-nine percent of the people in the agency understood back then. And you had that journalism thing. Most people come to us from the Marines or the FBI or someplace like that, where they learn to take orders and conform to the culture. But you didn't fit the pattern. You were a smart, rebellious kid who had studied Arabic in college and worked for *Time* magazine, of all things—and realized the goddamn house was on fire, and that you had to do something about it. That was what I liked about you. You understood what was going on. And you still do."

"I always thought you hated reporters."

"I do. They're losers. But I like you."

Ferris shook his head, thinking of all the braggarts and armchair generals he had worked with at *Time*. The news business was still riding high when he had joined the magazine in 1991. They had sent him to Detroit to cover what was left of the American auto industry.

He had been bored stiff and was going to quit after a year, but the barons of *Time* were interested in sending him abroad eventually because of his Arabic, so they brought him back to New York to cover Wall Street. That was worse than Detroit, and Ferris was going to quit for sure when *Time* assigned him to do a short piece on the radical Muslims who had surfaced in the 1991 attempt to bomb the World Trade Center. Ferris began reading the Arabic papers and visiting mosques. The more he talked to the sheiks, the more obvious it became: These people hate us. They don't want to negotiate anything. They want to kill us. Ferris knew he had stumbled into something important, but *Time* only ran a thousand words and when he complained, his editor lectured him about being a "team player." Ferris thought of writing a book about radical Islam, but he couldn't find a publisher who would give him an advance.

So he quit and went to graduate school. That was the only way he could follow what had become an obsession. His Arabic professors at Columbia were happy to have him back, although they disapproved of his studying Islamic extremism, as opposed to writing love letters to the downtrodden Palestinians. And then, six months in, there occurred one of those accidental encounters that in retrospect seem preordained: A former dean who had taken an interest in Ferris invited him to lunch. He beat around the bush for a while and at last, over coffee, asked Ferris if he ever thought of working for the Central Intelligence Agency. At first Ferris laughed. Thought about it? Hell, he'd been running away from it his whole life. Then it occurred to him: Stop running. This is who you are. And now, a decade later, he was in a hospital bed, with a steel pin in his leg, pleading to get back in the field.

Hoffman was smiling at him. "You remember what you said to me at that first meeting?"

Ferris tried to remember. The day he had graduated from The Farm, the director of training had summoned him and said that the head of the Near East Division wanted to meet with him. Right away. He made it sound like a very big deal. Ferris had been planning to spend a week in Florida, baking in the sun and drinking beer, but evidently that was out. He drove like a maniac up I-95, playing loud music the whole way, thinking how cool he was. When he got to Headquarters, the guard sent him to an office on the fourth floor. There was an ordinariness about the place that was suddenly obvious, now that Ferris was in. There were bulletin boards with notices of after-hours meetings that reminded him of high school. And there were little signs on the doors—"Electrical Closet," "Utility Closet"—as if they were worried that people would stumble into the wrong one by accident. At The Farm, they had told the Clandestine Service trainees they were joining the most elite intelligence organization in the world. But looking at the lumpy, hollow-eyed men and women plying the halls at headquarters, Ferris knew that could not possibly be true. He was wondering if he had made the biggest mistake in his life.

And then he met Ed Hoffman. What struck him in that first encounter was Hoffman's size. He wasn't overweight, just bulky, one of those people who took up a lot of space even when he was sitting at his desk. He kept his hair in a buzz cut, like a Marine recruit, but he was probably in his early fifties. He peered over the top of his reading glasses when Ferris entered the room, in a look that suggested surprise and impatience, as if he had forgotten that he had summoned Ferris. But that wasn't it. He was curious.

Hoffman was still sitting next to his hospital bed at Walter Reed, waiting for an answer. He was a little bigger now, a little softer in the middle. But he hadn't lost that surprising twinkle in his eye, the nimbleness that didn't fit with the heavy body.

"To be honest, Ed, I don't remember anything I said that day, except, 'Yes, sir,' and 'No, sir.' I was trying to make a good impression. I remember you told me we had something in common. You said we were both related to CIA washouts. I'd never heard my dad described that way, although it was true enough. And you told me about your uncle Frank, who was station chief in Beirut until he got mad at his boss and quit. I liked that. Where is he now, your uncle Frank?"

"Playing golf in Florida with everyone else. You're avoiding my question, Roger. Do you remember what you said at the end of our meeting, after I had quizzed you about the Islamic groups, and we had talked about bin Laden? You were the only person around Headquarters who seemed to know who he was, and you hadn't even gotten your first real paycheck yet. Do you remember what you said at the end of that meeting, when I told you I was sending you to Yemen to work on Al Qaeda? You remember your response?"

"Honestly I don't, Ed. It was a long time ago."

"Well, I remember. You looked me in the eye and said: '*This has to work.*' I never forgot that. When 9/11 happened, I thought, Get me that Ferris kid. Get him back from Yemen and make him my executive officer. I jumped you over about thirty people, did you know that? September eleven was a disaster for America, but for you, my friend, it was a good career move."

"Give me a break, Ed. I'm lying in a hospital bed with half my leg shot off."

Hoffman ignored him. "What you said back then is still true—now that we have Suleiman in our sights, now that you're heading out to Amman. These people are killers. They want to bring this war to every shopping mall and supermarket in America. So I'll play it back to you, Roger. *This has to work.*"

GRETCHEN FERRIS visited her husband every few days in the hospital. She was a dark-haired beauty, with a voluptuous figure that made the other men in the hospital stare at her and shake their heads. She never stayed very long. She always had to get back to the Justice Department. But she was devoted to Ferris, in her organized way. They had met as undergraduates at Columbia. She was smarter than him, at least by the conventional measures. She had nailed her law boards and sailed through Columbia Law School while Ferris was horsing around at *Time.* When he joined the CIA, she had come to Washington to clerk with a conservative circuit court judge, and when the Republicans took office, she was offered a job at Justice. She asked Ferris whether that would be a problem, both of them working for the government, and he said no. He was proud of her, just as she was proud of him.

She was a believer. That was the difference between them. For Ferris, most assumptions about life were inductive and open to revision. Gretchen worked the other way, from principle to practice. Maybe she had been less certain about things before, when they were younger, or maybe it was Ferris who had lost his bearings. The gap had worried Ferris a little before he went to Iraq, and it had grown wider. Gretchen didn't want to know things that would upset her. When Ferris tried to explain what had been so disturbing about Iraq, she would shake her head, as if Ferris weren't trying hard enough.

Whatever their differences, Gretchen knew how they might be bridged. Her appetite for sex was remarkable and, in a way, creative. It was something that set her apart from anyone's stereotype of a conservative lawyer. When she visited him in the hospital the first time, she opened her raincoat to reveal a bra, a garter belt, and milky white skin. She wanted to give him a blow job. Ferris resisted at first, feeling that he was betraying all the wounded Joes on the ward, but not for very long.

When Ferris told her that he was going to Amman, she got tears in her eyes—not just about missing him, but about the nobility of what he was doing. She talked about how they were both fighting in the same war, and how they were sacrificing their personal happiness for a greater cause. That's crazy, Ferris thought. Nobody stays married because it's the right thing for the country. Already he was beginning to wonder if it would last. He had become a hero to her, rather than a real person. At the airport the day he left, Ferris tried to explain that he wasn't sure he could stay faithful, being so far away for such a long time. But she cut him off. "Just don't ever tell me about it, and we'll be fine," she said. She kissed him and told him she loved him, and she meant it. Ferris said the words back, "I love you," but in his mind they sounded hollow.

6

F ERRIS PAID A CALL ON Hani Salaam at the General Intelligence Department the day after he returned from Berlin. A guard at the checkpoint stopped his armored SUV at the entrance to the complex and then waved him through. The word had evidently gotten around that he was a friend of the pasha. That was the thing about a country like Jordan, where life revolved around a royal court: Gossip flowed as freely as water; all the courtiers shared the same information, and everybody instantly seemed to know everything. The palace knew within a few days, for example, that Ferris had become acting chief of station a few weeks after his arrival, when Francis Alderson was expelled. That was supposed to be a big secret, but this was a company town, in more ways than one.

The GID's headquarters stood atop a steep bluff in Abdoun, not far from the U.S. Embassy. The building was hidden from the road, but when you turned a corner, it loomed suddenly like a stone castle. Inside the inner courtyard flew the ominous black flag of the Moukhabarat, bearing the Arabic script that translated: "Justice Has Come." On a clear night, the lights of Jerusalem were visible in the far distance. The GID was vast. Nobody knew how many people were on the payroll of the secret police, so they imagined the worst.

Was the person sitting next to you in the restaurant an informant? What about the *bawab* who guarded your apartment building, or the person in the next office at work? Probably all of them, and a dozen more who circumscribed every point of your life, but nobody knew. Young Jordanians sometimes played a game in bars, trying to guess who was from the Moukhabarat, but they dared to do so only if Daddy was rich enough to fix things if someone overheard. This was Hani's power, that in the absence of real knowledge, people imagined his men were everywhere.

Ferris was carrying a locked briefcase containing a set of NSA intercepts, chronicling the conversations of some members of the king's family who had lately been demanding more money from the palace. The intercepts were Hoffman's idea. They were an offering to Hani, to be presented as soon as Ferris could arrange an appointment. The message was: We deliver. Now you deliver.

Hani's secretary was waiting for Ferris at the front door and escorted him upstairs. Ferris walked past a bright mural on the first floor depicting the young king and his family, and then up a grand stairway. It was a bit like a fancy hotel lobby, decorated in lustrous teak and polished chrome. The elegant interior would have surprised most Jordanians, who imagined the intelligence headquarters as a Kafkaesque prison. But GID officers historically had treated themselves to the good life, sometimes to excess. One of Hani's predecessors had gone to prison after it was alleged that he been steering contracts to friends who, in their gratitude, had been depositing large sums in a secret bank account.

Ferris was escorted to the office of Hani's genial deputy, who proffered tea and made small talk. The director would be free in a few minutes, he said. Eventually an aide announced that the great man was ready, and Ferris was marched down the hall to a large office decorated with pictures of the young king and his father. Hani rose from his desk and strode toward the American.

"*Salaam aleikum, Hani Pasha!*" said Ferris. The American leaned toward the Jordanian and kissed him on both cheeks. Hani seemed amused at the show of respect. He took a puff of the cigarette in his hand and blew a perfect smoke ring in Ferris's direction.

"You are most welcome, Roger. We are sure you must be an Arab. You have such good manners. That is why we like you so much."

"I'm not an Arab. Just an American who can speak the language."

"Perhaps a little bit, long ago." Hani smiled. "A grandmother. A distant grandfather. I know it. I am never wrong."

"This time you are." Ferris smiled amiably. He never talked about his background. The agency frowned on giving away too many details, but it wasn't just that. Ferris didn't think his personal life was anyone else's business.

"*Y'allah!* Come sit down." Hani motioned for him to sit on the couch. He looked especially like Dean Martin this morning. He was dressed in a tweed jacket, an open-neck shirt and an elegant new pair of suede loafers he must have bought on a recent trip to London.

"You look well," said Ferris. It was true. The man was in the bloom of good health. He must have treated himself to a very high-class hooker in Berlin as a reward for his exploits.

"How is your leg, my dear? You were limping in Berlin. You tried to hide it, but I could see. I hope you are healed. I worry about you."

"I'm fine. All the better for seeing you, Hani Pasha."

"I got back yesterday from Germany. An excellent country, but they do not have an intelligence service. I don't think they ever realized I was there. When I got home, my people told me you wanted to see me. Right away!" Hani raised his eyebrows.

"It's Milan. The Europeans are going crazy. The White House is going crazy. And everybody's screaming at us."

"And at me." Hani threw up his hands. "I have put off liaison meetings with the Italians, French and British this morning, so that I could see you. Everyone wants results tomorrow. I think they do not understand intelligence very well. It is not a microwave oven. Ed Hoffman understands. He knows that what is done quickly is not done well."

"Your Berlin operation definitely got Mr. Hoffman's attention. He asked me to congratulate you. I think he was very impressed." Ferris stopped. He was on the verge of lying.

"Tell Ed that I am grateful for his praise. Someone else, I would think it was just flattery, because he wants something." He offered a thin smile, which rippled his lips like a shark's fin breaking water.

"We want to move fast on this, Hani Pasha. As you can imagine, Mr. Hoffman has lots of questions about the man we met in Berlin, Mustafa Karami."

"Oh yes, I can imagine."

"Specifically, Mr. Hoffman wanted to know how your second meeting went." Ferris didn't want to seem pushy, getting to the point so quickly, but you never knew how much time you had with Hani. The king had a habit of showing up at odd times, causing the intelligence chief to disappear for hours on end.

"The case is complicated," answered Hani. "It's a good case, but complicated."

"Why? You had that guy cold. 'Talk to your mother.' Best pitch I've ever seen. And you're going in a direction that interests us." Ferris left the thread out there for Hani to pick up, but he did no more than register Ferris's praise.

"We do have him 'cold,' as you say. The second meeting went well, and so did a third one I had just before leaving. He is our boy now. We own him, most certainly. But it's still complicated."

Ferris waited for Hani to explain, and when he didn't, he asked again, "Why is it complicated?"

"Because Al Qaeda is complicated. There are layers and layers and layers. Anyone who tries to move from one layer to another is suspect. You don't do anything on your own, you wait to be asked."

"But we can't wait. You know that. Especially after Milan. We hope you'll put Mustafa in play quickly."

"We can't wait, I agree. Waiting could get more people killed. But then, on the other hand, we must wait. I am a patient man, even when I am in a hurry. I took too much time setting up this operation to be rushed now. Even if Ed Hoffman wants me to move quickly."

Ferris paused before responding. Hani was being so careful. This was the right time to offer the gift he had brought along.

"Mr. Hoffman wanted me to give you something. You've been asking for these, I think. They're transcripts of phone calls in Europe and America from some of the members of the royal family who have been . . . worrying the king. You will be interested especially in the ones with the Lebanese banker in Paris who is handling some of the royal accounts." Ferris opened his briefcase and handed Hani the stack of transcripts.

"Ah yes." Hani glanced at a few pages and then closed the folder. He narrowed his gaze. "Well, that is very nice. His Majesty will be interested, I am sure. How nice of Ed to be so generous." Hani seemed slightly miffed at the gift, although Ferris wasn't sure why. The king himself had muttered to the director about his wayward siblings the last time he came to Washington.

"He wants to see you. He's coming to Amman."

"Yes, I know. He needs something, and I am wondering what it is." Hani smiled and lit another cigarette. Ferris didn't ask how he knew. Maybe Hoffman had told him; maybe he was only pretending he knew. It didn't matter.

"He's going to want to talk about the case," said Ferris.

"He is welcome. *Ahlan wa sahlan.* Just so long as he doesn't try to run the operation. He will make mistakes. That is why we like you, Ferris. You know what you don't know. You are young, you are smart, you speak Arabic, you respect your elders. You are a secret Arab." Hani gave him a wink.

"Can we get your debriefing of Karami?" asked Ferris. "That would help me with Hoffman."

"No. I am very sorry. That would not be appropriate. But I will summarize for you what he told us. Karami has contact with a man who was in the training camp in Afghanistan. This man is based in Madrid. They meet in Budapest. A man in Dubai who sends him money gets it from someone in Karachi, but we don't know his name yet. Karami was a courier in the USS *Cole* operation in 2000. He traveled once to Yemen, but they haven't used him on any operations since then. He's a sleeper. They're keeping him in place for something. Or maybe they've forgotten about him. I am sorry to say, *habibi,* this man by himself is not going to take us inside the tent. If he tries to go see the big men, they will say no. But I have another idea for him."

"What's that?" Ferris suppressed a frown.

"I can't tell you," said Hani. His face was so smooth, his black hair so full, his gray moustache so well trimmed. "That's not true. Of course I could tell you if I wanted to, but I don't."

"Why not? We are chasing the same target here. I'm sure of it. Why not cooperate?"

"Because it's my operation. You will share the take. But you need to let me run it the way I want. Because . . . let us be honest, my dear, because you have no choice." Hani smiled. Ferris found him irresistibly charming, even when he was saying things that would make Ferris's life difficult.

"Hoffman won't be happy," said Ferris.

"*Ma'alesh.* Too bad. He'll get over it. Who loves the Americans more than me?"

"Langley is paying a lot of bills around here."

"Is that a threat, my dear Ferris? How delightful. You are becoming a real chief of station now. Just don't make the same mistake as your predecessor, or we will have to throw you out, too."

The Jordanian smiled; the eyes sparkled with perfect confidence. Nobody wanted to talk about the transgressions of his predecessor, Francis Alderson, but nobody seemed to have forgotten them, either. Hani patted Ferris on the back. "You are representing the big boys at Langley. I understand that. But you are only showing your weakness when you threaten me in this way, so do not raise this subject again. And tell your division chief that if he so much as mentions money when he visits, he will regret it. We do not need to talk about this anymore, do we?"

"No," said Ferris. "But I can't predict how Mr. Hoffman will react."

"He'll be fine. You are at war. You have to trust your friends. Drink your tea."

FERRIS WENT HOME that night to his apartment in Shmeisani. It was on the top floor of a building owned by a retired Palestinian engineer, with a nice view of the milk-white city and the hills beyond. Ferris walked to the balcony. It was early evening, and he could see the play of shadows across the hills of Amman. He poured himself a glass of vodka and sat on his terrace, staring toward the faint twinkle of light that was Jerusalem. He liked being alone, normally—returning to the warm emptiness of a solitary apartment. People need safe houses in real life, but not all the time, and for Ferris, not that night.

Ferris thought briefly of his wife. Gretchen sent him love letters that mixed romantic passages she might have cribbed from *Cosmo* with descriptions of life in the Office of Legal Counsel. She had a compartment for everything—sex, law, politics—and she was adept at all of them. He wanted to think fondly of Gretchen, but the image of her just drifted out of his mind. Ferris couldn't hold on to it anymore. The Crazy Glue had come unstuck, and now her spirit presence floated away over the hilltops of Amman, back to America and her big oak desk at the Justice Department. Ferris realized that he didn't care if she was having sex with someone else. Perhaps that was a sign that he was already unfaithful himself, in his heart.

INTO THE EMPTY space in Roger Ferris's life had fallen a woman named Alice Melville. They had met three weeks ago in Amman. Ferris had liked her instantly, and he had removed his wedding ring before taking her to dinner, something he had never done before. He asked her home afterward. "Don't push your luck," she had said. When Ferris got a glum look, she kissed him on the cheek and whispered, "I take that back. Do push your luck. But not tonight."

He liked Alice partly because she was so different from his wife. Gretchen was a person for whom life's important questions were settled. Alice gave the sense that the basics were still up for discussion. She worked with Palestinian refugees and spoke about the suffering of the Arabs with great passion. Ferris's colleagues in the station would have instantly mistrusted her if they had met her, which Ferris was determined they would not. Most of all, Alice was mysterious. With Gretchen, everything was right there, cash on the table—brains, beauty, ambition. Alice was more elusive; Ferris sensed that she was like the Arabs—beneath her seeming openness was a deeper guile, and she never told you everything she knew.

Alice had sent Ferris a letter just before he left for Berlin. It was a continuation of a conversation they had been having the last time they were together, when they were drunk and talking about politics. The tone was serious and frivolous at the same time; that was Alice's style, Ferris suspected, but he didn't really know her yet. He had been keeping the letter in his pocket. He took it out and reread it in the dim light of his terrace, suspended in the black night.

"I hate this war, Roger," she began. "When did it begin, anyway? Did it begin in 2001, or the Crusades, or what? And who are these 'bad guys' your friends at the Embassy are always talking about? I assume it isn't all Muslims, but even if it's only the Muslims who hate America, that's still a lot of people. What are we going to do? Kill them all? And how will we ever get any of them to like us, if we keep on killing them? Maybe I'm stupid, but I don't get it. I hope we can have dinner again. We can go dancing at this new club in Shmeisani. Don't work too hard. I miss you. Do you miss me, even a little?" She had signed with a dramatic flourish of ink under her name.

Sitting on the terrace, nursing his second glass of vodka, Ferris knew that he missed her quite a lot, actually. He tried her cell phone, but she wasn't answering. Was she with someone else, or away traveling, or just mysterious?

Ferris knew he needed to write a letter. Not to Alice, whom he would be seeing soon enough, but to Gretchen. They were in an impossible situation. They both knew it, but neither wanted to admit it: If she had come with him to Amman, or if he had refused the assignment and stayed in Washington, they might have stood a chance. But in that case, they would have been different people. Gretchen didn't really want to be his wife; she would never have admitted that, but in fact she was too busy to be anyone's wife. She liked the idea of it, certainly. Being married to an intelligence officer fit her self-image—they were a couple of warriors, in her mind, except that they weren't really a couple.

Do it now, Ferris told himself. He went inside and sat down at the laptop in his study and began typing: My dear Gretchen . . . no, Dear Gretchen. We said we needed to talk when I left Washington in June, but we never really did. Now I think we have to. Our marriage is broken . . . no, Our marriage is in trouble. We both know it. We've been living apart for months and there is no end in sight. You don't want to leave your job and I don't want to leave mine, especially after what happened in Iraq. There is no space for us to be together as husband and wife. If we are not going to be together, then it's inevitable that we will meet other people . . . no. If we are not going to be together, then I think you should talk to a lawyer. . . .

Ferris stopped writing. He thought about the lawyers, and the fight over money, and whole nuisance of getting divorced. He saved the document, and then deleted it. He hated the idea of negotiating with her. She was smarter than he was, and she would earn far more as a lawyer than he ever would as an intelligence officer. She would quit the Justice Department in a few years, join a fancy law firm and make $400,000 a year. The only way Ferris could make that kind of money was stealing operational funds, which wasn't his thing, at least not yet. And she wouldn't make it easy.

Gretchen's problem was that she was intolerant of people who were weaker than she was, which included almost everybody. When they met at Columbia, she had told Ferris that she planned to vote Republican in the next presidential election. It wasn't a test so much as a warning. Ferris didn't care; politics bored him, whereas

Gretchen excited him. She was dazzling in her self-possession—with the easy confidence that used to be associated with ambitious young men. What was it that had made Ferris fall in love with her? It was partly that sheen: She knew how to be successful, and she made him feel as if he were somebody, just being with her. But she also understood what was under his skin. When he began chasing radical Muslims for *Time*, she was one of the few people who got it. "They're dangerous, Roger," she said. "Do something about it."

They stayed close because they were perfect. She always told him that. She was gorgeous, the sort of girl you would want to walk up Fifth Avenue with at Christmastime. She liked to wear red, listen to U2, get bikini-waxed at a fancy spa. She had a delightfully trashy, sloe-eyed, fuck-me look when she got drunk. And she was almost proprietary about her right to pleasure, as if she were depositing it all in a lifetime orgasm bank. When she wasn't making love, she slept like a cat, and Ferris would lie awake, wondering why he felt lonely.

They got married because . . . it seemed like the right thing to do. Their friends were all getting married. It was like a momentum trade in the stock market; everyone else is buying, so you buy, too. He certainly didn't love anyone else. She had waited for him two years while he was off in Yemen, and when he returned, she said, it's "our time." They found an apartment in Kalorama, and she started working at Justice just before September 11, 2001.

She had always been patriotic, but after 9/11 she had a sense of personal mission. There's something that happens when ambition fuses with principle that's like a chemical reaction, and it made her a subtly different person. At Justice, her ferocity began to attach itself to issues that Ferris dealt with in his own career, and it disturbed him. One evening she had asked Ferris about interrogation techniques. She was very specific about it. How much did you have to hurt someone before they would talk? How long did it take people to recover after interrogation? It wasn't an idle conversation about interrogation, if there could be any such thing, and Ferris suspected she must be doing legal research. He said he didn't know much, other than what they had taught him at The Farm, and she looked disappointed.

She had pressed him, and Ferris had finally explained that the only time he'd seen a rough interrogation was in Yemen. The local security service had captured an Al Qaeda suspect and had beaten him over three days. With a cricket bat, that was the detail that stuck in Ferris's mind. They had let him stay just conscious enough to appreciate each new wave of pain that was coming. Finally, in a spasm of fear, the prisoner had begun shouting the answers he thought the interrogators wanted to hear. But that had only made them more angry, so they had beaten him harder. Eventually, he died from loss of blood and trauma to the head. Ferris had watched.

"Did you tell them to stop?" Gretchen had asked.

"No. I kept thinking it would work. But then he was dead."

"Don't ever tell anyone else what you just told me," said Gretchen. "It was illegal. Technically."

When Ferris asked why she was so interested in interrogation, she didn't answer. She went off and made some notes, and then came back with the top buttons of her blouse undone.

The discussion had upset Ferris, and he wanted to believe that it had bothered Gretchen as well, but he wasn't sure. He had begun to realize that for her, the law was another kind of conquest. It was about removing restraints so that your client—in her case, the president of the United States—could do what he wanted. There was something sexual about it, a kind of reverse bondage. The law for her was about untying people so they could have their way.

She was proud of Ferris when he got wounded in Iraq. He had thought the scars would disgust her, but she liked to touch them— almost as if she were experiencing the event vicariously. But she couldn't: Ferris had seen into the abyss in that moment on Highway 1 when he thought he was about to die, and he had realized that she wasn't there with him. How could he tell her that? The sense of separation stayed with him during his convalescence, and it made him realize that there were things he didn't share with Gretchen, and never would.

FERRIS CALLED Alice's cell-phone number once again, and on the fourth ring, she finally answered. It was a sleepy voice. She had been dozing, and at first she seemed to have forgotten who Ferris was. He tried not to sound peeved. He had no right; she didn't belong to him.

"I've been trying to reach you," he said. "Where have you been?"

"Here mostly, and I went to Damascus for a day. I don't answer my cell phone sometimes."

"What were you doing in Damascus?"

"Shopping," she answered curtly. "I was wondering what happened to you, actually. I thought maybe you didn't like me."

"I was away. I had to leave the country, too."

"Mmmmm," she said doubtfully.

"I want to see you. Soon. Are you free tomorrow night?" The next evening was Thursday, the start of the Muslim weekend. There was a long pause.

"I don't know . . . ," she said.

"What do you mean?" Ferris held his breath.

"I don't know if I can wait that long." She laughed at the trick she had played on him.

When he put down the phone, Ferris went back to the terrace. Night had fallen, bringing the sudden chill of the desert. Amman was a bowl of light against the black sky. He felt, if not quite good, certainly less bad.

7

F ERRIS PICKED ALICE MELVILLE up at her apartment. It was down in the old quarter by the Roman amphitheater. Ferris didn't know any Americans who lived there. She was blond, wearing a sundress and sandals, with a sweater thrown over her shoulder. At first sight, her hair seemed to float in slow motion. "Hey, you," she said, bounding into the passenger seat and immediately changing the channel of the radio. God, she's beautiful, thought Ferris.

He took her to dinner at the Italian restaurant at the Hyatt Hotel. It was the most romantic place he could think of. They sat outside under the stars, with a gas heater next to them to ward off the evening chill. It glowed yellow and blue, like the embers of a fire. Ferris ordered a bottle of wine, and when they finished that, another one. The wine made her talkative, although Ferris didn't think that would be a problem even if she were stone sober. She was describing her work with Palestinian refugees. That was her job; she worked with an NGO that did relief work in the camps that still housed many poor Palestinians. Ferris referred to it as "Save the Children," though it was actually called the Council for Near East Relief.

"The refugees have no hope, Roger," she whispered, as if that were a secret. "What keeps them going is rage. They listen to the sheiks from Hamas and Islamic Jihad. They buy those bin Laden cassettes. When they go to sleep at night, I think they must dream about killing Israelis, and Americans. And now Italians, for heaven's sake."

"But not you," said Ferris. "They don't want to kill you." She was being so serious, but all he could do was look at her. The light of the gas lamp was giving her hair a reddish glow. He leaned over the table toward her, as if to listen. When she talked, he could see her breasts rise and fall through the opening of her dress.

"No, not me. They respect me . . . because I listen to them. Do you listen to them, Roger? Does the American government listen to them? Or do we just want to shoot them?" Ferris had told her that he worked in the political section at the embassy, which was his cover job.

"Of course I listen to them. The ambassador listens to them. We all listen to them. I even talk to them." He rattled off a few sentences in fluent Arabic, telling her that she was very beautiful in the moon-light and that he hoped she would come back to his apartment that night.

To his surprise, she answered in decent Arabic. She told him that he was handsome, but that his fate depended on the will of God. Then she added in English: "And don't try to sweet-talk me, Ali Baba. More people have tried to hit on me than . . ." She thought a moment. "Than Curt Schilling. And it won't work."

"Red Sox fan?"

"Of course."

"I won't sweet-talk you. I just have this problem that I am irre-sistibly attracted to blondes who speak Arabic."

Alice rolled her eyes and looked at the Arab men seated around the restaurant. "Welcome to the club. But seriously, Roger, I want to know what the embassy tells people. Do you tell them you're sorry that America is killing Muslims? Do you tell them you're sorry their houses have been bulldozed and their children have been killed? Do you tell them it only *looks* as if we've allied with these right-wing kooks in Israel? Do you tell them we made a mistake invading Iraq and busting it into a million pieces? What do you tell them, anyway? I'd like to know."

Ferris groaned. He wasn't a diplomat; he was an intelligence officer. "Do we have to talk about this?"

"No. You can tell me it's none of my business. Then I'll go home."

Ferris was startled at the thought that she would leave him. "Okay. Let me think. When people complain, I tell them I appreciate their point of view. I tell them I don't make U.S. government policy. Sometimes I say that I'll put their views in a cable. How's that? I'll put your views in a cable." He was trying to make a joke, but it didn't work.

"You really don't get it! You sit in the embassy all day and I'm out on the firing line. I mean it, Roger. I have to listen to these people screaming at me every day. Do you know they cheered in the camps this week when they heard the news about the car bombing in Milan? Cheered. Friends had to come over and protect me. They want to kill us. Don't you see that?"

The argument had colored her cheeks, so they, too, had the reddish glow of the gas fire. He knew he should be giving her better answers, but one of Ferris's problems was that he was bad at policy debates. They reminded him of what he had hated about journalism. Policy debates were for real State Department officers, or op-ed columnists, or people like this mysterious Alice who worked in refugee camps and wore a sundress to dinner. But he had to say something, or she would give up on him.

"I do see it, Alice. More than you might think. I'm on the firing line, too. We all are. That's what life is now."

She looked into his eyes, as if she were searching for something. Did she know what he really did? Had she guessed it? The thought made him uneasy. He excused himself to go to the toilet. As he walked there and back, he tried to disguise his limp, but his leg was bothering him in the evening cold, and she noticed it.

"What's wrong with your leg?" she asked when he returned to the table. "Are you hurt?"

"I was. Not anymore. I'm fine now."

"What happened? If you don't mind my asking."

Ferris thought a moment. He did mind her asking, but if this relationship was going to go anywhere, he was going to have to tell her more about who he really was.

"I got shot in Iraq. That was my last assignment before here. I was riding in a car, and a grenade went off, and I got a lot of shrapnel in my leg. I'm fine now. I just have this limp sometimes. It's made me much better in bed."

She didn't laugh at his joke. She was still studying him.

"What were you doing in Iraq?"

"I was in our embassy. I was supposed to be there for a year, but when I got wounded, they sent me here instead. Then I met you. See? I'm lucky."

"You weren't in the embassy when you got shot."

"No. I was outside the Green Zone. On a road north of Baghdad."

She took his hand, held it in the half-light and then let it go. "You don't work for the CIA, do you?"

"Of course not. Don't be ridiculous. I used to work for *Time* magazine, before I joined the foreign service. Look it up on Nexis. They'd never let an ex-journalist work for the CIA."

"That's good," she said. "Because then we'd have a problem."

Ferris felt a tingle in his arms, the little hairs bristling. He normally didn't mind lying about working for the agency; it was part of his job. But this was different.

"I admire you for being so brave, Roger. I just wish you could be brave for something else. I feel as if this war is destroying our country. People want to love America, but they see us doing these terrible things, and they wonder if we've become monsters. I'm frightened what's going to happen."

"I'm worried, too." Ferris rose from the table and took her hand. "It's a bad time." He pulled her gently toward him. She stayed in his arms for a long moment, and then moved away.

• • •

Ferris drove her down Prince Mohammed Street toward her building in the old downtown quarter. She was quiet in the car, staring out the window. Ferris was worried that she was angry with him when she suddenly said, "Turn left. I want to show you a place you've never been." She rattled a quick string of directions, back and forth in narrow streets of the old city, and in a few minutes they were several miles from the center of town, in a district that had none of the international patina foreigners usually saw. The streets were dank and ill-lit; donkeys carts trundled along the edge of the road. Walls were decorated with Palestinian flags and ancient, peeling posters of Yasser Arafat and crudely drawn anti-American graffiti.

"Stop," she said when they reached the crest of a hill and a small road, not much bigger than an alleyway, which was the entrance to a warren of stucco and cinder-block houses. Ferris scanned the area warily. It was a Palestinian refugee camp, one of the old ones where people had first arrived after the wars of 1948 and 1967. Ferris recognized it from a security briefing. This was one of the places where an embassy official absolutely should not go, the security officer had advised.

"I work here," said Alice, opening the car door. "I mean, it's one of the places where I work. I wanted you to see it. I thought maybe you would understand me better. Intimacy, you know?" Was she mocking him?

Alice strode toward the entrance to the camp. Ferris peered down the dusty roadway. Strings of twinkling lights were hung along the scattered light poles like Christmas decorations; a café was open just inside the wall, along with a few stores down the way. A few men were sitting in the café sharing a nargileh, sucking on the stem and blowing out smoke. They had been talking, but when they saw Ferris and his big SUV, they stopped. Ferris was edgy. Common sense told him they shouldn't be here this late at night.

"Come on," said Alice, walking toward the café. "Maybe some of my friends are here." Still Ferris lingered. It was like being in college, when someone who'd been drinking wanted to drive and you had to decide whether to be a spoilsport and say no, or go along.

"Come *on*, silly. I'll protect you." She grabbed Ferris's hand and pulled him toward the café. They sat in two plastic chairs on the concrete terrace, under a wooden arbor that kept off the sun during the day. The other men looked at Ferris guardedly and then began talking again. Ferris saw one of them gesture in his direction and heard him say in Arabic, "Who's the Jew?"

After a minute, the owner came out. Alice greeted him and he responded warmly. She asked in Arabic if Hamid was around that evening and the owner answered no, he was visiting his mother in Ramallah, thanks be to God.

"That's too bad," said Alice, turning to Ferris. "I wanted you to meet Hamid. He's one of my main contacts in this camp. He's one of the smartest people I know. You'd like him."

"You think so?" asked Ferris. "How come?"

"Because he's like you. He knows things, and he's tough. People here respect him. I thought maybe he would say some things better than I could."

"You know, Alice, I'm not sure your friend Hamid would want to meet someone from the American Embassy. We're not very popular around here."

"That's okay. You're with me. And I'm popular. I'll protect you." The look in her eyes said she meant it. This was her place.

"Yes, but he might get the wrong idea. Or other people might get the wrong idea."

"What idea is that?" asked Alice. He had trouble seeing her face in the dark. Did she know what he really did? Was that what she was saying?

"Never mind." Ferris was still tense. He scanned the perimeter, looking for signs of trouble, but it was quiet. Maybe Alice's nonchalance—her obliviousness to the possibility that it might be dangerous to be sitting in a Palestinian refugee camp late at night—was her protection. Or perhaps it was something else. Maybe she really did belong here, and in a lot of other places that were closed to Ferris.

The café owner returned with Turkish coffee, bittersweet like a bar of dark chocolate. They drank it down slowly. Ferris let himself relax a bit.

"How come you don't have a boyfriend?" he asked. "A girl as pretty as you must get asked out all the time."

She didn't answer at first. She took a last sip of her coffee and then turned over the cup and let the grounds dry for a moment on the side of the porcelain. She held the cup up to the light as if she were a fortune-teller.

"Good luck?" asked Ferris.

"Maybe. If you believe luck is written in coffee grounds. My old boyfriend believed that. And a lot of other crazy things."

"So you did have a boyfriend."

She looked away from Ferris, down the little alleyway and into the dark shadows. It was ten long seconds before she turned back to him.

"I loved him," she said. "He was a Palestinian. Very proud, very angry. I loved him, but he mistreated me."

Ferris reached out his hand for her, but she was too far away. "How did he mistreat you?"

"All the ways you can think of, and other ways, too."

"My God. I cannot imagine anyone hurting you."

"He couldn't help it. He was so angry. It wasn't me. It was everything. That's what I've been trying to tell you. These people are really angry with us. We think we can lie to them and steal their land and treat them like dirt and they'll just forget about it. But they don't."

"Why didn't you leave Jordan after that? I mean, how could you stay here, after he had treated you that way?"

"I'm stubborn, Roger. That's probably something we have in common. And the more I thought about him and his anger, I thought, No! Don't run away. That's what he would expect, and all the other Arabs, too. That we pretend to care about them and then, when real life bruises us a little, we run away. So I stayed. That's how I got over it. I kept loving the people who had hurt me. I wouldn't leave. I won't leave."

Ferris felt the unfamiliar sting of tears. He wiped his eyes, trying to disguise the gesture, but she took his hand and smiled in a way she never had before. He kissed her on the cheek, his own still slightly wet.

Neither of them wanted to leave. Ferris asked about her work in the camps, and Alice tried to explain. Helping these people was a matter of logistics: She purchased schoolbooks and medical supplies; she funded water projects and dental clinics; she arranged scholarships at American colleges. It was a job; she was good at it. But the animation in her voice made clear that she was doing the one and only thing in the world that mattered to her.

Ferris looked down the ruined street, to the darkened houses and the hidden places an outsider could never enter. He wished he could share Alice's belief that decent people could prevail, with enough schoolbooks and dental clinics. But he knew too much. This was a world seething with hatred. Its smiles were false ones; its true hunger was for revenge. The people had been damaged: by Americans, Israelis and the Arabs themselves. They were rats in a cage. Alice, brave as she might be, could not know the horror that was germinating in places like this. She didn't understand that these people wanted to kill her. Yes, *her*. It wasn't a misunderstanding that would be made right with more love. This was hatred. And it was the job of people like Ferris, who knew, to destroy the cells and networks and hiding places of the killers, so that people like Alice could survive.

"Don't look so serious," said Alice. "You'll spoil the party."

Ferris tried to smile. "Be careful, sweetie. That's all. Just be careful. The world isn't as nice as you are."

"I know what I'm doing, Roger. You underestimate me. I know where the lines are. It's you who has the problems. You're the one who practically got his leg shot off, not me. You're the one who needs to be careful."

Ferris took her hand again and whispered in her ear, "I want to hold you, but I can't here. Let's go back to your place." She smiled and rose from the little table. Something had changed.

• • •

THEY DROVE back past the old Roman ruins and the gold souk, and up the hill a few blocks to Alice's building. Something told Ferris not to press his luck that night, but he didn't want to let her go. As he walked her to the door, he asked if he could come up.

"Not this time, but maybe another time," she said. "Tonight was special. I haven't been this way with anyone for a long while. I just want to be sure I'm ready."

"I really like you," said Ferris. He wanted to say "love" but he knew that would sound crazy. He had only known her a few weeks.

"I like you, too, Roger. I'm glad you came with me to the camp tonight. Now you know who I am. A little."

They moved into the shadow of her doorway, away from the light of the street. He kissed her on the lips and she responded, her lips parting slightly, and then wider. He took her in his arms and felt her body against his. As he kissed her, he could feel her moving, softening.

"I want you," she said. Her voice was low and suffused with desire.

"You can have me."

"Not yet." She stepped back so she could look at him. "You're strong, but I think you're soft, too, in this place." She patted his heart. "Are you? Do you have a soft heart?" He wasn't sure how to answer that, so he just nodded. She kissed him on the cheek, her lips lingering on his skin, and then turned her back and walked up the stairs. He was standing there, looking up at her apartment, when he saw the light go on and a face in the window. He walked away in a kind of daze. It was partly the rush of emotion that he felt for her, but he was disoriented by what she had said. It had never occurred to him that he had a soft heart. He wondered if she was right.

8

E D HOFFMAN ARRIVED IN JORDAN a few days later. He was the Big American—big hands; big chest; big, ruddy face with the short bristle of hair on top. He was wearing sunglasses, which gave him the look of a Las Vegas tycoon—the sort of man who peels off cash from a wad of hundred-dollar bills. He arrived on a white Gulfstream jet whose only marking was the tail number. Ferris met him at the military airport, but Hoffman told him to go back to the office. The division chief went to his hotel to get some sleep, then to his favorite kebab restaurant. He finally arrived at the embassy in the early evening and immediately summoned Ferris to the secure conference room. He was waiting at the table, massaging his temples, when Ferris entered the room.

"My head hurts," said Hoffman. "I should remember never to drink the red wine at that restaurant."

Ferris extended his hand. Hoffman embraced him in a bear hug. "How's the leg?" he asked.

"Pretty good. They have me doing exercises. I'm fine. I just feel bad for the guys left in Baghdad."

"Well, don't. They couldn't begin to develop the rapport you've got with Hani. This Berlin thing is a big deal. You handled it just right."

"Thanks, but I didn't do anything except watch. It's Hani's baby."

"Hats off to Hani. Definitely." Hoffman pulled a foil package of peanuts from his pocket and popped a handful into his mouth. "But now it's our turn. I want to run it."

"You've got a problem, then. Hani wants to keep control. He wouldn't even give me a transcript of the debriefing. He says it's his operation, and we can share the take. That's it."

"I know, I know." Hoffman ate more peanuts. "And that's fine, because we don't really have to run it. We just have to manipulate it a little. That's why I'm here."

"I don't follow you." That was the truth. Ferris had no idea what Hoffman was talking about.

"Play it. Influence it. Make use of it."

"Sorry. But if it means screwing Hani, I'm against it."

Hoffman smiled. "Touching sympathy for your liaison brother. But you'll see. We can steer your pal Hani by controlling the information he gets, so he sees what we want him to see. Simple! Actually, it's not simple, it's pretty goddamn complicated. But the idea is simple. Believe me, he'll thank us for it when it's over."

"But Hani owns the agent. He can target him however he wants. And we don't have diddly."

"There's where you're wrong, junior. We have more than you think. I'm going to tell you a secret. You probably know it anyway, but you're not supposed to. The fact is that since September 11 we have captured a whole lot more Al Qaeda members than you realize. We have done all sorts of unpleasant things to get them to talk, which everyone is indignant about, but fuck them. And by the way, thanks very much to your wife for helping write the cover-our-ass memo. She is still your wife, right?"

"Yes, I guess so. We're sort of separated. By the distance."

"Whatever. The point is that we have a lot of information. We know which of these little bastards hates the other. We know who's paying off whom, and who thinks he got a raw deal in the payments, who's screwing who else's 'temporary wife.' We know where the rivalries are, where to plant the seeds of doubt. We have invisible strings on these guys, because we know so much about them—and because they don't understand how much we know. See, they don't even know who's been captured. They don't know if Abdul-Rahman from Abu Dhabi has been captured, or quit, or taken a better offer, or just decided to jerk off full time. They keep getting e-mail messages from people they think maybe we've busted, but they don't *know.* That's the thing. Which allows us certain opportunities for *deception.* Oops. I said it. We have never been very good at that fancy-dan stuff, but you know what? We're getting better. And with the help of our Jordanian friends, we're going to get better still. And it's going to take us to you know who."

"Suleiman?"

"Amen, brother. This is your case. You have a leg full of shrapnel to prove it. Hani is chasing the same thing you are. We're just going to give him a little help."

Ferris was silent for a moment, thinking about what Hoffman had said. Beyond all the razzle-dazzle, he was proposing that they deceive Hani. That sounded like a bad idea.

"You're the boss," he said. "But if you're planning to play games with Hani, my advice is don't. We need our friends now. After Rotterdam, Milan, the next Milan. Jerking Hani's chain sounds like a mistake to me. In this part of the world, you have to trust people or you don't get anywhere."

"Wrong. In this part of the world, you can't trust anybody, because they're all liars. Even Brother Hani. Sorry, but that's a fact. I have been in the Camel Corps a hell of a lot longer than you have. And you're right. I am the boss."

Ferris shook his head with resignation. "He'll be pissed if he finds out. And I'll have to take the flak. Until he throws me out. The way he did my predecessor."

"Well, obviously he would be pissed, if he knew. But he's not going to find out. Because we won't tell him, will we? America is paying the freight here, so it seems to me we can do what we like. And please. You are not Francis Alderson."

Ferris had wanted to ask the question for several months and had never had a chance, until now. "Why did the Jordanians PNG Francis? Nobody has ever explained that to me. There's nothing in the files, and nobody back at NE Division will tell me anything. What did he do?"

"Um, um, um . . ." Hoffman closed his eyes and thought a moment. "I'm not going to tell you. For your own good."

"Why? What did he do? Screw somebody's wife?"

"Hell, no. Everybody in Jordan does that. I wish it were that simple."

"So what is it?"

"Ask Hani."

"He won't tell me."

Hoffman smiled as he pushed his chair away from the table and got up to leave. "That's a good sign."

"Oh yeah? Well, here's my nightmare version, based on zero information. I worry that Hani tossed Alderson so that I would run the station. I'm young and I don't have much experience. He thought he could manipulate me, so he trumped up something against Alderson. That's why he took me to Berlin. So he could get more leverage over me."

"You're paranoid, my boy. A useful quality on occasion, but in this case, it's a reach. Hani didn't have to trump up anything on Alderson. Believe me."

"So what did Francis do? Come on, I want to know. I need to know."

Hoffman scratched his head and thought a moment. "Okay. I'll tell you, but only to keep you from imagining things. Francis Alderson's fuckup was that he tried to recruit one of Hani's deputies. He had gotten friendly with the guy, invited him out to dinner. The guy seemed ready for a pitch, so Francis pitched him. Offered him some money. It's normal. We do it every day of the year, somewhere around the world. But Hani went batshit. He said it was a betrayal of our relationship. We tried like hell to cover it up. Francis said the money was for the guy's kid to get an operation in the States. But Hani knew that was crap. He had us cold. So he PNG'd Francis, to make a point."

"And the point was: Don't fuck with me."

"Precisely."

"And now we're fucking with him."

"Look, Roger, for chrissake, lighten up. I told you, you have to cut me some slack on this. And like I said, he'll thank us for it in the long run."

HOFFMAN AND FERRIS went to see Hani the next morning. The Jordanian intelligence chief was at his most charming. He was dressed in a dark suit and tie to receive his distinguished visitor, but he loosened the tie and draped the jacket over the chair after they had talked a few minutes. He seemed to have a long history with Hoffman, to judge from the banter. Hoffman teased him about a woman he called Fifi, who seemed to have figured in one of their earlier joint operations. "A wonder of nature," Hoffman said, winking at Ferris, who had no idea what particular natural wonder he might be referring to.

When Hoffman offered Hani a cigar, the Jordanian brought out his humidor and insisted that the visitor share one of his. They lit up the stogies and both puffed away contentedly, sharing anecdotes about recent operations. But Ferris knew that the bonhomie was a delaying tactic on both sides, before they got down to the business that had brought Hoffman all the way from Washington. Hani didn't bring up the Berlin operation; he was too polite, perhaps. Or maybe he wanted to force the American to ask. Which Hoffman finally did.

"Maybe we should talk turkey," the division chief said. "I know you're a busy man, and the king is probably waiting for you."

"As you like. I know with Americans there is always this 'turkey.'"

The tone of his voice implied that he had, indeed, won a small victory by forcing Hoffman to go first. "You want to talk about Berlin, of course. I assume that Mr. Ferris has given you the details."

"As far as they go. I must say, you did a hell of a job spotting and developing this guy. It's a nifty operation. Just nifty. But I'm frustrated."

"Why are you frustrated, Ed?" The Jordanian was solicitous, and impenetrable.

"I'm frustrated because I want more input. I want to help you target the Berlin boy, Mustafa Karami. I want to see if we can steer him into the center of the center—to the network that is doing these car bombs in Europe. This is life-or-death stuff for us, my friend. These guys want to kill Americans. That's why I'd like to ask you, as a special favor to the United States, to run this as a joint operation."

Hani paused a good five seconds. He didn't like to disappoint Hoffman. "I am sorry, Ed," he said eventually. "But this is impossible. As you know better than anyone, there is no such thing as a true joint operation. There is always one side that knows more, and one side that knows less. So let me run it. I know my business. Have I ever failed you in the past?"

"No. This is the first time. And I don't like it. We want to help you run it. We can bring a lot to this case. It happens that we know quite a lot about this guy Karami. NSA has had him on watch lists for a long time."

Hoffman took a red folder marked with a string of code words out of his briefcase and put it down on the table. "I want you to do this right. But the problem is, I don't want to share my goodies unless you share control."

Hani looked at the folder, and then at Hoffman. Ferris could see that he was struggling with himself. "I am sorry. I do not want to play any games with you, Ed. I could tell you we will run it jointly, to make you feel better, but it would not be the truth. We found him, we recruited him, and we will run him. You will share in everything that we learn. I am sorry. That is the only way we can do business."

Hoffman scowled. He looked at Ferris, as if deliberating whether to send him out of the room, and then turned back to his host. "I would hate to have the president call His Majesty and complain about this. We are allies. That is why the U.S. Congress is happy to authorize covert payments that account for most of the operating costs of your service. And other, shall we say, activities of the Jordanian government. I would hate to do that. But you are putting me in a pickle, Hani. You are making me eat the shit sandwich. And I don't like it."

"Don't threaten me, my friend," the Jordanian broke in. His voice, usually so decorous, had a sharper edge. "Don't ever threaten me, Ed, because it won't work. The king won't stand for it, and neither will I. We would rather have none of your money than let you think that for a few hundred million dollars you have bought us. I told that to your young man here, Mr. Ferris, and I assumed he would tell you."

"Roger advised me against making this request. He told me you would be pissed off, and he was right. But I still want some control."

Hani shook his head. "You can't have it. As I told Mr. Ferris, this operation is complicated. It takes time. If you try to force it to get the big payoff, you will get nothing. That is why you must be patient."

"I know it's complicated. I'm not an imbecile." Hoffman patted the manila folder before him. "I've read the intercepts." He smiled. "So should you."

Hani looked at the folder again. "I'd like to," he said. This was the real card America had in the intelligence game—not its money, certainly not its HUMINT, but its ability to overhear almost any conversation in the world. "How good are the intercepts?" the Jordanian asked.

"Very good. They show that this guy Karami has been in contact over the past six months with an AQ operations man in Indonesia by the name of Hussein Amary. We heard about him from the Singaporeans. Is he on your radar?"

"Amary." Hani thought a moment. "No. I don't think so."

"Well, he should be. Because we think Amary is very dangerous. He's connected with the operations planner who we think is running these car bombs in Europe. We call him Suleiman. If Amary is also linked to Karami, that means he's more in the operational line than you seem to realize."

"This is very interesting," said Hani. He looked off balance.

"Yeah," said Hoffman. "Isn't it, though?"

"Can I have those files?" asked the Jordanian. "They may be helpful to us. As you say, we share the same enemy."

"What's in it for me?"

"Same as before. You share the take. The point is, we'll run a better operation if we know more. And you'll get more out of it. If there are ways to share more of the operational planning down the road, why not? I do not think His Majesty will object. But for now, we will run it. And we will be most grateful for the help of the United States."

Hoffman picked up the file. Ferris wasn't sure whether he was going to put it back in his briefcase. But after several seconds he handed it to Hani. "I like you," he said. "You play tough."

"*Ahlan wa sahlan*," said Hani. "You are most welcome."

"Don't screw me on this," said the American.

"We are allies, my dear Ed. We have a common enemy. We treat each other with respect." He held the file close, as if he had just won it in a fight. They shook hands, talked a while more and the Americans eventually departed.

NEITHER HOFFMAN nor Ferris said a word on the ride back to the embassy or the walk down the corridors. They talked only when they were back inside the bubble of the secure conference room.

"How did you do that?" Ferris asked. "By the end you had him begging for the thing you came all this way to give him."

"Easy. You just have to be a manipulative son of a bitch. That has never been a problem for me."

"Were those intercepts real?"

"More or less. Amary and Karami have definitely been in contact.

The first contact was, let me see, not long after the Jordanians started surveillance of Karami's apartment in Berlin."

"How did you know they had him under surveillance?"

"We're not completely stupid. Or at least, I'm not. You see, the Germans don't like people conducting unilateral operations on their territory. So when they noticed something, they let us know."

"Hani thinks the Germans are clueless."

"Well, that's one of his mistakes. He's a genius in his own environment, but that makes him a little arrogant when he leaves home base. Sorry to say."

Ferris was scratching his head. He was still trying to understand how the pieces fit together. "These conversations between Karami and Amary. Who initiated them?"

"Amary, of course."

"Why do you say of course?"

Hoffman pulled Ferris toward him. Even in the secure conference room, he couldn't be sure that he wasn't being bugged.

"I know because Amary is our guy," whispered Hoffman. "That's the game here. He's our guy. And the Jordanians are going to make his bones in Al Qaeda. They're going to plug him into Suleiman's network. And then it's showtime."

"Jesus Christ," said Ferris. "That's a nice piece of work. Except for tricking the Jordanians."

"Can't be helped. I tried to be reasonable and run the operation together, but your friend Hani refused. He shouldn't have, but he did. So we play it another way. I didn't make him take the intercepts. He practically grabbed that file. Anyway, this will be great for them. It will be the best operation of Hani's career. Yours, too. Wait and see. You just have to understand, your country is at war. Different rules now."

"That's what my wife keeps telling me."

"Well, she's right. We are at war with a ruthless enemy, and we cannot rely on the charity of our friends like the genial Jordanians anymore. We have to fight our own war, which means we need our own unilateral ops against Al Qaeda. Now. We have no choice. If we wait, people are going to get killed."

"I hope this works." Ferris closed his eyes as he said it.

"It will work. It's a good operation. And if it doesn't, we'll try something else. That's what you do in wartime. You improvise. So stop worrying, my boy, and get with the plan. I'm counting on you. Can I count on you?"

"Of course. Totally. And I'm not worrying. I'm thinking. They're different."

"Well, don't think too much. It's bad for the nerves." He put a meaty hand on Ferris's back. "Go get a bottle of whiskey and some ice. I need to get seriously drunk so I'll fall asleep on the flight back."

"You're flying back tonight?"

"Uh-huh. I promised Ethel I would take her to a show tomorrow night. *The Lion King*. I don't get it, frankly. I mean, how do you turn a kids' cartoon into a Broadway show? But she wants to go, and I'm a pussycat."

The notion of Hoffman being henpecked by a wife named Ethel pleased Ferris. He thought, not of his own wife, but of Alice, and how much he would like to take her to a Broadway musical, or a movie, or anything that would help them forget they were living on the sharp end of a knife in these dry, dusty hills. Ferris departed to go get the whiskey, leaving Hoffman smiling beatifically in the secure conference room, like an anti-Buddha.

9

ALICE MELVILLE FLEW BACK to Boston for the funeral of her aunt. Ferris drove her to the airport. She was dressed in a lime-green A-line skirt and a white blouse. She had a ribbon in her hair. The only thing that was missing to complete the effect was a circle pin. "What's with the sorority-girl outfit?" asked Ferris. It was a side of her he had never seen. "I don't want to scare my mother," she answered. "She thinks it's okay for me to be in Jordan because the king went to Deerfield."

Alice had adored the dead aunt, a doughty public-interest lawyer who had applauded her decision to go off to Jordan when everyone else was telling her she was mad. "Aunt Edith was even crazier than me," she wrote Ferris in an e-mail the night she arrived back home. She sent a few silly messages the first few days, including a short cartoon video she'd found on the Internet in which the United States drives Osama bin Laden crazy by hounding him with telemarketing calls. Then she went silent. She was too busy, evidently, or too sad about her aunt's death. Or perhaps, back home in the nest of privilege, she had forgotten all about him.

Ferris buried himself in his work. Hoffman's visit had been a shock to his system—a reminder that he was in a business where any action was sanctioned, so long as it worked. He asked himself whether he was doing everything he could to penetrate Suleiman's network with the tools he actually had in hand. He had only one, really: the address of the safe house where one of Suleiman's operatives had recruited Nizar, the unlucky young Iraqi who managed to get himself killed less than twenty-four hours after he met Ferris. The house was a villa in Jebel Al-Akhthar on the southern outskirts of Amman. The agency had maintained fixed surveillance there ever since Ferris first landed the intelligence. They had run a covert SIGINT operation to tap the phone line, and had data-mined every detail they could gather about the Jordanian family that lived there, looking for links to known Al Qaeda operatives. But so far it had been a dry hole.

The house was a simple villa, built of concrete blocks and surrounded by a dirty masonry wall. The owner was a Jordanian man in his early sixties named Ibrahim Alousi who had worked for an Arab construction company in Kuwait and recently retired. His two sons worked as engineers for the same construction company here, and their wives and children shared the villa. The family were all practicing Muslims. They went most Fridays to the mosque and rose each morning at dawn for the Fajr prayers, but they had no apparent connection with any of the Salafist groups in Jordan. Ferris's men had watched and waited and tracked, but they hadn't found any hint of a link to Suleiman or his network. Maybe the Alousis were just being careful, but the ops chief at NE Division had advised Ferris to end his surveillance. It was expensive, and it wasn't producing any intelligence. But Ferris hated to give up his one good lead, purchased at the cost of several human lives. And he thought the Alousi family was too clean, so innocent-looking they became suspicious.

Ferris decided it was time to take the offensive. He had been waiting for Suleiman to show his hand; now he would provoke him. He would throw something at the Alousis—a tantalizing provocation—and see how they reacted. And it happened he had the right bait to dangle in front of this prey. His predecessor, Francis Alderson, had recruited a young Palestinian named Ayman from a town in the

West Bank called Jenin. He was living in Amman now, and like most Palestinians, what he wanted most was a visa for America. The consulate had flagged him for the CIA station as a potential recruit, and Alderson had okayed a pitch right before he got booted. Now Ayman was on the books as an asset, but without any operational role. Ferris would give him one.

Ferris met Ayman in a room at the InterContinental Hotel at the Third Circle. Back in the 1980s, when the U.S. Embassy had been across the street, the hotel had been the hub of Amman's social life, but now it was safely out of the spotlight. Ferris was waiting in an upstairs suite when Ayman knocked on the door. The sun was shining bright through the window, glinting off the water in the pool down below. Ferris could tell from the young man's wide eyes that this was the fanciest room he had ever seen. He had the hard look of a young Arab: sinewy arms, taut facial bones, bad complexion partly hidden under the stubble of his beard. He was wearing a prayer cap of knitted white wool. He was perfect.

Ferris gave the young man his instructions. He was to go to the house in Jebel Al-Akhthar and ask to see one of the Alousi brothers. If they weren't home, he should ask when they would be back and return. When he was with one of the brothers, he should tell them one sentence only. *I have a message from Suleiman.* If they asked what the message was, he should tell them to come to an address in Zarqa the following day at seven PM. That was a hook; if anyone in the house had any link to the network, someone would have to follow that message up—if only to confirm that it was bogus.

Ayman looked uneasy as Ferris went through the instructions a second time. Ferris tried to brace him. Do this right, he told Ayman, and you'll have your visa to America. Make a mistake and we'll turn you over to the GID.

THE ALOUSIS' HOUSE was built on the side of a steep hill. It had two stories. Rusting steel reinforcing bars on the second-floor roof suggested that the old man had planned to build three stories but had run out of money. The neighbors walked the streets with their heads down, wrapped in their abayas or kaffiyehs, deaf and dumb. The wind whistled up the dusty streets and blew loose pebbles off the hillsides. Ferris had fixed surveillance across from the house, so he could watch on his monitor as Ayman approached the door. A woman answered, and then the old man, and Ferris shook his head, thinking the boys must be away. But eventually a young man arrived at the front door, dressed in a dirty blue track suit. He looked at Ayman warily, and then invited him in the villa.

Ayman was inside for nearly an hour. Ferris wasn't sure if that was good or bad. In an hour, they could ask enough questions to shred the thin legend Alderson had assembled for his young agent. But when Ferris debriefed Ayman late that night, he said the long wait hadn't been anything important. In fact, nothing had happened at all. He had passed the message, just as Ferris had asked. I have a message from Suleiman. Meet us at this address in Zarqa. But the Alousi boys said they didn't know anyone named Suleiman. How could there be a message from Suleiman, if they didn't know any Suleiman? It must be a mistake. Ferris asked what had taken so long, then, if they didn't understand his message. They had given him coffee and tea, to be friendly, Ayman explained, and asked him about his family in Jenin, and his friends, and if he had ever been arrested by the Israelis. Ayman seemed happy to have completed his assignment, whatever it was. When could he get his visa? Ferris told him it would be a few weeks, a month at most.

THE GID FOUND Ayman's body three days later, stuffed in a metal dumpster near the address in Zarqa where the meeting was supposed to take place. His tongue had been ripped out, leaving a blood-crusted stump at the base of his mouth. There were other signs of torture: broken ribs, missing fingers. One of Hani's assistants brought the pictures of the body to the embassy in an envelope, with a note that just said, "FYI." They knew Ferris had been in contact with Ayman, obviously. Ferris made himself look at the photos. He owed the poor boy that much.

Ferris called Hani's deputy and said he needed a favor. He gave him the address of the Alousi house in Jebel Al-Akhthar and asked him to raid it immediately and arrest anyone who was there. He said he would explain everything later to Hani. But when the GID team arrived at the villa an hour later, nobody was home. The residents seemed to have fled hurriedly in the night, out the back alley, throwing a few clothes in suitcases and running into the night. Hani's deputy called Ferris and said the GID would try to find the Alousis. But Ferris suspected they were already across the border—to Damascus or Riyadh or maybe Fallujah.

Ferris's dangle had worked: The safe house had been real, all right. But now it was blown. Whatever use they might eventually have gotten from their surveillance was lost. Hani never called, and Ferris was relieved he didn't have to explain how the young man from Jenin had ended up in the dumpster. He had learned something from his operation. The adversary was even harder to penetrate than Ferris had imagined. He had reached a wall, and none of the bricks were lose. Perhaps Hoffman was right. The only way to get inside was deception, but he didn't see how.

FERRIS WAITED for Alice's return. He hated the bureaucratic side of his job. Everything needed reports and permissions and cables, sent in the cover identities CIA officers called "funny names." In the cable traffic, Ferris was "Hanford J. Sloane," a pseudonymous identity that would have allowed him to invent a whole imaginary life of bogus operations and recruitments, if he chose. But Ferris actually liked the job of espionage. It was the paperwork he found dull.

The office tedium was relieved by a classified cable from his best friend from The Farm, Andy Cohen, whose funny name was "Everett M. Farcas." Cohen was a former grad student in Chinese who, like Ferris, had been suffering terminal boredom in the library before he joined up. He was tall and had a wispy goatee, which the instructors initially made him shave off but kept growing back. Cohen liked to bad-mouth everyone and everything. Unlike Ferris, who knew from his father how ordinary the agency could be, Cohen had imagined a world of Pierce Brosnans and Sharon Stones. When he met his dumpy, middle-aged instructors, he whispered to Ferris, "You gotta be kidding." Life at The Farm convinced Cohen that something was deeply wrong with the CIA. The night before graduation, he told Ferris, "You know, these people are total *losers*." But he had stayed in, sending Ferris regular reports on the incompetence and absurdity of his colleagues.

Cohen's first overseas post was Taiwan, where he had ignored the cautionary advice of his station chief and actually gone out and recruited Taiwanese agents. For that unforgivable display of initiative, he had been punished with an assignment to the Asset Validation Staff back at Headquarters. Created in the early 1990s to reduce waste and bureaucracy, AVS had become something of a cottage industry, providing employment for dozens of paper-pushing case officers. Its job was to vet agents and, where appropriate, decommission those who were no longer productive. Since Cohen regarded nearly all the agency's assets as useless, he was ready to fire the whole lot, but he had no interest in the AVS paper chase and its tedious scrub of each agent's Personal Record Questionnaire. So he did as little real work as possible, which left him time for trading foreign currencies online in his E*Trade account and sending tirades to Ferris.

"My colleagues in AVS are as dumb as *bricks*, Roger," the latest missive began. "They frighten me. I mean, this is where the people from The Farm who were too stupid to read the maps ended up. And the scary thing is that *they* get to decide who's worth keeping on the books. It's fabulous, really. The man in the next office is a Mormon from Salt Lake named Stan. He told me yesterday that one of the case officers he was vetting should be bounced because he had admitted on a polygraph that when he was a kid on the farm in

Nebraska he had sex with a sheep. Ridiculous, right? But Stan was really upset. He said the guy was a security risk. What did he think, that the sheep was going to blackmail him? Can you believe that? But just wait. Remember Aaron Fink from our CST class? Okay, next thing Stan decides that Fink's recruitments in Lima may be bogus because so many of them have Jewish names. Holy shit! I mean, Aaron is definitely a member of the tribe, but does Stan think he was recruiting these guys on orders from Baron Rothschild? Scary. So I looked at the list of Aaron's agents and most of the names were, like, 'Sanchez' or 'Ruiz,' just ordinary Spanish names, not Schicklegruber or Gottbaum, for God's sake. So I said to Stan, 'Hey, buddy, I think maybe you're out of line here. These aren't Jewish names and even if they were, so fucking what?' And Stan says, 'The names could have been changed.' Yikes. This is what we're dealing with here. Not just morons, but full-blown, anti-Semitic morons. I mean, really, the place is falling apart. Don't come back. Stay in the field as long as you can and then trade that bum leg for a full disability. I'm going to go work for Fox News so I can make shit up for real! Love, Everett M. Farcas."

Ferris sent him a brief reply and attached some jokes he'd found on the Internet. Cohen had a point. Much of the agency was laughably incompetent. But Ferris wasn't, and Hoffman certainly wasn't. So he would forget about the rest, and get on with it.

TO AMUSE HIMSELF, Ferris visited the library at the British Council. One of his hobbies was reading about World War II intelligence operations. He had read nearly every book there was about Bletchley Park, and the "wizard war" of the scientists, and the "Double-Cross System" the British used to deceive the Germans by manipulating their captured agents in Britain. The British had been losing that war, Ferris reminded himself. They had suffered the disastrous retreat at Dunkirk, and the ravages of the Blitz. Their enemies were stronger than they were, and more ruthless. The Brits had little in their favor, save one thing. They were good at puzzles. Ferris pulled books down off the shelves, hoping he would find something that would encourage him, or at least distract him.

A WEEK AFTER Alice's departure, Ferris was in his big, empty apartment, eating another solitary meal. A late October wind was rattling the windowpanes, a cold, dry breeze off the desert that settled in his bones. Gretchen called, as she usually did each week around this time. The conversation was more than usually empty. Ferris couldn't talk about work, and he didn't know what else to talk about. Gretchen was whispering hoarsely, telling him what she wanted to do in bed when he came home. Ferris told her to stop. He said his line was probably tapped, but that only seemed to arouse her more. "I hate this," Ferris said, by which he meant not just sex talk on a tapped line but the entirety of their relationship. "Oh, you're just in a bad mood, honey," said Gretchen. "Call me back when you're not such a *grouch*."

Admit it, he told himself when he had ended the call. You miss Alice. And there was something else: He was worried that she wouldn't find him interesting anymore, after she'd been back home in Boston mingling with the overachiever talent pool. His life was a perverse mirror image. He was married to one woman, whom he didn't love, and he was falling in love with another woman, who he was afraid might become interested in another man.

FERRIS LAY IN bed, waiting for sleep. As happened sometimes, the tape rewound to a moment in his life that was fixed in his memory. It was a wrestling match during his senior year at George Marshall High School in Fairfax. He was well ahead on points, and could have coasted to victory in the third period. His opponent was exhausted. But Ferris wasn't taking it easy. He was determined to pin the other boy and win outright. He had his opponent in a headlock and was driving his arm down hard so he could push the shoulder blades onto the mat. There was groan from the boy, not quite a word. And then he heard a sudden snap and a piercing scream, and he knew he had broken the boy's arm. The crowd was stunned and silent as the injured wrestler staggered off the mat cradling his wrist, and then a few people started to boo. Not many, but people had sensed that something bad was going to happen—that Ferris wasn't just determined to win, but to destroy his opponent. What Ferris remembered, when this scene came back to him, was the moment just before he heard the snap—when the boy groaned and tried to tell Ferris to stop.

Ferris shut his eyes against the image. He had been living with this memory for almost twenty years, and it still upset him. Violence itself wasn't the problem, it was the unintended violence—the possibility that he might unwittingly expose someone to harm. Ferris put the thought out of his mind—he could do that, will his conscious self away from what bothered him—and eventually he was asleep.

ALICE RETURNED AFTER ten days, and the first thing she did when she landed at Queen Alia Airport was call Ferris. "I'm sorry, but I missed you," she said, as if she were admitting to a character defect. "I thought about you a lot while I was gone, Roger. All the time, basically. That's why I didn't call, I was nervous."

"Yeah," said Ferris. "Me, too. Is that good or bad?"

"I don't know. Good, I think. But we're going to have to find out."

"Right. When do we start?"

"Well . . ." She paused, as if she were really deliberating the matter. "How about tomorrow night. I need to get some sleep. The man next to me last night snored all the way from Boston to London. And he had B.O."

"What time should I pick you up?"

"I hate that 'date' stuff. Can you cook?"

"Sort of. Not very well."

"That doesn't matter. Buy a steak and two potatoes and some red wine and we'll be fine. Can you do that? And some green beans, too, if they have them. Or broccoli. Or carrots. Okay?"

Ferris promised to do the shopping and hung up happily. He spent the next twenty-four hours in a pleasant state of desire, thinking not just about having sex with Alice, but about the pleasure of having her with him again—the bright blue, bottomless water that was Alice. He had the housekeeper throw away the old newspapers and other accumulated debris and sent her out to buy the food and lots of flowers. He put little candles in the bedroom and then decided that was too much, and put them away.

Alice arrived a half hour late. When Ferris opened the door and looked at her, he shook his head. Her face was radiant, with its own glow of anticipation, and her blond hair seemed almost to sparkle against the blue-black evening sky.

"God, you are so pretty," he said.

"Let me in the damned door. It's cold out here."

She entered the apartment, gave him a kiss and said, "Be right back. I want to take a look." She gave herself a tour, checking out every room—pausing in the master bedroom to give it a close review. She returned shaking her head. "God! You must be a big shot. This place is enormous."

"Embassy housing. They assume people have families, so the apartments are pretty big."

"Pretty big? It's huge. I'll spare you the lecture about how many needy Palestinian families could fit in here. So, come on! Do the host thing. What have you got to drink?"

"How about champagne?" She nodded, and Ferris fetched a bottle of Dom Pérignon he'd taken that day from a stock left by Alderson after his hasty departure. She studied the label.

"Is that supposed to impress me? Dom Pérignon? Because I have to say, it totally does impress me. A girl doesn't trust a man who buys cheap champagne. What's the point? It's like a woman buying cheap underwear. Do you know what I mean? Of course you don't."

Ferris poured two glasses, which they drank quickly, sitting on the couch, while she talked about her trip home, and her parents, siblings and cousins. Ferris filled their glasses again, and then a third time while she talked. She had told the family about Ferris, she said, although she wasn't sure why. That was why she had come back to Amman so eager to see him. She wanted to understand why she had missed him so much.

Ferris slid toward her on the couch and put his arm around her. She relaxed into his body and then pulled back to look at him.

"I know you, Roger. You think I don't, but I do. You're open, but you don't talk about yourself. You're brave, but you're scared of something. You worry that you have to take care of everything. But you don't. Tonight, you just have to be with me."

Ferris didn't answer. He put his hand to her face and gently traced the outlines of her cheek and lips. He pushed the hair back from her forehead. It was so soft and fine, almost like a baby's hair. He pulled her toward him. She tensed for a moment, then relaxed and turned her lips toward his. His kiss was gentle, his lips just touching hers. She opened her mouth and their tongues met. Ferris was aroused, and he pressed closer to her.

Her eyes widened, and then closed. "Not yet. I have to make you dinner."

Alice cooked the steak and potatoes, and the lima beans, which was what the maid had brought back from the market. She sang "It's Raining Men" while she cooked, in a surprisingly good voice. Ferris thought she was the most unselfconscious person he had ever met, and he tried to imagine what such a woman would be like in bed.

She caught the expression on his face. "Open the wine! Make yourself useful," she said, and Ferris went looking for the corkscrew.

They dined on the enclosed terrace. "Turn out the lights," she ordered. That side of the apartment faced away from the city, and in the inky desert night it seemed you could see every star in the heavens.

"Hold my hand," she said.

"Why?" Ferris was hungry.

"Because we have to say grace. Pay attention, Roger. This grace has been in my family for three hundred years. I want to say it because this is a special night. You have to learn it yourself by Thanksgiving. Close your eyes. *For thy tender care, dear Father, and thy blessings free, we would now, with loving hearts, render thanks to thee. Amen.* Say 'Amen.'"

"Amen," said Ferris.

She gave his hand a squeeze and then let it go. Ferris opened his eyes and looked at her. He felt suddenly guilty. She was so loving, and so trusting, and he knew that he hadn't been honest with her about something important—the most important thing, maybe. They ate for a while, as Alice talked about her trip home. She devoured her steak and potato but left the lima beans. When she had finished, she pushed the plate away and gazed dreamily at the stars, then turned back to him. She kicked off her shoe and began running her toes gently up his calf.

"I have to tell you something," Ferris said awkwardly.

"What's the problem? Don't you like girls?" She giggled.

"No, it's something serious."

"Oh, good. What is it?"

He shook his head. "I don't know how to say this. I'm ashamed to say it. But I'm married."

"I *know* that." She shook her head. "God! How dumb do you think I am?"

"How did you know? I never mentioned it. And I haven't worn my wedding ring since I met you."

"Because it's obvious. A single guy would have tried to jump me on the first date. But you were more patient. Mature. Married, like. That was one thing."

"I did want to jump you on the first date, and the second, and the third."

"It's not just that. There's something sad about you, even when you're having a good time. Like you need something that somebody hasn't given you. Not sex, but love. So that says to me, unhappy married man."

"That's true. I do need love. And I am an unhappy married man." He reached out his hand to touch hers, but she pulled it back.

"Plus, I asked."

"What do you mean, you 'asked.'"

"I asked at the embassy. One of the secretaries goes to my yoga class. I said I had met this really cute guy named Roger Ferris and she said, 'Watch out. He's married.' So I knew. But the other stuff is true. That's why I waited so long. I wanted to see if you were worth the trouble."

"You're not mad at me, for not telling you right away that I was married?"

"No. Because you did tell me, eventually. I might not have been willing to go to bed with you otherwise. No, that's not true. I still would have. But it's better this way. And you're going to dump your wife."

"It's true. I'm asking her for a divorce. I'm going to tell her, when I go back to Washington the next time."

"You should get a divorce, Roger, if you're not happy. But it's not about me, it's about you."

"I'm happy now."

"Yes, but not as happy as you're going to be." She took his hand and led him back toward the bedroom. There was a candle next to the bed. She had put it there secretly, when she made her first tour of the apartment. Now she lit it.

"Hold me," she said.

Ferris touched her hair, and then her lips, and pulled her toward him. As they kissed, she fumbled at his belt. While she tugged at his trousers, he put his hand under her dress. The soft fabric between her legs seemed to have dissolved. Their clothes came off in a pile, and he laid her body gently down on the bed and looked at her in the candlelight. Her cheeks were alabaster smooth in the light of the flickering candle. One hand modestly covered her breast, but she let it fall. She saw the wounds on his leg; in the candlelight, the welts of scar tissue were little hillocks, soft to the touch.

She opened herself to him, to his eyes and his gentle hands and the heat of his skin against hers. "I want you," she said, the words muffled in the breath of desire. She took him in her hand and guided him toward her.

He entered her slowly, but she pulled him deeper. Her body moved quickly, and she cried out for him. Before he could answer, their bodies reached the same sudden precipice of desire. He could feel her tightening around him, and then he lost himself in a shudder of pleasure that carried them together into white space. He laid his head on her breast, wet with his saliva, and listened to the beat of her heart.

10

S EVERAL DAYS LATER, Hani summoned Ferris to his office. Ferris went alone, around that bend in the road to the fortress set against the mountainside. Two sergeants led him upstairs this time, flanking him almost as if they were guards. And for once, he was not taken to the holding chamber of Hani's deputy, but brought immediately to see the pasha himself. Ferris wondered what was going on. There had been no sign that Hani had been upset; indeed, he'd heard nothing from Hani at all for days.

When Ferris entered Hani's office, he could see immediately that something was wrong. The Jordanian had none of his usual bravado. He had a heavy growth of beard and deep circles under his eyes, as if he hadn't slept for several nights. Hani gestured for his guest to sit in the chair opposite his desk rather than on the couches where they usually sat. He waited for the door to close, and then waited a moment more to compose himself.

"Mustafa Karami is dead," said the Jordanian coldly. "Our man in Berlin. He was murdered a week ago."

Hani spoke the words with a deep anger. It was an expression of frustration, of hurt, of regret at so much wasted effort. It wasn't the loss of the life so much as the man-years of work that had gone into setting up the operation, and the lives that might have been saved

Ferris wondered what to say. "Who killed him?" he asked finally.

"We believe it was one of his contacts from Al Qaeda. They got him in Madrid. What we do not understand is *why* he was killed." The Jordanian looked Ferris square in the eye. "Do you have any idea?"

Ferris paused a long moment, too long. "I have absolutely no idea," he said.

"*Absolutely no idea.* That is more than a no, and it makes me ask a question: Why do people feel it necessary to add extra words to their denials? When it would be enough to say 'no,' why does someone say 'absolutely not'? It is strange, don't you think?"

"Okay, Hani. I'll give you the simple version. I don't know who killed Mustafa Karami. Until I walked into your office, I didn't know that he was dead."

Hani was still musing about words. "With Arabic, there is something about our language that makes every statement a bit of a lie, you know? Even when you are telling the truth. Ours is a language for poets, not engineers. But English is simple. It is a language of 'yes' or 'no.' When people add something, it is for a reason. When someone says to me, 'Frankly, Hani . . . ,' or 'Honestly, Hani . . . ,' I always suspect that he is lying. If he were telling the truth, he would not need those extra words of emphasis. He would just say it. Am I right?"

"Yes, Hani. You are right."

"But I believe you, when you tell me that you do not know why Karami was killed. Because how could you know? I do not know myself."

"Thank you."

"But, my dear, we are going to find out. Isn't that good luck? You and I are going to find out why Mustafa Karami was killed."

"How are we going to find that out?" Ferris was suddenly nervous. He could feel his heart racing.

"By interrogating the man who killed him. The Spaniards seized him in Madrid and gave him to us. His name is Ziyad. He has been here almost a week. He is here now, right below us, in the prison beneath this building."

"The Palace of the Ghosts," said Ferris, for that was what Jordanians sometimes called the prison beneath the GID's headquarters. It was said you never left the prison the same person who went in.

"That is nonsense, my dear Ferris. There are no ghosts, and no broken bones. You know better than that. We do not torture people. The best interrogation technique is to let people break down themselves. Or bring in one of the sheiks, to read the Koran with them. They are much more effective than we could be."

"Not when you need information in a hurry."

"No, my dear Ferris. It is especially when you are in a hurry that you must be patient. That is the way I have behaved with Ziyad. When we brought him in a week ago, he was screaming through his hood that he would never talk. By Allah, he would shit on the moustache of the king before he would tell us a word. He was kicking and screaming, to show how tough he would be in resisting what he thought must be coming. I think he actually wanted me to beat him, to get his adrenaline going. But I walked away. I refused to say a word to him."

"Not a word, Hani?"

"Nothing. To him, only silence. The only sound was my praying, at prayer time. I came back the second night, and he was the same, but not quite so crazy. I sat behind him in the interrogation room and watched him for more than an hour. You could hear screams down the hall, but we always do that. The screams are recorded. He babbled for a while, telling me how tough he was. He said he was glad that he had killed Karami, because he was a traitor. He was glad. He shouted at me. He was waiting for the torture, but still it did not come. And I said nothing. Before I left, I prayed again. But not a word to him."

"He was disappointed. You wounded his dignity."

"You are precisely right, Roger. This is the Arab in you. Ziyad thought he was so important that we would have to beat him like a dog to get his information. But we were ignoring him. He could not understand it. It was an insult to his dignity, as you say. I came back last night and sat with him again. He had stopped screaming. I sat behind him again, just behind his head, so he could hear me breathing. I was silent for many minutes. Perhaps another hour, maybe more, I don't know. Finally he spoke. He wanted to know if I was going to ask him any questions. That's when I knew he was ready to talk. He was asking to be interrogated."

"So what did he say?"

"Nothing, because I still wouldn't talk with him. I whispered in his ear that he was in a great deal of trouble. I took off his hood and put a picture in front of him."

"His mother."

"Of course. 'Be careful,' I whispered. And then I walked away again. I wanted to give him twenty-four more hours of nothingness, so that he would truly need to confess to me. And now I think perhaps he is ready. He has been up all night again. Yes, I think this is a good time. Shall we go and see?"

"Yes," said Ferris. He knew he didn't have a choice, in any event. "One thing."

"And what is that?"

"Can I call Headquarters, to let them know that Karami is dead?"

"No." Hani's eyes were as sad as a dog's. "I am afraid you cannot call your Headquarters. That would be quite inappropriate."

"Why not?" asked Ferris, but Hani ignored the question. Then, for the first time since he had arrived in Jordan, Ferris felt afraid of his host. He was Hani's prisoner, and he had no doubt that for all the Arab man's subtle word play, he would kill Ferris if he decided it was necessary.

Hani rose from his desk and led the way out the door. Aides immediately jumped to assist him, but the boss waved them away. A guard at the end of the corridor mumbled deferentially, "*Ya sidi*," as

the chief passed. Hani nodded, then punched a code into an electronic lock, opening a heavy door. Ferris followed him, into the
Palace of the Ghosts.

Just past the door was a small elevator with no buttons. Hani put
a key into a lock and the elevator door opened. Inside, there were just
two buttons, up and down. This was Hani's private elevator to the
prison. They descended a long time; Ferris wasn't sure whether the
elevator was slow or they were going very deep underground, but it
seemed to take almost thirty seconds. Finally the door opened and
Ferris looked down a long, dank concrete corridor.

A group of powerful Arab men, the sort who looked like they
might shoot you on a whim, stood in the corridor. Hani approached
them and said something that Ferris couldn't hear. The American
shivered slightly. It was cold in this underground pit. A man might
freeze here, if he wasn't given adequate clothing. Hani beckoned for
him to follow down the corridor. There were heavy metal doors
every ten yards, with tiny openings.

"You can look, if you like," said Hani.

Ferris peered in one hole. He saw an emaciated man in his under-
pants, so glassy-eyed that he seemed barely alive. The smell in the cell
was of human excrement and urine.

"A hard case, that one," said Hani. "But he'll come around."

Ferris didn't want to look in any more cells. He was not a sentimental man, and he had seen before what America's friends and allies
were capable of when they decided to put the screws on someone. By
comparison, Hani was mild. But he did not want to be in this place.
They reached an intersection, where corridors of cells stretched a
hundred yards in either direction, and then another, similar intersection. Jesus, Ferris thought, half this country must be in prison.

"Here we are," said Hani when they reached a third intersection.
He walked to the left. There were no cells along this corridor, but
small rooms that appeared to be used for interrogation. He could
hear the sound of a man screaming. It began as a sudden wail of pain
and shock, as if a bone had been broken, and then grew in intensity,

as if someone were grinding the broken bone back and forth. Ferris didn't know whether it was real or fake. There was a pause, and then another horrifying shriek, as the victim whimpered and pleaded in Arabic.

Hani opened a door and gestured for Ferris to take a seat. Before him was a one-way glass panel, and just beyond that, the interrogation room, brightly lit by a fluorescent light overhead, with a desk and two chairs. The walls were painted blue. This was it. The blue hotel. On Ferris's side of the glass was a small speaker, so that he could hear what was said in the other room. "It's lucky you understand Arabic," said Hani. "I don't think this would translate very easily."

He left Ferris, entered the interrogation room and pulled his chair back against the wall, perhaps a dozen yards from the other chair. A moment later the far door opened and two guards led in the prisoner. He was unshaven, exhausted from lack of sleep but otherwise appeared unharmed. The guards sat the prisoner in his chair and strapped his arms and legs to the metal frame. Then they left the room. The prisoner looked at Hani almost plaintively.

Ferris waited for Hani to say something, but the Jordanian was silent.

"What do you want from me?" the prisoner asked. He repeated it, this time almost a wail. Still Hani was silent.

Several minutes passed. The prisoner stared at Hani with a haunted look. There were tears rolling down his cheeks, and then he was choking back a sob. "What do you want?" he pleaded.

At last Hani answered.

"Tell me, Ziyad, why did you kill Mustafa Karami?" His voice was soft. From the corridor came the sound of ceaseless screams.

"Because he was a traitor," the prisoner answered. "Because he was a traitor. Because he was a traitor."

Hani let the silence in the room build. It was like the pressure against the skull when a diver is too deep under water. After ten minutes, Ziyad grew desperate enough to speak again.

"Please. It is the truth. Mustafa Karami was a traitor."

"But Ziyad, how do you *know* that Mustafa was a traitor?" Hani's question was almost a taunt.

"You are tricking me. You already know!"

"There is no trick. Tell me."

"Because he was working with the Americans. He was a traitor, working with the Americans."

Hani paused, to register the words. "And how could you be sure of that?" The voice was as impossible to escape as a dream.

"You know the answer. You know, you know."

"Of course I know, but I want to hear it from you. You are an important man. I must hear it from a sincere man I respect, like you."

"Thank you, *sidi*. We were sure he was a traitor because he was in contact with their man. With Hussein Amary, who works with the Americans in Indonesia. That is how we knew that Karami must work for the Americans."

"Yes, the Americans." Hani's eyes were hard points of rage. "But how did you know?"

"We knew because Karami contacted Amary. At first it was the other way around. Amary calling Karami. He even asked us about it. Who is this Hussein Amary? Why is he calling me? But then, later, we learned that Karami had contacted Amary. He wanted to help Amary to travel to Europe, to meet with some of us. He asked about someone named Suleiman. And then we knew: You and the Americans were trying to insert him into our network. That was your trick. You were using Karami to put someone into our most secret places. That was when we knew that Karami could not be trusted. He was working for the Americans. And for you."

Hani was staring at the prisoner. Ferris could see the tautness in his face as he struggled to maintain his composure.

"Why didn't you kill Amary?" Hani asked.

"We tried to, but we could not find him. He disappeared. The Americans were clever. They hid him. They are very clever, the Americans. But they are Satan, and God will punish them."

Hani looked toward the glass mirror, at the spot where he knew

Ferris must be sitting. "Yes," he said quietly. "The Americans are very clever." He rose from his chair and left the room. There was a suppressed violence in his step, like a professional boxer walking toward the ring.

He opened the door to Ferris's listening post. Ferris wondered if the Jordanian was going to shoot him right there. Hani was clenching his fists—not as a prelude to violence, it turned out, but to regain control of his emotions.

"I do not ever want to speak with you again," he said, his voice wavering slightly. "We had a good and careful plan for Karami. He could have been a great asset for us both. Perhaps he could have taken us where we want to go. And now he is lost, because of your foolishness and your lies."

He looked at Ferris, still in shock. How could the Americans have been so stupid? He shook his head. It was over. He turned toward the door and then stopped and looked back at Ferris.

"I know what you have been doing. We have an expression for it in Arabic, called *taqiyya*. It comes from the time of the Prophet. It is the lie you tell to protect yourself from the unbelievers. They are the ignorant ones, so you can tell them any lie you want. That is what you and Ed Hoffman have been doing to me with your deceptions. *Taqiyya*. But you have made a very bad mistake."

"I am sorry," said Ferris.

"Do not say another word, Mr. Ferris. If you speak to me again, I will kill you." He turned again for the door and walked out, leaving Ferris in that foul pit deep in the mountain.

Through the window, Ferris watched as the guards unshackled the prisoner Ziyad and took him away. They would exploit him now that he had cracked, bleed him of every contact he'd ever had, every pot he'd ever pissed in, but the Americans would know none of it.

Ferris waited for a time, wondering if someone was going to fetch him or if he would be left there to join the detritus that was rotting under the ground. Eventually two soldiers came to collect him. They were the same two who had escorted him when he first arrived. They led him out a different way, down corridors that were dirty and ill-lit, and stank of shit. He could hear screams from cells as he passed, people who were in pain, or who had been here so long they had simply gone mad.

They came finally to an old gated elevator, big enough to hold a herd of cattle. This was the prisoners' elevator, Ferris realized. It reeked of men who had shat their pants in fear as they descended into the house of the dead.

The elevator made a slow, clanking ascent. The door opened to more dirt and debris, foul smells of captivity, a few faces caught in the lurid fluorescent light. The guards walked him toward a bolted door. A prisoner was pleading with Ferris, thinking he was a foreigner who might save him. The door opened and the guards gave Ferris a nudge. Darkness had fallen, and there was no moon in the bitter sky.

His SUV was across the road. He got in and started the engine, half expecting that it would explode. But no, that wasn't Hani's style. Ferris drove back to the embassy, sent a cable to Hoffman in the special channel and then, an hour later, talked with the division chief briefly by secure phone. Hoffman sounded upset, but not contrite.

THE NEXT MORNING, Ferris was on a flight back to Washington. He stopped at Alice's apartment and woke her up on the way to the airport. She could tell that something dreadful had happened.

"What's wrong, darling?" she asked. That was the first time she had ever called him darling.

"Something bad at work. They want me to come home, talk to people at the State Department."

"Are you in trouble? Something awful has happened, hasn't it? I can see it."

He looked at her stray wisps of hair across her sleepy face. "Nothing is wrong. Nothing that matters. But I have to sort out these work problems. And talk to my wife."

She nodded. "When will you be back?"

A muscle twitched in Ferris's face. He shifted weight off his bad leg. He didn't know when he would be back. If Hani meant what he had said, it might be never.

"As soon as I can," he answered. "I'll call you whenever I can while I'm away. Is that okay?"

"Of course. So long as you're really coming back."

He didn't answer at first. Pledges of commitment, in his experience, were only spoken if there was reason to doubt someone's fidelity. He thought of what Hani had said: Every extra word adds a measure of insincerity.

"I don't want to leave you." Each word carried the emotion he felt.

"Oh, Roger." She shook her head. There were tears in her eyes. "Promise me something. If you decide you're not serious about me, you must tell me. I don't want to be hurt. I have a good life now that makes me happy, and I don't want to be unhappy again."

"I could never hurt you," said Ferris. She nodded, and then turned her back. As she walked away, Ferris thought to himself: So this is what it feels like. This helpless feeling, this is love.

A CAR BOMB EXPLODED IN Frankfurt while Ferris was on his way back home. He called the watch officer in NE Division during his stopover in London, asking whether he should turn around and return to Jordan and was told no, that Hoffman wanted him in Washington, ASAP. You could tell, just by watching people at Heathrow, how frightened they were. They were crowding around the televisions in the airport lounges to watch the news. Several flights were canceled, because of the heightened security alert.

Ferris called Alice from London. She hadn't heard the Frankfurt news yet. Ferris told her to be careful, and she laughed out loud. "Me? *You* be careful. I'm not the one making the trouble." Ferris laughed, but it ached. He wanted to be back home with her. Not once in his marriage with Gretchen had he wished to hide away with her and let the world disappear. She was of the world; that was the point about Gretchen. She was mint-perfect, coin of the realm. Alice was in another space, still mysterious to Ferris, and he wished he could be there now.

Ferris brooded on the long London-Washington leg of the trip. They were losing ground. They had bungled their few, precious chances to get inside the enemy network. Ferris himself was no better than Hoffman. He had been impatient and greedy, and he had lost the trail of his adversary. The thought of returning to CIA headquarters was depressing. It wasn't the flat, linoleum feel of the place, or the instantly dated, 1960s "modernist" look of the architecture. It was the civil-service culture that permeated the corridors like dry rot. Ferris had heard the elite, band-of-brothers rhetoric when he joined. The agency had to be less smugly bureaucratic than Time, Inc., he reckoned, but he had been wrong. It was worse. It was a culture that had been lying to itself for so long that people had lost the ability to differentiate between what was real and what wasn't. Failure wasn't acceptable—so, as far as the agency was concerned, the CIA never made mistakes. These were people who believed their own PowerPoint presentations.

Ferris had brought along a book from the British Council library, and he read it now for comfort. The Brits had bungled, too—damn near crumpled in 1939 in the disarray of Dunkirk. Yet when they realized their very survival was at stake, they had found a raw ruthlessness in their character. The fumbling chess players and common-room eccentrics proved to be killers. That was the message of the intelligence histories Ferris liked to read. Facing an enemy they couldn't defeat head-on, the British found other ways. They raised lying to a form of warfare. They stole their enemy's Enigma cipher machines and recruited Britain's oddest and brainiest to break the codes. They captured German agents and played them back, creating a network of lies so intricate and believable that, for the Germans, it became reality. Knowing that they would not prevail unless America entered the war, they launched a covert action program to destroy the isolationists in America, spreading lies and gossip to defeat members of Congress they didn't like. The Brits maintained their guise as genial, patrician bumblers, until they bumbled their way to Berlin. They succeeded, lie by lie, day by day.

Ferris read the slim volume he had brought along about one particularly audacious piece of British deception, and as he turned the pages, he thought about his own adversary. Lacking a face to put to the name "Suleiman," he saw pure black when he closed his eyes. But he heard the sound of explosions—car bombs in Rotterdam, Milan, Frankfurt and coming soon, no doubt, to Pittsburgh and San Diego. The failure to destroy Suleiman wasn't the agency's failure, it was his own. He had grabbed at one of the far-flung roots when he recruited Nizar at the beginning of the year in Iraq. In Berlin with Hani, he had touched one of the nodes. And with Hoffman, it had seemed so easy to insert a probe into the enemy's flank. In his mounting frustration, he had imagined he could tease the enemy out of hiding in Amman. But all he and Hoffman had accomplished with their schemes was to sever the few connections they had. And all the while, the bombs kept going off.

They were back to the starting point, and they were running out of time. The Frankfurt bomb would make people panicky all over again. It was a particularly brazen act, in the middle of Europe's financial capital. It told people there was a network so cleverly constructed and well hidden that the CIA and its friends didn't know where to look. Your shield is gone, these car bombs said; you are helpless before your enemies.

In the drowsy stump of the long flight, Ferris pondered what Hani had said about *taqiyya,* the necessary lie. In the Islamic texts he had studied back at Columbia, the term usually applied to Shiites, who were taught to dissimulate when necessary to avoid danger. Indeed, this slipperiness was one reason Sunnis viewed them as inveterate liars. But there was a deeper meaning that went back to the Koran. It concerned a companion of the prophet named Ammar bin Yasir, who was imprisoned in Mecca with his family after the Prophet fled to Medina in the *hijrah.* Bin Yasir's parents were tortured and killed for their allegiance to Islam. Bin Yasir was more devious: He tricked the infidels by pretending to worship their idols, and then escaped to Medina, where he rejoined Muhammad. When he asked the Prophet if he had done the right thing by lying, Muhammad assured him that he had done his duty. Bin Yasir had surrounded the truth with a bodyguard of lies, as the British put it

many centuries later. He had treated the infidels with the contempt
they deserved. He had gone into the heart of their encampment and
deceived them, so that he could fight another day.

In the time of the Prophet, deception was the essence of survival.
Another story concerned the head of an Arabian tribe who was plotting to kill Muhammad. The Prophet advised his companions that
the assassin's weakness was his vanity. So when they visited him, they
complimented the sheik on his fine perfume, and asked him to lean
a little closer, so they could savor its pleasing scent, and a little closer,
handsome sheik, and a little closer. And then they chopped off the
vain man's head. The story illustrated an eternal truth of warfare.
Facing a difficult adversary, it is sometimes best to play upon his
arrogance. Lure him forward; draw him in. The right pressure on
just the right spot and he will collapse from within. That was what
the Muslims had done to America in Iraq, wasn't it? But it could
work in reverse.

The British book was still open on Ferris's lap, and he returned to
it now with greater attention. The operation it described had been as
much theater as warfare. In 1943, the British had needed to disguise
their true plan to attack in Sicily by convincing the Germans they
would be landing in Greece. They had created an illusion so perfect
that the Germans had leapt at it, thinking they were discovering a
great secret—not realizing that it was a lie. And it had worked.

Ferris sat upright in his airplane seat. He ordered some black coffee from the flight attendant and began scribbling notes to himself.
By the time the plane landed at Dulles, Ferris had the beginning of
an idea.

HOFFMAN WAS sitting gloomily at his desk when Ferris arrived.
He looked awful. The ruddy face had turned doughy, and there were
dark ruts under the eyes from too little sleep and too much drinking.
Even his brush-cut hair was limp. He didn't look like a tycoon anymore, but a bookie whose bets had come up wrong. His deputy was

sitting at the conference table looking at a thick binder, but when Ferris arrived, Hoffman asked the deputy to leave and closed the door.

Hoffman spoke in a low, raspy voice. He looked down at his desk rather than directly at Ferris. "I could apologize, but that would be bullshit. Nonetheless, I should have warned you in advance that the shit was about to come down on your head with Mustafa Karami. That was a mistake."

Ferris was startled. "What do you mean? You knew that Karami was dead? Before I saw Hani?"

"Yup. I heard it from the Spanish, at the same time they told the Jordanians. That's how we managed to get Amary out. We had a head start."

"Shit. You know what, Ed? You're right. You should have told me. Why didn't you?" Ferris was furious. He thought the situation couldn't get worse, and it just had.

"Because you would have told the Jordanians. Nothing wrong with that. I would have told them, too, in your place. But I couldn't risk that. And don't start sulking. I told you I was sorry."

"Actually, Ed, I think you said apologizing was bullshit. But it doesn't matter."

"Why doesn't it matter? Everything matters."

"Because Hani won't talk to me. I thought he was going to kill me when he realized what we had done to him. He was furious. I'm dead out there."

"Don't be too sure. He likes you. And you're a better bet than the next guy we'd send. So maybe he'll wise up. And for the record, I apologize." Hoffman puckered up his tired, beat-up face and made a kissing noise. Then he gave Ferris the finger.

Ferris laughed, despite himself. It was weirdly reassuring that Hoffman could still act like an adolescent after a disaster like this. He decided to let his anger go.

"You really think they'll let me back in Jordan?" Back to Alice's place, Ferris's place.

"Not entirely impossible. Let's wait and see."

"Hani is worth the trouble, Ed, if we can get past this flap. Not that you need my opinion, but I watched him break the man who shot Karami. It was the damnedest thing. The guy confessed everything—the hit, the fact they knew we were running Amary—without Hani ever touching him. He's good."

"Yeah, yeah, I know. He's a superstar. And we fucked him over. Et cetera. I'm sorry you had to be there and take his anger. I'm sure that wasn't fun. He called me up and screamed at me, too, for what it's worth. I told him to calm down. Bad things happen in war sometimes. Friendly fire. Get over it."

"Did he calm down?"

"Not really. But he shut up. I asked him to take you back, but he seemed to be off in another world, thinking about something. Long pauses, very strange. But he'll come around. He's a pro."

Ferris looked at his boss, wondering if he should say any more. "That's what bothered me, to be honest. Hani *is* a pro. He worked hard on that operation. Set it up, pitched the guy. And we were establishing a little trust, him and me. That's the one thing I've learned with the Arabs—it's all or nothing, total trust or zero. But we lost that. We became . . . nothing." He trailed off.

Hoffman put his ruined face in his hands and rubbed his sleepless eyes. When he spoke again, there was an edge of anger in his voice. "Okay. We did screw the guy. It was in a good cause, but if I were Hani, I would be pissed off. And if I were you, I would be pissed off. You had misgivings. You told me. Okay? We're all clear on that."

The division chief stood up. His bulky form loomed for a moment above his chair, and then in an impulsive burst of frustration, he pounded his fist down against his desk.

"But I am *not* Hani, goddamn it! And I am not you. I am *me*, and I have a job to do. And I am not going to guilt-trip myself into dropping the ball. We are at war, for chrissake. These shitheads are setting off a new bomb almost every day, while we jerk off. We've got things going you don't have a clue about, and you know what?

They're not working, either. The president asked the director at the briefing today whether the CIA had taken a permanent vacation.

"Jesus Christ," Hoffman muttered as he shook his head. "These people are trying to kill us, and we are running out of tricks to stop them. This Amary thing took me as long to set up as Hani's little operation did, and now it's all pissed away. So I'm going to worry about that, thank you very much, and not about how much we fucked over our Jordanian pals."

SILENCE SETTLED on the room. Ferris waited for another thunderclap from Hoffman, but he was sullen and withdrawn. His boss was losing it. They all were losing it. Hoffman was right. They were running out of tricks. They were waiting to get hit again, hoping they could find somebody in one of the networks and beat the crap out of him in time to disrupt the next attack. That wasn't a strategy; it was slow-motion defeat. Hoffman was still silent, and it occurred to Ferris that he was waiting for a suggestion. Ferris turned over in his mind the idea that had been forming on that long gloomy flight back to Washington. He thought of Hani's word—*taqiyya*. When the truth isn't working, you lie. When you're losing on one field of play, you create another.

"I have an idea," said Ferris. His words fell into a pit of silence. "Maybe it's crazy."

"Say what?" asked Hoffman. He wasn't used to Ferris making operational proposals.

"I said that I have an idea. It came to me on the plane. I'd been thinking about it before, but it seemed too weird. Now, maybe not. Want to hear?"

"Yeah, sure. What have we got to lose? Other than the whole fucking country."

"Okay. We have to get to Suleiman. If we don't, he's going to eat us alive. Just look at us. We're a mess. We have to get something going. Am I right?"

"Obviously. What's the idea?"

"It's something Hani said to me before I left. At the very end, before he threw me out. He talked about this Muslim thing called *taqiyya*. It's the lie you tell to get what you want. And I was thinking, suppose we just lie. Suppose we make Suleiman think we've already done it—that we're already inside the tent. We know we're failing, but he doesn't. For all he knows, we're sleeping under his bed, waiting for the right time. We lie, that's basically it. We pretend that we have him by the balls. And then we exploit his fear. Does that make any sense?"

"Maybe," said Hoffman. "If I knew what you were talking about."

"I'm talking about deception. *Taqiyya* is the only way we're going to penetrate Suleiman's network. We've been trying, and we haven't gotten anywhere. We could keep on trying. We could dangle people at every Salafist mosque in the world, and wait for someone, somewhere to take the bait. And maybe it would work, eventually. But we are running out of time. So if we don't have time to recruit a real agent, then let's pretend we've recruited one—and run him as a virtual agent. It won't be a real penetration of Al Qaeda, but a virtual penetration. But what's the *difference*, right? If we don't have the cards, let's pretend we have the cards. Let's bluff the guy—make him think we're inside, that we're running an agent. Hell, if we wanted to, we could pretend we've recruited Suleiman. We can pretend anything we want. If we're brazen enough, it will work."

Hoffman shook his head. He was smiling again. The gloomy thunderhead had lifted. "You know, I am going to have to revise my opinion of you. I had no idea you were this devious. This puts you in a whole new category in Eddie's book."

"I'm desperate," said Ferris. "So are you."

"That's a fact. So how do you propose we begin this razzle-dazzle? Assuming I was interested."

"That's what came to me on the plane. I was reading this book about a British deception operation in World War II, when they really, totally needed to snooker the Germans. And I thought, maybe we could play that game, too."

"Okay, Mr. Peabody. What's the book?"

"*The Man Who Never Was.*"

Hoffman closed his eyes and let it sink in. He saw it instantly—the dead body, the false message, the layering of lies. He went to his bookshelf and took down a dog-eared copy of the book Ferris had just mentioned.

"Operation Mincemeat. That's what the British called it, right? I must be getting old and stupid, that I didn't think of this myself."

"Just old," said Ferris.

"You know what? I like you, Ferris. You're a pisser. You really are."

"Thank you."

"To do this right, we would have to plug you into a new circuit. I have some people doing some pretty unusual stuff already. I tried to get you to join that shop after you got wounded in Iraq, but you blew me off. We can still make a fit, if you're really game. But don't raise your hand on this one too quickly. This isn't the Clandestine Service Trainee bullshit from the Farm. You sure about this?"

Ferris didn't think before he answered. We never do, when we make the decisions that change our lives.

"We have to get to Suleiman. This could do it."

"*Taqiyya,*" said Hoffman, still savoring Ferris's suggestion. He laid one of his big hands on the younger man's forearm. "You said it a long time ago, Roger. This has to work. We cannot lose. If we can't break Suleiman's network, a lot more people are going to die." He relaxed his grip on Ferris's arm and told him his secretary would call in a few days to set up another meeting. He had to make some arrangements, do some rewiring, before he could plug Ferris into that new circuit.

F ERRIS SLEPT IN A HOTEL his first night back in Washington. It was a rickety little inn off Dupont Circle that reminded him of the places where he had lived before he joined the CIA. And he needed to be alone, away from anyone he knew. He didn't want to see Gretchen until he had figured out what he wanted to say. She had a way of over-ruling his plans, or simply ignoring them. This time he wanted to set his own course. He called her at six-thirty the next morning, which he knew would be just after the shower, just before the makeup.

"Hi, Gretchen."

"Roger?" She was surprised, but happy.

"I'm back home," he said.

"No, you're not. You are certainly not home. *I* am home. You're somewhere else. Where are you?"

"In a hotel."

"What on earth are you doing there?"

"I'll explain. Can we meet for dinner?"

"Don't be ridiculous, darling. Come home, to your apartment and your wife. I have to work today, but I'll be home at seven. You have a key. I mean, of course you have a key. It's your apartment. So let yourself in. And get some rest. You're going to need it tonight."

Ferris wanted to caution her that it wasn't that kind of visit, but she was in a rush to get ready for work and hung up, telling him that she loved him and was *so* happy he was back. And she meant it. There wouldn't be any way to make this easy. He just had to tell her and get away.

The apartment was in a white-glove building in Kalorama, just off Connecticut Avenue. It suited Gretchen's sense of style. Rich people lived nearby, people with old money and social connections. Gretchen was like another daughter. She got to know the neighbors, visited them when they were sick, brought them little gifts from her trips. She had decorated the apartment lavishly; when they had lived together, she would always be dragging Ferris off to auctions and antique shops to add new bits of finery. When they invited the neighbors in for cocktails, the men always seemed to know what Ferris really did for a living, without asking him.

Gretchen was a self-taught aristocrat. That was what pleased the older neighbors, that this bright young thing was making an effort to join their world. Her father had sold insurance in Indiana, and he was a good, solid citizen, but not a man who had ever dreamed his daughter would join the Sulgrave Club. She had an older brother who had stayed in Indiana and worked as a regional sales executive for John Deere. That wasn't for Gretchen. She had put on her rocket pack at the age of eighteen, headed off to Columbia and created a new life. Ferris could admire her act of self-creation, but he no longer enjoyed being around it.

Ferris said hello to the doorman, who looked surprised to see him. He took the elevator upstairs and warily opened the door. In the entrance hall was a new writing credenza, he noticed, a fussy French thing with curvy legs that wouldn't be much use for actual writing. The apartment was tidy; traces of any other life she had been living while he was away had been removed. He went into the bedroom. Silver framed photos sat on the two bedside tables. He studied the picture of himself, looking rakish and still vaguely like a journalist, taken before they were married. There was no dust on the frame. Had she been polishing it, or taken it out of storage?

What he noticed, as he walked the apartment, was that the artifacts of his own real life had disappeared. There was no beer in the refrigerator; his subscription to *Sports Illustrated* had evidently been canceled; the clothes he had left behind had been removed from the closet to make more room for hers. Maybe this would be easier than he had expected. He was gone already.

Gretchen called just before six-thirty to say that she had been delayed at work but would be home at seven-thirty, and then once more at seven-thirty to say that she was just leaving. She finally returned home a few minutes before nine. She pushed open the door and said, "Hi, honey, I'm home," as if he had never been away. She was sorry to be so late, but it couldn't be helped. The attorney general had a crash project to finish, and she couldn't escape. Tried to, but it was impossible. It wasn't an apology so much as an assertion of a higher calling.

Ferris examined her. She looked the same as before, only more so: The lustrous black hair surrounding her face, in the style of an Italian movie star. The big bust, which was the first thing most people noticed about her, men and women, and which she used to intimidate or seduce, depending on the needs of the moment. The stylish suit, with the silk blouse cut low enough to show some cleavage.

She was waiting for a hug and a kiss, but when Ferris delayed she moved in and hugged him, pressing herself against him. He hugged back, but without much feeling. She knew something bad was happening, but tried to downplay it, hoping it would go away.

"What's wrong, Rog?" she asked. "Jet lag?"

"We have to talk," he said.

"About what?" She had a worried look in her eyes.

"Let's sit down."

"Do you want a drink? I'll go fix you something."

"No. Not right now. I want to talk."

"Here, sweetheart." She sat down on the couch, plumped a pillow and waited for him to join her. The pillows were new, Ferris noticed. They had a brocade edge that matched the cords on the drapes. Ferris took a seat in the easy chair next to the couch. He needed some distance, or he would never get it out. He tried to think how to begin, and when she started to fill the silence with chatter, he blurted out the words.

"I want a divorce, Gretchen. We don't have a marriage anymore."

"What did you say?" That was her last protection, to pretend that she hadn't heard.

"I said I want to talk about divorce. We are living apart, and that's because we have grown apart. I think maybe it's time to end it."

Her face looked as if she had been slapped.

"You bastard," she said. Her cheeks reddened, and then she began to cry. Somehow, Ferris hadn't anticipated this. He thought she would scream at him. She got up and went to the bathroom to blow her nose. She stayed there almost ten minutes, and when she returned, she had put on new makeup and regained her composure. She was in charge again.

"You can't do this, Roger," she said. "I won't let you destroy what we have together. We have the kind of marriage that people dream about. We're perfect for each other. You've been under a lot of stress. I understand that. I don't know what you think is wrong, but we can fix it."

"We can't fix anything if we don't live together. And I don't hear you offering to move to Jordan."

"I can't leave the department. You know that. I know how hard it is on you. I wish I could just pick up and come to Amman like those other wives, but I can't. Don't make me feel guilty about doing my duty."

He shook his head. This wasn't about guilt. "You aren't understanding me, Gretchen. I don't want to be married anymore. Our marriage is broken. I don't think it can be fixed."

"Anything can be fixed if people try. If there's something wrong, we need to repair it, rather than just throw everything away. You have to believe in yourself."

She wasn't listening to him. She was acting as if his request for a divorce were a sign of weakness that could be overcome by force of will, hers if not his. Ferris realized he would have to try a different approach. He had hoped he would be able to avoid it, but he couldn't.

"I'm seeing someone else, Gretchen." He waited a moment, expecting more tears, but her eyes were dry. "That's wrong, if we're still married."

"I *told* you . . ." She stopped. There was a controlled fury in her voice. "I told you that I don't care who you're seeing while we're apart. You can have as many little fuck mates as you want. I just don't want to know about it."

"This isn't a . . . fuck mate. I like this person."

"Don't be ridiculous, Roger. I don't care who she is, but she can't make you happy the way I can. You know that."

"I am not happy with you, Gretchen. I haven't been happy for a long time."

She ignored him. She was already off in her own space, plotting how to reel him back. "I was worried before. I was afraid you didn't love me. But if it's just another woman, frankly I had assumed that was happening. I would be surprised if it wasn't. I understand what men are like. Including you, Roger. You aren't as virtuous as you pretend to be."

Ferris began to respond, but she wasn't listening.

"Go make us a martini," she said. "I'll be right back."

She walked toward the bedroom before Ferris could protest. He sat in his chair for a while, and then decided he did need a drink, even if she had suggested the idea. He went to the bar and fixed two vodka martinis. As he shook the mixture, he could feel his fingers stick to the bitter cold of the shaker. He added an olive for her, a twist for himself. In a perverse way, he really was back home. He wondered if he would be able to restart the conversation; maybe he would just have to walk away.

He carried the drinks back to the living room and waited for her to return. What was taking so long? But he knew. And he didn't move. He took a sip of his martini, and then another. The taste was quicksilver cool on his tongue. Eventually, he heard the bedroom door open.

She was dressed in a lacy black nightgown. As she walked slowly toward him, her heavy breasts swayed back and forth under the fabric. Roger shook his head no. But he looked at her body.

"I don't want to argue anymore." She sat down beside him, and let the gown slip open a bit, so that the voluptuous curve of her breast was visible, and then relaxed on the couch so that the gown spread open all the way and exposed her nakedness. There was no hair between her legs, Ferris saw. That was new. He didn't want to be aroused by the sight of her, but he was.

"I need you," she said. "I need my husband." She leaned toward him, her bosom brushing against his shirt, and began to unzip his fly.

"Don't," he said, taking her hand away. "This is the wrong time."

"Stop teasing. I want you." She moved her hand back to his zipper and then pulled at it. He couldn't stop her now, he realized. It had been too late the moment he had agreed to make drinks and let her leave the room. He made one last effort and pushed her away again. This time it made her angry.

"What's wrong with you?" she said, pulling back. "I've been waiting for you for five months, and you don't want to touch me?" She thought a moment, as if recalculating her strategy, and then gave him a pouty look. "I'm so lonely," she said. Her legs spread slowly apart. She was waxed smooth as pink marble. Ferris tried not to look, but she had him now.

"Stop it, Gretchen." He was surrendering. This was how she always won arguments. She undid the buttons of his shirt and then removed his trousers, shoes and socks. He was helpless. She took him in her mouth, and then straddled him, so that his head was buried between her breasts, the nipples grazing his eyes. She rocked on him, up and down, until she came with a wail. Then she led him to the bedroom, and made him do it again, and again.

Early the next morning, when Gretchen was in the shower,

Ferris gathered his clothes and snuck away from the apartment. He felt disgusted with himself. He was too weak to resist the feral power of his wife. Next time, he would have to let a lawyer speak for him. As he closed the door of his apartment, he knew it was for the last time.

13

F ERRIS SPENT TWO DAYS in the flipperless pinball machine that was Headquarters, waiting for a summons from Hoffman. Because of the Frankfurt bombing, the lights were blinking red from every overhead sensor and watch list. There were meetings and briefings and urgent summonses from policymakers. The Frankfurt bomb had been parked across the street from Citibank's German headquarters and detonated during the afternoon rush hour. A dozen people had died; three times that many were seriously injured. Ferris found a cubicle in the NE Division's ops center and tried to manage things back in Amman, long distance. Every few hours he stopped by Hoffman's office down the hall, but the division chief was never there. The deputy chief would ask solicitously if he could help, but Ferris would shake his head. After a while it got embarrassing and Ferris stopped checking. If Hoffman wanted him, he was easy enough to find.

Hoffman eventually sent a brief e-mail on the secure system. "Meet me at Mincemeat Park at 9:00." Ferris smiled. Already Hoffman had appropriated his idea. A separate message from Hoffman's secretary provided directions to a part of the Headquarters complex Ferris had never visited—in the new building, on the other side of the cafeteria, near the north loading dock. Ferris wondered why they weren't just meeting at the usual NE Division office on the fourth floor.

When Ferris reached the specified door the next morning, he found Hoffman's secretary waiting for him. It turned out this location wasn't his actual destination, but a false address. The secretary led him back along a long corridor to an unmarked door, where she punched in a code, applied her thumb to a biometric scanner and waited until the door clicked open. Inside was a key-operated elevator; they descended for perhaps fifteen seconds. When the door opened, she led Ferris through another set of cipher-locked doors that opened onto a large workspace—a windowless underground cavern decorated in blues and greens and filled with banks of computer screens and big monitors. Dozens of people were working at desks and cubicles in a room the size of a basketball court. Ferris looked up to the cool white fluorescent lights above; he reckoned they must be somewhere under the north parking lot. Hoffman was standing by an open office door halfway down the room. He beckoned for Ferris to join him.

"Mincemeat Park?" asked Ferris.

Hoffman beamed. "Cute name, don't you think? Bletchley Park and all that. I was going to call it Taqiyya Park, but I was worried that nobody could pronounce it." He gestured to the large room and its busy employees. He looked pleased with himself, given all the bad news. "This office doesn't exist. If you ever tell anybody you were here, I'll swear you were lying and then have you fired. Just so we're clear."

"Got it. But what *is* Mincemeat Park, now that I'm here?"

"We used to call it the Near East Operations Advisory Group, until yesterday. NE-OAG. That sounded vague and bureaucratic. The short version is we run the division's black ops here. The serious CT ops."

"What's the long version, if you don't mind telling someone who has been doing the unserious ops?"

"Don't be an asshole, Roger. By 'serious,' I mean off the books. The counterterrorism operations we run out of this room are, shall we say, 'unofficial.' They are deniable because the president isn't notified about them in any formal, put-it-in-writing sense. And being officially unaware, how can the president tell Congress? Mincemeat Park is what the CIA would be, if it wasn't so fucked up. It is a clandestine intelligence organization. As such, it can take risks, break laws, ignore bureaucratic requirements, tell people who aren't cleared to fuck off. And it's invisible, tucked away under the Green Parking Lot. We're like Platform 9¾ in those dumb Harry Potter movies. Just a brick wall, until you punch the invisible cipher lock and see what's really there. And then, poof, you are inside another world, where the wizards still have some magic. So, what do you think? Come on! Admit it! You're impressed."

"This is where you've been when I couldn't find you?"

"Yup." He was beaming.

Ferris scanned the room. It had the feel of the operations room at Balad, only funkier. There were big screens on the back wall, and the unmistakable flickering images of Pred Porn. But the real action was in the pit, where the operatives worked. They didn't look like any collection of CIA people he had ever seen. They were young, in their late twenties or thirties, mostly. They were dressed in jeans and T-shirts and tight skirts. There wasn't a necktie in the room. And the walls of the cubicles had the look of a wacked-out college dorm, with pictures of various bearded adversaries, maps showing the locations of known operatives, the spidery lines of "link analyses" connecting members of the underground network. The analysts were hunkered over their desks like submarine chasers studying their sonar, trying to locate the unseen killers and force them to the surface.

"You built your own CIA," said Ferris.

Hoffman nodded. "Yes, I did. These folks may not exist, officially speaking, but they're working their invisible asses off. And I'll tell you why. Because they know they are the last best hope. They know that one of these days, the bomb that goes off in Milan or Frankfurt or New York is going to be a nuclear bomb. And if they don't find it, it's going to take a million people with it. So they're working every hour, every day, to find that bomb and kill the people who want to plant it. That's why I love them—every overworked, maladjusted one of them. They may not look like killers, but they are."

Ferris surveyed the rows of cubicles. Women occupied at least half of them. They did look wired, you could see that; snapping on their chewing gum, tapping their toes; you could tell a lot of them would be smoking cigarettes if it were still allowed. Some had a tough, worldly look, a bit too much makeup—you could imagine them as blackjack dealers in Vegas. Others had a deceptive sweetness, but in their eyes was the stone-cold look of an adder.

"Hey, Gwen." Hoffman turned to a thirtysomething brunette at the closest desk. "Tell him what you're working on."

She looked quizzically at him. Hoffman nodded.

"I'm tracking a cell in Syria. They were in Damascus last night. Today they're in Dayr al-Zor, on their way to the Iraqi border. But something tells me they aren't going to make it over the border to Husbaya. We have ninjas nearby. Something tells me that as soon as I get a lock on them, they're dead."

She smiled the cool thin smile of a professional assassin. Ferris turned to Hoffman. "Who do the ninjas work for?" he asked.

"Nobody. That's the point. That's the only way we're going to get out of this mess. People like Gwen, here."

Hoffman took Ferris's arm and pulled him toward an open office door. "Come on. There's someone I want you to meet."

Inside the office, a thin dark man in wire-rimmed glasses was typing furiously at a computer terminal. He was dressed in a black cashmere sweater and appeared to be in his late thirties, perhaps a few years older than Ferris. As Ferris got closer, he saw that the man was an Arab—a North African, to judge from the honey-brown tint of his complexion. The man looked up at them over the top of his glasses and then back at the screen. His fingers continued dancing over the keyboard for another fifteen seconds and then he stopped, hit "Enter," and looked up.

"Sorry to keep you," he said. "I just liquidated the bank account of a Salafist leader in Riyadh. He's going to think another man from his prayer group stole his money. And if we're lucky, he will try to kill that man." He smiled at the thought of all these good outcomes flowing from a few keystrokes on his computer.

"Meet Sami Azhar," said Hoffman. "He runs day-to-day operations down here in the pit. He's much too smart for people like you and me."

"Certainly too smart for you, Ed," said Azhar, looking over the top of his glasses again. "You appear to be smart, but you're simply over-caffeinated. When you aren't overintoxicated. I don't know about your guest. We'll have to see." He stuck out his hand and greeted Ferris.

"Sami used to be a quant on Wall Street. He was born in Egypt, but he came to America to go to graduate school. He has a doctorate in mathematics and another one in economics. He got very rich working for a hedge fund. So rich that he decided to give something back to his adopted country. Have I got this right, more or less, Sami?"

"It is true that I was well compensated, Ed, but I also invested wisely."

"Sami used to do some fancy freelance work for the agency and the NSA in the nineties, helping us understand the crazies who were trying to kidnap his religion. But after 9/11 he realized that the world had gone off its rocker and that only a complete idiot would keep working for a hedge fund. As a Muslim, he felt a special responsibility to help stop the loonies. Am I right?"

"Yes, indeed. Or as you would say, Ed, 'Fuck yes!'"

"Right. So he asked if he could do something important for me, off the books. Because I knew Sami, I thought he might be just weird enough for what I had in mind here. I'd read the file on him: a math genius when he was a kid in Egypt; got a scholarship to go study in

America; made so much money on Wall Street he stopped counting zeros. He was an oddball, in other words—one of a kind. Smart and ruthless, but he also gave a shit. He was special."

"Actually you are wrong, Ed. I am not special. Most people on Wall Street are smart and ruthless. The difference is that I am less selfish, at the margin. I should also point out that I am not especially weird for a mathematician. I'm just angrier. There's a difference."

Azhar turned to Ferris. "I tease Ed, but I truly enjoy working here. We are attempting what everyone always talks about but rarely accomplishes—which is to think 'outside the box.' In fact, we are so far outside the box that I'm not sure we will ever find our way back in again."

"Enough bullshit," said Hoffman. "We need to talk." He closed the door, sat down at the conference table and motioned for the other two to join him. A large screen was mounted on the wall across from Azhar's desk.

"Here's the drill. We are creating something new, from scratch. To do that, Roger, I'm going to read you into some secrets that are very close-hold, even around here. Just want to be sure you understand what the deal is."

Ferris nodded. "The deal is that I will not disclose the information to anyone else, even within the agency."

"Well, yes, obviously that. But I was talking about something else. After you leave here, you are going back into the field. That's why I didn't tell you about all this stuff before. It's dangerous. I can't share it with people who might get caught. But I've thought about it, and I don't see any other way. So the deal is, if some bad shit happens and you are captured, you *cannot* reveal this information. You must take appropriate measures. You follow me?"

Ferris sat back with a start. He thought he understood what Hoffman was saying, but he wanted to make sure. "Appropriate measures," he repeated.

"If captured, you would have to take 'appropriate measures' if you thought you couldn't resist interrogation. And let's be honest, nobody resists interrogation for very long, despite what they tell you at The Farm. So we give you a gel bridge to put in your mouth when you go back into the field. If you're *in extremis*, so to speak, it will do the trick. When you bite down hard on it, it releases a poison—very quick, very easy. It even tastes good, or so I am told. I haven't had the pleasure, although I take one of these little suckers with me every time I travel. Anyway, do we agree on that? I won't think you're a pussy if you say no. I'll just end the conversation here."

Ferris thought a moment. He had been pulled into a world that hadn't existed for him fifteen minutes ago. It was the zenith of his chosen vocation, or perhaps the nadir, but it didn't matter which. It was at the farthest edge. He thought fleetingly of Alice, and then her image slipped out of his mind.

"I'm in," Ferris said.

"Good boy." Hoffman shook his hand. "Fact is, I would never have asked you unless I was sure you'd say yes. Okay, this is the conspiracy, right here. The three of us and that's it. Nobody else will know all the pieces. Are we clear on that?" The two coconspirators nodded, and Hoffman continued.

"I briefed Sami on your off-the-wall idea, Roger. And guess what? He loves it. And he thinks they will swallow the bait. Isn't that right?"

Azhar nodded. "A very creative idea."

"So the first thing we need to do, obviously, is find a body. Any suggestions, Roger?"

"He has to look like a case officer, that's the main thing. He should be about my age, early-mid-thirties, someone who would be assigned to handle a penetration of Suleiman's network. He should be Caucasian. Healthy. Good muscle tone. And certifiably Christian."

"Meaning what?"

"Meaning he shouldn't be circumcised. If the bad guys don't find a foreskin, they'll think he's an Israeli."

Hoffman shrugged and turned to Azhar. "That right, Sami?"

"I am afraid so. Arabs are, so to speak, Jew-crazy. I am sorry."

"That's what the body should look like," continued Ferris. "But how do we get one? Can the FBI find a body in a morgue somewhere?"

"God, no," said Hoffman. "I wouldn't trust the FBI to find a stray dog. This is a job for our military brothers and sisters in Special Operations. They'll just do it, deliver the body and not ask questions."

"So let's tell the military to get us a body," said Ferris. He was beaming. It was really happening.

"I already have. Contacted MacDill yesterday. It may take a few weeks. You'll probably be overseas again by the time we get our man, so I want your proxy. Sami and I will build a legend. Backstop his cover. I already have a name for him. Harry Meeker. It's a clean identity we built for an operation a couple years ago. Like it?"

"Any name you like, so long as it's not Roger Ferris."

"We've been doing some thinking, me and Sami, while we were waiting to get you wired up here. And we think we need some collateral, to make your *taqiyya* thing work. We have to really drive these guys nuts—make them think their whole world is coming apart. To do that, we need layers of deception that reinforce each other. Otherwise, Suleiman is going to smell a rat. That make sense?"

"Sure," said Ferris. "But I want to help run the collateral."

"That won't be a problem, Roger. As a matter of fact, you are going to be doing most of the work. I'm too old and Sami is too weird, so that leaves you. Sami, why don't you explain for our contestant what he's just won?"

Hoffman flipped a switch and dimmed the lights. Azhar stepped toward the computer next to the projection screen, his curly black hair and cocoa-butter face projected in gray shadow behind him.

14

LANGLEY

S AMI AZHAR FIXED HIS GLASSES on his nose and fiddled
with his computer, queuing up bits of information he wanted to
share. He seemed lost in time for a moment, somewhere between this
place, here and now, and the little elementary school in Cairo where
he had astonished his teachers long ago with his ability to multiply
large numbers in his head. Ferris studied him and thought perhaps
he was like the refugees who had helped Britain and America win
World War II. Growing up in Cairo, he must have sensed the great
Muslim crack-up that lay ahead, and wanted to escape it. But it
turned out that was impossible. The war was everywhere.

"You will forgive me, I'm sure, if I start with the object of our pursuit," Azhar began. "In the months since you heard the name
Suleiman in Iraq, the team here has been doing some research. We
know a bit more about this gentleman than you might think."

Azhar touched a computer mouse and the first image appeared
on the screen. It showed a thin Arab man with a neat beard and
a knitted white prayer cap on his head. It was an intelligent face—
displaying not the rough demeanor of a killer but the austerity and
asceticism of a scholar. What struck Ferris was the intensity of his
eyes. They were small fireballs of rage.

"We were very lucky to get this picture. It is from an old passport, before he vanished. Now, he is a will-o'-the-wisp. He is everywhere and nowhere. In the radical mosques, people whisper his name as if he is a phantom. They write poems about him; we have even found a few underground CDs that talk about his exploits. But he leaves no traces. In the diffuse world of Al Qaeda, he has become the true operations planner. He is the man who has fused the Class of 1996 from Kabul with the Class of 2006 from Baghdad. He is the bridge between the old Al Qaeda and the new. You have been looking for him. We have been looking for him. The Jordanians have been looking for him. But none of us can find him."

Ferris studied the face, wanting to commit it to memory. Part of him was angry that Hoffman had kept this information from him for so many months. But a larger part of him was curious—and eager to understand how Hoffman and Azhar wanted to flesh out his idea of *taqiyya*.

"We know where Suleiman is from," continued Azhar, "even if we do not know where he is now. He is a Syrian, from Hama. His real name is Karim al-Shams. The male members of his family were all killed by Hafez Assad's troops in 1982—father, uncles, brothers. They were senior figures in the Ikhwan Muslimeen, the Muslim Brotherhood. After the massacre in Hama, the brotherhood in Saudi Arabia adopted Suleiman. He studied electronic engineering and then physics in Riyadh. He also studied some biology. He is very intelligent, I am sorry to say. We have some IQ testing that was done on him when he was at university in Riyadh, and it's quite startling. We also found documents in Afghanistan that show he experimented in considerable detail with both nuclear and biological devices."

"Tell him about Milan and Frankfurt," said Hoffman, "and the car bombs."

Azhar clicked his mouse and a new slide appeared. It showed what was left of the car bomb that had exploded in Frankfurt a few days before, across from the Citibank office. "We know that Suleiman likes car bombs. We intercepted a message after the car bombs in Baghdad really began to take a toll, saying that a senior Al Qaeda member, we didn't know who, wanted the suicide bombers to come to Europe and America—to kill Christians and Jews, not Muslims. Suleiman wanted the terror to move to the West. It wasn't him speaking, but it was someone in the network we think is close to him. That was the first connection. And then we have the detonator from Milan."

Another click on the mouse, and the screen displayed tiny shards of metal. "I won't go into all the forensics, because I don't understand them. But the FBI thinks the Milan bomb has the same signature as ones the Baghdad station traced to Suleiman's network several years ago in Iraq. The initial forensic reading from Frankfurt is the same, too, isn't that right, Ed?"

"Yup," said Hoffman. "Afraid so. Suleiman thinks big. He has a network of sleepers who can operate under our radar. They are able to build the car bombs, put them in place and escape. And they know their shit, these guys: They use stolen cars; they wear disguises when they are moving the cars. We have surveillance photographs from Milan and Frankfurt showing those cars on the way, and in both cases they show the face of the driver. The police in Europe have been going nuts pounding the pavement, trying to come up with matches, but so far it's been useless because they're in disguise. Their tradecraft is too good. We think Suleiman is coming to America next—maybe with nuclear or biological. Do you remember the KGB mastermind guy Karla in the Le Carré novels? Well, I've decided that Suleiman is Al Qaeda's Karla. He has all the strings in his hand. And one of these days, he's going to pull them."

"Does the White House know all this?"

"Of course not. Remember, we don't exist. And if they knew, they would just go even more batshit. No, they just know the crap they get from the CT analysts."

Ferris studied the picture. They knew so much, and so little.

"Let me ask the dumb question," said Ferris. "Why haven't we been able to get a bead on him—you, me, Hani? Why is he such a hard target?"

There was an awkward pause. Ferris sensed there was something they weren't telling him. He looked to Hoffman and made a motion with his hand, as if to say: Come on, say it.

"*Obviously*, that's what the Amary operation was about," said Hoffman. "To drive Suleiman up into space where we could listen to him. If Hani's man in Berlin had reinforced Amary's legend, we were going to have him send messages we could track as they made their way to Suleiman. Marked cards. Or if that didn't work, we would have jerked their chain and tried to make Suleiman think we knew where he was. So that he might have panicked and moved or contacted people. That's one of Dr. Azhar's specialties. Tell him, professor."

The Egyptian nodded. "On Wall Street, I dealt in the world of observables. If I could monitor something, I could observe its movement and then correlate that movement with other observables—mapping weather forecasts against the future price of corn, to take a crude example, or bond spreads against oil prices. In my analytical work, I tried to push information that had not previously been quantified or monitored into spaces where it could be observed—so that small differences could be arbitraged. That is how I made my money. What I do now for Ed is to apply that same methodology to his targets."

"Isn't he cool?" said Hoffman in a tone of genuine wonderment. "Tell him the rest, Sami."

"Very well. In dealing with Al Qaeda, the challenge is to push them into spaces that we can monitor. If they're not talking on cell phones we can intercept, our task is to frighten them into changing their procedures. Because every time they move, they throw up new signals. They buy new cell phones—without realizing that you can't buy new phones or cards in Pakistan that we haven't tagged. Or they get nervous about their computers, so they decide to buy new ones without understanding how completely we own that space. Thanks to our diligence, there is not an e-mail server in the world to which we do not have access. And as for computers—well, I have to laugh.

We can get into anybody's hard drive, anywhere. And thumb drives. Their couriers love to carry those around from place to place. But they have electronic signatures. Everything has a signature. That is the lovely thing about the digital world. It is so precise."

"We're driving them into our trap," said Hoffman, picking up the narrative. "We own the communications space. When we disrupt these guys, it's partly to make them nervous and push them into circuits we can track. Let's say we arrest a bunch of guys in London, or Uzbekistan, or Bumfuck, Indiana. What do you suppose we're after?"

"Interrogate them," said Ferris. "Send them to Gitmo. Send them to Hani. Whatever."

"Well, sure, interrogation," said Hoffman. "That helps. But that's not the real pop. Even if the guy we capture doesn't say shit, the bad guys have to assume he has blabbed. So they'll have to change their cell-phone numbers, and their Internet addresses, and even their hardware, and get new stuff. And sooner or later they're going to call someone on our watch list—even if it's a kebab place in Karachi. And then, blam, we've registered whatever new communications device they're using. They just have to touch one hot wire and the whole circuit lights up. Or we force them to change locations. And you know what? Movement is *dangerous*. We may be stupid, but we're not so utterly stupid that we can't monitor every airplane, bus and train that crosses a national border."

"But you haven't got Suleiman," Ferris cut in. "So Suleiman is different, obviously. These techniques you and Sami are describing that worked so well on other people haven't worked with him. He's still maintaining radio silence. That's why we need something new."

"Amen, brother," said Hoffman. "Now we have reached ground zero. But you already know the answer."

"*Taqiyya*," said Ferris.

"Just so. When you said it the other day, it was like, bing, a light went on. Just like you said: We have to make Suleiman think we have done the thing we in fact have been unable to do, which is to get inside his net. And then we can play with his mind. Jealousy. Vanity. Pride. Those basic emotions will crack Suleiman open like a fat oyster. We will introduce information into his sphere that is so upsetting, so confusing, so threatening that he must find out what it's about. And at that point, he must contact others. *Must.* And then he is observable. Quantifiable. Destructible."

THEY BROKE FOR coffee. A message had come in for Hoffman from the director, urgently asking him to call about Frankfurt, so he excused himself and went into his office, adjacent to Azhar's, and closed the door. Ferris took advantage of the break to ask Azhar if he could see the operations room.

"I'll give you the tour," said Azhar, "but you have to understand that a lot of what we do here is to build illusions. We are backstopping a magic show. This room is the back office for the Al Qaeda Shopping Mall, which we have created to satisfy the needs of members of the underground—so that they lower their guard, unwittingly, and do their business through us. Let's start with the travel agency."

Azhar walked Ferris to a cluster at the far end of the room. At the desks sat a group of three young recruits, none of them more than thirty. From their pasty faces, it looked as if they hadn't been aboveground in months. To Ferris, they had the look of the supernerds who had won all the science fairs back at George Marshall High School. Azhar turned to the oldest of them, a woman with a bad complexion and gel in her hair that made it spike like a punk rocker's.

"Adrienne, explain to our visitor what you're doing here. I told him you guys were the travel department."

"Well . . . okay." She looked distressed at the prospect of revealing anything to a new guy, but Azhar gave her a little wave of his hand. "So, like, the people in Al Qaeda have to travel, right? But they know we can monitor anything that has a computerized record. So they're looking for untraceable ways to make reservations. And we've, like, put ourselves in that business."

"Show him an example," said Azhar. Adrienne walked Ferris toward the next computer pod, where a young brown-skinned man was furiously typing.

"Right, so this is Hanif. He oversees our cutout in Karachi, whose real name we don't know, but we call him Ozzy. Like Ozzy Osbourne. Don't ask me why. Anyway, our man Ozzy in Karachi specializes in untraceable travel. He's very good. He went to a madrassa, he has good family connections in the Kashmiri underground. If you're a jihadi and you want to make a plane reservation to fly from Karachi to London under a phony name and passport, he's your guy. He'll handle all the arrangements. Cheap, too. People in the underground tell their friends. They love Ozzy. But the thing is, see, we look at all the bookings, so we can match up the travelers with people on our watch lists. Ozzy's place is set up with digital cameras, so we can monitor in real time everybody who comes into the shop and match faces with people we're interested in. Show him, Hanif."

The young Pakistani-American toggled a switch on his computer, and they were instantly watching an Internet feed from a hidden camera in the bucket shop in Karachi. A swarthy man with a pock-marked face loomed into view, badgering the clerk about a ticket for Morocco.

"We'll find out who that is," said Adrienne. "We'll sell him the ticket, let him travel, watch where he goes. Maybe we'll grab his cell phone when he's not looking and copy the SIM card, so we know who he's been calling. We are so *bad*."

Hanif and the other kids clustered around began laughing, and so did Ferris. This was a level of the game he had always hoped the CIA could play but suspected was beyond its reach.

Azhar led him to another cluster of desks, which he described as the banking section. Here again, it was the same basic mission. Members of the terrorist underground needed to move money around the world clandestinely. America and its allies had shut down all the easy ways—they had pressured the banks and the Islamic charities and even the *hawala* money changers. That made it harder for jihadists to move money from one cell to another, and they needed skilled people. To satisfy this demand, Azhar and his bizarre gang had created their own supply. Using a handful of people Hoffman and Azhar had strung together, they had created a chain of people who could move money covertly. Often, they didn't know about their agency contact. But all the information they collected came flowing into Azhar's databases.

"You have to think the way they do," explained Azhar. "That's my advantage. I grew up with them. I know how they think, what they need, how they move. And then, once I understand what they need, I figure out a way to provide it—airplane tickets, passports, money transfers, secret hideaways in strange cities, cell phones, computers. They never see my face. But I am there to serve them, every day, twenty-four/seven. That's my business plan."

The Egyptian gestured to his banks of computers and the hopeful young faces studying the screens—looking for ways to understand and deceive the enemy. Ferris had read about Bletchley Park—the collection of geeks, queers and other social misfits who had cracked the Nazi codes and allowed Britain to survive and win the Second World War. Hoffman and Azhar had created something equivalent—a system that would tag the cells of Al Qaeda and watch them as they moved through the bloodstream. It was brilliant, except for one thing. It hadn't forced Suleiman to the surface. Ferris had given him a name, and now he would have the job of luring him into the open.

15

HOFFMAN WAS BACK IN Sami Azhar's office, wearily rubbing his eyes, when they returned from the tour of Mincemeat Park. "This is what happens when people think they're losing a war," Hoffman said, shaking his head. "Everyone starts screaming, 'Off with his head.'" He didn't explain, but Ferris could guess: The director had just chewed him out for the lack of progress on Frankfurt, but that was because the president had just chewed out the director, and the news media had just hounded the president. People didn't like being frightened. They wouldn't put up with it for very long. They wanted to fight back, and they felt powerless when intelligence officers couldn't find the enemy. All the shit seemed to be falling on Hoffman for the simple reason that he was the only person in the government who had a clue what to do. Some people tighten up under that kind of pressure, but it seemed to make Hoffman looser.

"The director is having a fit," said Hoffman. "The White House just ordered him to testify before the Senate Intelligence Committee tomorrow on Milan and Frankfurt. 'Intelligence failures.' He told me to write his testimony. I could sympathize with him, really I could, if he wasn't so stupid."

"'A great empire and little minds go ill together,'" said Azhar. "That was the observation of Edmund Burke, I believe."

"Cut the crap, amigos. They want me back in the building soon, so we need to finish up. Okay, Roger, this is Taqiyya 101. We've been working stuff up the past few days to complement your man who never was, Mr. Harry Meeker. Your idea, with the blanks filled in by me and Sami. I think we've got something that will dig the knife in very deep." He motioned to Azhar to restart his computer.

"Okay, Sami, put up the Sadiki slide." Azhar clicked his mouse and a new image came up on the screen. It was a photograph of an Arab man in his late thirties, dressed in a business suit. He had a well-trimmed beard and the look of a man who took fasting and prayer seriously.

"This is Omar Sadiki. He's a Jordanian architect from Ma'an in the south, a very religious and conservative city. He lives now in Amman, where he works for a firm that specializes in Islamic design. He's a good Muslim, active in a bunch of charities the Saudis sponsor. For the past decade, he has traveled regularly to Zarqa, north of the capital, to attend Friday prayers. Several members of his Koran study group have disappeared, and we think they joined the underground. We think Omar himself was approached about going to Afghanistan when he was a kid, but he decided to stay in Jordan and study architecture. This is why people at the mosque trust him. Because he's not knocking on anyone's door, not pushing. Some people in Zarqa think he is already a member of Al Qaeda, but he isn't. He's just a smart, tough, religious guy."

"Stop!" Ferris help up his hand. "I don't want to sound petty, but how do you know so much about someone on my territory? Omar Sadiki, whoever he is, is not one of my agents. I've never heard of him. Did you find out about him from Hani? Are you running a parallel station? What the hell is going on?"

"Jesus, don't be so turfy," said Hoffman. "Hani is clueless about Sadiki. I'm not making the mistake of bringing him into anything again. Sadiki is one of the good Dr. Azhar's projects. He was think-

ing of using him as a front for a Muslim architecture and construction ruse—so we could build Al Qaeda's offices for them, in addition
to making their travel arrangements and doing their banking."

"Fine. But how did you guys spot him?"

"Well, let's just say that Sami knows his family."

"Meaning what?"

"Meaning that his brother is on my payroll," broke in Azhar. "He
works in Dhahran, for UBS, and he's doing a little business on the
side. He doesn't realize it's for us. It's what I believe you call a 'false
flag.' Saudi investors in my old hedge fund began coming to him,
and they brought their friends. Now many people are using him to
launder money. That's how I am building out the little counternet-
work I was just showing you, using friends of friends and cousins of
cousins. The gentleman in Saudi Arabia told us about his pious
Muslim brother in Jordan, and there we are."

Ferris studied the photo on the screen, and then smiled and shook
his head. He saw it, in a flash, just as Hoffman had.

"Got it," said Ferris. "He's part of my *taqiyya*. We're going to
pretend he's our guy, even though he isn't. Are we on the same
page?"

"Yes, indeed." Hoffman reached over and patted Ferris's cheek.
"Honestly, I love this shit. I mean, it's so totally off the wall, it might
just work."

"It will work, if we do it right," said Ferris, his mind spinning.
"We make it appear that Omar Sadiki is part of the enemy's network.
We move him around, send him on missions, burnish his legend. We
make other people worry about him. Maybe we make it look like
Sadiki is horning in on Suleiman's territory. Maybe we make him a
car bomber, too—a freelancer, competing with the master. We make
Suleiman jealous. We make him nervous."

"We make him *crazy*!" said Hoffman. "We make Sadiki seem like
such a player that the big man *has* to find out what he's up to. It's
driving him nuts. He's wondering if he's been cut out of the action,
or if we've turned his network, or what the fuck? How can he not

know about this Omar Sadiki? And then Suleiman surfaces. He contacts his people. He has to. He thinks he's been penetrated. He doesn't
know what's going on. He's acting weird, Suleiman is. His people are
starting to wonder about him. Maybe *he's* the mole. And then, pow!
We drop the ringer. The proof that Suleiman is a rat."

"Harry Meeker?"

"Just so. And then we've got him. Sami, next slide."

The screen displayed a building façade in downtown Amman. It
was white stone, like everything else in the city. There was a neat sign
out front that said in English and Arabic, "Al Fajr Architects," over
a corporate logo that showed a rising sun.

"This is where Omar works," said Hoffman. "His company does
a lot of business in the Gulf. We have the address and phone number
for you." Another slide appeared. "And here is a picture of Omar's
brother, Sami's friend who works for UBS in Dhahran. I don't think
you'll ever need to meet him, but here's what he looks like, in case
you get in trouble and we have to bust his balls."

"Let's do it," said Ferris.

"Work with Sami. He has pulled together some basics. He has you
working for a bank that wants to hire Sadiki to design a new branch in
the UAE. When you get back to Jordan, you'll have to put together the
other parts of the operation, but Sami can help you with the starter kit."

"You keep saying 'when you get back to Jordan.' How do you
know that Hani will let me back in? He was seriously pissed when I
left. He said he never wanted to talk to me again."

"He's calmed down. He informed the embassy yesterday that you
are still welcome as liaison to the GID. Actually, he said that you
alone would be welcome—if we try to send someone else, no dice. He
says it's too much trouble breaking in a rookie. Besides, he likes you.
He's basically demanding that you come back. From a Mincemeat
Park standpoint, it would be easier to run you as a singleton, unde-
clared to anyone. But we can't afford to fuck with Hani any more
than we already have. So you'll be back in Amman when you aren't
on the road. Don't worry about that."

"When do I leave?" Ferris was thinking about Alice and how many new secrets he would be keeping from her.

"Hell, I don't know. Whenever you're ready."

"I'm ready now. I want to get back to Jordan as soon as I can."

"Don't you want to see that wife of yours?"

"Not particularly. I told you back in Amman that we're sort of separated. I told her two days ago I want a divorce."

"Fine. Whatever. None of my business. Everybody else around here seems to fuck up their marriages, why not you? You can leave whenever you want. But I want you to stop on the way and see some folks in Europe."

"And who might they be?"

"Our ninjas in this operation. They're from MacDill. They are sitting in Rome, trying not to blow their covers while they wait for someone to tell them what to do. That's going to be you, with help from Sami. You'll get a kick out of them. They are some crazy fuckers. Much too out-of-control to work with our shop upstairs, which is why I like them so much."

Hoffman stood up suddenly. "I've got to see the director. I can't tell you how much I would prefer to stay here with you thinking of ways to mess with Suleiman's head, but duty calls. And Ferris, remember what Sam Snead said: If you aren't thinking about pussy, you aren't concentrating."

FERRIS SPENT THE rest of that day and most of the next with Sami Azhar, preparing for his trip. He and Azhar worked up a script for the initial contacts with Omar Sadiki. They researched the places in Abu Dhabi where the meetings would take place. They got Support to prepare a disguise that Ferris could wear to his meetings with Sadiki. They began to weave the cloak of false information they would gather around Sadiki—that would make him appear to be part of a network to which he had no real connection. Azhar proved ingenious in tapping lawyers, computer consultants and financial intermediaries who could, in various ways, burnish the legend.

"I am afraid we will need explosives, to make him truly believable as a car bomber," said Azhar.

"Not a problem," answered Ferris. "I'll talk to the ninjas about that in Rome." Hoffman could not have said it with greater assurance. Anything was possible, once you decided to invent a new game.

As Ferris prepared to leave, Azhar seemed awkward. Ferris thought at first that he must be envious, that Ferris was going somewhere the ex-quant from Wall Street could never follow. But it wasn't that. He handed Ferris a little plastic box in the shape of a hemisphere, like the kind of box children use to hold their retainers or mouth guards. Inside was the gel bridge, containing its drops of deadly poison.

"This is in case . . . ," said Azhar. "I trust you will never need it."

"Nothing bad is going to happen," said Ferris. "Don't worry, Sami." But he saw that his colleague's hand was shaking slightly when they parted, and he knew he was right to be worried. Ferris was headed into a space that had no boundaries or rules, where literally anything could happen. Ferris realized that he had one more thing to do before leaving Washington, which was to see his mother.

16 CHARLOTTESVILLE, VIRGINIA

JOAN FERRIS LIVED ON THE western edge of Charlottesville in a rambling ranch house with a view of the Blue Ridge. She had bought it with her husband a few years before he died. He had tinkered and fiddled with it so that there were electrical outlets every few yards and a phone jack in every room and a hundred other ingenious features he never had a chance to enjoy. Tom Ferris never quite got the timing right. At his funeral, Roger had read "Sailing to Byzantium," which summed up his feeling that his father somehow had been born in the wrong country and wrong century, trying to please people who weren't worth the effort. Guests at the funeral congratulated Roger for getting through the poem dry-eyed, which made him feel worse.

Roger had grown up in Fairfax County, just off the Route 50 highway that connected the Virginia suburbs to Washington. Most of the families in their subdivision were linked in some way with the Pentagon or the CIA. His father had raised the flag in front of the house every morning when Ferris was a boy, and then stopped, as if he had lost faith in the enterprise. Ferris asked him why and he pointed down the street to the neighbors' houses. "We have too many flags around here," he said bitterly, "and not enough patriots."

Ferris's mother took a job teaching English at George Marshall High School, the same school Ferris attended. He grew up with the sense that something was wrong and that his All-American life had a hidden flaw. His father would lose the job he could never talk about; his mother would tire of her husband's sullen despair and just not come home one afternoon.

Ferris wanted to make his parents happy, partly to protect against the risk of family meltdown. He was one of the top students in his graduating class, in addition to lettering in football and wrestling. In both sports, he was known for "gutting it out." He was starting linebacker on defense, but he had also played offense the second half of his senior year after the starting fullback got hurt. In wrestling, he had reached the state championships by outlasting better opponents who collapsed in the third period, when Ferris always seemed to be able to summon a last gulp of effort. The "favorite quote" next to his picture in the high school yearbook was Vince Lombardi's motto, "Winning isn't everything. It's the only thing." His problem in high school, to the extent he had one, was that he was too smart to be a jock and too athletic to be a wonk. That put him in between the various cliques, and he learned to suppress his emotions so that people never knew exactly what he thought. His main secret back in high school was how much he wanted to lose his virginity, but once he put that behind him senior year, he found other things to conceal—especially his ambition. He had no secrets from his mother, however, least of all the fact that he wanted to escape her suburban household and the sense of failure that had settled into the walls.

Ferris didn't like coming home, even to the new house in the Blue Ridge. It reminded him of his father, whose memory was an unfinished conversation. Another discomforting thing about the Blue Ridge house was that it was full of memories of Gretchen. They had come here often before and just after they were married, and had made love in almost every room, and much of the outdoors, as well. Thinking of Gretchen gave him a chill. He wanted to call Alice, but she had been unreachable the past few days. She was off somewhere, or not answering her phone. Ferris missed her.

Joan insisted that he stay for dinner. She made him what she always claimed was his favorite dish—a concoction of ground beef, canned peas and tomato sauce that she called "wheezing hash." It had never been his favorite dish, or even close to it—something about the name made him wonder if it was very healthy. But he hated to disappoint his mother, who seemed to take such pleasure in making it, as if it proved she was a good mother, after all. She was odd that way. "I sometimes feel as if I'm a fraud and everyone knows," she would occasionally say late at night, talking in the kitchen after dinner. Ferris would try to talk her out of it, but she would get a faraway look in her eye that conveyed that he didn't really understand what she was talking about.

Joan Ferris was a genuine intellectual; she read widely and deeply, and Ferris always thought that she would have made an ideal college professor. She loved ideas and would discuss them for hours with Ferris while his father was off puttering in his craft shop, turning out meticulous woodworking pieces that had absolutely no practical use. Theirs was a house in which no one ever turned on the television Sunday afternoons to watch the Redskins. Joan Ferris had loved it when Roger went to work for *Time*, and been mystified when he left to go work for the "State Department." But she could see that he liked his new job, and of course she knew, after all those years with her secret-keeping husband, where Roger really worked. What was more, she understood that he was evening a score.

After dinner, Ferris wandered over to the photo albums stacked neatly in the pantry. He tried to disguise his limp around his mother, but it never worked.

"Your leg isn't getting any better, is it?" she said.

"It's fine," said Ferris. "I'm healthy as a horse."

The albums were stacked and shelved in neat rows, with dates and places marked on the spines. Ferris pulled down the volume marked "Grandma and Baba." Those were his father's parents, who had lived outside Pittsburgh. His mother's parents, who had lived in Upper

Saddle River, New Jersey, were genteel folk known as "Honey" and "Gramps." There weren't that many pictures; Grandma and Baba had mostly kept to themselves. Ferris had always thought they were embarrassed: that they lived in Pittsburgh; that Baba had worked in the steel mills; that they hadn't melted into the pot enough to suit their assimilated son and his WASP wife.

Baba was muscular like Ferris, but darker. His skin had a rich tone, a color like virgin olive oil, and his hair had the tight bristle of a scouring brush. "I wish we knew where Baba's family came from," said Ferris. He had asked his father often enough, but the answers had always been vague. The Balkans. Someplace that ended up as part of Yugoslavia. The closest he ever got to a precise location was, "Maybe Bosnia."

"There's a guy I know in Jordan who tells me I must be an Arab. Maybe he's joking, I don't know."

"I think not." She laughed. "Baba said he was from the former Ottoman Empire, which covered a lot of territory. I always imagined he was from someplace unpronounceable east of the Danube, like Bosnia-Herzegovina, or Abkhazia. He said his family had Muslim neighbors, I remember that. But he didn't like to talk about it, and your father didn't press him. Everybody got jumbled together in Pittsburgh, and I guess they didn't like being called 'Bohunks,' or 'Polacks,' or whatever they happened to be. So they just thought of themselves as Americans. Or so I always imagined."

" 'Ferris' doesn't sound like an Eastern European name, though, does it? Dad told me once it had been changed, but he said he didn't know what it was before."

"He told me the same thing, before we were married. I think he was embarrassed. He always said there were papers somewhere, but he never wanted to dig them out. I thought that was sad, that your father seemed to care so little about his background, but that's what he loved about the agency: Whoever you had been before just disappeared. I tried to get him to help me do a family genealogy once, but he wasn't interested."

"Baba's family was Catholic, right?"

"I think so. He always went to Mass with Grandma. He didn't mind that I was a Protestant, but Grandma did. When I told her I was a Congregationalist, she said, 'Not Jewish?' to make sure. They were both quite rare in Pittsburgh, I gather."

Ferris studied the photo of his grandfather again. "He looks like me, doesn't he?"

"A bit. Though you are better-looking, my dear."

Ferris put away the album. He had been stalling, wanting to put something off, but it was getting late, and he would be driving back to Washington early the next morning.

"I've told Gretchen I want a divorce," he said. "We aren't living together anymore. And we weren't very happy before, when we were. So I think it's time to be honest and make a break, before we have kids and it gets any more complicated."

"I see. And what does Gretchen say?"

Ferris remembered all the different versions of "no" that had emerged during his evening with Gretchen. He was still ashamed that he had allowed her to seduce him so easily, and in her mind, at least, to obliterate the resolve he had tried to express about ending the relationship.

"She wasn't happy. She claims we're a good match. I'm sure she doesn't want to be bothered looking for another husband. She's very busy."

"Oh yes, I've always known that about Gretchen. She looked busy the first day I met her, at your graduation."

"So what do you think, Mom?"

"Gretchen is a very successful woman. I wish I had her drive. But I was never sure she made you happy. So if you have decided to make a change, and you're ready for all the pain, then you should do what you think is right. Follow your heart. And since I'm being motherly, I'll go ahead and ask the obvious: Is there another woman?"

"I don't know yet. Maybe. I would want a divorce in any event.

But I did meet someone I like a lot in Amman. I hope things work out with her. We'll see."

Ferris gave her a kiss and said he was going up to bed. His mother said she would just stay a moment and tidy up the kitchen, but she remained motionless at the table. There was a look of worry and helplessness on her face that Ferris had seen every time he had said goodbye.

GRETCHEN HAD been calling Ferris's cell phone. He had ignored the calls from her home, office and mobile numbers, and he hadn't responded to any of the various messages she left. But the phone rang again as he was driving back to DC, and since he didn't see one of her numbers on the display, he answered. He recognized her voice immediately. She was using someone else's phone, and she was almost shouting.

"Where are you, Roger? Damn it! Why haven't you answered my calls? You can't do this to me. You can't. I'm your wife. Everybody knows."

"I'm driving back from my mom's. I told her we're getting divorced."

"We aren't getting divorced. You love me. You know you do."

"Let's not go through a whole show, Gretchen. I don't love you. I want a divorce."

"You liar. You are so weak and pathetic. How could you fuck me like that the other night, if you don't love me? Nobody made you do that. Nobody made you fuck me. What do you think a judge will say about that?"

"What does a judge have to do with it? You can't make someone stay married. The law doesn't work that way. Even I know that. Divorce isn't a mutual decision. It's the end of mutual decisions."

"You came inside me. Three times."

"Look, Gretchen, I am sorry that I succumbed the other night. You are very sexy. You always have been. If good sex were enough for a good marriage, we'd be fine. But it's not."

"You treat me like a whore. You think you can fuck me and then walk away from me, but you're wrong. If you go ahead with this, you will regret it. I am telling you. I will make it very hard for you."

"Don't threaten me, Gretchen. I have to deal with people every day who are much scarier than you. Believe me."

"Don't be so sure, Roger. You've never made me angry before. When I'm fighting on principle, I do not compromise. I do whatever is necessary. You will regret this, I promise you."

Ferris was going to try to calm her down, suggest that they talk to a counselor before he left. But she had cut the connection.

17

FERRIS CHECKED INTO A SMALL hotel near the Piazza Cavour in Rome, in the gray district framed by Vatican City and the Tiber. The hotel itself was threadbare and anonymous, not fancy enough for Americans or charming enough for Europeans. The arrangements had been made by the kids on Azhar's staff, who must have thought it would be a good place to hide. Ferris was to contact the ninjas by calling a cell-phone number when he arrived and wait for a callback from "Tony," the chief of the little Special Forces cell. He made his call the afternoon he checked in, but there was no response that day or the next.

That first night, he called Alice from a pay phone. He wished they could meet in Rome, take long walks in the Centro, live on love and the occasional cappuccino, but as it was, he couldn't even tell her he was there. It turned out she had been away from Amman on a trip, to refugee camps up near the Syrian border, she said. Ferris scolded her for taking risks, but she cut him off. "They need me!" she insisted. She was all cranked up about the latest news; more dead in Lebanon, more dead in Iraq. What was the world coming to? Ferris had no answer for that.

"I love you," he said. He had never used those words with her before.

There was a long pause, and then Alice said, "Oh my."

"I told Gretchen I want a divorce."

"Good," she responded. "I mean, good that you told her, not good that your marriage is breaking up. If you hadn't told her, I would have worried that you were one of those people who don't know how to be happy. Or that you were a chicken."

Ferris laughed and then repeated, "I love you."

"Come home, so I can love you, too."

Ferris promised he would be back soon, but it might be another week or two. He felt something like physical pain when he ended the conversation.

Ferris waited two days for "Tony," walking the cobbled Roman streets to wear down his nervous energy. He tried to imagine his Special Forces colleagues among the crowds of Americans at the Piazza Navona or the Fontana di Trevi. Muscular men, shirts not quite big enough for their chests, necks the size of pine trees; not talking, scanning the pavement through wraparound sunglasses. Everyone in Rome looked slightly outlandish to him, even the bums down by the muddy embankment of the Tiber.

Each afternoon he would return to his hotel to find . . . nothing. And then, on the afternoon of the third day, there was a slip of paper in his message box and the name "Antony." Close enough. Ferris called the contact number from a pay phone across from the Palace of Justice.

"Sorry, things got fucked up," said the voice on the other end of the phone. "Security problem. We had to cool down."

"So, what's the temperature now?"

"Cooler. We'll be positively chilling by tomorrow morning."

"Where should I meet you?"

"Temple of Faustina. Villa Borghese," said the Special Forces officer. He had trouble in pronouncing "Borghese."

The next day Ferris took a cab to the Via Condotti, wandered in and out of the shops for a while to see if he could pick up any surveillance and then took another cab to the Villa Borghese across the river. He told the driver to deposit him near the Temple of Faustina, by a little lake that bordered the Zoological Garden. There, planted in the ground as if he were wearing concrete boots, stood a burly man who had to be "Tony." It turned out his real name was Jim, or at least that was what he said. He was dressed in jeans, a knit shirt and a V-neck sweater. He looked like a million other young men, except for the set of his eyes, which were continually scanning the middle distance.

Ferris shook his hand and studied his face when they were close up. "Do I know you?" he asked.

"Possibly, sir, but not likely."

"Balad," said Ferris. "Early this year. You were running ops with Task Force 145. I was operating over the wall. Until I got banged up."

"Well, far out, sir. I guess that makes us buddies."

They were instant friends now, having served in the shithole of Iraq. Normally military people didn't think much of their CIA counterparts, at least the ones who hadn't come out of the military themselves. But Ferris was an exception. He had been in Iraq, and he had nearly lost a leg because of it.

"So what's up?" said Ferris. "You said on the phone you had a security problem."

"These crazy Italians." Jim shook his head in embarrassment. "One of my guys got in a traffic accident. It wasn't his fault. The Italians don't drive the same way we do. Anyway, the local cops began asking questions about where he was living and what he was doing, and they sent some Carabinieri people to our safe house, which all of a sudden wasn't so safe. We were operating out of an apartment over by the university, a mile or so from here. Now we're in temporary lodgings."

"Where's the temporary base?"

"The Cavalieri Hilton, up on Monte Mario."

"Jesus! That place is five hundred bucks a day."

"Roger that, sir." A trace of a smile came over Jim's face. "It's good cover for Americans, with the swimming pool and the girls and all. We don't look out of place. And we shouldn't be fighting the global war on terror on the cheap, sir."

Ferris laughed out loud. "How long have you guys been here? And cut the 'sir,' crap, please."

"A month. We haven't done much other than set up cover and commo, which I guess we sort of screwed up. The colonel said you would tell us the real drill. He said what you're doing is super-black, and the general at MacDill had signed off on it, and we should just do what we're told. I'm not sure the colonel knows. He sounded sort of pissed off about that. The way he talked, he made it sound like somebody had sprinkled you guys with fairy dust. Sir."

"Let's take a stroll," said Ferris. He gave up the effort to dispense with "sir." As far as Jim's little team was concerned, Ferris was the rain god. They walked until they came to a bench that offered a clear view across the water and of the approaches to the lake from the zoo. Ferris motioned for Jim to sit down.

"So here's the deal. We are running a very sensitive operation against the folks who are setting off all these car bombs. The operation isn't CIA, exactly. It has its own compartment. My boss has cleared it with your boss, and that's all we need to know. Right?"

"Roger that. But what's going down?"

"I can't tell you that. But I want you to be ready to do two things. The first is to be ready to pounce if one of our high-value targets surfaces. How many people do you have in your team?"

"Four, sir, plus me."

"Okay. You need to be ready to move out anytime we register one of our bad guys. You should have kit, weapons, the whole thing ready, anytime. Have you done any of these takedowns before?"

The Special Forces officer nodded, the muscles in his neck rippling as he tilted his head forward. "Iraq. Indonesia."

"Good," said Ferris. "So you know the drill. Stealth. Nobody sees you coming. Nobody sees you leaving. It has to be invisible for forty-eight hours, so we can put the guy on a plane and mess with his network. And whoever we're targeting has to come out alive. I know that's hard, but it really matters on this one. We can't bust this network unless we get intel from the folks we capture. Are your men all good to go? I mean, have they done this stuff before?"

"Yes, sir. All except one, and he'll be cool. He's from Biloxi, like me."

"Well, be sure to remind him about pocket litter. The little stuff they've been squirreling away in their pockets because they're too paranoid to throw it away. Charge slips, phone numbers, cell-phone cards, receipts from money orders, thumb drives. You've got to make sure they don't destroy that stuff after you bust down the door. When you do your ops plan, think about multiple entry points, so you can stop them from destroying anything."

"Roger, sir." The Army officer was scanning the horizon as he listened, watching for any hint of surveillance.

"And you need to do a really good search when you grab them, even though you're in a hurry to get out of there. These guys carry everything on them—all their commo, all their files. They're paranoid, because they know we're coming after them. So they'll have their laptops with them, and their cell phones, and a couple of different SIM cards, and their address books. They have it all with them, twenty-four/seven. Which means if we can take them down and grab all the pocket litter and paraphernalia, we're in fat city."

"Heard, understood, acknowledged, sir. You said there was a second thing. What's that?"

Before answering, Ferris surveyed the area. He noticed a man walking toward them from a street that bounded the pond on the north side. He had a dog on a leash. "Who the hell is that?" said Ferris, rising from the bench.

They walked five minutes more, to another bench that commanded the view of a neatly terraced formal garden, before Ferris resumed his briefing.

"The second part is a little weird," he said.

"We can do weird."

"You're going to need some explosives. They have to be the same type that were used in the Frankfurt and Milan bombings. Same tags. My people will help you get them. And we're going to need detonators, the right kind. We'll give you those specs, too."

"Roger, sir, and what are we going to do with all this stuff?"

"You're going to make a car bomb."

Jim stared at Ferris. For once he didn't say "Roger that," he just nodded. "And what are we going to do with the car bomb, sir?"

"Well, basically, we're going to set it off."

"Holy shit. I guess this has all been approved. Right?"

"Yes," said Ferris. "More or less."

"You want to tell me any more, sir?"

"No. I've told you everything I'm authorized to say. The only thing to add is that if you knew everything I know, you would say, 'That's a pretty fucking cool operation.'"

FERRIS LEFT Rome the next morning for Geneva, where he was to initiate contact with Omar Sadiki. Ferris's cover name was "Brad Scanlon," and he worked for a company called Unibank, as its site development manager for Europe and the Middle East. He had business cards, fax forms, an Internet address for e-mail. He reread the script he and Azhar had drafted. The bank was planning a new branch in Abu Dhabi . . . Islamic ambience . . . need to negotiate the contract quickly . . . schedule a time to meet at the site . . . need contact numbers . . . will send literature . . . must respond by week's end. It looked seamless, but then it always did, until the seams pulled apart.

FERRIS PLACED the call to Omar Sadiki the next morning. When the architect came on the line, Ferris introduced himself as Brad Scanlon, and made a brief pitch about Unibank and its new branch.

He asked if Al Fajr Architects would be interested in bidding on the project.

"I don't know," said a cautious voice on the other end of the phone. "Our clients are Arab companies."

"You have been highly recommended by our Arab friends." Ferris read off a short list of Arab companies that had retained Al Fajr, which Azhar had compiled when he first thought of using Sadiki many weeks ago. "If you're interested in bidding, we would want you to come look at the site in Abu Dhabi. Would that be possible?"

"Perhaps. If my manager agrees." He was cautious, but not unduly so. Business deals in the Middle East always began cagily. Ferris needed to make the link before he went any further.

"Who would represent Al Fajr, if you decide you are interested?" asked Ferris.

"That would be me, sir," answered Omar. "I do all the on-site evaluations for new projects."

Ferris didn't want to sound too eager. He expressed regret that the general manager himself would not be coming and then offered to send the details of the project immediately, by e-mail or fax. Omar requested fax, and was assured the documents would be on their way from Geneva by the close of business. Ferris said he would need an answer within five days, and a meeting at the site in Abu Dhabi soon after that, if they were interested.

"May I ask, please, what is the fee associated with this project?"

Ferris named a handsome figure—a bit more than what such a project might normally command, but not so wildly generous that it would raise suspicion. Omar promised that he would respond within the week.

When he hung up, Ferris smiled. It had gone more smoothly than he expected. That was the only thing that made him nervous.

Ferris contacted Hoffman, through a new communications link they had established that bypassed NE Division. Hoffman congratulated Ferris and asked him where he was staying. Ferris gave Hoffman the name of the hotel. "Check your e-mail," said Hoffman.

• • •

IT DIDN'T TAKE Sadiki long. Two days later, on a Wednesday, the architect called to say that Al Fajr wanted to bid on the Unibank project. There was a new tone in his voice, almost of enthusiasm. He wanted to arrange a date when they could meet in the Emirates. Ferris studied his imaginary calendar and then proposed they meet the following Thursday. Omar consulted his real calendar, proposed that they meet a day earlier or three days later. He wanted to be home for the Islamic weekend, evidently. Good boy. So the meeting was set for a week hence, in Abu Dhabi.

The only odd thing was that the Jordanian seemed to want to check his new client's identity. He asked him to spell the name slowly, S-C-A-N-L-O-N, asked where he was from in the States, seemed almost to want to keep him on the phone. Ferris wasn't worried; his cover identity was solid. Someone would have to know Ferris's voice intimately to make any connection, and the chance of that was close to zero.

Ferris messaged Hoffman to report success and ask if he could stop in Amman on his way to the UAE. He wanted to see Alice, but Hoffman said no. That would be insecure. He needed to do his initial development of Omar outside Jordan, where Hani wouldn't find any loose threads.

HOFFMAN SENT Ferris an encrypted e-mail a few days later. He had the body. Harry Meeker was on ice in a cold locker in Mincemeat Park. There would be time later to dress and barber him and fill his pockets with the debris of his imagined life. The poison pill had arms and legs and, soon, a personal history. Now it was Ferris's job to create the provocation that would lead the enemy to ingest the pill and swallow it down whole.

18

F ERRIS WATCHED OMAR SADIKI make his way through the shimmering midday heat toward The Fishmarket Restaurant on Bainuna Street. He was tall, reedy man with a narrow face and a neatly trimmed beard. He was wearing a gray business suit for his meeting, but it was easy to imagine him in a white robe and kaffiyeh. The maître d'hotel seated him at the table Ferris had requested, while Ferris looked on from across the room, checking for surveillance. He studied Sadiki's face: He looked composed, purposeful, as if he knew what he was after. The only thing that perturbed the Jordanian was the heavyset German man a few tables away who was drinking a beer and reading *Stern*. It must be the beer, thought Ferris. That was oddly reassuring.

Ferris emerged from the shadows and introduced himself as Brad Scanlon from Unibank. The name wasn't his only camouflage. Ferris was in a disguise that would have confused his own mother. His hair and eyebrows were a sandy blond, rather than the normal dark brown. He had a thin moustache, and a pair of black-framed eyeglasses that overwhelmed his features and dimmed the spark of his eyes. Padding around his waist and bottom made him appear thirty pounds heavier. To anyone who knew Ferris from Jordan, he would be unrecognizable as Brad Scanlon.

The Jordanian offered a limp handshake, a sign of good manners in the East. Ferris apologized for being late; Sadiki apologized for being early. A Pakistani waiter was hovering behind them, menus in hand. Ferris studied Sadiki's face: The Jordanian had a callus in the middle of his forehead from bowing so passionately in prayer each day. The prayer mark hadn't been visible in the photo Azhar had displayed. He was ostentatiously devout. That was another good sign.

"I'm so sorry," said Ferris, nodding toward the German. "I didn't know they served beer here. We can go somewhere else."

"This is not a problem, Mr. Scanlon. He is not a Muslim. He can do as he likes." Sadiki offered a dour smile.

After the waiter took their orders, Ferris pulled from his briefcase some documents he had brought along. The first was an aerial view of an empty lot in an upscale Abu Dhabi neighborhood called Al Bateen, near the fancy downtown area that overlooked the Corniche and the Gulf. He had a drawing of the site, and pictures of some of Unibank's other branch offices. Sadiki joined in; he emptied his own briefcase and displayed a sheaf of documents about his firm and its work.

Ferris saw that Sadiki had brought along his laptop computer. That was unfortunate; it would complicate things.

The Jordanian started his pitch awkwardly but gained confidence. He showed Ferris photographs of some of the buildings that Al Fajr had designed. A shopping center in Fahaheel in Kuwait; two offices buildings in Amman; a dormitory for the Jordanian College of Technology in Irbid. They were good, if uninspired, designs. Sadiki had a second folder of photographs, and Ferris asked to see them. This was Al Fajr's Islamic portfolio: The firm had designed small mosques in the Palestinian towns of Halhul and Jenin in the West Bank; one in the Jordanian city of Salt, and a big one in Sanaa, in Yemen. Ferris remembered that he had seen the Yemen mosque when it was under construction, during his stint as a case officer in

Sanaa. The last photos were of two big mosques in the Saudi cities of Taif, along the Red Sea Coast, and Hafr Al-Batin, near the Jordanian border. These were massive, domed structures, with spindly minarets that soared gracefully above the buildings.

"These are beautiful," said Ferris. "Did the Saudi government commission them?"

"We built them for a private Islamic charity," Sadiki answered. "They are for the believers, not the government."

Ferris nodded respectfully, and smiled inwardly. He was beginning to understand why Azhar had selected Omar Sadiki to star in their play. He was connected to the network of Islamic charities that had funded Al Qaeda in its early days. Indeed, he had all the necessary attributes of a member of the underground. When Sadiki finished his presentation and closed his portfolio, Ferris saw that his firm's logo was a red Islamic crescent bisected by a bold blue triangle. Below the logo were the words "The Islamic Design Solution."

SADIKI WENT to the men's room to wash his hands before the meal, and Ferris was left staring out the window, almost in a trance. Through the glass, he could see the white hulls of some of the yachts that were docked in a marina behind the breakwater. The big boats sparkled in the sun. They must have cost tens of millions of dollars each, yet Ferris suspected they were rarely used. They were for decoration; perhaps once every few months, a prince of the desert would take a retinue of pliant Western ladies out for a pleasure cruise—have them strip down to the buff and entertain his business clients. The marina was part of the show—the theme park of modern life made possible by the shower of oil wealth. It was hard to imagine that the older men seated at this restaurant had, as boys, lived in the harsh desert with their camels and sheep, or dived for pearls, or smuggled cargoes to Persia in their dhows. The Emirates had been so poor in the 1930s that people had worried its economic fortunes would be destroyed forever by the rise of the Japanese cultured pearl industry.

Ferris thought of Alice while he waited for the food. The loneliness snuck up on him again—a wish that he could share the place with Alice, a yearning for the sound of her laugh or the touch of her hand. He wondered what she would think if she could see him in his disguise—other than that he looked fat. It would be nice if she could laugh out loud at how preposterous it all was, but he knew she would have a different thought: Ferris was living a lie, wrapped in a lie; his whole world was lies. How could a liar ever make her happy?

THE WAITER brought a traditional Arab mezzeh of ground chickpeas and eggplant, stuffed kibbeh, tabbouli and halloumi cheese. That was followed by a grilled hammour from the Gulf and some grilled shrimp. Ferris made small talk, but not much. He let Sadiki fill the silences with polite questions about Ferris's family. The Jordanian offered reassurance when Ferris said he had a wife but no children. Eventually, Sadiki got around to what evidently was bothering him.

"Why do you want to hire Al Fajr for this job? We are good for mosques, not office buildings."

Ferris had anticipated this question when he and Azhar wrote their script. He explained that the building site was in a neighborhood that had been very Islamic, with only a few expatriates from the West. Now that was changing with completion of the gleaming Emirates Palace Hotel a mile away. Unibank wanted to put its local branch in the newly fashionable Al Bateen area, but also be respectful of the Islamic character of the neighborhood. And Al Fajr came highly recommended. So the choice was easy.

Sadiki praised God and mumbled something appropriately humble in Arabic. He seemed content with Ferris's answer and sat back and cleaned his teeth with a toothpick. He was easier than Ferris had expected.

Ferris's fake moustache was itching and he was ready to go back to the hotel, but he had several more items on the agenda. He invited the Jordanian to visit the site, and Sadiki readily agreed. He had brought along a digital camera and an architectural sketchbook. They headed down Bainuna Street in the rented Lincoln Town Car, turned left on Sheik Zayed the First Street and then parked in front of a fenced lot with a sign that said "Unibank" in big bold letters. The Abu Dhabi station had done its set decoration handsomely.

The afternoon sky had a hazy quality—a pinkish white at the horizon rising to a thin blue. The asphalt was soft under Ferris's feet, and his scalp was sweating under the wig. A few Mercedes and BMWs plied the streets, their windows rolled up tight, but most people had gone home for their afternoon naps.

Sadiki toured the property, took a soil sample, shot photographs from various angles and made some measurements. He spent nearly an hour examining the site, and then asked some technical questions. The Jordanian seemed almost to be putting on a show of his own. They sat in Ferris's rented car with the air conditioner blasting while Sadiki went through his list: How many employees would be using the office? How many customers it would serve? What floor space was desired? How many stories tall? Had Unibank already contacted a local construction contractor? Did it have building permits? Ferris had answers for most of his queries, all drawn from the briefing book Azhar's team had prepared.

The Jordanian mulled the matter, but not for very long. When Ferris explained that Unibank had an option to buy the property that would expire at the end of next week, he agreed to submit a bid and some very preliminary sketches by next Thursday noon, before the Islamic weekend. Ferris asked if Sadiki could meet him in Beirut, where he had other business next week, and the Jordanian agreed to that, too.

Ferris had just one more request. He wondered if Mr. Sadiki could come to the office of Unibank's local lawyer, Adnan Masri, and sign a letter of intent. It was a formality, but a necessary one for any new vendors of services. Sadiki balked at first, but after a cell-phone call to someone in Amman, he said yes, Al Fajr would sign. Ferris apologized that the lawyer's office was in the Al Markaziyah district, near the old souk, rather than in the fancier part of town. Sadiki shrugged; it made no difference to him.

The lawyer Masri was an older man, bearded and dressed in the traditional white robe and gold-threaded black cloak of the region. He spoke with Sadiki in Arabic, offered him tea, explained the papers to him. Soon enough, the paperwork was done. If Sadiki was suspicious, he didn't show it. And why should he be? He could not have imagined the deception that Azhar and Hoffman had assembled behind this façade: He could not know that Adnan Masri was part of Azhar's network of money changers who moved funds for the underground; or that as Masri talked with Sadiki, a camera installed secretly in his office was taking pictures of the encounter; or that one of the photographs would soon find its way to the UAE's intelligence service as part of its regular surveillance of Masri; or that a copy of the photograph would land on the desk of an Al Qaeda sympathizer inside the UAE security service who was always looking for ways to protect fellow members of the organization; or that this local Al Qaeda sympathizer would transmit a copy to his contact in the organization, to warn him that one of the brethren had been caught in a surveillance by the local Moukhabarat.

Sadiki knew none of it. That was the point. He existed in other people's imaginations now more precisely—and certainly more potently—than he did in his own.

FERRIS LINGERED at Masri's office before saying goodbye to the Jordanian architect and wishing him a safe flight home the next morning. He wanted to give the Support team that had been working over Sadiki's hotel room time to finish. They were collecting and copying everything they could find—date book, address book, all the useful pieces of paper in the pockets of the clothes Sadiki had brought from Jordan.

In his finicky architect's way, Sadiki had been carrying his laptop with him everywhere. But Support took care of the computer problem in the middle of the night. Around three A.M., one of Hoffman's boys pulled the fire alarm at Sadiki's hotel. The Jordanian groggily followed directions from the fire marshals down to the lobby. He wasn't gone long, only fifteen minutes or so, but that was time enough for the CIA team operating out of a room down the hall to download everything on his hard drive. They got his e-mails, his personal files, the list of pious Muslim friends to whom he sent cards of welcome at the Eid al-Fitr at the end of Ramadan, even the members of the Ikhwan Ihsan, the Brothers of Awareness, which appeared to be a study group of believers at his mosque. When the new day dawned, the men and women of Mincemeat Park had the additional fabric they needed for their cloak of illusion.

19

FERRIS'S FLIGHT OUT OF Abu Dhabi was delayed by a sandstorm, and it was past midnight when he landed at Queen Alia Airport. He presented his diplomatic passport to the control officer; usually he was whisked through, but not this time. They made him wait a good thirty minutes, politely of course, plying him with tea and sweet biscuits in a shabby anteroom on the second floor of the airport while a GID captain made frantic telephone calls. Ferris protested loudly—his passport was in order, his residency stamp was valid, he should be free to enter the country. He asked to use his cell phone so he could call Alice and tell her he was back, but the captain ignored him. The Jordanian officer kept gesturing with his thumb and forefinger—*shway, shway,* slowly, slowly—for Ferris to be patient. Finally his phone rang and, after a muffled conversation, he handed it to Ferris. It was Hani.

"My dear Roger, I wanted to welcome you back to Jordan myself. I am so glad you have decided to return to your true home."

"Thank you, Hani Pasha. I'm afraid your welcoming committee at the airport wasn't informed that I was such an esteemed guest. They've held me up for half an hour. I want to go home and get some sleep."

"Take it as a sign of flattery. We only harass important people. The rest—well, who cares? And it is my fault, really. I wanted to welcome you back myself. I would have come to the airport to greet you personally, but it is so late, and I have such an attractive guest with me at the moment. But we need to talk, don't we? Yes, I think so. Let us have breakfast the day after tomorrow. You Americans always like breakfast meetings, don't you? We'll meet at eight-thirty at the Officers' Club in Jebel Amman. Near the British Council. Do you know it? I'm quite sure we won't be disturbed there at that hour. Arabs detest breakfast meetings. Now let me speak to the captain."

Ferris handed back the phone, while the officer in charge of the little group received instructions from the pasha about what to do next. Having inconvenienced Ferris, they now put on a show of hospitality that was as annoying in its way as the delay had been. He was whisked to the VIP waiting room, where more tea and pastries arrived while they collected Ferris's luggage from the carousel downstairs. A motorcade was assembled to accompany Ferris's embassy SUV, police patrol cars front and back and a half dozen motorcycle outriders. The caravan made its way into downtown Amman, lights flashing and sirens blaring. It was hardly the way for an acting CIA chief of station to return home, but that was evidently the point Hani wanted to make: Whether Ferris was detained at the airport or coddled in a motorcade, he was under Hani's control here.

By the time they left the airport, it was one-thirty A.M.—too late for a telephone call, normally, but Ferris called Alice anyway. He'd reached her the day before from Abu Dhabi to say that he would be back soon, but he'd wanted his actual arrival to be a surprise. He awoke her from a deep sleep, so that her first words were unguarded and spontaneous.

"Hello, darling," she said. "Where are you?"

"Darling," Ferris repeated. "I'm back in Amman. They finally let me come home."

"That's nice. Whoever 'they' are. What time is it? Where are you?" She still wasn't quite awake.

"It's almost two A.M. I'm on the airport road. Can I come see you?"

"Now? No, of course not."

"I miss you."

"I miss you, too, Roger, but it's the middle of the night and you've been away for almost three weeks. I need to brush my teeth. Let's say tomorrow night for dinner, at my place."

"I love you," said Ferris. He hadn't planned to say that. It just came out.

"Hmmm," she answered. "We'll see about that."

PEOPLE AT the embassy were happy to see Ferris was back, if a little surprised. When he had left so suddenly, the rumor was that he had been expelled, like Francis Alderson. The ambassador, who resented the CIA station's ties with the palace, actually looked a bit disappointed when Ferris stopped by to pay his respects. So did the operations chief, who had been running the station in Ferris's absence and undoubtedly had hoped to continue. Ferris hit upon a solution that would make them both happy. He told the ops chief that he could handle all the routine paperwork while Ferris was traveling the next few months. He could sign off on rents for safe houses and meet CODELs from the intelligence committees and update the agents' Personal Record Questionnaires. He could manage everything except contact with Hani Salaam, which Ferris would keep to himself. The ops chief seemed delighted. He would be a paperwork prince, just like a real station chief.

The embassy staff was on edge. New security rules had been adopted during his absence. Embassy personnel weren't allowed to travel in many parts of town without an escort. Military personnel weren't allowed to travel in uniform. There was an elaborate new drill for travel between residences and the embassy—varying routes, carpooling in armored vehicles. The embassy security officer had posted new instructions on what to do if the embassy was attacked with biological weapons or a dirty bomb. New shelters were designated in the chancery, as well. You could see the effect of all this security mania from the look in people's eyes: They blinked, glanced away, started at any strange sound, even as they kept up the regimen of embassy life. It was the false bravura of people who know they are targets.

Ferris left the office at four-thirty despite the entreaties of his secretary, who had a stack of correspondence she wanted to go over with him. Ferris told her it could wait; he wanted to take a nap before his date with Alice. He tried to sleep but was too keyed up, so he watched a televised soccer match from Qatar until it was time to get ready. On the way to Alice's apartment, he stopped to buy flowers. He chose an elaborate arrangement—orchids and lilies—big, showy flowers that were too loud for someone like Alice, but made a statement. The florist took endless care wrapping them, slowly adding sprig after sprig of ferns, spraying them with lacquer and tying them in such an elaborate arrangement of ribbon and string that Ferris wasn't sure she would be able to get them undone. He looked at his watch and muttered that he was late, but the florist gave him a knowing smile and continued with his fantasy bouquet.

Alice's apartment was in an old stone building that dated back to Ottoman times. In its day, it must have belonged to a wealthy merchant, for the stone and tile work were of very high quality. Ferris climbed the stairs to the second floor and knocked on a door gaily painted in pastel colors. When Alice emerged, Ferris stood motionless for a moment, admiring her. Her face was luminous, the skin soft and ripe. Her blond hair was tied behind her, exposing the fine lines of her neck, and there was a look of playful expectation in her deep hazel eyes. She wore a black dress with a scoop neck that showed off her figure.

"Hi, there," she said, giving him a dazzling smile and taking his hand.

"You look . . . incredible," said Ferris. He stood in the doorway, dumbly holding his enormous bouquet of flowers.

"Aren't these *sweet*," she said, taking the flowers. Her tone was slightly mocking. She pulled him by the arm into the apartment. "Now, you sit down in the living room while I put these in some water." She tore at the elaborate packing that encased the bouquet and tossed it in the trash while she searched for a vase big enough to hold the small arboretum Ferris had brought.

The apartment was like an oriental jewel box. It contained treasures fashioned long ago by the original owner, which a visitor could not have imagined from the outside. The walls and ceilings were inlaid with fine woods, mother-of-pearl and gold leaf. There were handsome murals depicting scenes of the Arab world—the teeming Levantine harbor of Alexandria, a snowcapped Mt. Lebanon, the gold dome of the Al Aqsa Mosque in Jerusalem, the rich farmlands of the Damascus plain. The far wall was an array of leaded glass windows opening onto a garden below that had a small bubbling fountain surrounded by plants and shrubs. A few were in bloom, even in November. There was the low sound of Arabic music; as Ferris listened, he realized it was the voice of the Lebanese singer Fairuz, who sang of the distantly remembered pleasures of Arab village life in a way that was said to bring tears to the eyes of men and women who listened to her. Alice emerged from the kitchen bearing the float of blossoms in an oversized vase.

"Pretty amazing apartment," said Ferris. "You didn't tell me it was so nice."

"You didn't ask. Anyway, it was obvious when you dropped me off that you felt sorry for me, living down here in the old city. You had that look that said anything this old, without air-conditioning, can't be very nice. So I thought, screw him. He doesn't appreciate a good thing when he sees it." She winked. "Actually, I wanted to save it for you, as a surprise."

She brought a bottle of wine from her little fridge and set out a spread of appetizers—fat pistachio nuts bursting from their shells, little quail eggs with rock salt and pepper, fine olives and crunchy peppers and carrots. Ferris was still a little dizzy over seeing her. He sat down next to her on the couch and took her hand. It felt tiny. He didn't really want to talk, he wanted to hold her; but he had to say something.

"I missed you, Alice," said Ferris. "I'm sorry I was gone so long. Every day I was away, I wanted to be here with you."

She waited a moment before answering. "I got frightened, Roger. After you had been gone two weeks, I began to think you weren't coming back. I talked to my friend at the embassy, and she said nobody knew when you would return. When I heard that, I just burst into tears. I was so scared that you wouldn't come back to me. I thought you would be swallowed up in all this mess."

Ferris wrapped her in his arms, and her body eased into his. It took him a moment to realize she was crying.

"Don't be sad," he said. "I'm here now."

"I'm not sad. I'm happy. I just don't want anything to happen to us. The world is going crazy. I want to hide away in this beautiful place."

Dinner would wait. She took him by the hand and led him into her bedroom. It was a room for an Arab princess. She had decorated it with sprays of flowers and scented candles so that it was like a magical garden. They undressed each other slowly, each piece of clothing coming off in its own time: a dress slowly falling to the floor; the buttons of a shirt plucked one by one; a belt undone, and then a slow tug at a zipper; the clasp of a brassiere unhooked and the straps falling, and her chest soft against his. When they were naked, they were two perfect creatures. The lacerations on Ferris's leg had vanished, in her mind and his. He took her slowly at first, wanting to stretch out each moment, but their bodies were too eager to wait very long. It wasn't until he was finished that Ferris realized she was crying again.

"I love you," she said through her tears. "I love you. I love you. I love you."

Ferris cradled her body against his. He was worried. He loved her, and she loved him, and what were they going to do now?

• • •

SHE LAY AGAINST his chest on the fresh sheets. A fan turned lazily above them, making the candles flicker and blowing a cool breeze over their bodies. She got up eventually and busied herself, first in the bathroom and then tidying their clothes from the floor. As she picked up Ferris's jacket a small plastic box fell out of the pocket. Ferris watched it hit the floor and quickly leaned out of bed to pick it up. It was the dental bridge that Hoffman had given him back at Langley. Alice's cat, Elvis, bounded across the room and bumped the plastic case with his nose.

"What's that?" she asked.

"Nothing," said Ferris, taking the jacket from her and putting the plastic case back in the pocket. She was looking at him strangely, and he knew he should give her a better answer. He popped open the lid, so she could see the semicircular ring of plastic. "It's just a bite guard. So I don't grind my teeth."

She smiled, back to normal again. "Somehow, you don't strike me as the tooth-grinding type."

"You never know. We all worry about something." He gave her a smile and hung up the jacket. How could he lie so easily to someone he loved?

FERRIS ROSE at six. They made love again, noisily, and then Ferris went home to his apartment to shower and change before his meeting with Hani. He felt light-headed from so much sex and so little sleep, and he had a nervous feeling in his stomach. In the shower, the image that fell into his head was the scene from twenty years ago when he had broken the other boy's arm without meaning to. Or had he meant to? He winced at the recollection. Where was the line? When did the bone stop bending and begin to break?

HANI WAS waiting for him at the Officers' Club. It was deserted, as he had predicted. The Jordanian looked very pleased with himself this morning. He was wearing a double-breasted blazer with shiny brass buttons; his shirt was one of those two-tone models they sell on Jermyn Street, with white collar and cuffs and gaudy regimental stripes. He greeted Ferris with an appraising eye.

"Long night?" the Jordanian asked. "You look a bit . . . tired."

"Jet lag," said Ferris. He wondered if Hani had him under surveillance. Of course Hani had him under surveillance.

They sat down to a proper English breakfast, served by a waiter in white gloves. The club was all musty leather and dark wood paneling. It must have been built back in the days when Glubb Pasha imposed British discipline on the Hashemite army. Hani ate like a trencherman, talking between bites of his kippers and scrambled eggs.

"We forgive you, Roger," the Jordanian said. "That's what I wanted to say. We are sorry that we lost our temper. But we were provoked." He was speaking about himself in the royal plural. Even the king didn't do that.

"That's okay," said Ferris. "If I had been you, I would have been pretty angry, too. And I'm glad you decided to let me come back. I like it here."

"We know you do. And we are watching out for you. You are our little brother."

Was that a warning? "Thanks," Ferris said. "I appreciate the thought. But I can watch out for myself."

"As you like, my dear. And I trust you. Even after what happened to my poor man in Berlin, Mustafa Karami. Because I know it was not your fault. But I will be honest. One reason I wanted you back in Amman is because I worry about Mr. Ed Hoffman. He is the one I do not trust."

"Well, don't ask me. Hoffman doesn't tell anybody what he's really up to, including me."

"Oh, I doubt that. I doubt that. You are his boy. What is the expression? His 'fair-haired boy.' I suspect you know quite a lot about Mr. Ed Hoffman and his plans. And I don't want to get burned again, you see? That is what worries me. I can hear Ed's footsteps. I can hear him breathing. But I do not see him. That bothers me, I am afraid."

"Can't help you there. Sorry. Deaf and dumb. You know the rules."

"Yes, yes. Don't worry. I am not going to try to 'recruit' you. I will not be as rude as your predecessor, Francis Alderson, and try to suborn a member of a friendly intelligence service. Put away that fear, please. But I want you to understand something. We are not as stupid as you and Mr. Ed Hoffman seem to think we are. Truly. Do not make that mistake."

"I know you're not stupid. The truth is that I have great respect for you. You are my teacher, *ustaaz* Hani."

"How nice," said the Jordanian. "I will remember that expression of friendship. This is a part of the world where friendship matters. But you know that. You are an Arab yourself. Or so we like to think."

FERRIS WAS in the embassy later that morning, trying to clear his desk of all the accumulated cables and reports, when his secretary pushed open the door and asked if he had heard the news from Saudi Arabia. Ferris shook his head.

"Two bombs exploded in a little while ago in Riyadh. One outside the Four Seasons, another near the local branch bank of HSBC."

"Oh shit," said Ferris, shaking his head. "How many people are dead?"

"They aren't saying. The news is just coming over now."

Ferris turned on CNN and went to his secure computer. The television network had better information at that moment than the CIA, as usual. Ferris called Hani, who had gotten back to his office a few minutes before Ferris. The Jordanian said he had already ordered a lockdown of everything he could in the country. Extra security was on its way to the American Embassy and every other potential target in Amman.

The next call Ferris made was to Alice. He tried her office number, but she was out, so he called her cell phone. He could tell from the sound of the wind that she was outside somewhere. He told her the news from Riyadh, and she didn't say anything for a few seconds.

"This is going to keep happening, more and more," she said. "Don't you see? Milan, Frankfurt, Riyadh. Afghanistan, Iraq, the West Bank. We won't stop, and they won't stop."

"Where are you?" asked Ferris.

"I'm at one of the Palestinian camps outside the city. I'm trying to get them new computers for their school."

"I think you should go home, or at least back to the office. It's dangerous today. I'm worried about you."

"I'll be okay. It's dangerous every day. And there are lots of people here to protect me." She paused. "You know, Roger, this is the sort of day when I shouldn't be hiding. I should be here with people, to show them that we aren't all crazy, that I'm their friend, and I won't be scared away. Tell me you understand that."

This is why I love her, Ferris thought. "I do understand. I'm just anxious for you. I can't help it. I love you."

"I love you, too," she said slowly. "Pick me up tonight. I'll cook dinner for you. We can stay at your place, if that makes you feel better. I'll even let you hold the TV remote control. How's that?"

"Better." Ferris smiled. He knew that she was right. This was a day when she should be out with her Arab friends—unless it wasn't, but you would never know that until it was too late. He went back to CNN and the secure CIA computer, and spent the day bouncing messages around the world and pretending that he was making a difference. By the end of the day, nineteen people had died at the hotel, and another dozen outside the bank. On a day like this, you operated on autopilot, running through a series of procedures that were laid down like a script.

Ferris was worried about Alice, but he was on the roller coaster now. The long clanking climb up the hill was past. The car had crested the top and now it was all gravity and momentum. Alice could make nice to every Palestinian on the planet, but it wouldn't stop people like Suleiman. Ferris was going to take him down. He was going to find a way into his viscera, inside his bloodstream. He would destroy him from the inside out. Otherwise, this would never end.

20 BEIRUT / AMMAN

O MAR SADIKI LOOKED SHEEPISH when he arrived at Ferris's suite at the Phoenicia Hotel in Beirut. He seemed impressed by the hotel, which kept its sheen amid the ruined majesty of Beirut. The Jordanian kept smiling awkwardly, and as the grin grew wider, it had the effect of compressing the prayer mark on his forehead into a red dimple. Ferris wondered why he was acting so oddly, until he saw the bid. Al Fajr had estimated a project cost that was nearly double what Ferris had expected. He could only imagine the kickbacks that would be flowing from contractors in Abu Dhabi back into the pockets of Al Fajr's principals in Amman. No wonder Sadiki had the shit-eating grin: He was ripping off the infidels. Ferris had to think a moment how Brad Scanlon would react. He stroked the tufts of his false moustache as he thought about what to say.

Ferris led Sadiki to the terrace and sat him down in a wrought-iron chair. The view was splendid—across the Bay of Beirut to Jounié and the rugged slope of Mt. Lebanon. It was a late fall day, but the sun was bright and the air so crisp and clean you could see to the top of the mountain. The generations of bomb damage were invisible. Ferris ordered coffee from room service and then sat down with the cost estimates and contractors' bids. He kept shaking his head as he studied the numbers. Occasionally he would take out his calculator and do some imaginary estimates of his own, jotting sums down on a white legal pad. When he had reviewed it all, Ferris took off his thick black glasses and rubbed his eyes.

"This is too expensive," he said. "My manager will never approve this."

"Mr. Scanlon, please. With Al Fajr, you know you will get the best. That is why we have our good reputation. Because our work is high-quality. That is why you came to us. Yes?"

"Listen, Omar, my friend. Of course we want the best, but we are not building a palace here. You have to understand, we are a bank, and we have to be careful about money or people won't trust us. And as I said, I could never get this approved, even if I accepted it. It would be the most expensive Unibank branch in the world. We need to negotiate this down."

Sadiki nodded, and Ferris thought he had done the right thing. Of course the initial estimate was inflated. Life was a bazaar. If the Americans were stupid enough to pay too much, why stop them?

"With any design, changes are always possible, sir. We could ask some of the subcontractors in Abu Dhabi to rebid their estimates. You gave us very little time, so the numbers are a little rough. What did you have in mind, when you were thinking about how much to spend for this project?"

Ferris studied his white legal pad, punched some more numbers in his calculator. He was winging it, hoping Sadiki wouldn't become suspicious. "The number I could get approved would be about twenty-five percent lower, I think."

"You don't know too much about the construction business, I think, Mr. Scanlon." Ferris moved uneasily in his chair. There was something in his tone that made him worry that Sadiki was on to his game.

"What do you mean by that?" said Ferris sharply.

The Jordanian immediately backed away. "Twenty-five percent is a big cut, Mr. Scanlon. You would have to sacrifice quality. I do not think you would be happy, at that price."

"Well, tell you what. You give me your best price. Come as close as you can to my twenty-five percent reduction. I won't hold you to every penny, but try as hard as you can to make economies. If you can do that and get me a better number, I am sure we will end up happy."

Sadiki said he had to call Amman and talk to the general manager. He haggled with him in Arabic for a while, made some notations on the sheets of his bid estimate, then called a number in Abu Dhabi. In the midst of this second call, the muezzin's call to prayer sounded from a nearby mosque and then echoed from a half dozen other mosques in West Beirut. Sadiki excused himself and went off to pray.

When he returned, he looked refreshed. He was a believer, no question about that. He apologized for the delay and resumed his telephone calling. After badgering two subcontractors in the Emirates, he went back to his work sheets and a few minutes later he proposed a reduction in price that was about half what Ferris had requested. That was where Ferris had suspected they would end up when the process started, so he agreed, and proposed an additional meeting in two weeks, in Amman, to go over final estimates and construction plans. Meeting in Jordan would violate the operational rules he had established with Hoffman, but it would be just once, and he didn't want to leave Alice any more than necessary.

"There's one more thing," said Ferris, as they were about to shake hands on the deal. "While you're in Beirut, I want you to meet our security consultant, Hussein Hanafi. He's an unusual fellow. I think he used to be involved with the . . . well, you know, the extremists." Now Hanafi did consulting for international companies, Ferris explained. He knew everything about firewalls, electronic funds transfer, Internet security. Because he would have to sign off on the final designs, it would be useful to get his recommendations now. Sadiki nodded and smiled. Nothing seemed to bother him.

The consultant worked in the Fakhani district of West Beirut, long ago the headquarters of Yasser Arafat's guerrilla fighters and in recent years an informal gathering point for Beirut's small circle of Sunni fundamentalists. Sadiki seemed slightly uncomfortable as the driver took them deeper into the warren of alleyways—worried not for himself, but for his host. This was bandit country, not a place for an American like Mr. Brad Scanlon.

When they reached Hanafi's address, they saw a sign in the second-floor window for his business, "HH Global Solutions." Sadiki took Ferris's arm protectively and steered him toward the small office building and up the stairs. Who's in charge here? Ferris wondered, but he let Sadiki take the lead. The office was brightly lit and recently painted; the furniture was new and clean. At a desk sat a woman in a headscarf. She buzzed the intercom as soon as they entered, and a beady-eyed Arab man with thick glasses emerged to greet them. He introduced himself as Hussein Hanafi and led them back to his inner office, which had several computers and a book-case filled with technical manuals from Microsoft, Oracle and Symantec.

Hanafi was a computer nerd; that much, at least, was no illusion. The Lebanese Deuxième Bureau had kept an eye on him ever since he returned from Afghanistan in 1998. He ran his little business and did some consulting for jihadist Web sites—which was how Sami Azhar learned about him. If he had any suspicions who he was really working for when Azhar recruited him into his string of covert serv-ice providers, he didn't voice them. He was a valuable catch—a real face and name that people in the movement would recognize. Hoffman's team had secretly wired the office, installing two tiny cameras and a microphone.

Hanafi spoke to the architect in a mix of English and Arabic, banging through a list of computer-security issues that were relevant to the design of a new building. Ferris feigned difficulty in under-standing, and after ten minutes he excused himself and said he would leave the two of them to figure out what was best for the Abu Dhabi project. After Ferris left in his car, Sadiki and Hanafi talked for another hour, occasionally laughing and joking. It turned out they even had a few friends in common. All the while the tape rolled and the digital cameras made their record.

FERRIS HAD a new assistant in Amman named Ajit Singh. He was a small, lithe Indian-American, with burnished brown skin and a perpetual, opaque smile. In the manner of people his age, he liked to wear a baseball cap, sometimes backward, sometimes frontward, sometimes sideways. Azhar had sent him to Amman to help with technical details.

Ajit was an interesting case: His father had made a good-sized fortune in Silicon Valley, initially by creating an inventory management program that he had sold to Wal-Mart, later by investing his money wisely in companies where his Indian engineer friends were working. Young Agit, fresh out of Stanford and heading for some fantastically lucrative career himself, had joined the agency as an act of vengeance. He had spent a family holiday in Kashmir after graduating from university. Six months later, several of his relatives were murdered by an Al Qaeda suicide bomber. After discussing the matter with his father, who was deeply patriotic in the way of successful immigrants, Ajit Singh applied to the CIA. Because of his unusual computer skills—even in his first months, he was one of the agency's best hackers—he soon came to the attention of Azhar, who lured him into his brainy black hole.

Ajit Singh could do anything with computers. He had a similar facility with languages, which were just another set of symbols to him, like a computer program. He had taught himself to read and write Arabic in the months after he made payback his life's mission. Singh could create Web sites, manipulate Web sites, tag Web sites with special "cookies" so the intelligence community could track who went in and out. When he set up shop in Amman, Ferris gave him Francis Alderson's old office, which was still empty. Singh filled it with servers, flat-screen displays, peripherals of various descriptions. The local NSA listening post had to send over a technical team to get him fully wired up.

Singh had hung a little sign on his wall that said: "People Are Stupid." That was the secret of his success. People were stupid enough to type their passwords into computers that had been rigged to monitor every keystroke; stupid enough to forget that when they visited a Web site, they picked up an electronic marker that accompanied them from site to site; stupid enough not to understand that when their computer was online, its hard drive was open for the picking; so stupid, in fact, that they failed to realize that every laptop or cell phone with a Bluetooth connection was effectively a broadcasting antenna. Best of all, it was in the moments when people thought they were being clever and taking special precautions that they were likeliest to do the stupidest things of all.

Singh's job in Amman was to manage the electronic side of Ferris's operation. He had gathered up all the names and addresses that had been picked up from Omar Sadiki's hotel room in Abu Dhabi. He had taken the data on the hard drive of Sadiki's computer and turned it inside out, looking for bits of information that could be manipulated and redirected. His colleagues wondered if he slept on the floor, because he always seemed to arrive before anyone else and still be there when they left. Occasionally, members of the station would see him in the cafeteria, listening to music on his iPod and eating french fries. But otherwise, he was a ghost.

After Singh had been in Amman for about ten days, he asked Ferris for a meeting. He seemed quite excited, and Ferris was curious what he had cooked up. They met in Ferris's office, late that afternoon.

"I see the *nodes*," announced Singh with an unusually big smile. He was wearing a T-shirt that said "Hysterics," advertising a New York punk band he liked, and a yellow bracelet that made a striking contrast with his dark skin.

"Good man," said Ferris. He had no idea what the young Indian was talking about.

"The nodes," Singh repeated. He looked disappointed at the possibility that Ferris might already understand what he was going to say. "I've found the nodes for this network you're trying to penetrate. Or whatever you're doing. Don't tell me. I don't need to know. The point is, it's all there. I've been working it over with Sami and his people back home, and we totally *get it*. Your nice architect Mr. Sadiki has visited a *ton* of jihadi Web sites. We're inside the servers of about half the ones he has visited, so we know who else is using them. And we know which ones are just day-trippers and which ones are serious. So we have this picture of, like, his community. His virtual community, I mean. Isn't that cool?"

"Very cool. But I want you to focus on his fellowship group at the mosque, the Ikhwan Ihsan. Those are the links we have to start with. They're airtight. He knows those people. They make the legend real."

"For sure. I've cross-tabbed the people in his group—*and* their brothers and first cousins—against my list of visitors to jihadi Web sites that we know have received and posted operational messages from Al Qaeda. We're running their names and credit-card records against our algorithms back home. If they ever bought a souvenir in Karachi or made a call from a pay phone near a Salafi mosque in Birmingham, we'll know. We have a real network here. Now we just have to light it up."

"Cool," said Ferris again, with genuine appreciation. "But remember, we need to make Sadiki believable as a jihadi. Not just someone who visits Web sites, but someone who is planning and carrying out operations."

"Ye-aa-ah." Singh drew out the word, as kids often did, as if to say, ob-vious-ly. "So what I'm ready to do now is send messages from Sadiki to some of the people in that community, some of the nodes, who are real jihadis. I've created an account for him that he'll never see. But I need help. What messages do you want me to send? You have to write them. I'm just the technician."

Ferris thought a moment. The messages had to be suggestive, but also vague. They had to imply that Sadiki had higher authority from someone, without being explicit. And they had to point toward the operational date he and Hoffman had set, which was December 22, just before the Christmas holidays.

Ferris thought it over for perhaps 30 seconds, made some rough notes and then wrote out three short sentences in Arabic, which he read aloud to Singh: "The teacher has told me to prepare the lesson. We are looking now for the right place to preach. We send greetings to our brothers and ask for God's help."

"Nice," said Singh. "The teacher. The lesson. That works."

"We're going to need a couple more, so everybody doesn't get the same one. And we need some answers, to send the people who write back. Give me a while to think." Singh put his earphones on and listened to music while Ferris doodled in Arabic.

"Listen to this," said Ferris several minutes later, tugging on the cord of Singh's headphones to take him out of his rock-and-roll reverie. "In the name of God, we thank the brothers who have prepared the path for us. The feast day is coming. God is great."

"That totally works," said Singh.

Ferris labored for another hour writing messages and follow-ups. Singh took them away and began sending them out as e-mail messages from Sadiki to a dozen or so people they had selected from the virtual community of their virtual agent. To each, Singh attached a message in Arabic that said, "Dear brother, if we meet, you will forgive my silence." That way, if anyone actually did query Sadiki directly—and heard him protest that he had sent no message—they would assume he was just covering his tracks.

Singh waited for the electronic harvest. A few people didn't respond at all. Others replied to what they thought was Sadiki's e-mail account—with their messages instead going to Singh. He responded with the brief, tantalizing responses Ferris had written— which hinted at further details of the Christmas plot. Three of the recipients forwarded Sadiki's original message to other e-mail addresses with curious comments that said, in effect: Is he ours? Is this real? That gave Azhar's team more e-mail addresses and servers to monitor, and an electronic path that was moving them closer, byte by byte, to Suleiman.

21

Ajit Singh amused himself with a new toy while Ferris prepared for his third meeting with Omar Sadiki. It had become something of a game within the intelligence community to build fake jihadist Web sites, but Singh thought most of them were useless. The graphics were too slick and the Islamist rhetoric over-enthusiastic. Sometimes the bogus sites would even suggest that new users "register" by providing useful data like their cell-phone numbers. Ajit wanted to build an Islamic portal that wasn't so obvious—that would include militant Muslim material streamed amid lots of other tame stuff about love and life. "Think of it as a cross between Osama and Oprah," he explained to Ferris. Ferris told Singh to go ahead, so long as it didn't take much time. But the young man had already been working on the project for days and was, in fact, nearly ready with a "beta" version.

The name Ajit had chosen was *mySunna.com*—the "right path" online, in Arabic and English. He built it like a commercial site, not too fancy, but with lots of useful features that would pull traffic. He included a pull-down electronic "Zakat Calculator," for example, so that devout Muslims could calculate the proper tithe. They would type in their total assets, including cash, bank balances, stocks, investment property and gold and silver, and then hit "Calculate Zakat," and, *Y'Allah!* For news with a Muslim tilt, he had RSS feeds from *Khaleej Times* in Qatar and the *Dawn* in Islamabad.

Once Ajit got going, he couldn't stop. He added a pull-down menu that invited visitors to enter a *mySunna* store. Inside "mysouk" were framed pictures of Osama, Zawahiri and Zarqawi; there were prayer rugs woven with bin Laden's image. Another click away was "mymovies," with a portfolio of videos shot by jihadist gangs across the Muslim world. The titles included *Iraqi R.A.W.* and *Iraqi R.A.W.2*, with amateur footage of fighters in Iraq setting off IEDs and firing mortars at U.S. bases. Another Iraq video was *The Lions of Fallujah*, taken from the insurgents' side during U.S. attacks. For those wanting jihadist action on another front, Ajit offered compilations from Chechneya—*Russian Hell*, Volumes 1, 2, 3, 4 and 5. There were bin Laden tapes, too, as originally broadcast on Al Jazeera. A last offering was *Riyadh Bombers*, a chilling compilation of the video "last wills" of the men who carried out the May 2003 bomb attacks in the Saudi capital. Ajit didn't bother filling orders—he forwarded traffic to other Islamic Web sites that were offering the same products.

Ajit was proudest of his Islamic advice column. "Talk to *mySunna.com*—What's haram and what's not? Your intimate Islamic questions answered." Users were invited to send in queries that would be answered online by a real sheik. He tried to make these as personal and tasteless as possible, to draw traffic. "Check it out!" said Ajit proudly when he gave Ferris a tour of the beta version. "This is going to pull some eyeballs!"

ANAL INTERCOURSE:
Question: Is a Muslim allowed to have anal sex?
Answer: This act is strongly Makrooh (but not actually Haram). There is no objection to the couple getting pleasure from the entire body of one another. But it should be taken into consideration that some actions are beneath human dignity.

Question: When a women is in her period, can she have anal intercourse?

Answer: If wife is consenting to it, it is permissible. But it would be extremely abominable.

HAND-SHAKING:

Question: Is shaking hands with girls allowed?

Answer: It is not permissible.

MASTURBATION:

Question: What about masturbation? Is it okay if there is no wife available?

Answer: It is not permissible.

Question: If the wife asks the man to masturbate in front of her, is it permissible?

Answer: It is permissible, but it is preferable if the wife uses her hands, and not the man.

MIRRORS:

Question: Can husband and wife have sex while looking at each other in a mirror?

Answer: It is permissible.

ORAL SEX:

Question: I am really sorry that I have to ask this type of question, but since I grew up in a Western country, I really don't know much about our religion. Brother, my question is, can we have oral sex?

Answer: Oral sex act is permissible, provided that no liquid is swallowed.

"Where did you get this stuff?" demanded Ferris. "It's hilarious. Did you just make it up?"

"No way. How would I know what's *haram* and what's just *makrooh*? No, this is all real."

"So where the hell did you get it? Did you pay some sex-obsessed imam?"

"You won't believe this, but I actually got it off a Shiite ayatollah's Web site. It's all there, man. They have a bunch of religious scholars in Najaf deciding whether it's okay to come in a girl's mouth. For real."

"Ajit, you have made my day," said Ferris. It was reassuring to think of the enemy worrying about the theological implications of anal sex.

A few days later, *mySunna.com* was up on the Web, with its online video boutique, and its Islamic advice column, and chat rooms that within a week were regularly visited by people wanting to exchange real messages. Ajit, the invisible face on the other side of the screen, had added some features that allowed the agency to monitor and manipulate that message traffic, too.

FERRIS HAD his third meeting with Omar Sadiki, in Amman. He was careful about surveillance, operating by "denied-area" rules. It was crucial that Hani know nothing about his contacts with the architect. On the appointed day, Ferris left the embassy with a colleague in a car with darkened windows. They drove until Ferris was sure they were free of surveillance. As the car slowly turned a remote corner in Jebel Amman, Ferris opened the door and gently rolled from the passenger seat to the sidewalk. As he left the seat, a pop-up rubber doll inflated, filling the space where Ferris had been sitting. That trick had been used many times in Moscow. With the darkened windows, an observer couldn't have seen that Ferris was missing.

Another car was waiting for Ferris in an alley. He made his way to the underground parking garage of a large apartment building where the agency maintained one of its many Amman safe houses. Ferris took the elevator up from the basement; once in the apartment, he donned the disguise he had used in his two previous meetings with the Jordanian architect—the same wig, moustache, black glasses and padded gut. Ferris barely recognized himself when he looked in the mirror.

They met in a suite at Le Royal, a big hotel in the middle of town owned by an Iraqi billionaire. Sadiki looked as solemn and pious as ever. He presented the final bid documents, new plans and drawings, new details from subcontractors. Payments had already started flowing to Al Fajr for the work, thanks to the agency's cooperative relationship with Unibank. When it was time to cancel the contract in a few months, Unibank would pay Al Fajr a nice "kill fee" for the aborted project; that had been arranged, too.

Ferris was looking for signs of stress in Sadiki—anything out of the ordinary that would suggest he might be suspicious of his contact with "Brad Scanlon," or that some of Hoffman's deceptive schemes might have become known to him—an odd word at the mosque, or an anxious call from a relative, a tipoff from Hani's men. But there seemed to be nothing. Sadiki was as cool—and as bland—as before. The two spent several hours going through the paperwork, eating lunch in Ferris's suite while they talked.

Sadiki excused himself to pray in the middle of this meeting, just as he had in Beirut. Once again, he returned looking cleansed. This was the part of Islam that Ferris genuinely admired, even if he didn't understand it. For believers, the daily prayers were like bathing in a pool of spring water. There was a sense of release and purification that seemed to come from the rituals of kneeling, bowing, confessing, praising. That was what "Islam" meant—submission to God's will.

Ferris could have embraced these slaves of Allah, in another lifetime. But for him and his colleagues, it was now and forever the day after September 11, 2001. He made himself think about the people on the upper floors of the World Trade Center—the people who couldn't escape because the floors below had been destroyed by the impact of the hijacked airplanes. He made himself imagine how it had felt as the carpet under the victims' feet got so hot it began to burn, and the air around them filled with flames and smoke—and how the physical and mental anguish became so unbearable that these desperate people chose to jump from windows eighty stories up to splatter themselves on the ground, rather than remain in that living hell one more instant. This is a war, Ferris told himself. You are a soldier. More people will die unless you do your job.

22 THE KING'S HIGHWAY, JORDAN

WHEN ALICE PROPOSED A WEEKEND outing, Ferris happily agreed. They couldn't just sit in Amman and wait for the next car bomb. And he needed a rest. He was so wired when he left the embassy that it would take him an hour or two, and several drinks, to calm down. They were together almost every night now, switching back and forth between the two apartments. She quizzed him less about his work; people learn not to ask questions when they don't want to know the answers.

Alice suggested that they head south, along the ancient route known as the King's Highway, which had carried Hebrew wanderers, Christian crusaders and Muslim pilgrims across the wadis and barren hilltops of southern Jordan for more than two millennia. The embassy security officer would have objected to a route that took them through too many Bedouin towns in the restive south, but Ferris didn't ask him. As acting chief of station, he could go where he liked. Rather than commandeering one of the embassy's armored SUVs, he rented a little Mitsubishi.

"Cute car," she said when he picked her up. She noticed the Jordanian license plates and smiled. "Going native?"

She gathered up her maps and guidebooks and directed Ferris

south out of the city onto the narrow winding road that skirted the Dead Sea rift. The landscape pitched down toward the shimmering surface of the salt sea, which had the misty unreality of a mirage. As the car descended toward the lowest spot on the planet, Ferris could feel his ears adjust to the change in air pressure. Across the Dead Sea was the West Bank and then, barely visible atop a far ridge, the urban thicket of Jerusalem. Alice directed him toward a Swiss resort hotel along the Dead Sea coast where she knew the manager.

"I'm taking you for a morning swim, my dear, except that you're not going to swim." She explained that the Dead Sea water was so salty you couldn't push your arms and legs under the surface, so you just floated. She pulled Ferris in to meet her friend the manager, a tidy Palestinian who had been polished to a Swiss shine in Lausanne. He gave them towels and the key to a cabana by the water. And soon Alice was tugging him into the luminescent Dead Sea water.

Alice floated away from shore gracefully. The suit molded to her body like rubber. Her nipples showed through the fabric, stiff and round.

Ferris dove into the water but, just as Alice had warned, his body bobbed like a cork. The water actually stung, burning into his skin as if it were rubbing alcohol. There was a sulfurous smell, too, but Alice didn't mind. She let the water carry her as if she were lying upon a liquid bier; she drifted under the November sun with a look of pure pleasure on her face. Ferris tried to relax with her, but his mind kept going back to bombs and bombers.

THEY SHOWERED and changed, and soon they were back up on the ridge tops and tooling down the King's Highway. Alice wanted to show Ferris the Crusader castle at Kerak—the fortress where the odious Reynauld de Chatillon had made his headquarters. Alice walked him through the stone portals and along the walls and parapets, recounting stories of Reynauld's perfidy—how he used to plunder the poor Muslim pilgrims on their hajj journeys down the

King's Highway to Mecca; how he encased the heads of his victims in wood before he threw them off the castle walls so that they would remain conscious and feel all the pain of their broken bones. That was what Muslims remembered when they called Americans "Crusaders."

They looked west from the castle walls toward the wadis that drained the rainfall off the hilltops. It was a landscape that hadn't changed much in a thousand years; effaced more by nature's hand than by man's. In the far distance where Jerusalem stood, the sky was sapphire-blue at midmorning. Alice cocked her head and turned toward Ferris. Tendrils of her long hair had escaped from her pony-tail and were wisps in the wind.

"The Crusades began with a big lie, too," she said. "Did you know that?"

Ferris knew he was going to get one of Alice's lectures. He didn't mind them anymore. They were as much a part of her as the golden hair streaming in the breeze.

"Is that right?" he asked, playing the straight man.

"Yes, it is. Pope Clement didn't claim that the Muslims had WMD, but it was almost as bad. He preached that the Muslims were robbing and torturing poor Christian pilgrims in the Holy Land. That was a complete fabrication, but it was the Middle Ages. People were gullible and superstitious and stupid, so they believed the pope and they all marched off to kill the Muslims. They went to war for a lie. Isn't that terrible?"

Ferris nodded. Yes, it was terrible.

"Once they got to Holy Land, they were in for a shock," she continued. "Because the Muslims actually fought back. And then the crusaders were stuck. They were far from home, and now they had a real war on their hands, so they had to keep sending more crusaders, and more, and more. And then, eventually, they were defeated and the ones who survived had to crawl home. Notice any parallels? Any remote connection with recent events?"

"No," said Ferris, smiling. "None that come to mind."

"Oh! You make me so angry." She stood on her toes and whispered in his ear, "Learn from history."

Ferris scanned the horizon. It was a landscape that contained sediments of nearly every epoch of the human experience. Many miles to the south was the incomparable Roman city of Petra, secreted away in a hidden valley and carved out of the rock in eternal perfection. To the north, several hours' drive, were the magnificent ruins at Jerash, Pella and Um Quaiss—three of the ten trading cities of the Near East that the Romans called the Decapolis. The ruins dotted this landscape, eerily intact. There were great plazas formed by stark Ionic columns, colonnaded streets with the original paving stones underfoot, Roman theaters in perfect order with stone seats surrounding the empty stages as if the audience and players had suddenly fled on the wind.

"What happened to them all?" Ferris said, half to himself, staring out at this landscape of time. "The Greeks, the crusaders, the Romans."

"They are dead," said Alice. "Or so I have been led to believe."

Ferris smiled and put his arm around her. "What I meant was, why did they disappear? The Romans built to last. Their cities are still here, two thousand years later. They were in total control. And then they lost it. What did they do wrong?"

Alice looked at him. "Do you *really* want to talk about this, Roger? Because I don't think you're going to like my answer."

"Yes. I want to know what you think. "

"Okay, the Romans disappeared because they made mistakes. They had bad rulers. From Hadrian to Commodus is just sixty years. That was all it took for Rome to go from greatness to decline. That's how quickly it happens. So wise up." She poked him gently in the ribs, but Ferris wasn't ready to concede.

"Come on, it wasn't just that. The Romans got soft. They got weak. The Roman legions lost their discipline, and the barbarians were able to defeat them." He set his jaw. Didn't she understand? A warrior ethic was the best antidote to decay.

"Yes, my gimpy-legged darling. They did get soft, and that was part of their downfall. But that was much later. What started the death spiral was bad leadership. When the decline began, Rome was still a superpower—militarily. The Praetorian Guard had too much power, not too little. It was the political institutions that got weak. The corruption and ruin came later. Rome rotted from the inside out. Trust me on this. I did the extra-credit reading."

Ferris looked at her. She was shaking her head at Ferris's incomprehension. The ponytail swished from side to side like a horse's mane. What was it about her that captivated Ferris so? Was it the fact that she teased and taunted him, and talked back against his certainties? That she cared enough about him to tell him he was wrong? That she knew things he didn't, whole layers of experience that she veiled beneath her blond tresses and beguiling hazel eyes? In that moment, she was infinitely precious. He didn't care if the new barbarians destroyed every skyscraper in America, so long as they spared Alice. "I love you," he said.

"Oh good, he's admitting defeat." She tugged at his hand, pulling him away from the rough stone of the castle wall.

ALICE HAD packed a lunch of French bread, wine, cheese, prosciutto and melon. They found a perch in the late November sun, atop some rocks in the keep of the crusader castle, and sat down to eat. Ferris cut open the cantaloupe with a big pocketknife and layered the slices with strands of prosciutto. Alice laid out the bread and cheese and uncorked the wine—a Kefraya red from a hundred miles away in Lebanon's Bekaa Valley. The flavors were perfect, each one registering its own precise notes on the tongue. When they finished the meal they lay on the ancient stones, basking in the sun.

ALICE HAD one more stop. She wanted to take Ferris to the town of Mu'tah, a few miles distant. It was famous in Muslim history as the site of one of the first battles between the Muslim army exploding out of Arabia in the seventh century and the legions of the Byzantine Empire. Mu'tah was a university town now, and like Zarqa to the north, it was a center for Muslim fundamentalists.

Ferris frowned when Alice proposed the side trip. Mu'tah was thought to be a dangerous place for outsiders. During the time of his predecessor, Francis Alderson, a CIA case officer had tried to pitch a member of the Muslim Brotherhood in Mu'tah and had briefly been kidnapped by friends of the enraged man who had been his target. It was also rumored to be a center for the Ikhwan Ihsan, the Brothers of Awareness.

"Let's go home," he said. "I'm tired. I want to take a nap, and then make love."

"But you *must* see Mu'tah. It's charming. And there are shrines nearby in El Mazar for the Prophet's son Zaid bin Haritha and his deputy Jaffar bin Abi Talib. This place is famous to Muslims. How are you going to understand them if you don't know their history, Roger? It's like being in Boston and not stopping to see Faneuil Hall."

"I've never been to Faneuil Hall. Let's go home and make love."

Alice pouted. "If you force me to go home, you can forget about sex. And not just tonight. Besides, I have a letter I want to give to one of the teachers in Mu'tah. He has been helping some of our students part-time. I brought it all this way to give it to him. So we have to go."

Ferris knew by her tone that she wouldn't be budged. They got back in the Mitsubishi and bounced the few miles down the road to Mu'tah. Alice sang "Big Yellow Taxi," hitting almost all the notes. She was happy to be drawing Ferris deeper into her world; and perhaps she sensed, too, that she had made the right bet about him. Ferris hid his worries, but he scanned every house as they entered the outskirts of Mu'tah. There were no Jordanian special forces here; only a few useless police. The women wore headscarves; some were fully veiled. The men had the flinty look of Bedouin, and many of them had long beards—an outward sign that they wished to be, not of this world, but of the seventh century.

"I don't like the feel of this place," said Ferris, interrupting Alice in the middle of her song.

"It's *fine*."

"I don't know. I definitely feel like we're outsiders here."

"I'm not an outsider. I have a letter to deliver to a friend named Hijazi. He's in this religious group. The Ikhwan Ihsan, or something like that. He has been so helpful. If you're nervous, I'll just drop off the letter and then we'll go. How's that?" They were pulling into the center of town now. The university was a hundred yards away.

"Jesus, Alice. You didn't tell me this guy was Ikhwan Ihsan. They're bad news."

"You really don't know what you're talking about, Roger. They're not bad news at all. Quite the contrary. They are very helpful to our projects. They send teachers and professional people. I work with them, and a lot of other people you wouldn't like, and I'm just fine. Now, you sit here in the car and I'll be right back." Ferris protested once more that he wasn't comfortable here, but she was out the door and striding down an alleyway that led to the university.

Ferris turned off the engine and went to get a coffee in the café just ahead. It was only when he opened the door of the Mitsubishi that he noticed a half dozen men off to his right, seated outside the local mosque. Their heads moved in unison as they watched Ferris walk across the square. They had the hard-eyed, intense look of people who studied, prayed and trained together. Ferris had seen dozens of groups like them during his time in Iraq, along the roads, gathered in alleys. It was intuition, rather than anything specific, that told him they were trouble.

"Alice!" he called out. "Come on. We need to go. Now!"

She had disappeared from view and either couldn't hear him or wouldn't respond. His call had been useless in terms of getting her back, but it had focused the attention of the group by the mosque.

Now they knew from Ferris's voice that he was American, and that he was worried.

Ferris continued toward the café, eyes down, hoping to avoid any move that would call further attention. An old man was sitting outside, smoking a nargileh. He edged away when Ferris approached. The whole town was sullen. This was a place, Ferris remembered, where the people rioted when the king tried to remove subsidies on common staples like bread, a town of professional malcontents. Ferris ordered a Turkish coffee from the waiter, medium sweet. He drank it slowly, waiting for Alice. The young men across the way huddled a last time and then dispersed. Where were they going? And where was Alice?

Ferris had to piss. He wished now he had drunk less of the Kefraya red. He stood and entered the dark of the café and asked where the toilet was. The barman didn't answer; he had a look of fear and confusion, and his eyes darted into the shadows. Ferris sensed danger, and he was turning to leave when he felt a sharp blow to his head. His vision went black and then exploded into white rays of pain as he tumbled to the floor of the café.

When Ferris opened his eyes a moment later, men were fumbling in his pockets looking for his wallet. Two men had him pinned down, and two more were talking in Arabic. Did they know who he was? Had they followed him here?

"Please, I'm a friend," said Ferris in English, worried that his Arabic would only give him away as an intelligence officer.

They found his wallet and were looking at the Jordanian identity card that listed him as a member of the U.S. Embassy. That sent them into a dither; they had a real prize now. The man who had hit Ferris with the club prodded him with one of his feet.

"Why do you come to Mu'tah? To spy on Muslim people?"

"No, no," said Ferris. "I'm just a diplomat. I came see Kerak. Now I will go back to Amman." Ferris was trying to think what to do. Nobody at the embassy knew where he was. If he was kidnapped, it would be many hours before anyone realized he was missing. He felt in his pocket for the plastic box that contained his poison dental bridge. He never wore it. Why did he carry it? They would find that next. He was debating what to do when he heard the cracking sound of the front door being kicked open. Lying on the floor, he couldn't see what was happening, but he heard a woman's voice speaking in strong, forceful Arabic. It took Ferris a moment to realize that it was Alice.

"Let him go. Now! My friends in the Ikhwan Ihsan will be very angry that you have treated a guest with such disrespect."

"Ikhwan Ihsan?" said the man with the club. *"W'Allah!"*

They backed off. Ferris rose from the ground and stood next to Alice. She had a steely look, unblinking, unyielding. She did not shout, she did not threaten. But by her posture and her well-phrased Arabic, and most of all her fearlessness, she commanded respect from these young men.

"Thank you," she said in Arabic. "May God grant you good health." They responded with ritual phrases of greeting and peace.

A young man in a long white robe walked into the room and stood next to Alice. The circle of young men who had jumped Ferris drew back farther, respectfully. This must be Hijazi, Ferris surmised, the man Alice had come to visit. He extended his hand to Ferris in greeting and then turned to the men gathered around, who a moment before had seemed ready to kidnap Ferris.

"Brothers," he said, "you shame the town of Mu'tah and the blood of the Prophet's companions that was shed here. This visitor has come here with Miss Alice Melville, a friend of the Arab people. You are worse than the *jahil*, the ignorant ones, to treat our visitor this way. Please apologize to him and beg his forgiveness for your uncivilized and ignorant behavior." The men murmured their apologies and shook Ferris's hand. They looked genuinely sorry, not for clubbing Ferris but for offending Hijazi. Ferris stared at Alice in wonder.

Hijazi insisted that they take tea and sweets with him. Ferris wanted to leave, but he knew it would compound the embarrassment to the town if they refused this ritual of apology. A local doctor came over to attend to Ferris's head wound. As they sat in the café, gifts were brought out: simple local handicrafts, mostly. They offered dates and sweets, and the man who had hit Ferris tried to give him money, in the manner that tribesmen always settle their feuds, but Ferris refused. Eventually, when it was nearly dark, the ceremony of regret was over and they were allowed to depart.

When the Mitsubishi was safely back on the King's Highway, Ferris pulled off to the shoulder. He stared at Alice, who had become in these few minutes a different person for him. As much as he had loved the irreverent free spirit, he loved even more the iron-willed woman he had just watched.

"You may have saved my life back there," he said.

"Maybe. I don't think they would have done anything. How's your head?"

"It hurts."

"I am *so* sorry." She leaned over and planted a kiss on his head. "You were right. We shouldn't have gone into Mu'tah. The town is too small, and the people are too angry. It's my fault. Will you forgive me?"

Ferris nodded. All the pieces of Alice seemed to have come together into one assembly. She appeared to be one of those rare people who lived her values completely and transparently.

"I liked your friend Hijazi," said Ferris. "He was a lifesaver. How do you know him, anyway?"

"Like I told you, his group has been helping us. They're professional people from all over Jordan. They are very religious, but very sweet, too. Most of them wouldn't hurt a flea. They have a little group that works with us regularly in Amman. Two doctors, a lawyer, an architect. All really nice guys."

Ferris stopped smiling, stopped moving. He could feel his heart beating. "No kidding? An architect? Why would he care about a school?"

"I don't know. But the architect is one of the nicest. He's a tall guy, kind of quiet, but really sweet. Has this cute mark on his forehead from praying so much. He volunteered to do some designs for the new school we want to build."

Ferris looked away from her and closed his eyes. His world was going black again. "What's the architect's name?"

"I forget. But he's a nice guy. Wait, I do remember. His name is Sadiki, like 'friend' in Arabic. Omar Sadiki. Sweet guy. They all are. And we need the help, God knows."

Ferris froze, eyes still shut tight. He felt as if something in the center of his body had just collapsed. He had put her in danger; he had touched her with the poison of his work. He took her hand. He couldn't look at her. He had to think quickly what to do, how best to protect her—and he decided in that instant that he must do nothing. If he said anything—gave her a push in any direction—he could expose her and Sadiki and everything else that mattered to him to great danger.

"Hey, you, what's up?" she said. "Your hand is cold as ice. We better get you back home. You've had a shock."

"Yeah," said Ferris, turning back to her. "I guess I am a little cold. Maybe we should get going."

Ferris pulled away from the shoulder, back onto the King's Highway. The sun was falling fast now, and he turned on the heat. Alice fiddled with the radio. Ferris could barely bring himself to look at her. By the time they reached Amman, the sun had set over the western hills.

23 AMMAN / WASHINGTON

A N URGENT MESSAGE ARRIVED for Ferris that weekend from the CIA inspector general, requesting that he return immediately to Headquarters to discuss a "matter of interest." The cable gave no further details. Ferris sent a flash message on Monday to Hoffman asking him to call as soon as he got into the office. He had to wait seven hours for Hoffman's response. Ferris read the brief cable to his boss. "What's this about, Ed?" he asked. "They make it sound like I'm under investigation."

"You are," answered Hoffman. "I just found out about it. That's why I was late calling you. I had to see some people."

"What have I done?" Ferris's first thought was expense accounts.

"That's the problem. I don't know, and my spies in the IG's office wouldn't tell me. Or couldn't tell me. Or maybe they don't know, but I doubt that."

"Can you turn it off? I mean, it's not like I don't have other things to do right now. If we're going to make your December twenty-second window, it's crunch time."

"I'll try. But these guys in the IG's office are total assholes. Think of the Internal Affairs Department in the most screwed-up police department in the world: The cops are getting hammered, the crim-

inals are having a field day and meanwhile the IAD guys are inves-
tigating guys for taking free donuts at the 7-Eleven. That's the IG's
office. They make their bones destroying case officers. I'm sorry, but
that's a fact."

"But I haven't done anything wrong. At least nothing I can
remember. Have I done anything wrong?"

"God, I hope so. But I can't remember anything offhand."

"This isn't funny, Ed. Not for me. What should I do?"

"You've got to come home. Pronto. Next flight out. Talk to these
guys and find out what this is all about. Then we'll figure out how to
make it go away."

Ferris thought of Alice, and Omar Sadiki, and felt the tightening
knot in his stomach again. "I really don't want to leave Amman now.
Things are cooking. It's the wrong time for me to leave."

"I understand. But you have no choice. These guys are pricks. If
you don't come when they call, then they send someone out to bring
you home in handcuffs. Don't fuck with them. Take my word for it.
I crossed them once and they almost broke my ass. I had a good
lawyer. I'll call him and see if he can help you out. But first you have
to see them. Call today and set up the appointment—day after
tomorrow, first thing, and go alone. After you've talked with them,
go see the lawyer and figure out what the hell to do. If you show up
with the lawyer, they'll just try harder to screw you."

FERRIS MET Alice for coffee that afternoon at the InterContinental,
near her office. He said he had to return home urgently, the first
RJ flight out to Europe early in the morning and then on to
Washington. His mother was sick, he said, and she was alone. He
needed to be with her. He had thought about what lie to tell, and this
seemed the safest.

"I knew you were worried about something Saturday," she said.
"You got all sad as we were driving home. You knew then, didn't
you?"

"Yes," Ferris lied.

"I'd love to meet your mother someday."

"You will, darling. You'll meet everyone."

She examined the wound on his head, pronounced that it was healing well, and then took his hand in hers and held it for a long while. She wasn't one to attempt a false expression of optimism about something she didn't understand. It was Ferris who broke the silence.

"That group you're working with in your project, the Ikhwan Ihsan. You should be careful about them," he said.

"Why I on earth should I be careful?" She let his hand drop. "They are lovely men. They want to help some of these poor Muslim boys and girls. And I seem to recall that one of them came to your rescue on Saturday in Mu'tah. What could possibly be wrong with them?"

"You never know with these guys. They're fundamentalists. They don't like America very much."

"That's all the more reason to work with them! So they'll see we aren't all homicidal maniacs—that we don't see terrorists in every mosque, for goodness' sake. Let's not have this argument now, Roger, really."

He studied her face, trying to decide what to do. Her fair skin was flushed with emotion. She wouldn't listen to him. To tell her any more would only put her in more jeopardy. Her best protection was her lack of knowledge. Nobody who spent any time with her could doubt her sincerity. He took her hand again and squeezed it tight.

"Just be careful, darling," he said. "I'll be back as soon as I can."

She kissed him on the cheek. "You always say that. 'Be careful, darling.' But you're the one who should be careful, Roger. You're the one who knows the real crackpots and killers. Not me."

"Maybe you're right," said Ferris quietly.

"Well, there's a job waiting for you at my place when you get back. You can make lunch for refugee boys and girls coming in from Iraq. How's that?"

"Excellent. Maybe I'll convert. Become a Brother of Awareness myself."

She accompanied him to his apartment and stayed while he packed, chiding him for taking dirty shirts and underwear because he hadn't done his laundry. An embassy car waited downstairs, and he dropped her at home on his way to the airport. On the long journey back to Washington, he thought of her in the Levantine neverland of her apartment, hidden away from the world that seemed to be closing in around him.

THE FIRST THING Ferris noticed when he arrived at the main entrance at Headquarters, thirty-six hours later, was that his badge didn't work. They had suspended him already, electronically. Two men from the Office of Security came downstairs and took him to a windowless conference room in the back of the old building. The lead investigator from the Inspector General's Office was waiting, along with an attorney from the CIA General Counsel's Office named Robert Croge and an FBI agent with a Slavic name that Ferris couldn't remember. Holy shit, thought Ferris. What have I done? The IG representative was a tough, tight woman with a pageboy haircut and a pin-striped suit. She introduced herself as Myra Callum and advised Ferris that her office was conducting a criminal investigation into matters that involved him. The FBI agent introduced himself and said the interview was being taped and read Ferris his Miranda rights, which scared him all the more. Ferris asked if he could speak privately with the young lawyer from the General Counsel's Office, who he gathered was there to protect the agency—if not exactly to protect him. After a hasty consultation, the group agreed and adjourned to the hallway. On his way out, the FBI man turned off the tape recorder.

"What in God's name is this all about?" asked Ferris.

"I can't tell you," answered Croge. "Listen to their questions. You'll get a good idea from what they ask you." He was a smooth-faced young man in a gray suit. He reminded Ferris of pictures he had seen of John Dean, the Watergate lawyer. He had a face that seemed to have been leached of any color or emotion.

"Do I have to answer their questions?"

"No. You can refuse to answer anything you want. Just take the Fifth. It won't look good, but that's your problem."

"Are you my attorney?"

"No. I represent the agency. You can get your own attorney. Though I would advise you to listen to their questions first. If you refuse to cooperate, they'll put you on administrative leave immediately, and you could be in limbo for a long time. This matter is highly classified, so by the time you get a lawyer with appropriate clearances, it could be months."

"I'm *fucked*! And I don't even know what this is about."

"Sorry, pal. My advice is talk to the lady from the IG's office. If the questioning strays too far into operations, I'm going to cut it off anyway. Talk to them. Basically you have no choice." Ferris nodded his assent, and the lawyer stuck his head out the door and called them other two back.

Myra Callum returned looking even more teed off than before. The FBI man turned on the tape recorder again. They each introduced themselves again, for the record. Ferris did the same. They asked him if he was waiving his right to have an attorney present and Ferris muttered yes. Apparently they were worried that he hadn't spoken loudly enough, so they asked him to say it again.

"I am going to ask you some questions about your past activities," said Callum. "During 1999 and 2000, were you assigned to the CIA station in Sanaa, in the Democratic Republic of Yemen?"

Technically, the answer to that question was classified. Ferris looked at the lawyer from the General Counsel's Office, who nodded that it was okay to answer.

"Yes, that's correct," said Ferris.

"And was your position in the station deputy operations chief?"

"Yes," answered Ferris. "At first, I was just a CO. But after six months someone left and they made me deputy ops chief."

"And in that role," continued Callum, "did you maintain regular liaison with the security services of the host country, Yemen?" Her voice was dry and stern; it sounded as if it came from somewhere behind her, as if she were a ventriloquist's dummy and someone unseen was projecting the voice. Ferris didn't like her, and he truly didn't like the idea that he was being quizzed like a criminal.

"Obviously." He spoke with an edge that betrayed his anger. "Of course I maintained liaison with the host service. That's what agency officers do, all over the world. That is, the ones who are actually out in the field, as opposed to those back at Headquarters who make trouble for the people who do the work."

Croge, the agency lawyer, shook his head. Don't make these people mad.

"A yes or no will be sufficient, Mr. Ferris," said Callum. "And you can save your snide comments about the agency for your future bedmates in prison."

"What the hell is that supposed to mean?" said Ferris.

She ignored him and continued with her questions. "Now, on February seventeenth, 2000, did you have occasion to meet with members of the Yemeni intelligence service, known as the *Mouk-ha-ba-rat?*" She said it phonetically, for whoever would be transcribing the tape.

"How should I know? I don't have my calendar."

"Perhaps I can refresh your memory, Mr. Ferris. On February seventeenth, February eighteenth and February nineteenth, did you assist the Mouk-ha-ba-rat in interrogating an alleged Al Qaeda member named *Sa-mir Na-kib*, who was in their custody?"

"Fuck me," Ferris whispered to himself. It hit him suddenly, with the force of a hammer against his head. *This is about Gretchen.* She had snitched on him. She had remembered a long-ago remark he'd made about interrogation in Yemen. He had told her that an Al Qaeda prisoner had died in captivity while he was present. She had admonished him never to repeat to anyone what he had done, because technically it was illegal. Ferris had forgotten about it, but she had held on to it these past few years, saving it in case she ever needed leverage. And now she was using it.

"Mr. Ferris, I am waiting," said the nasally voice of Myra Callum.

"Where did you get your information?" said Ferris angrily. "From an informant, right? An 'anonymous' informant."

"Where we got the information is irrelevant. Just answer the question. Did you meet with members of the Yemeni intelligence service on February seventeenth, eighteenth and nineteenth, 2000?"

"I decline to answer."

"On what grounds?"

"It's classified."

Croge interjected. "Speaking on behalf of the agency, I can assure you, Mr. Ferris, that Miss Callum, Agent Sackowitz and I all have proper security clearances. We are authorized to receive this information."

"Sorry. I've never seen any of you before today. I want it in writing from my boss, Ed Hoffman, chief of the Near East Division. Otherwise, no way."

Croge looked fatigued. Callum looked furious. The FBI agent looked bored. "Just continue with the questions," said Croge. "I'll call the fourth floor in a minute."

"In the course of interrogation of Sa-mir Na-kib on the aforementioned days, did you witness the beating of the prisoner?"

"I decline to answer."

"Why?"

"Same reason. It's classified. It would be a violation of law for me to answer without proper verification of your clearances by my superior."

"Did you witness members of the security service threaten the prisoner, Sa-mir Na-kib, with a cricket bat, and then hit him with the bat? In the head?"

"Classified. Classified."

"Did you at any point attempt to stop the members of the Yemeni Mouk-ha-ba-rat from these activities, as required under U.S. Executive Order 12333 and other relevant agency internal orders?"

"Classified. Classified. Classified."

Callum looked at Ferris with a black dart of pure hatred in her eyes. To her, he was one of the bad ones; one of the men who had taken away her promotions, held her back from advancement, taken risks that caused trouble for everyone else, made messes they expected other people to clean up.

"Mr. Ferris, I reject your reason for declining to answer. I am *fully* authorized to receive this information. You are insulting me and the Office of the Inspector General in questioning my clearances, and you are stalling. In addition to being in potential violation of U.S. criminal statutes, you are arrogant, and I'm going to make sure you pay for it."

Ferris looked at her and smiled for the first time since he had entered the room. He had gotten to her. He had ruffled her lawyer's confidence. That was worth something. "Just get Ed Hoffman," said Ferris. "Show me written authorization from my boss that I am allowed to discuss these matters, and then I'll talk to you. Maybe."

THEY ADJOURNED the session a short while later. They were getting nowhere, and Croge was worried that Ferris might actually be right about needing written authorization to discuss details of liaison activities, which were among the agency's most closely guarded secrets. They gave Ferris a temporary badge. When he had left Headquarters, Ferris called Hoffman and asked him to meet him at the Starbucks in the McLean Shopping Center.

24 WASHINGTON

STARBUCKS WAS NEARLY DESERTED in late morning. The only person nearby was a frizzy-haired student typing on her PowerBook and listening to music on her iPod. Ferris was sitting in a dark corner eating an oversized banana-nut muffin in the hope that all those calories would make him feel better. Hoffman ordered an almond Frappuccino and was slurping it through a fat straw when he sat down beside Ferris.

"Well, at least I know now what this is about," said Ferris. "It's my wife, Gretchen. I told her once about some bad stuff that happened in Sanaa when we were interrogating an Al Qaeda prisoner, and how I didn't do anything to stop it and the guy eventually died. Now she's using it to squeeze me because I want a divorce. Believe it or not, that's what this is about."

"I'm impressed," said Hoffman, putting aside his drink. "She must really love you. But that doesn't alter the fact that you are in some serious shit."

"You don't mean they take this nonsense seriously?"

"Unfortunately, yes. My spy in the IG's Office says their informant—your charming wife, presumably—has a lot of political juice. Friends in high places, clout with the White House. So when the informant passed along the information, the IG's Office had to pursue it. My spy says they don't think it's much of a case. If you wanted to prosecute all the guys who've sat in on nasty interrogations, half the DO would go down. But they have no choice, unless their informant recants. I talked to my lawyer, Mark Sheehan, by the way. He has all the clearances, and the General Counsel's Office says it's fine for you to talk to him. In fact, I think the GC wants this to go away. He knows it doesn't smell right and that it's trouble. Sheehan will see you this afternoon, at five or six. I forget which. I told him we need you bad on something and we can't waste time with all the legal crap. We need to *move*."

Ferris thought a moment, over the sucking noise of Hoffman draining his Frappuccino. "So if the informant withdraws the complaint, the IG's Office would drop the investigation? Is that what you're telling me?"

"Yeah. Maybe. Ask Sheehan. That's the sort of stuff he's good at. The thing is, they can't prosecute without witnesses. And if nobody talks, they don't have diddly. I mean, God knows, the Yemenis aren't going to talk. They killed the guy. And the victim isn't going to talk, because he's extremely dead. So what have they got, actually, at the end of the day? Fuck-all. So keep cool in Kabul. This is a case without witnesses. Did you tell anybody else about this, other than your wife?"

"No. I put a note in the file to the effect that this guy had died after interrogation. That's what they must have found. But I didn't put in any details. I didn't even tell you. At least, I hope I didn't."

"No way," said Hoffman. "If you had, I would have had to report it. Now get out of here. Go see Sheehan. A good lawyer can fix anything. I need you back in Amman. The clock is ticking."

MARK SHEEHAN'S office was in a fancy building on Pennsylvania Avenue. It was like entering another universe. A secretary sat Ferris down in a waiting room that could have received royalty. He was early—it turned out that the appointment was for six, not five, but that didn't matter to Ferris. They had comfy chairs and glossy magazines and there were real paintings on the wall, rather than lame prints like the ones at the agency. Sheehan over the years had become a guardian angel for case officers in trouble. He was one of the top criminal lawyers in the city, and he made a very good living representing corporate malefactors who probably deserved to go to jail. But Sheehan was an ex-Marine, and it made him angry to see good CIA officers being hounded by congressional committees and showboating lawyers and anybody else who felt like taking a whack at them. So he represented DO clients pro bono. Ferris relaxed in the temporary embrace of a white-shoe law firm. The secretary brought him coffee in a china cup and saucer, and then a Diet Coke and some cookies, and eventually they summoned him to meet Sheehan.

Ferris went through his story carefully. He described Gretchen's role at the Justice Department, and his suspicion that she'd played a role in drafting the DOJ interrogation policy. He also recounted, in grim detail, the three-day process of interrogation in an underground prison in Sanaa—the threats, the tools they had used, the spurt of blood from the head, the puddle of blood on the floor. He painted it the best way he could; he hadn't known they would use the cricket bat; he hadn't realized how seriously hurt the man was. But the basic fact was inescapable: The man had been tortured to death.

"Was any other American citizen present when the prisoner was beaten?" asked Sheehan. When Ferris said he had been the only person there from the station, the lawyer seemed relieved. That meant the only available "witness"—indirectly—was his wife, Gretchen Ferris. And her testimony could be impeached.

"What should I do?" asked Ferris.

"It would be nice if your wife changed her story. If she called back whoever she talked to and said that she wasn't so sure now. That would make things easier for everyone, including her."

"Look, I know what she wants. She wants me to call off the divorce. But I'm not going to do that."

"Understood," said Sheehan. "But maybe there's something she *doesn't* want. I'm not giving you any advice, obviously. But sometimes an informant realizes that it's not in her best interest to pursue a matter."

"Her best interest," repeated Ferris. That was certainly a concept Gretchen understood.

FERRIS WAITED until nine that night and then called Gretchen's apartment. He made the call standing in an alley outside her building. When she answered, he cut the connection and went upstairs and rang the doorbell. She had the door chained and didn't let him in at first. Ferris thought she might have another man with her, but it wasn't that; she was doing her makeup.

"What a surprise," she said, unbolting the chain. "Have you come to your senses?"

She was wearing a long black sweater over the skirt and blouse she'd worn to work. From the inflection in her voice, Ferris suspected she'd already had her martini. She was trying to ruin him. He had to remember that as he looked at the beautiful woman who stared up at him with her lips parted ever so slightly.

"I know what you're doing, " he said. "You're trying to destroy me. But it won't work."

"Don't be ridiculous, Roger. How could I destroy a big, strong CIA man who isn't afraid of *anybody*? You must be having delusions. It's you who is trying to destroy me, by demanding a divorce."

"I met today with the inspector general, and after that I hired a good lawyer. I know what's going on, and it won't work. There's no evidence, no witnesses, just your word against mine. And you are an angry soon-to-be-ex-wife, so nobody's going to believe you. I never told you anything about Yemen. I will swear that in court. You made it up to get revenge. The case is a loser. The problem is, I don't have time to go through all the legal maneuvers. So I want you to withdraw the compliant. Say you were mistaken. Say you're sorry. Just make it go away. And then we're even."

Her laughter was forced and slightly drunken. "That's absurd. You really are pathetic, Roger."

"Make it go away," Ferris repeated. "This is no joke." His voice was cold and unyielding, and for a moment she was taken aback. But she recovered quickly, and named her price.

"I'm not going to lift a finger to help a man who is trying to divorce me. The only one who can solve your problems is you. It's in your hands . . . darling. As a wife, I could not possibly testify against my husband. But as a soon-to-be-ex-wife, as you so coldly put it, that's a different story. So you have to decide."

"No. That's my decision."

"No, what?"

"No to your blackmail. I won't stay married to you so I can beat a bullshit rap about something you think you heard me say. If I agreed, then the next time you were angry, you'd invent something else. Anyway, I'm not here to ask you for anything. I'm here to tell you something."

"What's that, tough guy?" She said it tauntingly, but there was an undertone of uncertainty.

"Unless you withdraw your complaint immediately, I am going to take action to defend myself."

She laughed again, even more unconvincingly. "How's that? By recruiting one of your ridiculous CIA agents to come after me? I'm petrified."

"I'm going to defend myself by telling the truth. I'm going to say that I asked you for a divorce, and you went into a jealous rage and invented a false story. And then I am going to show them—and by that I mean show *your* employer as well as mine—that you are an unreliable person. An untrustworthy person."

She looked at him and then shook her head. "You've lost your mind, Roger. I know these people. The people on the White House staff are my friends. I am part of their world. They're not going to believe the word of someone like you from the CIA, which they *hate*, against someone like me, who's their friend. It will never happen.

"It won't be my word against yours. I have records. Letters. Pictures. Documents. I can take you out."

This explicit threat, rather than frightening Gretchen, seemed to enrage her, summoning a contempt for him that had been there all along. "You don't have the balls for this, Roger. You're too polite. I know you. You're not a killer."

"Try me. I put up with your tantrums and sexual demands, and I let you have your way. But this is different. I am fighting for my life. If you don't back off, I will destroy you. I mean it. Watch me."

He turned and walked out the door. She called after him, and then began cursing—screaming his name and joining it with vile obscenities. People down the hall began to open their doors. But it was too late for Gretchen. The elevator door had closed and Ferris was on his way out of the building.

FERRIS WENT to his mother's house in the mountains, where he had taken the precaution of storing his private files when he went overseas. She tried to soothe him, realizing that something was wrong, but he was in another world. He gathered his material and began to sift it—papers, old e-mails he'd saved on discs, digital photographs that he had never printed, handwritten letters. He locked himself in his old bedroom and spent nearly a whole day going through this record of his life with Gretchen, deciding what would be useful to him now. He narrowed a big pile down to a smaller pile, and then sifted the items, one by one.

She had cheated on her college loans. That was probably his best weapon. Ferris had helped, and sent her an e-mail confirming that it was done. And she'd pulled a fast one in law school, crediting far more hours to her supposed campus job than was warranted. She had bragged about that in an e-mail, too. That was really Gretchen's problem. She had trusted too much in Ferris's decency. She had lied about drug use, too, in her interviews with the Justice Department. Ferris could prove that, as well, because she had sent him an e-mail asking for advice when she first applied for a job. Ferris told her, jok-ingly, to tell the truth and say she'd never used drugs. So she lied, and it worked, and she was so relieved and grateful that when it was over, she sent Ferris a gushy e-mail. The FBI would enjoy that.

Finally, there were her taxes. In the year before they got married, when she was still filing separately, she'd had an unusually large tax bill. She had been desperate to pad her expenses, so she had gathered up all her charges for lunches and dinners and pretended they were business meals and entertainment. She'd even included a trip they had taken to the Virgin Islands that Christmas. Ferris had kept copies of the receipts. Gretchen had been wrong about him. He had kept some ammunition from the first.

FERRIS'S MOTHER could see that he was preoccupied, searching through his old files. And she didn't bother him until he had finally finished, well past midnight. But when he was done, she brought him downstairs in the kitchen and made him a cup of tea. It was early December; the leaves were down across the Shenandoah Valley and the winter winds were rattling the windows of her big, empty house.

"A man from the FBI came by," she said. "Or at least he said he was from the FBI. He showed me some kind of badge."

"Oh? What did he want?"

"He said he was updating your security clearances. He wanted to know if we had any family files. Old records, letters, that sort of thing. From your father's family."

"No kidding. That's strange. Did you give him anything?"

"A few papers for him to copy. I didn't have much to give. I let him rummage around for an hour or so. They did that before, when you first joined the agency. And they did it with your father, so many times. So I didn't think anything of it."

"Did he find anything he didn't like?"

"No. He seemed quite happy when he left. He said everything was in order, and not to worry. The update was fine."

Ferris shrugged. Hoffman must have sent the security man when Ferris joined Mincemeat Park. It didn't matter. He had no secrets. And right now he had bigger things to worry about. He said goodnight to his mother and caught a few hours' sleep before heading back to the city.

FERRIS COPIED two sets of the records. One he left with his attorney, the other he took with him to Gretchen's apartment. She had a beaten look from the moment she opened the door. There were deep circles under her eyes, and Ferris suspected she hadn't slept much since he had last seen her. She knew that he had the leverage. What she had never imagined was that he would use it.

Ferris laid the material out on the floor, item by item. He explained what each one was, in case she had forgotten, but it was obvious that she hadn't. He said that a copy of the same file was already with his lawyer, who had instructions to deliver it to the Office of Professional Responsibility at the Justice Department at ten the next morning unless he heard from Ferris to the contrary. He had expected her to defend herself when he laid out the evidence—to claim it was all lies, or denounce his perfidy in keeping these personal records for so many years. He had thought there might be tears, too. But she remained silent, shaking her head occasionally. When he finished, she turned to him.

"I loved you," she said. "But I don't love you now. Not after this. Go away. I have to think." She walked to her bedroom and closed the door. Ferris picked up the papers and let himself out of the apartment.

Early the next morning, the Inspector General's Office received a call from a lawyer acting on behalf of Gretchen Ferris. The attorney said that Mrs. Ferris had discovered additional information concerning her husband. She was not prepared to testify against Mr. Ferris and was withdrawing the allegation that he had violated any laws or federal regulations as a CIA employee. Gretchen's attorney then telephoned Sheehan and recounted the conversation with the IG. He said that Mrs. Ferris had also instructed him that she was prepared to grant her husband a divorce.

Ferris felt empty in victory. He knew he had violated a trust. She had tried to hurt him but it had been for love; he had tried to hurt her back for his own protection, and that had broken the spell. Once love was gone, there was no more reason for Gretchen to care. She wasn't one for fighting lost causes, and she would be besieged with suitors soon enough. She was a prize, and she knew it. Ferris had counted on her rationality, but he hadn't realized how quickly it could turn.

"GET BACK to work," said Hoffman. He was calling on the STU-3 with the news that the IG investigation had formally been dropped. He told Ferris an agency plane would be waiting for him that afternoon. He didn't say where Ferris would be heading, but it obviously wasn't Amman.

"I want to meet Harry Meeker," said Ferris.

"Harry is waiting for you in the cold room. He's not going anywhere, trust me. And we're almost ready to drop him into Suleiman's cave. But there are a few more details we need to prepare. That's why I got you the plane. We're almost to H-Hour. We have to do these last few stitches nice and neat."

Ferris paused. He was ready to go—eager to go, even. But there was a little question lurking in the back of his mind, one of the many little eddies of mystery that Hoffman left in his wake.

"Can I ask you something?"

"Sure. Ask whatever you like. Whether I'll answer is another thing."

"Why did you need a lawyer? What had you done that Mark Sheehan had to get undone?"

Hoffman sounded weary, as if the act of remembering drained something from him. "You don't really want to know," he said.

"Yes, I do," answered Ferris. "It's something we both have in common, right?"

"Let's just say I crossed a line. A big red line. And Sheehan convinced people that it would be better for everybody to pretend that I hadn't."

"What line had you crossed?"

"That's the part you don't want to know."

"Don't give me that, Ed. I'm going out to do the dirty work, and you're playing games with me. What line did you cross?"

Hoffman sighed in exasperation. It was easier for him to explain than to fight any more with Ferris.

"I crossed the line that says you aren't supposed to kill people. Nobody likes to admit that about our business, but we do what has to be done. And I did. It was something like what happened to you in Yemen with the prisoner, but there were more people, over a longer period of time. Don't ever ask me about it again. But don't forget: When it comes to operations, I mean it when I say that I will do whatever it takes."

25 ANKARA / INCIRLIK

A WHITE GULFSTREAM JET BEARING Ferris landed in Ankara two days later. He took a taxi from the dowdy airport to the Ankara Hilton, an antiseptic tower set amid the diplomatic quarter. It was a bitter December day. The wind whipped into the city from the Anatolian plain; Turks hurried along the sidewalks, wrapped in scarves and sweaters and hunched over against the cold. A gray froth of steam emerged from cars and buildings and people's mouths. Several decades before, this had seemed like a city of a hundred mosques but no Muslims, so tightly had the army applied the secular tourniquet. But now Turkey had found its Islam, and it was rare to see a woman outside the international area of the city who wasn't wearing a headscarf.

When Ferris had settled into his room, he called Omar Sadiki in Amman. He spoke in his Brad Scanlon business voice, but his tone was urgent. A serious problem had arisen. Unibank's engineering chief for the Middle East had reviewed Al Fajr's plans for the branch office in Abu Dhabi and had raised questions about the specifications for insulation and the building's ability to retain air-conditioning efficiently. The climate in Abu Dhabi was extreme, with summer temperatures over 115 degrees, and the consultant wasn't sure that

Al Fajr had planned adequately. The insulation they had specified might work in Jordan, but not in the Emirates. Too much of the cold from the air-conditioning might escape, which would make the building very expensive to operate.

Sadiki sounded surprised. "The insulation is good," he insisted. "It's the same as we use in Saudi Arabia. Hafr Al-Batin is even hotter. No problem there, for sure."

"Well, you need to explain it to our regional engineer. He's here in Ankara with me. He's a Turk. He needs to see you right away. Otherwise he says he's going to put a hold on the project."

"What does that mean?" asked Sadiki.

"It means you won't get paid. Sorry. I'm as disappointed as you are. It won't take long. You can go and come back in the same day. Our travel agent can make the arrangements and deliver the tickets to your office." Ferris tried not to sound anxious, but much depended on the success of this ploy.

"When do you want me to come?" Sadiki sounded curious rather than agitated. Construction projects always had unforeseen delays. "Wednesday. The day after tomorrow," said Ferris. "That's the only day that will work for the chief engineer. I'm sorry, but I have to ask you to do it. He won't talk to anyone else."

"Wait, please." Sadiki put Ferris on hold while he had a conversation, presumably with one of his superiors. It took several minutes. Ferris began to worry that the answer would be no. He and Azhar had a fallback plan, but it wasn't as good.

Ferris heard static as Sadiki came back on the line. "So, are we all set?" he asked.

"You will pay?" asked Sadiki.

"All the costs. Fly you business class. And we'll expedite payments, once this is resolved. We're really sorry."

"Okay, then. I will be there Wednesday, December the twenty-first, if the God wills." Ferris gave him the details of where to meet, in a building in the old Islamic quarter of the city. He said the airplane ticket would be delivered to Sadiki's office in Amman first thing the next day. Sadiki said not to worry, he understood. The Jordanian was always so pliant. Perhaps that should have worried Ferris, but it didn't.

FERRIS TOOK a U.S. military helicopter late that afternoon to the big air base at Incirlik, 250 miles southeast of Ankara, which had been one of the staging points for American air operations over Iraq before the war. It was dark when he arrived. Waiting to greet him at the ramshackle military terminal was an agency officer Ferris remembered from somewhere, perhaps just the cafeteria at Headquarters. He was a balding, stoop-shouldered man in his mid-forties, who identified himself as a member of the Ankara station. NE Division had asked him to help with logistics. He led Ferris to the pallet where they had strapped his bag, and then to a waiting Humvee that drove them a half mile to an unmarked Quonset hut.

Inside the hut, propping his feet on his pack and reading a dog-eared copy of *People* magazine, was Jim, the Army officer Ferris had met in Rome. Jim had his wraparound sunglasses propped over his forehead, even in the evening dark, and he was wearing a work shirt with rolled-up sleeves in the chill of mid-December. He looked tighter and tauter than he had in Rome, as if he had spent most of the intervening weeks in the gym.

"Hey, stranger," said Ferris. "What do you know?"

"Not much, sir. Except you agency guys are pretty weird."

"That's a fact," said Ferris. "We're the Central Weirdness Agency."

The Ankara officer looked uncomfortable. "Hey, I'll leave you guys alone," he said. "I'm leaving the Humvee outside. They said you'd need one. I'll be back tomorrow morning at oh six hundred to take you to the chow hut. If you're not here, you'll have to find it yourselves. They stop serving at oh seven thirty." He excused himself and left the two younger men facing each other in the half-light of the makeshift office. Ferris put down his bag and looked in the little refrigerator in the back of the hut for something to drink.

"So, did you bring the boom-boom?" asked Ferris when he had drained the soda.

"Definitely." Jim nodded toward a big suitcase on roller wheels in the corner. "I've got enough plastic explosive in there to blow us from here to Tel Aviv."

"And did you get a car?"

"Volkswagen Golf. Same car they used in one of the Istanbul bombings. One of my guys parked it over by the BOQ, like you wanted. "

"Perfect," said Ferris. "So we're ready to rock."

Jim was scratching his head. It was obvious that something was bothering him. "Are we actually going to use this shit, sir?"

"Yeah," said Ferris. "Pretty much."

"Cool," said Jim. "But, like, how? Because that's a lot of explosive. Trust me."

Ferris went over the ops plan before Jim got any more spooked. He took the operational specs he and Azhar had prepared out of his briefcase and laid them down on the table between them. He walked his Army partner through each step of the plan. It took nearly an hour to summarize all of the interlocking pieces.

"And nobody gets hurt?" asked Jim when Ferris had finished. He had a very graphic idea of the damage this much explosive power could cause.

"Not if we do it right," Ferris said. "It just *looks* like people get hurt. A lot of them."

Ferris looked at his watch. It was past ten o'clock. "We've got six hours," he said.

"Let's lock and load," said Jim.

Ferris thought that he had never been in a situation with a military man when he didn't say, at some point, "Lock and load." They said it before having drinks at a club, before watching an NFL game on TV; maybe they said it to their wives before having sex.

"You lock, I'll load," said Ferris. "How about that?"

Ferris gathered his equipment—flashlight, maps, security gear to monitor the perimeter while they were working. He removed a pair of night-vision goggles from a compartment of his bag. Jim gingerly steered the wheelie bag toward the door of the Quonset hut. He had another bag over his shoulder that contained fuses and timers and communications gear. They carefully stowed the gear in the back of the Humvee. Ferris took the driver's seat. He studied his map for several minutes, to make sure he had the coordinates right.

"The BOQ is about ten minutes from here. We're going lights out, but the area should already be clean."

Ferris adjusted his night-vision goggles until the night air glowed bright with false light. He put the square-nosed vehicle in gear and set off down the rough macadam road. He made several turns along the way, following his map, until he saw a checkpoint up ahead manned by two U.S. soldiers. It was the only entrance to a fenced compound, roughly the size of a football field, which was ringed with razor wire. This was the Incirlik Bachelor Officers' Quarters, the compound where most pilots operating out of the air base were billeted. It was close enough to the perimeter of the base that people living in nearby towns and villages could see if something went wrong, but far enough away that they couldn't conduct close surveillance.

Ferris slowly pulled toward the zigzag line of concrete barriers that protected the entrance. He flashed his lights three times; one of the guards flashed back twice. When they reached the checkpoint, Ferris leaned out the window toward the guards and said a code name. They both saluted, and one of them pushed a button lowering the big metal flange that blocked the path ahead.

Ferris drove forward toward a three-story wooden building. There were Humvees and some civilian vehicles in the parking lot, as on a normal evening. The curtains were drawn, but most of the lights seemed to be on. With all the light, they wouldn't need the goggles.

"This is it," said Ferris. "The last folks pulled out two hours ago."

"Why are all the damn lights still on, sir?" asked Jim. He obviously preferred working in pitch-dark.

"To make people think the Americans are still here," said Ferris.

"Oh. Right. Roger that."

"Where's the car?"

"Around back," said Jim. "By the dumpster."

They drove slowly to the far corner of the building. There, deep in the shadows, sat a red Volkswagen Golf with Turkish tags.

"Let's get to work," said Ferris. He set up his electronic surveillance that would warn them of movement inside the perimeter of the compound. Then they unpacked the rest of the gear from the back of the Humvee and moved it next to the red VW.

"You ever make a car bomb before?" asked Ferris.

"Negative, sir. But let's pop the cherry."

Jim slowly unpacked the plastic explosive from the wheelie bag and began handing it gently to Ferris, who arrayed it in the trunk of the car. When they had lined the floor of the trunk, Jim stopped. "How much?" he asked.

"All of it," said Ferris.

"That's going to take down the whole damn building."

"If we do it right."

Ferris could see the wary flicker in the Army officer's eyes. "You're sure none of our buddies will be in here when it goes off?"

"Most of the guys are on leave, but the Turks don't know that. The ones that are still on base are bunking temporarily in the enlisted men's compound nearby. That's the plan, anyway. And you have to trust the plan."

"That's what they told us about Iraq."

Ferris smiled. "Just do it. And you sure you got the right plastic, with the right tags?"

"Oh yeah. When the Turkish bomb squad checks this shit out after it's over—the residue and what's left of the fuse and the timer— the address will be Al Qaeda all the way. It's the same stuff they used in the Istanbul bombings in '04."

"Nice touch," said Ferris.

They worked in silence. When all the explosive had been moved into the trunk, Jim went to work on the fuses and then the detonator and timer. Ferris went around to the main entrance. The door had been left open. He went downstairs to the basement fuse box that controlled the building's lights. He installed a timer that would maintain illumination over the next seventy-two hours on a regular schedule, keeping the lights blazing when the putative inhabitants of the building would normally be awake and turning them off when they would be asleep.

Ferris returned to the side of the building, where Jim was still at work double-checking the fuses and timer for faults. Then, with infinite precision, he attached the last wires.

"When should I set the timer?" asked Jim when he had completed the installation.

"Set it for oh seven hundred, Thursday morning. And don't fuck up."

"We leave that for the agency, sir," Jim said. He set the timer as instructed and then closed the trunk of the car. If anyone should somehow happen to wander by the building over the next two days, they would not see anything out of order. Ferris retrieved his sensors and then did a thorough search of the area to make sure they hadn't left anything behind.

Jim was lingering by the Volkswagen, not quite ready to go. Something was still bothering him.

"Sir, I'm just thinking. What if some Turk wanders in here Thursday morning? Or what if one of the officers who lives here returns early from leave before Christmas? Have we got some kind of sentry who will keep an eye out and shoo people away if they're here at the wrong time?"

"No sentry. Sorry."

"Excuse me for asking, sir, but why not?"

Ferris paused. He had asked Hoffman the same question when they had gone over the plan at Mincemeat Park. How do we avoid killing innocent people by accident? "We pray," Hoffman had answered, and when Ferris had pressed him, he had admonished him about limiting information to the fewest number of people possible. Looking at Hoffman, Ferris had realized: He's willing to lose people to make it work.

"Operational security," said Ferris. "We can't risk having a sentry. Sorry, but those are my orders."

"HUA, sir." The Army officer had the robotic look that comes over soldiers when they know it's time to stop asking questions and get on with it.

They replaced the rest of the gear in the Humvee. They drove back through the checkpoint and returned to their Quonset hut. Ferris offered Jim a beer, and the two men drank together, but it was mostly in silence. Then they went to their bunks to catch a few hours' sleep.

The Ankara case officer arrived at 0600, as promised. Jim was already eating a foul-looking MRE. Ferris told his Ankara colleague he wouldn't be going to breakfast, but to the flight line to catch a chopper back to Ankara. As he was leaving, Jim gave him a punch on the shoulder—hard enough that it hurt. "Merry Christmas," he said.

26

THE DECEMBER DAWN turned the eastern sky an ochre-red. Through the window of the Black Hawk helicopter, Ferris could see the washboard plain of Anatolia. The flight had been logged with the Turkish military, so there was no need to be flying so low to the ground, but the pilot was getting his jollies. They followed the riverbeds that scored southern Turkey, banking left and right so tightly that Ferris could feel the Gs in his stomach; they buzzed terrified flocks of sheep, scattering the animals in every direction under the wash of the rotors; they skimmed over empty fields, swirling the deep grass into a Van Gogh landscape. The pilot was having fun, pulling the Black Hawk up suddenly when he approached power lines, and occasionally dipping recklessly below them. He knew Ferris would never report him, and that if he did, nobody back on the flight line would care.

Ferris had a busy day in Ankara. He met with Bulent Farhat, the Turkish agent who would be posing as Unibank's chief engineer. Farhat had been an Afghan traveler long ago; the Turks had sweated his jihadist passion out of him when he returned and had set him free on condition that he continue reporting for them, at first in Salafist circles at home and then, when they trusted him, from mosques in

Germany. The CIA had picked him up in Germany and ran him as a unilateral, even though he was still on the books of the Turkish service.

Ferris took Bulent to the office where he would be meeting with Omar Sadiki. It was on a busy commercial street near the city's oldest mosques. The office itself was modern, but nondescript—hard to remember; harder still to find again. Ferris gave the agent some Unibank business cards and a briefcase with the company logo on the side. He ran through the script: Bulent would quiz Sadiki about the cold retention and heat resistance of the insulation Al Fajr had specified; he would complain that it wasn't dense enough and suggest a change in the design specs. He should offer to pay for the change order if Sadiki balked. In any event, he should make sure that as they talked, he handed drawings and designs back and forth. The camera and microphones in the office walls would do the rest.

Next, Ferris called Ajit Singh back in Amman to confirm the cyberspace portion of the December 22 operation. Singh described his kit of electronic tricks: he would send cryptic messages later that day from the Sadiki e-mail account he controlled, hinting in coded language that an operation against an American target was ready; he had prepared a communiqué taking responsibility for the Christmas bombing and announcing a militant new Salafist group, which would be posted on an authentic jihad Web site several hours after the bombing became public; he had a buzz of congratulatory messages that would pass among the networks; he had postings ready for Islamic chat rooms on *mySunna.com* and a dozen other jihadist Web sites—explaining the origins and theology of the new group that had staged the bombing. The postings would explain that the new group believed Al Qaeda was going soft—attacking civilian targets in Europe rather than American military targets. A few messages would even accuse Al Qaeda's leaders of being in the pay of the CIA.

"You are a genius," Ferris told his young assistant.

"If that's true, why can't I get laid?"

"I'll take you out when I get back," said Ferris. "Find you a girl. How's that?"

"I want two, please."

Ferris laughed. He wondered if his wired assistant might actually be a virgin. "Okay, fine. Two girls."

SADIKI ARRIVED the next morning. Ferris sent a car to meet him at the airport. The Jordanian had been delayed at passport control, which meant his name must be on watch lists. Ferris was waiting at the office, in his usual disguise, with Bulent. The meeting went off as planned. After about an hour's haggling, they agreed on terms for respecifying the insulation. Bulent insisted on taking Sadiki to a celebratory lunch at a neighborhood restaurant. Ferris excused himself, saying he had other business, so the other two went off to a favorite gathering place for Islamist politicians and pamphleteers; it was a restaurant where they would be seen—by pious Muslims connected to the underground, and by the Turkish security men who were watching them. The car took Sadiki back to the airport after lunch, and he caught the late flight out that night.

THE NEXT MORNING, Thursday, December 22, a large bomb detonated at the Incirlik air base in southern Turkey. The fireball could be seen from many miles away, and the roar of the explosion quickly drew a crowd outside the air base. Local stringers for the wire services sent out bulletins thirty minutes after the bomb attack, and CNN Turk got video footage, shot with a telephoto lens from outside the perimeter of the base, that showed a thick column of smoke rising from what was left of a building. Two hours after the bombing, CNN Turk was quoting Turkish sources saying that the target had been an American barracks.

Ferris called Hoffman by secure phone a few hours later to confirm that everything had gone off as planned. He was worried, just as Jim had been the night they set the explosives, that something might have gone wrong.

"It was almost perfect," said Hoffman.

"What does that mean?" asked Ferris.

"It means that some dumb-fuck enlisted man went to the officers' barracks because he heard there were a bunch of empty rooms. He snuck past the guards. They identified his body thirty minutes ago."

"Oh, Jesus." Ferris had let this happen. He had seen this deadly mistake coming and hadn't done anything to prevent it. What was happening to him?

"Don't worry about it. This guy violated orders and entered a no-go area. That's not your fault. It's not my fault. It's his fault. So don't get all gooey and lose sight of what's important. We're getting close now. Suck it up."

Ferris didn't answer for a moment. He let Hoffman's words sink in. "You don't really care that this guy is dead, do you?"

"No. I guess I don't. And neither should you."

Ferris didn't try to respond. He just said goodbye.

THE U.S. AND Turkish militaries did their best to keep a lid on the story, and because it was a military base, they had some success. But at ten that morning, the prime minister's office in Ankara held a press conference for Turkish media and said there had been a large blast at Incirlik. There were casualties, but none of the dead or wounded were Turks. The prime minister's spokesman told the Turkish reporters on background that the target of the blast had been the U.S. Bachelor Officers' Quarters at the base, where many of the pilots lived. The spokesman said most of the building had been destroyed, but that the Americans were treating the casualties in their own field hospital, which normally handled emergency evacuations from Iraq.

People in the States were just waking up when the Pentagon issued a statement, at 1400 Ankara time and 0700 in Washington. The Pentagon confirmed that a car bomb had destroyed the U.S. officers' barracks, that American casualties had been limited because many officers were away on Christmas leave. The Pentagon refused to release the names of the dead and wounded, pending notification of their next of kin, and a few reporters were advised in a gaggle afterward that there might not be a public announcement of the casualties because some of them had been stationed at Incirlik on classified missions. That wasn't a surprise. The Pentagon press corps knew Incirlik was a base for special operations inside Iraq: a deniable "black" facility that everybody knew all about. The pictures told the story: They showed the devastation—a massive bomb blast that had destroyed a symbolic target, the base used by the very airmen who had dropped bombs on Iraqis.

When the claim of responsibility was posted on the Islamic Web site, the story went into a new gear. The statement criticized other terrorist groups as pro-American sell-outs. The group taking credit, "Nasr al-Din Albani Revenge Brigade," was previously unknown. But by late that day, analysts in London and Washington were speculating that the group might be an important new offshoot of Al Qaeda. The man for whom the group was named was a watchmaker from Damascus who, before his death in 2000, had made a name for his free-form interpretation of the sayings of the Prophet Muhammad, known as the "hadith," that challenged the dry orthodoxy of the official canon. He was a modern saint to some of the more extreme proponents of Salafist Islam, people who wanted to purge the corruption of modern life and re-create the purity and fighting fellowship of the days of the Prophet. Albani's followers were scattered in Syria, Saudi Arabia and Jordan; the movement's center point was a mosque in Zarqa, where many of Albani's followers had taken refuge after fleeing Syria. The intelligence analysts knew, but didn't tell reporters, that one member of the Zarqa mosque was a mysterious Jordanian architect who had been gaining prominence in jihadist circles.

There were more snippets of evidence, courtesy of Ajit Singh. Analysts noted similarities between the Salafist rhetoric in the Albani Revenge Brigade's communiqué and that of postings that had been made on jihadi Web sites in recent months. There was a frequently repeated Arabic phrase, for example: *"Nahnu rijal wa hum rijal,"* which translated as "We are men and they are men." For the jihadists, the statement meant that the traditional mainstream interpretations of the Koran and hadith were no more valid than those of Salafist radicals. That was the essence of Albani's call for radical reinterpretation. A story in the *London Daily Telegraph* cited British analysts noting another quote, from a radical Salafist sheik named Abdel-Rahim al-Tahhan, which had appeared on a number of sites, in part of the communiqué: *"La khayra fi qur'an bi-ghayri sunna, wa la khayra fi sunna bi-ghayri fahm salafna al-silah."* That amounted to a declaration of independence from the traditional canon for Sunni Muslims, known as the Sunna: "There is no good in the Koran without the Sunna, and there is no good in the Sunna without our righteous Salafist understanding of it." These were the new killers, warned the *Telegraph*, more dangerous even than those who had detonated the car bombs in Milan and Frankfurt.

It took twenty-four hours before the first leaks emerged from the joint Turkish/FBI team that was doing the forensic examination of the site of the blast. Their findings made front-page news around the world. The Incirlik bombing was definitely linked to the Al Qaeda network. Technicians had matched the explosives and the detonator with those used in a previous Al Qaeda bombing in Istanbul.

No real operation is perfect. But as Ferris followed the shadow play of virtual events, he could only conclude that falsehood was perfectible in a way that true life was not. He remembered something from his journalist days in the early 1990s—an observation by astringent critic Janet Malcom, who observed that there is only one kind of narrative where the accuracy of what's described on the printed page cannot be questioned, and that is fiction. So, too, with the Incirlik bombing. The truth that the world understood was that an angry new group of car bombers could hit Americans inside their own bases. It was a shock—most of all to the real car bombers.

•   •   •

FERRIS RECEIVED an e-mail from Gretchen. He was worried at first when he saw the sender, but the message was reassuring, in its way. The subject line was "You Blew It." The message itself was the text of an item that had appeared that morning in the gossip column of the *Washington Post*, reporting that a soon-to-be-divorced Justice Department lawyer had been seen that holiday season on the arm of a senior White House aide who was among the town's most attractive bachelors. Ferris could only smile in appreciation; Gretchen was a force of nature. When one path proved to be obstructed, she had changed course and chosen another. That was her gift, that she did not complicate the business of life with introspection. She decided what she wanted and then went out and got it. Now the future lay open for Ferris, too. He was going home to Amman to be with the woman he loved. There was one impediment: At the center of his relationship with Alice Melville was a lie.

27

H ANI SALAAM SUMMONED FERRIS the day he returned from Ankara. All he said on the phone was that it was urgent and that it concerned Incirlik. The media frenzy over the bombing was still gathering momentum, and Ferris was worried that Hani might do something to pull apart the web which he had worked so hard to spin.

When Ferris arrived at GID headquarters, he noticed that the management had installed a new portrait of the king in the front lobby. In place of the old painting that showed His Majesty relaxing in short sleeves with his wife and children, as carefree as if they were at a beach resort, the new tableau portrayed the monarch in his Special Forces uniform, scowling toward the middle distance where the enemy lay in wait. It was a sign of the times, Ferris thought. The easy talk about reform and renewal was over; the Arab leaders were caught in the bottle now with the scorpions.

Hani looked elegant as ever, and impervious to the battles around him. He was wearing a royal blue shirt, open at the neck, with thick gold cufflinks. His gray suit had the fit that could only have come from a tailor: the trousers that broke just so over the tops of his shoes, the jacket gently shaped at the waist. He was wearing a little

Christmas candy cane on his lapel, whether in deference to his American visitor or to his handful of Christian employees, Ferris couldn't say.

"Merry Christmas," said Hani, taking Ferris's hand and holding it for a moment, while he mulled a question. "Assuming, that is, that you are a Christian. I don't think I ever asked, but you Americans are so religious nowadays. It's worse than Saudi Arabia. Still, Christmas is for everyone, isn't it? Here in Jordan, even the Muslims have Christmas trees."

"I'm not a believer," answered Ferris. "I like to sing the hymns, but I stopped going to church years ago, when I couldn't say the Creed. I felt hypocritical, like a Muslim who drinks. But thanks for asking."

"And how is Mrs. Ferris?" Hani had never asked about Gretchen before. The comment couldn't be accidental.

"We're getting divorced. The papers should be final in a few weeks."

"Yes, I heard something about that. I trust that everything is all right."

"It's fine, Hani. Everything is just fine." The Jordanian was showing off—making sure that Ferris realized he knew about his private life. He probably had heard about the inspector general's investigation, too, but on that subject he opted for discretion.

Ferris didn't want small talk. He was tired from the hectic activity in Turkey, and still troubled by his last phone call with Hoffman. "You said on the phone you had something important, Hani. As we say in America: 'I'm all ears.'"

"Yes, my dear, I was getting to that. I think we can help you on that dreadful Incirlik attack. My greatest sympathies, by the way." He pulled a photograph from a file on his desk and laid the picture before Ferris.

The photograph showed Omar Sadiki. He was dressed in a business suit, with his neat little beard and his wary, pious eyes. It appeared to be an enlargement of a passport photo.

Ferris stared at the picture, trying not to move a muscle in his face. He had been dreading this moment—when Hani would begin sniffing around Sadiki. Hoffman had advised Ferris to deny he had any links to the architect.

"Who is he?" Ferris asked, staring blankly at the picture.

"His name is Omar Sadiki. He is an architect with a firm here in Amman that builds mosques in Saudi Arabia. They work for the charitable foundations, the ones that fund the madrassas. He is also active in a mosque in Zarqa that we have been watching for a long time. We know quite a lot about him." Hani paused and studied his visitor's face as if he wanted to make sure of something.

Ferris kept still. He was aware of each breath. He waited for Hani to say more, but the Jordanian was biding his time, wanting to be asked.

"Does he have any connection with Incirlik?" ventured Ferris.

"We think so. The evidence is not so hard, but it points us in that direction. He flew from Amman to Ankara the day before the bombing. It was supposedly business. But we have talked to the Turks, and they tell us that while he was in Ankara, this Omar met with a Turk who went to Afghanistan. Our Mr. Omar stayed only a few hours in Turkey. Just long enough to do a little operational planning. If that is what it was. And then he came back home to Amman."

Ferris paused and thought a moment. Months of work would be lost if he wasn't careful. "Good stuff, Hani. What are you going to do with it?"

The Jordanian regarded him curiously and then took a cigarette from the pack on his desk and lit it. He held the smoke in his lungs for a long moment before exhaling.

"That's why I asked to see you, Roger. We want to watch this Mr. Sadiki, see who he talks to. He is the best lead we have had in some time. I do not plan to arrest him, for now. I hope you will not try anything unusual, either. That would be a mistake, I think."

Ferris turned away from Hani and paced toward the couch. He was relieved but tried to hide it. If the Jordanians arrested Sadiki, the consequences could be disastrous. The architect would stutter his protestations that he had nothing to do with Incirlik; in a few painful hours it would be obvious he was telling the truth and the game would be up. He turned back toward Hani, who was still puffing slowly on his cigarette.

"I think you're right," said Ferris. "Don't arrest him. Leave him in place."

Hani's eyes narrowed to a crinkle. "Yes. Watch and wait. That is usually the right course of action. I knew I was right about you. But you must promise to stay away from him. No little rendition job in the middle of the night, because I will be watching. Can you give me your word on that?"

"Oh yes, absolutely. We won't get near him. And you won't. We'll all watch and wait. Right?"

Hani nodded and offered a slight smile. "You should call Mr. Ed Hoffman. He would want to know, I think."

"As soon as I get back to the embassy, I'll tell him. He will be very excited. This is great work, Hani. Nobody could have cracked this but you. We owe you our thanks."

Hani stubbed out his cigarette. He still had a curious look in his eye, or maybe Ferris was just imagining it. "We are allies. How can we not help each other?"

The two men shook hands. Ferris asked Hani if he needed any technical help in the surveillance of Sadiki. That was one area where the Americans always had something to offer. But the GID chief said he would be fine, unless Sadiki started moving outside Jordan. Ferris asked Hani if he would be informing the Turks or any other friendly services, and the Jordanian gave another half smile.

"Not for now," said Hani. "This will be our secret."

WHEN FERRIS narrated the conversation for Hoffman forty-five minutes later, he got nervous all over again. Hoffman kept saying, "Shit!" as if he knew bad news was coming. When Ferris got to the end and Hani's promise to leave Sadiki in place, Hoffman's response was a relieved, "Thank God." Ferris realized then just how nervous his boss had been that the operation might be blown.

"Do you think he knows?" asked Hoffman.

"What do you mean?"

"Do you think he realizes we're playing games with Sadiki?"

"Maybe. He's smart. But I don't think so. The collateral is all there. The more he goes looking, the more he'll see the trail I've laid."

"The legend is there, for sure. And Hani isn't a genius, as I keep telling you. I think we're okay. You want me to come out and talk to him?"

"Not unless you plan to read him into the operation. He would just get suspicious if you came out. He would think you were pulling some razzle-dazzle stunt on him again."

"Which I am."

"Right. But let's not make it too obvious."

"Merry Christmas," said Hoffman. For it was, in fact, Christmas Eve.

FERRIS MET Alice that night at her apartment. She was wearing a red Santa hat, askew, and she had rouge on her cheeks, making her look slightly like a woman who might appear in the Christmas ads for Scotch whiskeys or snow blowers. Ferris had been away for several weeks, and he had worried she might go home to Boston to spend Christmas with her mother. But here she was, better than any imagining.

She clasped her arms around his neck, stood on tiptoe to kiss him and then hugged him tight. Ferris could feel her hands against his bony ribs.

"What happened? Did you stop eating? You feel ten pounds lighter."

"I've been busy. Skipped a lot of meals."

"Well, you're down to skin and bone. Just so long as you've got a little left for tonight." She gave him a sly smile.

She led him upstairs to the secret garden of her apartment. She had a Christmas tree in the living room, a bent-over cedar that had barely survived the trip from Lebanon but was aglow with lights and glass ornaments and even tinsel. Where had she found that in Amman? The King's College Choir was singing Christmas carols on the CD player, and a half dozen brightly wrapped presents were under the tree. Ferris had just found time to go shopping himself that afternoon, and he took his gifts from the bag and laid them gently down.

Alice retreated to the kitchen and returned with two glasses of wine. They drank enough to feel slightly tipsy, and then Alice began to trace her finger along the seam of his trouser, and then his zipper.

"Not yet," said Ferris. "I'm still getting in the Christmas spirit." In truth, he wasn't ready for intimacy. There was too much he hadn't told her since he had left Amman so suddenly. In his few phone calls, he hadn't wanted to say much—he was sure Hani had her phones bugged by now—so he had been clipped and tight. "Can't talk now," he would say. "Explain later." And she would understand. She had fallen into the rhythm of his life to that extent—that she realized he had secrets, and that there were times when she had to give him space and wait until he could say more.

So he told her. Not everything, not even a full slice of everything, but a taste. He explained that he had gone home to face a legal investigation. His wife had threatened to retaliate when he first demanded a divorce, and she had taken her revenge by digging up some dirt from his previous assignment at the U.S. Embassy in Yemen. He'd had to convince her to back down and stop making trouble before she would agree to the divorce.

"What did you have on her?" asked Alice.

"Just dirt. It doesn't matter. Mostly financial things. Anyway, I made it go away."

"How?" She still wanted to know.

"By convincing her that it would be unwise to continue."

"That sounds like blackmail."

"Sort of. Let's just say that my wife, my ex-wife, left a lot of loose ends. She knew I was aware of them, but I don't think she expected I would use them. Too gallant."

"So you *did* blackmail her. That's a little scary, isn't it?"

"I had no choice. And it shouldn't scare you. You're as clean as the snow on the North Pole."

She poured them both another glass of wine. The choir was singing "The Twelve Days of Christmas" on the stereo.

"Where did you go then, after Washington? Not to the North Pole, I bet."

"I went to Turkey," said Ferris.

"Oh God. I hope you weren't there when that terrible bomb went off. They still haven't said how many Americans were killed. There must have been a lot. That's why they're trying to cover it up."

Ferris flinched. That was a measure of the success of his operation. He had managed to hoodwink his girlfriend.

"I was in Ankara. The bombing was at an air base in the south. I was nowhere near there. I did my business, and then I came home. To my girl."

He drank some more wine, but it didn't taste right on his tongue. "How about you? How were things here in Amman while I was gone? Everything good at work?"

"Pretty good. The Palestinian kids got out of school for winter holiday—they're not supposed to say 'Christmas.' Some of them came around the office. And we got a new grant from the Malcolm Kerr Foundation, which will help pay for those computers. These nice people from Cisco Systems say they'll put in broadband connections at all the schools. That was sweet. They must have wanted to put it in their corporate Christmas card. The only bad thing was that we lost some of our Jordanian volunteers. That made me sad."

"Oh yeah? Who?" Ferris's body reacted as if a switch had been flipped.

"That group you didn't like. The Ikhwan Ihsan. The architect man I told you about came by yesterday to give us a check. He said it was their last gift. And then today we got a visit from a man from the Moukhabarat. He said he was sorry, but we couldn't have any more contact with the Brothers. He said they were going out of business. New rules for Muslim groups. Too bad for us. We need the money."

"You talk to the Moukhabarat?"

"Of course, silly. This is Jordan. Everyone talks to the Moukhabarat."

Ferris felt a perverse sense of relief. He wished the Jordanians weren't cracking down quite so obviously on Sadiki's friends, but he was glad that Alice wouldn't be in contact with them anymore. It had been too messy the other way. People could get the wrong idea if they realized that Alice knew Sadiki, and Alice knew Ferris. They might make a connection.

"Maybe it's for the best," he said. "Those Muslim groups can get freaky."

"Not these guys. They were sweet. Sadiki even gave me ideas for projects."

Ferris spoke cautiously. "He's dangerous. The GID wouldn't have come to see you if he wasn't. Trust me. You'll find other donors. There are plenty of fish in the sea."

She pulled back from the warmth of his chest and sat up straight on the couch.

"What aren't you telling me, Roger? Don't lie. Do you think I'm stupid? Every time this guy's name comes up, you get the willies."

"Don't ask me that. There are some questions I can't answer. You know that. Forget I ever asked about Sadiki. Forget everything."

"Tell me, Roger. If you love me, you'll tell me."

Ferris felt a kind of vertigo. He wanted to pitch himself over the lip of all his lies and into the release of confession. But he knew he couldn't, and he steered himself back into the deception that would protect her.

"I'm sorry. There are just some things we can't talk about. It would be dangerous."

"What do you mean? How can the truth be dangerous? It's lies that are dangerous."

Ferris put his arm around her. At first she pulled away, but he tried a second time and she let the arm rest on her shoulder. He held her gently, until her body relaxed and she gave up on the questions, or at least on the hope they would be answered.

"Stay away from this war, Alice. Please. It's destroying too many people already. Nothing good can come from it, except when it's over."

She went away to the bathroom, and when she returned, she was quieter and more careful. Something had changed. Ferris knew it, but he couldn't do anything about it. They opened their presents that night under the tree. Alice had bought him a beautiful Arab robe, embroidered with gold and fit for a prince, and a red tarboosh to wear on his head, like the old Ottoman pashas. Ferris had bought her clothes, too—a beautiful Ferragamo dress that he'd found in a boutique at the Four Seasons. But the main gift he saved for last. It was in a small box, and it was a diamond engagement ring.

When Alice opened the box and saw what it was, she began to cry. She left the room for a moment and composed herself. When she returned, she kissed Ferris and said she loved him. Then she put the ring back in its box and returned it to him. "I can't accept this now, Roger. Not until I know who you are."

28

F ERRIS WAS CALLED BACK to Headquarters the day after
Christmas. He had spent the holiday with Alice, long silences,
sentences that began but didn't finish. What does a man say to
woman who has rejected his proposal of marriage? What does a
woman say to a man she knows is lying to her? How does the man
convey that if he tried to answer the woman's questions, it would
make everything much worse? "For the sake of kindness, I cannot be
kind," wrote the poet Bertolt Brecht. For the sake of truth, Ferris
could not speak. Alice tried to be festive, roasting a turkey she had
managed to find in the markets of the city; she wore her red Santa
hat until Ferris made her take it off. And then Hoffman called on the
cell phone, which he never did, and told Ferris to come home as
quickly as possible. To Ferris, it was a relief to leave. He wanted to
believe that Alice was safer with him not around.

There was heavy snow back in Washington. Cars were skidding
out along the George Washington Parkway, and even the entry to
CIA Headquarters was slick with ice. Ferris ran his rented car into a
drift in the North Parking Lot (which the agency administrators, in
their cheery, color-coded way, had renamed the "Green" lot) and
made his way to Hoffman's high-tech rat hole. He had his own bio-

metric badge now, one that scanned him past the hidden doors and down the elevators that didn't exist to Mincemeat Park. The chief was more manic than usual; his face was red, and Ferris at first thought he'd had too much to drink at holiday parties, but he was actually pumped up by something else.

"Ho, ho, ho," said Hoffman. "Merry Christmas."

"Very funny," said Ferris, jet-lagged from the long flight home. "This had better be good."

"Good? I should say so. ' "The time has come," the Walrus said, "to talk of many things: Of shoes and ships and sealing-wax—of cabbages and kings. And why the sea is boiling hot—and whether pigs have wings." ' To quote the estimable Lewis Carroll."

Oh Jesus, thought Ferris, he has gone completely, barking mad.

"To be precise," continued Hoffman, "I am quoting *Through the Looking Glass,* and that is where we are about to go, my friend, through the looking glass. With our guide, Mr. Harry Meeker."

A smile dawned on Ferris's face, a walrus smile. They had arrived. Hoffman took him by the arm and pulled him down the corridor, past the desks of analysts and officers manipulating their imaginary jihadist Web sites and tracking their targets around the world. He got all the way to the end of the room, to a set of glass doors that, in Ferris's memory, had always been closed. Hoffman put his badge on a reader attached to the wall, put a keycard in the slot and the door opened. He continued down a dark corridor and made a right turn, where he opened another door.

It was freezing inside this last room, literally. Azhar emerged from the shadows, wearing a thick coat and gloves to stay warm. It was dark, except for a fluorescent glow from the corner. The low light had a crystalline quality, as if they were seeing through tiny chips of ice. Ferris followed Hoffman toward the light. There on a table he saw the body of a man, rigid as a piece of wood, the pale skin coating the bones of his face like a layer of paraffin. He was dressed in casual clothes, a pair of pleated slacks and a white shirt.

"Here's your boy," said Hoffman.

Ferris touched the cold, waxy skin. He was so dead. This was his first actual encounter with the body he had encouraged Hoffman to procure, and he had the peculiar sensation that he had killed the man himself. Ferris thought of the *The Man Who Never Was,* the dog-eared British intelligence book that had given him the inspiration for his plot. Sixty-five years ago, the corpse's name was Major William Martin of the Royal Marines, and he had washed up on a beach in Spain. It had worked then, but the Germans were stupider than Suleiman.

"I love this guy," said Hoffman, patting the corpse's icy cheek. "He's my kind of case officer. Goes where you send him, doesn't talk back. Keeps his mouth shut, permanently."

But Ferris wasn't listening to the banter. Looking at the stiff and lifeless body, he wondered whether it would work—whether the series of reflecting mirrors they had assembled would all point in the right directions.

IT WAS TOO cold to stay with the corpse for very long, so Hoffman and Ferris adjourned to a conference room nearby, leaving Azhar to minister to the dead man. On the conference table stood an open metal briefcase that was dented and discolored from frequent use. Attached to the handle of the case was a metal chain, connected at the other end to a thick metal bracelet, like a handcuff. Arrayed nearby was a series of manila folders. Hoffman stood at the head of the table.

"Time to bait the hook. This was your idea, Roger. What do you want in his briefcase? What should Harry Meeker, CIA case officer extraordinaire, be carrying with him when he is shot trying to make contact with an access agent in Al Qaeda? Run me through the drill."

Ferris closed his eyes and tried to put himself into the fantasy world they had worked so hard to create.

"He's carrying a message for Suleiman," said Ferris. "That's the detonator. He has a message from the CIA to Suleiman. When other people see it, they will think Suleiman is working for us. You have that ready?"

Hoffman nodded. "A message for Suleiman, to be delivered via an access agent in Pakistan."

Ferris continued, "Harry will be asking Suleiman for help in dealing with a dangerous new threat. And that threat is Omar Sadiki, whose dossier Harry has been assembling."

"Precisely," said Hoffman. "Sadiki has crossed a line. Suleiman had just been killing Europeans, but the new man is killing Americans at the air base in Turkey. So Harry is contacting his supersecret source in Al Qaeda. He wants Suleiman to stop the new splinter group Sadiki is running, outside Suleiman's control."

Ferris shook his head in wonder. "I just hope they will believe we're this devious. And this smart."

"Of course they will. They think we're Superman. That's why they hate us so much."

"Do you have the paperwork ready?" asked Ferris.

"Yup, but I want you to look at it before we load the torpedo."

Ferris walked along the row of manila folders, looking at the contents, and then returned to one folder. He pulled a grainy photo that showed Sadiki meeting with Bulent Farhat in Ankara. "We use this one, for sure. This proves Sadiki was in contact with an Al Qaeda guy in Turkey just before Incirlik. If the agency was making a dossier against Sadiki, this would be Exhibit A."

"Into the briefcase," said Hoffman, placing the photo inside. "What else?"

Ferris took a second photo from one of the early folders. It showed Sadiki in Abu Dhabi, meeting with the lawyer who had once been part of Al Qaeda's money-transfer system. "We need this. This is Harry's proof that Sadiki moved the money for the Incirlik bombing."

"For sure. What else?"

Ferris pulled a document on FBI letterhead and date-stamped that day. It purported to be an analysis of the plastic explosive used at Incirlik, matching it with the explosive used at the HSBC and Israeli consulate bombings in Istanbul in 2003. "Harry Meeker would want this one. It nails the Al Qaeda connection."

Hoffman laughed as he took the document. "This will make Suleiman's people crazy. How could they not know about a guy who has the same stash of plastic explosive they used for earlier ops? How could they be in the dark? Unless . . . *unless* . . . Suleiman is jerking them around. Unless Suleiman is not what he appears. Unless a worm has been eating at their insides. They won't know what to think!"

Ferris studied a third photograph. A caption said it was the office used by the Brothers of Awareness in Amman. Ferris recognized the neighborhood. It was near Alice's office, in the old part of the city.

"What's that?" asked Hoffman.

Ferris was still looking at the picture, lost in thought. "You don't need this one," he said very quietly, his voice barely audible. He put the photo back in the folder.

"What's the problem? Photo not interesting enough?"

"No. Leave this one out. It doesn't do anything for us."

Ferris added a few more items. He found a surveillance record from the UAE intelligence service about Sadiki's movements in Abu Dhabi. Harry Meeker would have studied that. And he added the airplane receipts, to and from Ankara. Those would have been in the dossier. And he had the report from the Turkish immigration authorities, forwarded to the agency by Turkish liaison, about Sadiki's entry and departure on December 21. It made a neat kit— evidence that Sadiki was part of an important new breakaway cell of Al Qaeda, which the CIA urgently wanted to contain. He took the briefcase in his hands and held it, feeling its weight.

"I hate these bastards," said Hoffman. "That's why I love this play. Because it will make them destroy themselves. The stuff in that briefcase gets passed up the chain, and it makes *all* of them wonder if the CIA is running their main man. We introduce that seed of doubt in the organization, and then we just let it do its work. They begin to doubt everything. Their whole world gets turned upside down. This is the poison pill. If they swallow it, they are dead."

Ferris nodded. It was his idea. He wanted to believe it, but he worried that they had missed something.

"So I'm Harry," said Ferris, holding the briefcase. "I've been working the Incirlik case for the agency. I've got all the evidence I need to prove that Omar Sadiki did it. I want Suleiman's help. How do I get to Pakistan?"

"Here's the itinerary," said Hoffman. "First, Harry goes to London and Paris to brief the allies. We'll have someone in a Harry disguise brief midlevel people at SIS and the DGSE to backstop the legend. He'll be flying on the same Gulfstream that's carrying the corpse. We've got pocket litter for London and Paris. Restaurant receipts for dinners, taxi receipts, all that shit. Harry will go see *Cats* in London, and he'll send a text message to his girlfriend on his cell phone, telling her how great it is. When the Al Qaeda boys find Harry's phone, they'll like the *Cats* thing. So American. We just added that yesterday."

"Lovely. But when does Harry get to Pakistan? That's all that really matters."

"He flies to Islamabad from Paris. He goes to see the ISI, first thing. We assume the ISI is penetrated, so we're sending the man in the Harry disguise. He briefs the Paks. But then Harry goes unilateral."

"He goes to see his Al Qaeda contact in Waziristan."

"Precisely. He and the base chief in Peshawar and a half dozen Special Forces guys go up into the mountains, supposedly to meet a Pashtu tribal guy named Azzam, who worked with Suleiman when he was in Afghanistan. We've been meeting with this guy Azzam for real, paid him some dough, trying to recruit him as an access agent. It hasn't worked, but the bad guys don't know that. And Harry is going to be carrying his message for Suleiman, addressed to 'Raouf,' which we know from intercepts is the code name Suleiman uses with his people. And the letter is . . . well, I'll say it, because Sami wrote it. It is a work of art."

Hoffman handed him a message, written in Arabic on paper that was so stiff it could only have come from America. Ferris read it aloud, translating it into English. "In the name of the Prophet, peace and blessings be upon him et cetera, I send you greetings, Raouf, via our good friend and brother Azzam. We ask your help in the matter of a renegade Jordanian brother whose photograph and dossier I am giving to Brother Azzam. We ask that you take appropriate measures, as in the past. Peace and blessings be upon you."

"Let's include this photograph." Hoffman displayed a small picture of Omar Sadiki. Ferris handed the Raouf letter back to his boss, who attached the photo with a paper clip and put it in the metal briefcase, ready for Harry Meeker.

"He won't bleed," said Ferris. "You realize that, right? When Harry gets shot in this mountain village, he won't bleed."

"Of course he won't bleed! He's dead, for God's sake. But he will *ooze*. He will *seep*. We've done tests. It will be fine."

"Are we crazy?" said Ferris, half to himself.

"Maybe, but you know what? When Suleiman's pals see all this stuff and begin trying to figure out what it all means, they are going to be even crazier. It eats away at people, not knowing what's true and what isn't. It makes them wonder whether they believe anything at all. It's the great destroyer, doubt. It does the devil's work for him." Ferris nodded his assent. He tried not to think about the other ways in which Hoffman's statement might be true.

29

T HEY RAN HARRY MEEKER through a final checklist, as if they were firing a human cannonball. Azhar stood over the corpse with a clipboard, reading off items while members of the technical staff confirmed the answers, and then said, "Check!" The first concern was body temperature. They had brought Meeker up a few degrees in the last week, to the level at which he would be transported. The agency's pathologist recommended a gradual process of increasing his body temperature so that it would reach the ambient air temperature a few hours before the body was discovered. They did various measurements with the surgical equivalent of a meat thermometer before Azhar announced, "Check!" and passed on.

They inventoried each pocket. Gum wrappers from London, Paris and Pakistan. (Hoffman had decided that Meeker should have chewing gum in his mouth when the body was found—a natural touch—and had designated Azhar to prechew it.) Some change: Two euros, a fat British two-pound piece and a handful of Pakistani rupees. Check! Then the wallet itself: the credit card receipts from the Exxon station on Route 123 and the laundry in McLean Center, the driver's license and credit cards, the autographed picture of the imaginary girlfriend, "Denise," the ticket stubs and matchbooks and condoms that added up to Meeker's identity.

And then the cell phone: Azhar had already constructed his pastiche of "Received Calls" and "Dialed Numbers." While they were doing the final review, he decided he wanted to add a string of three "Missed Calls" from Denise. If someone got curious and dialed the number that had made those missed calls, they would hear the breathy voice of a young woman saying, "Hey! This is Denise. Leave me a message or whatever."

And finally, Harry's clothes: He had a warm overcoat now; the body would be discovered in the tribal areas between Peshawar and the Afghani border in late December. They had bought a parka with a fleece lining from Lands' End, and that seemed right—except that it looked too new, even after a half dozen dry cleanings. So Hoffman put out a group e-mail message for Mincemeat Park that said "Clothing Drive" asking for a used size 44 regular men's outdoor coat, preferably fleece-lined. Two jackets came back: One looked newer than the one they already had; the other was shiny with wear, with a small tear on the sleeve and a lining that was matted from perspiration. Hoffman pronounced it perfect. The wool trousers still worked, and so did the white shirt, and the trekking shoes. During the last check, before they were going to load Harry Meeker into the refrigerated container for his last trip, Hoffman noticed a crease in the trousers.

"Jesus Christ!" he shouted. "Who tramps around the Back of Beyond with a goddamn crease in his trousers? What is wrong with you people?" Azhar, who was prepared for anything, had a steam iron and quickly removed the creases from Harry's pants.

FROM THE OPERATIONS room at Mincemeat Park, Hoffman and his team were able to follow Harry Meeker's progress. They monitored the plane's landing in London, Paris and, finally, Islamabad. While Harry stayed in his box, a real case officer from NE Division in disguise left the plane at each stop and went to the local CIA station and from there to the offices of the friendly services, where he briefed officials on the latest in the Incirlik bombing. A short item appeared in *Le Figaro* the day after the Paris visit, reporting that the United States had new information about Incirlik implicating a breakaway Jordanian cell of Al Qaeda.

When the plane landed in Islamabad, the Harry decoy visited the Inter-Services Intelligence headquarters and traveled that night to Peshawar. He would return the next day to Islamabad and then, by a string of commercial flights, fly back to Washington. Harry himself—the "real" Harry, on ice—went to Peshawar overnight, stowed in the back of a truck.

Alex Smite, the Peshawar base chief, met the truck. He knew what was coming, but still, when he got his first look at the body, he called back to Hoffman. "You're sure the director has signed off on this?"

"Relax. It's going to work, and all the paperwork has been filed," Hoffman said. He couldn't blame his man in Islamabad: Life at the agency was about second-guessing.

The corpse was transferred to Smite's Land Rover, a soft-skinned vehicle with darkened windows. The corpse was propped in the right-hand back seat, the place of honor for the visiting guest. A tight seat belt held the body firm. Hoffman called on the encrypted phone, asking for a check on the body temperature. Smite used an actual meat thermometer, which left a hole but was all he could find. The body was about right. It would approach air temperature of thirty-five degrees in about twelve hours. Another twelve hours after that and the body would begin to decompose. But by then Harry would be "dead." Or, to be more precise, his dead body would be full of bullet holes and sprawled on the back seat of the Land Rover.

SMITE MET his Special Forces team in the hills outside Peshawar, at a camp that had been used the last several years as a basing point for mostly fruitless efforts to capture top Al Qaeda officials. He didn't care if the rendezvous was under surveillance. Hell, he wanted to be seen. They formed up a little three-car convoy; there was an armored SUV riding ahead of the Land Rover, and one to the rear. Each SUV carried four heavily armed men from SOCOMM. For the first fifty miles, a Pakistani army escort accompanied the vehicles. But the outriders withdrew when they entered the badlands, and the Americans continued on alone toward Kosa, a village just south of Mingaora in the Northwest Frontier regions. One of Smite's Pashtu agents had radioed ahead to Kosa to advise Azzam that American visitors would be coming.

The arrival in Kosa was carefully choreographed. Ferris watched much of it in real time, thanks to imagery from a reconnaissance satellite overhead. As the convoy neared Azzam's house, gun barrels protruded from the windows of the two SUVs. That was standard procedure in these areas—enough force to intimidate, but not so much that it provoked hostile fire. What wasn't visible from the overhead camera, or to the Pashtu men on the ground, were the four other Special Forces officers who had been hiding in the mountains and had slipped into town that morning.

When Smite arrived at Azzam's house, he followed the same routine as on his last visit to the village four months before. He waited in the Land Rover while a village boy fetched Azzam, and the Pashtu emerged after several minutes with his bodyguards. Smite stepped down from the Land Rover and beckoned for Azzam to join him, and the tribal leader came, just as he had previously. He wanted his money.

"Easy, baby, easy," said Hoffman as he watched the image on a monitor and listened to the sound transmissions. It was like sitting in a tree over the village, peering down on the action.

Smite spoke to Azzam in Urdu, loud enough to be heard by the tribal leader's men, standing twenty yards away. He said he had a special visitor from Washington who wanted to speak to him privately. He had come a long distance to meet the great leader of Kosa and to bring him greetings.

Azzam walked slowly and ceremoniously toward the car. You could imagine him thinking: Why not take the money of these fools from America? Smite held the door for the tribal leader to climb into the back seat of the Land Rover. When Azzam was seated, Smite triggered an electronic lock that prevented anyone inside the vehicle from opening the doors. Then he walked calmly toward the lead SUV and got inside.

When Azzam saw Harry Meeker's body propped up in the back seat, he must have sensed something was wrong, but it took a few moments to register. Perhaps he was avoiding eye contact, being deferential in the manner of the East to a visitor who was going to give him money. Or perhaps they had done such a good job with the disguise that Azzam just waited for the man in the parka to say something. After about five seconds, it registered: A piercing scream was audible on the circuit transmitting from the Land Rover back to Langley. By then it was too late. Azzam couldn't get out.

The Special Forces team heard the scream through their earphones. At that signal, their commander shouted to Azzam's chief bodyguard to put down his weapon. The Pashtu shouted back, and weapons were raised around the clearing. Armed standoffs happened all the time in the frontier areas, and usually the tension was defused with some more shouting and, occasionally, warning shots fired in the air. But this time there was a sudden rip of automatic weapons fire, and two of the Pashtu guards fell to the ground. The other guards opened up on the SUVs, but their small-caliber AK-47 rounds couldn't penetrate the armored skin. As the barrage increased, the thin-skinned Land Rover was pierced with bullets, and then raked stem to stern. To the Pashtus, it felt like a ferocious battle, but it was a setup.

Azzam's men couldn't have known that the initial volley of fire had come from the second Special Forces team behind the SUVs. The hidden Americans had kept the bodyguards in their sights the whole time. One of them carried an AK-47; he concentrated his fire on the Land Rover, spraying a few shots on Harry Meeker's side of the vehicle to make sure he would be hit, too. Azzam's body bounced wildly inside the Land Rover as the bullets tore through him. That was also part of the plan. They wanted Azzam dead, so that the documents in Harry Meeker's briefcase would be the only explanation for what had happened. Harry's body didn't bounce, and it didn't bleed much. But it did ooze.

Smite and the two SUVs retreated under fire back to the main road; the hidden team quickly pulled back into the hills, where their own vehicles were waiting. On the way out, they left behind a battlefield souvenir: an American body, flown out of Afghanistan a few days earlier. The local boys would feel better if they thought they had killed an American soldier in the exchange. Another body would reduce the likelihood that anyone who analyzed the events later would doubt their authenticity.

Smite and his two SUVs roared out of town. Helicopter gunships arrived several hours later, in what seemed a mission to evacuate the American body from the Land Rover—and any sensitive papers he might have had with him. They landed in the village clearing, established a perimeter around the Land Rover and searched the car for twenty minutes. But by that time Harry Meeker was gone. The body and the briefcase had been carried into the mountains by Al Qaeda men, as Hoffman knew they would be. In a few hours, one of the organization's trusted lieutenants would be breaking open the metal briefcase and trying to make sense of its contents. And then they would begin to wonder.

Wire service reports later that day confirmed the ambush of U.S forces and said that an American soldier had been killed. No mention was made of a second American, in civilian clothes, who had been gunned down in his car while meeting with a local tribal leader in the outer circles of Al Qaeda. But no broadcast was needed for that report. By that night, Azzam's meeting with the American was the talk of every village in the border region, and it was openly whispered that Azzam must have been working for the CIA. The hook was in.

• • •

HOFFMAN KNEW it was working. They picked up the chatter on cell phones and Internet links. Suleiman's men were struggling to make sense of what they had found, but they were too junior to make decisions. The senior operational leaders in Al Qaeda would have to decide what to do. ISI captured a courier heading to Karachi. The message was an urgent call for a council, a meeting of the *ulema*, about a matter so serious it might require a decision by the *khalifa* himself. The NSA began to pick up voices it hadn't heard in several years. The members of the network had been forced to break their usual operational security. The worst thing that could happen was happening to them.

Luck is the residue of good planning. Hoffman had done plenty of the latter, and he began to get a bit more of the former. The voiceprint of an NSA intercept from a cell phone in Vienna showed a voice that resembled one on the agency's highest-priority watch list. There was static on the line, but careful technical examination showed that it was the voice of a Syrian-born operative from Hama, Karim al-Shams, who had taken the operational name Suleiman. The master planner was surfacing. The meaning of the call was hard to understand because it was spoken in a private code, but he talked about the martyrdom of Hussein, who was tricked into his death by jealous rivals. Hoffman's analysts thought they understood the essence of what Suleiman was saying: He had been the victim of a trick.

With the NSA's help, the Austrian police were given the likely radius from which the cell-phone call had been made. They cordoned off the neighborhood that night and raided a half dozen apartment buildings. Just before dawn they found the phone, but the man who had been using it evidently had fled.

FERRIS WANTED to get back to Amman for New Year's Eve with Alice, but Hoffman asked him to stay another day. He wanted a celebration. The problem was that the revelers, who knew the secret, were all part of Mincemeat Park. The very fact they worked together was a secret. So Hoffman decided to bring New Year's Eve in to them. He smuggled booze and food into the office. He designated bartenders from among the analysts, and for DJ, he picked a case officer who had always dreamed of being a hip-hop singer. Ferris tried to lose himself in the drink and the music. He even danced with a drunken young woman who worked for Azhar, who slid up and down against his body as if he were the pole in a strip joint.

But Ferris wasn't really there. He felt wasted, now that the operation was over. Whatever would happen now Ferris couldn't control, couldn't even see. The only thing that filled that void was the thought of Alice. He had sometimes wondered, in the years he was with Gretchen, what it felt like to be in love. Now he knew. It came to him that this New Year's Eve he needed to make a resolution. He looked for Hoffman, thinking he should say something to him, but he had disappeared.

Ferris had spoken with Alice earlier in the day, as she was getting ready to go to a party at the Four Seasons with some Jordanian friends. She hadn't tried to make him feel guilty for not being there. She had passed beyond that, into a silent space. Ferris had called her cell phone at midnight Amman time, but she hadn't answered, and it had upset him not to be able to say her name as the year turned and to kiss her by telephone, at least. He had left a message; his cell phone didn't work inside Headquarters, so he couldn't tell if she had tried to return the call.

Ferris left the New Year's revelers and walked to an empty office and dialed Alice's number. Even with the door closed, you could hear the thump-thump of the amplifier. Alice answered on the third ring. She sounded sleepy, a little groggy, even, as if she had taken a sleeping pill.

"There's something I have to tell you," Ferris said. "I've made a New Year's resolution."

"What?" she answered. It was obvious she wasn't really awake.

"I'm ready."

"What?"

"I'm ready for us to be together. The rest doesn't matter."

"Everything matters. When are you coming home?" Her voice was faraway; she sounded almost lost.

"Tomorrow," said Ferris. "I'll fly back New Year's Day and be there late on the second. I'll make you dinner. I'll love you. I'll give you what you wanted."

"That's nice." She was waking up now. "What do you mean?"

"I'll tell you the truth. I won't live any more lies. I don't have to anymore. That's over."

"I don't know what you're talking about, but it sounds sweet."

"That's okay," said Ferris. "I know what I'm talking about."

FERRIS STAYED in the empty office for a while, thinking about Alice and about what he would do in the New Year, if he was serious about his resolution. He would tell her everything. That meant he would have to resign from the agency. There was no other way. It was getting near midnight when Hoffman banged on the door. He was carrying a bottle of champagne and two glasses.

"Open up, you bastard," he grumbled. "We need to talk." He was quite drunk, and the alcohol had dulled his usual exuberance. He seemed almost melancholy. He sat down across the desk from Ferris and filled the glasses with champagne. Ferris waited for him to give some rascally, bravura toast, but he was silent. Eventually Ferris spoke.

"We did it," Ferris said, raising his glass. "I didn't think it was possible, but we pulled it off. We're inside their DNA."

"Yeah, maybe," said Hoffman glumly.

"No maybe about it. Not after they picked up Suleiman's call. He's in trouble. Otherwise he never would have surfaced. We've picked up so many new leads in the last few days, we're going to be able to roll up networks from London to Lahore."

Hoffman was shaking his head. It wasn't just the booze. Something was bothering him. Ferris didn't want to worry about Hoffman's problems, he wanted to think about his own.

"Lighten up, boss. Take a victory lap."

"We haven't won yet."

"We're a lot closer than we were a week ago. Drink up." He clinked glasses with Hoffman and drained most of his own, but the older man didn't drink.

"It's too perfect," said Hoffman. "Something has to be wrong."

"What are you talking about? For chrissake, why don't you take 'yes' for an answer? It worked. God only knows how, but we did it." Ferris didn't want to hear about self-doubt or loose ends. Now that his part of the operation was done, he was thinking about a new life. He wanted Hoffman to go away and leave him to his own future.

"Something's not right. Suleiman should never have surfaced the way he did so quickly. I never expected that. It's almost as if he's probing us, trying to see how much we know."

"Come on, Ed, you're being paranoid. You've been living with this too long. You're suffering postpartum depression. Let it go, man. You have a nice, perverted baby."

"You think so? Why did Suleiman leave his cell phone for us to find? And who's he talking to about betrayal? We still don't have anything real. It's making me crazy."

Ferris laughed and poured himself another glass of champagne. He was tired and, in truth, he wasn't interested in Hoffman's problems. He gave him a kiss on both cheeks, close enough that he could feel the bristle of his whiskers and smell his sour breath. People outside the door were shouting and dancing and chanting the boss's name: "Hoff-man! Hoff-man!" It was almost midnight. People were counting down the seconds. They wanted their boss.

Hoffman emerged from the little office. He was too much of a leader not to take this turn. He got up on a table, lifted his bottle overhead and shouted to the crowd, "Happy New Year! Thanks for so much hard work. More to come. I love you all." He finished a few seconds before the clock ticked down to zero. Perfect timing, as usual. The crowd roared; they were drunk, happy and exhausted. People were singing, and a conga line was forming behind a voluptuous woman who targeted terrorist cells. In the frenzy, Ferris was probably the only one who noticed that Hoffman had slipped away to an empty office and closed the door.

OMAR SADIKI disappeared on New Year's Day. Ferris heard the news as he was heading to the airport to catch his flight back to Amman. The Amman station had been monitoring Sadiki's phones to make sure he didn't get into any mischief. He hadn't answered phone calls on New Year's Day, and the Amman operations chief, who was running things in Ferris's absence, eventually got nervous. Late that afternoon Amman time, he sent one of his Jordanian agents to Sadiki's house to call on him. Inside, the agent found a roomful of confused women and children. Sadiki's wife said her husband had gone out with some visitors that morning and hadn't come back. They had asked for him at the office and at the mosque and at the coffeehouse where the members of Ikhwan Ihsan liked to sit in the afternoons. But there was no sign of him. The wife said her husband had been preoccupied about something. And now whatever it was had caused him to vanish.

Ferris called Hani on a secure phone after talking to the Amman station. Hani said he had already heard the news and apologized repeatedly. He didn't know how Sadiki had slipped through his surveillance. It was his fault, he kept saying. The GID should have watched more closely. They shouldn't have let him disappear. Ferris had never heard Hani sound so remorseful.

"Shit," Ferris muttered to himself when he had finished the conversation with Hani. He had known that something bad would eventually happen to Sadiki, from the moment he had met him in Abu Dhabi. He was too vulnerable, too much a pawn in other people's games. Ferris had willed himself not to worry about the consequences; if you thought too much about what might happen to your agents, you would never run an operation. But Sadiki wasn't even an agent. He was a nothing. He knew nothing. Perhaps that would make it easier for him when his captors began to interrogate him. There was a deeper fear eating at Ferris. He barely wanted to admit it to himself. It wasn't Sadiki he cared about, really, but the fact that Sadiki knew Alice Melville.

"WHY DIDN'T I take him out of Jordan to protect him?" Ferris asked Hoffman when he reached him an hour later. "Why did I just leave him there? He was a sitting duck."

"He'll be fine. They'll bleed him, and he'll say what he knows, which is nothing. He'll deny that he had anything to do with Incirlik. He'll say that he was in Turkey on an architecture project for an American bank. He'll tell them about Brad Scanlon. They won't know what to believe. They'll beat the shit out of him, which will only make his confession weirder, and by the end they'll be more confused than when they started."

"They'll kill him."

"I doubt it, but so what if they do? Like I always tell you, shit happens. If we worried about every Joe who got burned, we'd never get anything done."

"Jesus. You are a cold-blooded bastard."

"So are you," said Hoffman. "You just don't want to admit it."

Hoffman really didn't care. The human beings involved might as well have been pieces of plastic on a checkerboard.

"They'll make *me*," said Ferris. "When they interrogate Sadiki, he'll give me up, and they'll have my identity."

"No, they won't. They'll make your alias, but so what? The disguise was fabulous. The legend was tight. It's backstopped all the way. Stop worrying. Omar will come back to work, maybe missing a few fingers and toes, but so what? You can hire him to build you a beach house."

"They'll interrogate Sadiki about other Americans in Amman. They'll try to find if he had other connections to the embassy, through people who might have known me."

Hoffman sounded exasperated. "Look, Roger, what are you trying to tell me? Because I've got other things to do."

Ferris debated whether to tell Hoffman the black secret that was in his heart—that Omar Sadiki knew an American woman, who knew an American man who worked at the embassy. Whose name was Roger Ferris. But he couldn't bring himself to do it. That was the moment he stopped trusting Hoffman. When he hung up, Ferris began calling Alice Melville. There was no answer, at home or at work or on her mobile. Maybe she was out. Maybe she had a hangover. Maybe she was on a trip. Maybe she had a new lover. Ferris took the night flight for London in a growing panic. He had pushed the bone to the breaking point, and now it had snapped.

30

QUEEN ALIA AIRPORT HAD A stale, post-holiday feel when Ferris arrived late on the afternoon of January 2. The officer at passport control barely looked at the computerized watch list as he stamped him through. The Christmas displays were still up in the duty-free shop, hawking booze and cigarettes to Muslim travelers, but the store was empty. Even the porters who tried to hustle tips by pushing your luggage cart a few dozen yards seemed bored. Outside, a dust storm was blowing in from the desert; Ferris emerged from the terminal into an eerie half-light. The cars were phantoms, visible only at the last minute when they emerged from the brick-red dust. When Ferris breathed deeply, he could taste tiny grains of sand against his teeth.

Ferris called Alice when he landed, but she didn't answer, so he decided to go straight to her place in the old city. He had his own key now, and she always said she liked surprises. He tried to stay calm and positive: If she was out, he would wait for her, yes—maybe make dinner, light the candles, gather the blanket of love around her. They would make a new start—an end, and then a new start. It would take an hour or two, and probably a few glasses of wine, to dissolve the awkwardness. But after a while, she would be making wisecracks about people at work and hectoring him about America and the Arabs. And as they relaxed, he would begin unraveling the lies and stitching something that was real.

Ferris had the airport taxi drop him at her building on Basman Street. He rang the bell downstairs but there was no answer, so he let himself in and climbed up a flight to her apartment. Alice's door was ajar, and at first Ferris was relieved—thinking that she must be home after all. He pushed the door open wide and called into the apartment. When she didn't answer, he went to the bedroom, hoping she might be there, and then the bathroom, calling out her name every few steps. Alice's cat, Elvis, was flopped on the bed, but otherwise the room was empty. The bathroom door was closed, and when he saw that, he imagined that she must be inside and that in a moment he would hear her singing a bluesy Joni Mitchell song. But the bathroom was empty, too, and Ferris began to worry in earnest.

He retraced his steps, pacing each room and calling for her as if she were hiding in the walls. He hadn't looked closely at the apartment on the first pass, but now he noticed things that weren't right. The rug in the entry hall was askew. Alice was a natural tidy-upper; she would never have left it that way. In the salon, the bookshelves were messy. Some of the books had been pulled down and left on a table; others had been shoved back on the shelf upside down or with the spines against the wall. In the kitchen, a breakfast meal was half made—a box of cereal was open, and a carton of milk left out on the counter. Ferris smelled the milk; it hadn't gone bad yet.

Ferris walked down the hall to the small room Alice used as an office; the drawers of her desk were open and some of the files were strewn on the desktop. And her laptop was gone. That was the moment his real fear began—when he realized that whoever had been in the apartment had taken Alice's computer and its electronic files. Perhaps it was a burglary: Alice had gone to work that morning in a rush, left her breakfast half eaten because she was late, and then after she left, a thief had broken into the apartment. Ferris used the phone in the kitchen to dial Alice's number at work; her office phone was ringing, but nobody answered.

It was only as he was hanging up the phone that he saw the blood marks on the floor below the counter. Ferris's cry was almost soundless, a scream of white anguish. He saw more drops of blood just beyond the kitchen, and then a trail every few feet toward the door. Oh Jesus. Where was she? He struggled to keep himself from screaming. The worst thing he could imagine, the thing he had seen in the far distance like a speck on the horizon, was now hurtling toward him. He sat down on the couch and tried to think. Don't panic, he told himself. Make sure she's really missing. He called the main number of the Council for Near East Relief and asked for Hoda, a Palestinian woman who was Alice's assistant. She sounded frightened, too. Alice had never arrived for work that day, she said. Everyone at the office was worried, because that wasn't like her. But then they thought maybe she was with her American boyfriend.

"This *is* her American boyfriend," said Ferris, trying to control his voice. He told Hoda not to summon the police or do anything else until he called her back. He had to think, but on what template? Hoffman's or his own?

The weight of it pressed against him. He had let this happen. Alice had been kidnapped. Someone had broken into her apartment and taken her away. Ferris tried to think rationally. Should he call the embassy security officer and have him contact the Jordanian police? That would be standard procedure for an American abroad. Or call the CIA station and get his deputy over to the apartment now with the FBI man at the embassy, to do the forensics right away before the Jordanians screwed them up? Or call Hani and ask for special help? In the end, he did all three. He didn't care any more about operational cover. That set of worries had disappeared along with Alice. The only mistake now was not doing enough to save her.

. . .

THE TEAM from the embassy arrived first. The FBI agent did a quick sweep of the apartment, taking several blood samples from the floor and dusting for prints in the kitchen, where the assault seemed to have begun. Ferris sat on the couch, his head in his hands, while they gathered the evidence. The ops chief from the station who was acting as his deputy sat down beside him. He was older than Ferris, and had sometimes been prickly in the past, but not now.

"This is your girlfriend, right? What can I do? Just tell me. No rule book on this one."

"I don't know," answered Ferris. "I'm scared something really bad has happened."

"Can you talk about it?"

"Not now. It's too complicated. There's too much you don't know, that nobody knows. But I think she's been kidnapped."

"Hoffman wants to talk to you. I called him right after I heard from you. He wants you to call him ASAP on a secure line."

Ferris shook his head. "Not yet. I have to think."

"Whatever, man. He'll be pissed." The deputy put his hand on Ferris's shoulder. He was going to say more, then stopped himself. Ferris was right. There was too much he didn't know.

Hani Salaam arrived a few minutes later with a technical team from the GID. They secured the scene, put on their plastic gloves and went to work. The radios crackled with calls for additional help. From what Ferris could hear, they were already setting up road-blocks and checkpoints, to stop any cars that might be carrying Alice. Out the window, Ferris could see men in the dark blue uniforms of the Jordanian special forces.

Hani walked toward Ferris, who was at the far end of the salon, back among the mirrors and rosewood. The Jordanian kissed the young American on both cheeks. Ferris could see the concern in the Jordanian man's face, and for the first time, he let himself go a bit. His eyes filled with tears and he put his head on Hani's shoulder, the way he might have on his own father's, and Hani patted his back gently, the way you might do with a child. "It will be all right," he said several times.

Ferris was silent for long while, eyes closed, trying to think what to do. When he opened his eyes again, he asked Hani to come with him to the bedroom, where they could talk. His deputy and the FBI man made to follow, but Ferris waved them off. He closed the door and retreated deep into the bedroom. He reached for the phone at Alice's bedside and detached the handset from the base, and then unplugged the phone itself from the wall. Nobody should overhear what he was about to say. He sat down on the bed and motioned for Hani to sit next to him.

"I need help," Ferris said, his voice shaking slightly. "Will you help me? I need to know that before we talk."

The Jordanian nodded. He was dressed in his usual elegant way, but his manner was grave.

"I think I know what happened," said Ferris. "I'm scared."

"Tell me. We can find her, if you help us."

"I think Al Qaeda has her. They kidnapped her."

Hani shook his head benignly. "Why would they do that? She's a social worker, your girlfriend. She works with Palestinian children. Isn't that right? Why would anyone want her?"

Ferris was entering forbidden territory. He should call Hoffman first and figure out a game plan. But as Ferris considered the CIA's rules and requirements, he tapped a well of self-disgust. That was the thought process that had put Alice in jeopardy. He needed to talk to Hani now and get him mobilized before it was too late.

"Listen to me, and please try to forget about the parts that don't help Alice. Be my friend, please. Can you do that?"

"Of course, my dear. I have always been your friend. Even when you were not mine."

"Okay. The reason they grabbed Alice is that she knows a man we have been working with. He's the Jordanian architect we talked about, Omar Sadiki."

Hani's eyes widened. "She knows him? The Sadiki who is a suspect in the Incirlik bombing? But how have *you* been working with him? How can that be, my dear? Are you telling me he was your agent?"

"Don't ask. Not now. But I'm certain that when Sadiki went missing New Year's Day, it wasn't an escape. The Al Qaeda network must have grabbed him, to find out what he knows. They will be pumping him for any connections he has with the United States. They won't see our hand—it's pretty well hidden. But they will find out that he was friendly with Alice Melville. She met him often through her charity."

"Oh dear," he said abruptly, "I am sorry." It was the worst thing he could have said, for it confirmed Ferris's sense of the extreme danger that surrounded Alice. The Jordanian said nothing for a moment, then spoke again.

"Does she work for you, this Alice? Is she under nonofficial cover?"

"God no. She hates the CIA. She works for that NGO, trying to help people. That's not her cover. It's real. She's exactly what she looks like."

"But someone might think she was working for the agency?"

Ferris stared at Hani. "Yes."

"They might think that, because she knows this fellow Sadiki. And because she knows you."

"Yes." Ferris's voice was barely audible, smothered in the bitterness of his regret.

"And now you need to find her quickly. Before they use any unusual methods to gather information from her."

Ferris was shaken by those words, "unusual methods." He reached for the Jordanian's hand. "Please, Hani. Please help me. I can't get her out without your help."

"And this is no trick?" It was a cruel question, but given what had happened months before, not an unreasonable one. At some level, Hani was still angry. Ferris sat on the bed, his head in his hands again, the picture of powerlessness and remorse.

"Forgive me, Roger. I am sorry I said that." He put his arm

around Ferris's shoulder. "Of course I will help. We have a few deep contacts in the Al Qaeda network we can reach on short notice. We use them only in emergencies, but this is an emergency. They can tell me if she has been taken. I am sure of that. Whether they will know where she is, I cannot say. But let me go now and talk to my men, and begin."

He pulled Ferris to his feet. "Come on. Stand up. God is testing you. He has the power, and you are his slave. *Abd-Allah*. The slave of God. That is what we say. You cannot escape your fate. You must only have trust and faith. So come out with me and talk to my team. We will get started now. You must be strong. If people see that you are weak, they will only be more frightened."

Ferris rose from the bed, went to the bathroom and washed his face, and then walked back to the group that was gathered in the salon.

31 AMMAN / WASHINGTON

THE WIND ROSE OVERNIGHT and the dust storm grew worse. It was a hot wind, blowing in from Saudi Arabia and the Sinai, carrying the Arabian sands in a vast cloud that stretched hundreds of miles. Traffic in Amman slowed to a crawl that evening. Cars put on their blinkers, but even then they were barely visible until you were on top of them. The traffic backed up on the main streets and traffic circles, and the ghostly fleet of motionless automobiles looked like freighters at anchor in a deep fog. The few pedestrians out on the streets wrapped their heads in checkered kaffiyehs and leaned against the wind; all you could see of their faces were the eyes through the narrow openings of the scarves. Nothing could fly, nothing could move. It was kidnappers' weather, a gritty, red-brown world in which you could hide almost anything.

Ferris stayed up most of the night at the embassy, waiting for information. He called Hoffman on the secure phone that evening, when he finally left Alice's apartment. Hoffman was angry at first because of the delay, but when he realized how upset Ferris was, he backed off. He didn't try to apologize. He said the agency had mobilized every asset to try to locate Alice Melville. The trick was to conduct the search in a way that didn't reinforce her captors' belief that she was, as he put it, "a person of interest."

"We'll find her," Hoffman said. He was trying to sound hopeful, but for some reason, his words sank Ferris to a deeper level of despair. He had to put the phone aside for a moment as Hoffman called out, "Hello, are you there?" When Ferris came back on the line, Hoffman told him to get some sleep. Ferris said he would, but he knew that if he lay down on the couch in his office, all he would see were images of Alice: bound and gagged in the trunk of a car, or in a dank basement. Or worse, images of her being interrogated—of an arm being twisted to the breaking point and then snapping.

"You should have told me about Alice, buddy. The fact that she knew Sadiki, I mean. We could have put her on ice for a while."

Ferris didn't answer. He knew it was a lie. Hoffman wouldn't have done anything. He was just covering himself now, after the fact. Ferris's voice was shaky; he was having trouble holding on.

"Now listen to me," said Hoffman. "The most important thing is to let all the normal things happen. The embassy needs to announce that your Alice has been taken. Someone needs to call this outfit she works for, the Near East whatever, and have them issue an appeal. And the person who calls them shouldn't be you, for chrissake. Get the embassy PAO to do it. He should contact the Jordanian papers and give them a handout about Alice. Her boss at this center should call the Arab papers, too, and Al Jazeera and Al-Arabiya, and tell them people have kidnapped a woman who spends all her time helping Arabs. That's what's going to get her freed, okay? The truth. The CIA doesn't have a goddamn thing to do with her. I've talked to the State Department, and the ambassador is going to contact prominent Palestinians and see if we can open up some private channels. He'll say we won't pay to get her released, but obviously we will. Everybody knows that. So sit tight."

All Ferris could do was mumble his assent. He was glad in that moment that Hoffman in his cold-blooded way knew what to do. The announcements were made; the quiet calls went out. By the next morning, Alice's kidnapping was front-page news in every paper in Jordan and America. Most of the stories quoted Alice's boss, the director of the Council for Near East Relief, saying that Alice Melville was "the best friend the Arab people could have" and that her kidnapping was "a terrible mistake." An *Agence France-Presse* story was the first to mention that Alice Melville had a boyfriend who worked as a political officer at the U.S. Embassy. The AFP story quoted an unnamed "Western diplomat," who had to be from the French Embassy, speculating that Melville's relationship with the unnamed American diplomat might be a factor in her kidnapping.

HANI'S MEN from the GID were efficient and, under the circumstances, relatively quick. They matched the blood on the kitchen floor against strands of hair on Alice's brush. The lab technicians at King Hussein Hospital stayed up late and they eventually reported a DNA match: The blood was Alice's. They found lots of prints in the apartment, but most of them turned out to belong to Roger Ferris. They had hoped to find prints in the kitchen, where Alice had evidently been seized, but there weren't any good ones, and the FBI agent said the people who had abducted Alice had probably worn gloves. There were several of them; they had ascertained that from footprints on the floor. The kidnappers had picked the locks downstairs and at the apartment door carefully, with minimum damage. They were skillful professionals, rather than amateur bunglers. Ferris didn't know whether that made it better or worse for Alice.

Hani came to see Ferris at the embassy the next morning. That was unusual; normally the pasha insisted that people come to him. But this was different. They met in a secure conference room the station used for meeting with GID liaison officers. Ferris had a ruined look; the skin of his face, usually taut and tan, was sallow and baggy. The circles under his eyes looked as if they had been drawn with charcoal. He was an image of stress and suffering. These were no longer the same eyes that had once danced with curiosity. Now they had looked to the bottom of the well.

The GID chief embraced Ferris, kissed him three times on the cheeks and then once on the forehead. He could see that the younger man was in pain, and that there was no way to relieve it until Alice was found. Hani tried to stall, out of a habitual politeness, or maybe his fondness for Ferris, but the American took his hand imploringly. He was under Hani's protection now.

"Tell me what you've heard, no matter how bad."

"We reached one of our contacts in the network. He is in Syria, but he knows about operations in Jordan."

"What did your source say?" A note of hope crept into Ferris's voice. He didn't intend it, but he could not stop himself from wanting to hear good news.

"He said it is true. An American woman was seized in Amman. It is just as you said. They have been watching her for some time. They wanted to understand her connection with Omar Sadiki. They do not understand Sadiki. It is very important for them. They took her yesterday morning and moved her quickly out of the city. They put her in the trunk of a car. It is a very high-level operation. Whoever wants this information about her must be very senior. That is good news."

"Why?" Ferris looked at him desperately.

"Because the big ones will be more careful than the little ones. They are not thugs. They want information. They will not hurt her for no reason. So ease your cares a little, my friend. It will be all right."

Ferris dabbed at his eyes with his sleeve. It embarrassed him to cry. "Where is she?" he asked. "Do you know?"

"I cannot say. Our contact would not answer that. I don't think he knows. When we pressed him, he said he thought she was in Syria. I suspect she was taken across the border last night during the dust storm. They would not keep her in Jordan. It would be too dangerous. I think they have taken her to Syria, to talk to her."

"And then what will they do?"

Hani leaned toward the American. He spoke quietly, soothingly. "They will release her. When they realize she can't give them the information they want, they will let her go and try to get it some other way. They are killers, these people, but they are not stupid. That is one thing we have learned."

"What can I do?" asked Ferris. It was his powerlessness that weighed most on him. He felt the same way a parent would feel toward a child who is in mortal danger: Let it be me, not her. Take me. Let me suffer. Why should an innocent person suffer for something she would have despised, if she had known about it?

Hani looked at him with knowing eyes. He wanted to be reassuring, but he could not be. "There is nothing you can do, my dear. Except wait."

THE CIA STATION chief in Vienna called it "Suleiman's Nokia." It was the cell phone the Austrian police had seized, after the NSA had picked up the voice of the Syrian master planner following the uproar over Harry Meeker in Pakistan. The head of Austrian intelligence had turned it over to the station chief, who had sent it back to Langley on the first plane out. Hoffman's technicians had examined it in minute detail, but they had failed to find anything useful. The SIM card, it turned out, had been used to make only the one call they had been able to trace. But Hoffman plugged the phone into a charger to keep it alive, just in case.

On January 4, "Suleiman's Nokia" rang, just once. It wasn't a person calling, but a text message. When Hoffman read it on the display, he was dumbfounded, and then worried. It was as if a plumbing line had clogged and the sewage was backing up, through the telephone, right into his office. The text message said: *"Mr. Ferris, please call Miss Alice, 963-5555-8771."* It was a mobile telephone number in Syria. The NSA and the agency could hunt down the Syrian paperwork about who had purchased the SyriaTel SIM card for that number, but not the caller himself. The phone number was like a onetime pad. It had been used once and then discarded. Hoffman thought for a long while about what to do, and then decided he had no choice, operationally. He called Ferris and read him the message.

32

A s Hoffman read the brief text message, all Ferris could think was that it meant she wasn't dead. The people holding her knew about her link to Ferris. They wanted to trade her, to release her in the hope they could entice her CIA boyfriend. They realized now that she didn't know anything, and so they would use her as bait. But to save Alice, someone had to take her place. Ferris had written down the number as Hoffman spoke, and now he stared at it. He was sweating in the winter cold of his office.

"She's alive," murmured Ferris.

"Probably she's alive," Hoffman cautioned him. "At least, they want you to think she's alive. That's the good part."

"What's the bad part?"

"Well, they know about you. They know you work for the agency. They're sending you a message on Suleiman's phone, which they know we have. So that tells us two things: That the people who have Alice are high up in the network, close to Suleiman. And that they've learned enough from 'Miss Alice' to know that she's your pal. Which is to say, they have interrogated her."

A shiver spiked through Ferris. His mind raced through different scenarios, each darker than the one before.

"I have to call the number," said Ferris. "I have to talk to her."

"I agree. You should call the number. At first I thought it would be a bad idea. It's obviously a trick, to lure you in. But then I decided, so what? We have to play out the hand. But first we have to set things up, okay? We have to have everything in place and ready. This may be our only chance—to get Alice, obviously, and to get a line on Suleiman. This is our best shot. So we want to do it right."

"What does that mean? Do it right? What I care about is Alice."

"I know you do. And if I were in your position, that's all I would care about, too. But there's so much riding on this. You may not realize it right now—and I understand that, really—but our little operation is actually working. They're confused; they don't know what's going on. That's why they grabbed Sadiki. That's why they grabbed Alice. That's why they sent us this weird message. They don't know which end is up. We are getting close."

"I don't care about that anymore. I just want to save Alice. If we wait, she could get killed." Ferris waited for Hoffman's assent, but it didn't come. "For God's sake, don't you understand? I got her into this nightmare."

"Slow down, Roger. We'll do anything to save her—except one thing, which is to screw up this operation. I understand that you feel guilty about putting her in harm's way. And you should feel guilty. You made a mistake not telling me you were involved with a woman who knew Sadiki. That compromised your girlfriend, and all of us. But you aren't going to make it better by going off half cocked. People's lives are at stake. Shit, millions of lives. The country is at war. This isn't just about you and your girlfriend. Are we clear on that?"

Ferris's head was pounding. He didn't say anything, and the silence built on the secure phone line until it was almost a voice itself. Ferris was listening, not to Hoffman, but to that other voice. And then it was obvious.

"Yes," Ferris said. "We're clear on that. You can count on me."

"Attaboy. I know how stressful this must be, but it will work out. You'll get your girlfriend back, and a medal, too."

"A medal," Ferris repeated. But he was already somewhere else.

FERRIS TOOK the Syrian mobile telephone number he had written down and put it in his wallet. He told his deputy he was going home to shower and get some rest. Then he left the embassy and drove himself to GID headquarters. He arrived unannounced and told the chief of staff, who came downstairs in a dither, that he needed to see Hani Pasha immediately. He was asked to wait, but only for a few minutes, before he was escorted to Hani's spacious office.

Hani studied Ferris when he entered the room. Instead of a kiss, there was a handshake, which in the moment was more intimate. "You look terrible, Roger," he said. "I am very sorry for what has happened to you."

"Thanks for the concern, but don't worry about me. I am not the issue. I may be the problem, but I want to be the solution. That's why I'm here."

Hani looked at the American curiously, as if assessing his state of mind. "What are you talking about, *habibi*? You are not making sense today."

But Ferris knew exactly what he was talking about. It had become obvious to him, in a moment of absolute clarity. The light went on in his head and all the elements there had shifted their coordinates slightly to form a new pattern, one quite different but no less precise.

"Ground rules," said Ferris. "This conversation did not happen. I am speaking only for myself, not as an employee of the United States government. You will not inform anyone at the agency about my visit or what we discussed. Ever. Agreed?"

"Unusual rules. Perhaps I can agree. But you tell me so little."

" 'Perhaps' isn't good enough. This one has to be 'yes' or 'no.' What I want to do won't hurt Jordan, and it probably will help. And you will have the advantage of knowing what I'm doing and using it however you want. I don't care. But I need your absolute promise that you will protect me."

Hani tilted his head to one side and lit a cigarette as he pondered the request. He eyed Ferris as if he were measuring him. He took several puffs on the cigarette. The Jordanian seemed almost pleased.

"My dear Roger, I have always said you are one of us. That means you put people before things, and that you put personal honor before anything else. I thought I knew that about you, but until now I could not be sure. So the answer is yes. Of course I will protect the confidence of this conversation. The room is ours alone. But now you must tell me what you want."

Ferris drew near Hani. His voice became low. So far as he knew, the agency wasn't bugging Hani's office. But then, there were many things he did not know.

"Can you make me disappear? So that nobody will find me—including and especially the U.S. government. And then, can you get me into Syria, so that no one will know?"

"I suppose so. That is not difficult for us. We control this space. But what is it that you want to do?"

"I want to contact the people who have kidnapped Alice Melville. I want to offer myself to them as a trade. They don't want her. They want me."

"W'Allah!" Hani opened his palms. "Are you crazy, my friend?"

"No. I just got sane, as a matter of fact. Before, I was crazy."

"But how will you contact them? They are not in the Yellow Pages, Al Qaeda. They are not so easy to find. Even for me."

"They contacted us. They sent a message to me, supposedly from Alice, asking me to call a mobile phone in Syria. Hoffman wants me to wait, so he can figure out some game. Some sting that he thinks will trick them. But his games are all bullshit. You know that better than I do. The only ones we're fooling are ourselves."

"But this is very dangerous, Roger. You know too many secrets. They will want them. It will be . . . unpleasant."

Ferris touched his pocket, and the plastic box that contained the dental bridge and its poison. He had kept it with him for these months, but he had never really imagined he would need it.

"I'll deal with that. But it's the only way to get her out. They won't let her go unless I offer myself in trade. That's obvious, isn't it? Hoffman will never let me do that, which means she's going to die. I have no choice. I have to do this. And I'm going to do it, no matter what you say. But I want you to help me. That way, I'll have a better chance of saving Alice."

Hani didn't say anything. He wasn't a man who made promises easily. Ferris took the Jordanian's hand in both of his own and held it. He would have knelt and kissed it, if he had thought it would do any good.

"Please help me," said Ferris. "I am begging you to help me."

Hani looked at him and smiled. It was an elusive smile, barely a trace on the lips and impossible for Ferris to read, but still there.

"Yes, my dear. Of course I will help you. You are a brave man, and you want to give yourself to save someone that you love. Only a dead heart could refuse you."

HANI MOVED quickly. One of his men drove Ferris's car to Zahran Street and parked it on the street near the Four Seasons. When Ferris's colleagues at the embassy realized that he was missing, they would waste some precious time looking for him at the hotel. Hani made a few phone calls and met alone with his deputy; then he escorted Ferris to the GID garage where his big BMW limousine was parked. They took seats in the back and Hani closed the curtains. In a country where the GID's authority was unquestioned, they were now all but invisible. Ferris patted his pocket again, for reassurance.

They drove north from Amman toward the Syrian border. Hani opened the curtain once they were on the highway so that he could see the scenery, but Ferris left his side closed. They avoided the four-lane route through Al-Mafraq and instead took the old Highway 15 that crosses the Syrian border a few miles west, at Dera'a. As the big sedan rolled north, Hani explained his plan. Ferris asked a few questions, but only to make sure that he understood. Ferris's cell phone rang once. It was his deputy from the station. Ferris said groggily that he was trying to sleep and would be in the office the next morning after stopping at the gym.

Just before the Jordanian border town of Ramtha, Hani ordered his driver to take a side road that wound along the border. When they reached a little village called Shajara, they turned onto a dirt road and then into the driveway of a small compound of cement-block buildings whose roofs were topped by a bristle of antennae. In the driveway was a rusted Mercedes taxi with Syrian license plates. The border was less than a mile away. Hani led Ferris into one of the buildings. GID officers in plain clothes, who had been awaiting his arrival, greeted their chief with kisses and a tray of cookies and sweet tea. Hani waved them off and asked for a quiet room on the top floor. He closed the door and turned to Ferris.

"Now is the time to make your phone call," Hani said.

"Do you have a clean phone?" asked Ferris.

"Of course." Hani removed a new Samsung clamshell phone from his coat pocket and handed it over. Hani had an extra earpiece, so he could listen in. Ferris managed a thin smile at the Jordanian's careful preparation. He took out his wallet and found the number he had scribbled down while Hoffman was reading the text message. He dialed the number carefully on Hani's phone, 963-5555-8771. It rang three times before someone answered.

"Hello," said the voice in English. They were waiting for him. This phone could only have one caller.

"This is Mr. Roger Ferris from the CIA. I want to talk to Miss Alice."

"Okay, mister. Thanks God you are calling. I have question for you, to make sure you are you, please."

"Fine. What's your question?"

"Where do you take Miss Alice for dinner, first time?"

Ferris felt a well of nausea. They had gotten that out of her through interrogation. Either that or he'd been under surveillance.

"The Hyatt Hotel in Amman. The Italian restaurant."

"Yes, okay. Thank you, sir. And what is the name of the cat Miss Alice keep in her apartment, please?"

"Elvis. The cat's name is Elvis."

"Right. I think you are you. Mr. Ferris."

"Okay, can I talk to Alice now, please."

"Yes, but I am very sorry. Miss Alice not here. But she ask me to give you the message, if you call."

"What is the message?" Ferris was brusque. He wanted to cut the haggling and get to the point.

"If you want to see Miss Alice, you must go to where I say. You only. No trick, or Miss Alice will not be alive."

"Where should I go?"

"To Syria, please."

Ferris's eyes gleamed with tension and exasperation. "Yes, fine, but where in Syria?"

"Yes, mister. To Hama. That is where Miss Alice is."

Hani was nodding as he heard the name of the meeting place. Hama was Suleiman's hometown. It was where the ruinous history had begun, with the destruction of the Muslim Brotherhood in 1982.

"It must be a trade," said Ferris. "Unless I see Alice, I will not come to you."

"Yes, sir, yes, sir." The Arab voice on the end sounded eager, as if he could not believe that the American was actually going to give himself up. And he had a proposal all ready. "Sir, you will see Miss Alice at the *norias,* the waterwheels on Orontes River, in the center of Hama. You see her there. You see that she is safe and free. Then you call number and you wait for us. We will be watching. You leave, we will be killing Miss Alice, and you, too."

Ferris paused and looked toward Hani. He would need backup of some sort, to make sure that Alice would be protected once she was released. Hani seemed to have read his mind. He nodded and whispered the words, "We will be there."

"I agree to the trade," said Ferris. "What is the number I should call, once I see that Alice is free?"

"Sir, please call 963-5555-5510. Not me. I am only relay man. When they answer, tell them in Arabic that you are Mr. Roger Ferris from CIA and that you are ready to meet them, right now in Hama. You want number again?"

Hani had scribbled the number on a piece of paper and handed it to Ferris.

"Let me read it back to you, to make sure I have it right. 963-5555-5510."

"Yes, sir."

"And I should tell the person who answers that I am Roger Ferris from CIA and I am ready to meet them now in Hama."

"*Mumtaz*, mister. Very good. Okay. And when will you meet us in Hama, please?"

Ferris looked to Hani. The Jordanian scribbled a few words and gave the paper to the American.

"I will be in Hama tomorrow morning, at eight A.M., at the old waterwheels on the river. If Alice is not there, the deal is off. Do you understand?"

"Oh, yes, sir. I will tell them. I am relay man only. I think you are in a big hurry." He said it curiously, as if he could not fathom why Ferris was so eager to be tortured.

"Just make sure Alice is there. Then you get what you want. Otherwise, nothing." Ferris broke the connection.

"*W'Allah,* Roger, you are a brave man," said Hani, taking his hand. "No matter what happens to you, Alice Melville will know how you loved her. I will make sure of it. You will live in her heart."

THE MERCEDES taxi was downstairs. The driver was smoking a cigarette, ready to leave. The neighborhood beyond the compound was alive with the sounds of an Arab village at dusk. Children home from school, playing soccer in the dirt; mothers shouting out orders and complaints as they prepared the evening meal. The world had that sense of time suspended, as the shadows lengthened, the colors deepened and daylight gradually disappeared.

It was time to go, Hani said. He outlined his plan for Ferris. The car would take Ferris north into Syria through the Dera'a crossing. The driver was a smuggler, and the GID had used him often before. He had paid his bribes over many years to Syrian customs officials, who were so thoroughly corrupt that it was all one big family. Ferris would ride the few miles across the border in a compartment under the back seat. The uncomfortable part would only last thirty minutes or so; then Ferris could ride in the passenger seat. Hani would send two chase cars north to accompany the taxi through Damascus and then up to Hama. They would have to drive all night. Hani would have another team waiting in Hama. The moment Alice was released, they would surround her and bring her back to Jordan. There would be plenty of guns in case anything went wrong, but the Jordanian assured him that nothing would go wrong. And then, when the moment was right, Hani's men would do their best to rescue Ferris.

Hani handed Ferris a small electronic device that appeared to be a Bic lighter. "If you are in trouble and you can't wait, press the button," he said. "We'll come get you." Ferris took it and thanked his friend. The talk of rescue was generous. But Ferris knew that this was a one-way trip.

33

F ERRIS WENT DOWN TO MEET the Syrian taxi driver alone. The man was in his forties, with furtive eyes and a thick moustache that hung over his lips like a paintbrush. The driver opened the back door of the corroded red Mercedes, pulled a hidden latch and yanked up the back seat, revealing a compartment just big enough for a body. A matted carpet was laid over the bare metal and there was a bottle of mineral water. "Business class," Ferris muttered. The driver nodded, uncomprehending. Ferris climbed in and contorted his body into the small space. It smelled of sweat and urine. Evidently Ferris wasn't the first hidden traveler. The driver said he would tap three times when it was safe for Ferris to come out. Then he lowered the seat, and Ferris was encased in darkness.

Ferris wasn't a morbid person. As a child, he had worried about death the way most children do, trying to comprehend the idea of his own nonbeing. The idea was too complicated and depressing, and so he mostly forgot about it. He had a period in his mid-teens when he feared that he would die a virgin, but after Priscilla Warren took care of that he stopped thinking about nothingness. Now, lying in the dark and smelly hold of the taxi, Ferris was forced to contemplate the prospect of his own nonexistence. He wasn't afraid so much of dying, but of the pain that would precede it. His poison dental bridge was in his pocket, and he pondered when he should use it. If he waited too long, it might be too late: They would take it from him before he could bite down on the poison and save himself from agony. But if he used it too early, he might kill himself unnecessarily, in the moment before rescue or reprieve. He would squander the chance to live a normal life, grow old with Alice and have children. That last negation bothered him most. He would have lived for nothing, as far as the species was concerned. That truly was an unproductive life, worse even than dying a virgin.

The taxi slowed as they neared the Jordanian border post. Ferris tensed, but the stop was quick and painless. Hani must have put in the fix. The car rumbled forward into no-man's-land, and Ferris sank again into his black reverie. If he lived, perhaps he could have children with Alice; if he lived, perhaps he might grow old with her. "Perhaps" was all he had. His hope was the same one that sustains the cancer patient even as his body shrivels and he can't eat or swallow—the idea that somehow the sentence of death will miraculously be lifted; that he will drag his brittle bones to the everlasting gate and trick the gatekeeper into another few hours, days, years. Ferris understood, in the abstract, that pain could become so awful that he would want to pass into nothingness—but not if there was a chance of rejoining Alice. They could smash his legs with a crowbar, shatter his kneecaps, pound his spine with a sledgehammer—yet in each moment of agony he would be thinking of Alice, and of staying alive for her.

The image of her was clear and perfect, and in a rush of certainty, Ferris did something impulsive. He removed the dental bridge from his pocket and laid it down on the dirty rug of his secret compartment. If he kept the poison, he would be tempted in his fear to use it; and if he used it, he would give up not just life, but love. He would die for nothing. He had made a promise to Hoffman to protect the secrets, to kill himself before he betrayed things that might kill others. But keeping that promise would mean breaking another that now surmounted it. He pushed the poison farther away, deeper into the blackness.

THE TAXI halted suddenly, and Ferris heard a murmur of Arab voices. His driver was addressing someone he called "Captain." Ferris caught an edge of fear in the driver's voice. The door opened and then slammed shut, and he heard footsteps around the car. Something was wrong. The captain was shouting at the driver, in the way of military officers who know their power in the moment is absolute. The border was closed, said the captain; it was too late; the driver knew the rules. The driver kept repeating a name. Abu Walid said it was okay. Abu Walid said no problem. Ask Abu Walid. Ferris heard the sound of boots on the pavement, the voice of the driver protesting that it was a mistake, and then they were both gone.

Ferris remained huddled against the floorboard of the taxi. He was frightened, in a new way. What if he died right there—or just as bad, was taken away, put in a Syrian jail and then sent back to Jordan? Alice would surely die: The kidnappers would be waiting for Ferris in Hama, and when he didn't arrive, they would kill her. That was the worst thing, Ferris realized—not his own death, but Alice's. The only meaning his life had now was the possibility of saving her. If that were lost, then he would kill himself and be done with it.

The wait stretched to many minutes. Ferris heard occasional shouting in the distance, from what must be the captain's headquarters. Ferris's head hurt from breathing in the dust of the road and the fumes of the gas tank. His legs throbbed from so long in the cramped position. The pain had grown from a prickly feeling of pins-and-needles to sharp spasms in his joints and muscles. He began to think he would prefer anything—capture, even—to this pain. But he knew his mind was playing tricks. In comparison to the pain he would feel later, this was just a pat on the cheek.

Ferris waited. It might have been thirty minutes, an hour. In the dark of his crypt, he lost his sense of time. With the engine off, there was no heat in the car, and the January night air was bitterly cold. He couldn't move to warm himself, so the chill crept into his bones. Ferris wanted to die, but even more, he wanted Alice to live. He felt for the poison and remembered it was gone, deep into the recess of his hiding place. He was glad to be rid of the temptation.

He heard more shouting, from a voice that sounded like the captain's; and then the submissive voice of his driver, and heavy footsteps approaching the Mercedes. The driver had given him up. He sounded meek as a mouse now; Abu Walid hadn't bailed him out and, in the glare of an interrogation room, he had decided to give up his passenger so that he could live to smuggle another day. The footsteps got nearer, the metal studs on the boots clicking against the pavement until they were next to the car. A door opened. They must be opening the back door; in another instant they would be hauling Ferris out of the compartment and it would be over.

But the driver was opening the front door. In his wheedling voice, he was thanking the captain, telling him that Abu Walid would be very grateful for the captain's help, and wishing that God grant the captain long life and good health, and the captain's sons, good health to them, too, yes, sir, thank God. The door closed. The key turned, and the ignition sparked to life. The driver put the Mercedes in gear and pulled away from the border post, calling out a last pliant farewell.

They stopped for a customs check, but it was perfunctory. Ferris was frightened when he heard the trunk open, but it closed just as quickly. A customs man thanked the driver for the carton of cigarettes and waved him on.

THE TAXI rumbled along for another twenty minutes, moving slowly through the narrow streets of Dera'a and then faster as it connected with the main highway again. Ferris heard a whoosh of air each time the Mercedes veered left to pass other cars and trucks. He worried that the driver might keep him in this box all the way to

Hama, but the car at last began to slow and swerved to the right. Ferris heard the crunch of gravel under him as the taxi pulled onto the shoulder and lurched to a stop. The driver opened the back door, pounded three times on the seat above Ferris's head and then tugged up the seat. Ferris couldn't move at first, his legs and arms were so stiff. The driver had to pull him from the compartment. He gave Ferris an old cap to cover his face and a frayed wool jacket of the sort a Syrian taxi driver's friend might wear, and sat Ferris next to him in the front seat. Ferris didn't think until later that he had left the poison behind in the secret compartment. He didn't try to retrieve it.

THEY DROVE through the night. Damascus was crowded and noisy, even at midnight. The Palestinian refugee camps that lined the southern edge of the city were twinkling with the sweet fellowship of the poor. The coffeehouses were open, the men tugging at their narghilehs and blowing out clouds of smoke; the bakeries were selling fresh pastries and sweets for those with a late-night sweet tooth. In the cinder-block apartments down the narrow alleyways of the camp, you could see the flickering blue lights of the television sets, each with its own satellite dish, connecting people to a modern world they loved and hated at the same time. When they reached the city center, people were still out strolling. Many of the women along the sidewalks were dressed primly in headscarves and shapeless smocks; others were done up like tarts, in low-cut blouses open even on this winter night. A few made eye contact with Ferris. Perhaps they really were prostitutes, but Ferris knew that in Muslim eyes, it didn't matter whether they were paid for their services or not. They were defiled by the ways of the West.

After they left Damascus, Ferris dozed off for a few minutes. He awoke suddenly with the image of Alice bound and bloody in a basement. It wouldn't go away. They stopped for food and coffee at a place the driver knew, just south of Homs, which he insisted was clean, but when Ferris went to use the toilet, it was a hole in the floor that stank of shit. It was nearly three A.M. The next big city north on the highway after Homs was their destination of Hama. Ferris told the driver he wanted to rest until six-thirty in the restaurant parking lot. The police wouldn't bother them there, and he didn't want to get to Hama so early that he would have to wait conspicuously for the rendezvous. A few other cars were stopped in the lot; he wondered if any of them were Hani's men. Ferris dozed again, fitfully. He was awakened by first light. The orange rim burst over the barren landscape to the east, turning the nearby sky from purple-pink into bright yellow-white; he wondered if he would live to see another sunrise.

THEY REACHED the center of Hama around seven-thirty, still too early. Ferris told the driver to drive to the northern suburbs and then turn back. As they drove, he looked at the buildings along the road. Some were ruined shells, and he realized that this must be one of the neighborhoods that had been destroyed when Hafez al-Assad rolled his tanks into the Muslim quarters of the city nearly three decades before and fired at point-blank range, leveling the houses and destroying anything inside. The Muslim Brothers had fled to caves and tunnels in the old city, near the river, but they had been driven out by flame throwers, gas and bullets. This was the world that had created Suleiman. The hatred that had been spawned here was now focused on America and, this day, on Roger Ferris.

The driver parked the taxi at the bus stop near the Orontes River. Ferris sat in the car and watched for Alice. It was nearly eight. He told the driver he was going for a walk and that if he didn't return in two hours, the driver should leave without him. He gave him a hundred dinars, which he knew was too much, but what was he going to do with money when he was dead? He got out of the car and began walking toward the ancient wooden wheels that spooned water from the river and deposited it into the town's aqueducts. He looked all around, wondering where Hani's men might be, if they were there at all. Better not to look too curious. He put his head down and turned up the collar of his jacket against the chill. His bad leg was stiff from the long, cramped ride, and he was limping more than usual.

It was a cloudless morning. The winter sky was azure at the horizon, rising to a deep royal blue. Ferris sat down on a bench by the Orontes, near the entrance to the biggest of the waterwheels. The river was a placid blue-black, and in the stillness you could see reflected the old Al-Nuri Mosque and the other stone buildings that lined the banks; in the bright morning sun, the wooden wheels had a golden glow. He sat for ten minutes, then fifteen, scanning the riverbank. There were more than a dozen waterwheels arrayed on the two sides of the river, and he couldn't be sure where she would be. He got up once and made a tour of the area and then returned to his bench. He had the sense that he was being watched, but he couldn't tell the touts and vendors from the terrorists.

Ferris was squinting into the morning sun when he saw a group of Arab men approach the *norias* from the western side. A woman was with them. She was wearing a long black dress and a headscarf, but there was something about her walk that made Ferris look twice. He rose and moved toward the group, which was now about seventy-five yards away. As he did so, the group stopped and parted. One of the men said something to the woman, it was like an order, and she removed her scarf. The man gave her a little push and then he and his friends ran away, so that she was standing alone by the riverbank.

Ferris moved more quickly toward her, so that he could see her face and be sure. In an instant that stopped time, he knew that it was Alice. The blond hair, the graceful body, the wide smile as she sensed that she was free. They must have cleaned her up, but Ferris didn't want to think about that. All he knew was that she was free. He called out her name and began to run toward her, but his bad leg was wobbly and he stumbled and fell. In the wind and street noise, she didn't hear him, but that was all right. She was free.

As Ferris moved toward Alice, he saw three Arab men, not like the others, but well dressed, converging on Alice. They were much closer to her, and Ferris could hear one of them calling out Alice's name. He was frightened for a moment, but he realized that he recognized the voice, and as he looked more closely, he saw that it was Hani. The Jordanian had traveled north overnight to rescue Alice himself. Ferris cried out her name again, but Hani had reached her now and had his arms around her, and he and his men were leading her toward a van that was parked nearby. She seemed relieved to see him, almost as if he were a lost friend. Ferris shouted as he tried to run on the gimp leg, but a Syrian policeman moved toward him, thinking that in his cap and ragged coat Ferris must be a Syrian, so he slowed. He called out, but she couldn't hear. Now Hani was opening the door of the van, and Alice was in the back seat with a guard on either side, and the van was backing away.

Ferris stopped calling Alice's name. The van was moving quickly, back toward the Damascus highway. Tears came to his eyes. The impossible had happened. The kidnappers had been true to their word. So had Hani, in his promise that he would protect her when she was released. The only piece of the bargain left unfulfilled was Ferris's. He thought about running, but he knew that Alice would be vulnerable until she was out of Syria. He needed a trick, a ruse, something to buy time. They were waiting for his call. He took out the cell phone and then put it back in his pocket. Let them wait. He felt a dark contentment, for he knew now that Alice would survive, no matter what.

34

THE CELL PHONE RANG five times before Ferris answered. An Arab voice asked if this was Mr. Roger Ferris, and he said yes. "We are waiting for you, sir. Why you have not called, please?" Ferris apologized and then hung up. He didn't want to die if he didn't have to. He stood up from the bench and began to move away, wondering in which direction he could run. But as he took his first steps, he saw two bearded men in winter parkas walking toward him.

Ferris reached for Hani's electronic pager; it was in the pocket where, until a few hours before, he had kept the poison. He pressed the button of the mock-lighter once, and then again. The two men were on either side of him now. He felt the blunt muzzle of a gun against his ribs. The man holding the gun had bright eyes and a face that was hammered gold, the color of wild honey. He looked Egyptian. Ferris thought he recognized his face from the agency's mug shots of Al Qaeda operatives, but he couldn't be sure.

"You are Ferris?" asked the Egyptian.

"Yes." The gun pressed deeper into his side at the confirmation.

"This is no trick?"

Ferris shook his head. "No. This is no trick. You did what you promised. I will do what I promised."

"And what is that? What will you do for us?" queried the Egyptian. He had an odd smile and a cruel set to his eyes. He was trying to hide a lifetime of hatred.

"Wait and see," said Ferris. He looked for Hani's men out of the corner of his eye, but he saw no one. They were taking care of Alice. That was all he had asked them to do; he was expendable. That was the deal. But Ferris was truly frightened now, smelling the acrid garlic breath of the two men and knowing that he was slipping into their control. He wanted to scream, or bolt and run, but he knew that would only hasten his death and he had resolved to hold on to life as long as he could.

"We are sorry we treat you like a prisoner," the Egyptian whispered in his ear. "We do not know if you tell truth or lies, so we must make you prisoner. I am sorry."

Ferris stared at his captors. Who were they kidding? Of course he was a prisoner. He wondered now if he should have discarded the poison and decided yes, the temptation to use it would have been too great. He might already be dead.

The two men walked him to a yellow Hyundai that was around a corner from the main square. A driver was sitting at the wheel; next to him was a bearded guard, cradling a gun across his lap. This was the bridge of no return. Ferris reached one more time for his coat and pressed Hani's pager, but the gunman pulled his hand away. He patted Ferris's pockets. "What is this?" he asked, pulling the device from Ferris's pocket. It looked like a lighter, but it didn't seem to work. He pressed and pressed, waiting for the flame, and then grunted and tossed it away.

"Maybe you will trick us?" The Egyptian scowled. Ferris began to protest, but a hand quickly gagged his mouth, and then tape. They patted him down in earnest now, and found the cell phone tucked in the pocket of his trousers. The Egyptian took that, too. The other gunman fished Ferris's wallet and passport out of his pockets and put them in his parka. They pushed him into the back seat of the little Hyundai and arrayed themselves on either side. The car rumbled a few hundred yards and turned into a dusty alley and rolled down it far enough that they couldn't be seen from the main road; there they blindfolded Ferris, bound his wrists and ankles and pushed him to the floor of the back seat.

"We are sorry," said the Egyptian again to the bundle that was now Ferris. He and the other captor moved to another car that was waiting in the alley, and the convoy departed. Why were they apologizing? He was a dead man.

THEY TRAVELED for several hours. Ferris wasn't sure how long—the blindfold was so tight he had no sensation of light or dark—but he felt the air get cooler, and he sensed that it was afternoon. He guessed that the cars had been heading north, toward Aleppo, or east, toward Iraq. The convoy stopped eventually. They left him there hog-tied on the floor, while his captors climbed up some stairs. After a few minutes, people returned and opened the back door of the car. They pulled Ferris out headfirst and carried him like a rolled-up carpet, manhandling his neck and feet, up some stairs and into a building, then downstairs again into what Ferris assumed must be a basement. So this is where it ends, thought Ferris.

But it wasn't. Two men trundled downstairs, grunting Koranic aphorisms at each other. They left Ferris's blindfold in place but untied his hands and feet, gave him water and food and let him use a stinking toilet. Then they tied him up again and dropped him on a dirty mattress and told him to sleep. And he did, a fitful sleep, broken by every sound from the floor above.

They moved Ferris again the next morning. The blindfold had loosened from the sweat and pressure. This trip wasn't as long—no more than half an hour. Ferris guessed that they were moving him from one safe house to another—probably in Aleppo. Iraq was too crazy a place to hide, even for them. They went through the same routine, hauling him about like a bound-up rug, carrying him upstairs and down. In this second safe house, he was again given food and water and allowed to use the toilet. This one didn't smell so bad, and the toilet actually had a seat. Ferris had to move his bowels. They sat him down and turned their backs. Then they bound him again and left him sitting in a chair, but not for long. There was noise upstairs, the sound of several cars arriving, muffled voices of welcome, the sound of prayers.

Ferris dreaded each time someone came downstairs, thinking that now the torture would begin. So when he heard the creak of the stair board, his stomach tightened. But the voice that greeted him this time wasn't so gruff. He undid Ferris's bonds, hand and foot, then his gag, and then, to Ferris's astonishment, his blindfold. It was the same honey-colored face that had approached him in Hama and put a pistol in his side. The Egyptian handed Ferris a razor, shaving cream and a towel and led him back to the bathroom. Ferris could see now that it had a shower. "Make yourself clean," he said. "You are our guest."

They were softening him up. Ferris didn't know what that meant, but it couldn't be good. He closed the bathroom door, turned on the shower and let the water run down his body. He was filthy, from riding in hidden compartments and on car floors and sleeping on a grimy bed; he watched the dirt swirl down the drain and imagined for a moment that his whole body could dissolve into that hole in the ground, too. It felt good to be clean, and better to be clean-shaven. He looked at his eyes in the mirror. They were sunken, rimmed with dark shadows. The spark was gone; what was left was hard and gray and implacable. He wondered if Alice could love such a face, in the event that he should survive to see her again. But then, she must have been changed by the nightmare she had lived. They were not the same people. Ferris toweled himself, combed his hair and prepared to meet whatever awaited him upstairs.

They came for him at midmorning, after another car had arrived. He was blindfolded again, but only loosely, and then led up two flights of stairs to a large room in the back of the building. The room itself was dark, curtains drawn, but they turned on a bright light and sat Ferris down in a chair and told him to wait. From behind his head, someone untied the blindfold and let it drop. In the shadows at the far end of the room, Ferris saw what looked like a video camera mounted on a tripod. Oh dear Jesus, he thought: They are going to film my beheading, just the way they did with the others. A white jolt of fear lit up his body. He closed his eyes to try to calm himself. At least it would be quick, when it finally came, he thought. He hoped he could meet it in silence.

AFTER TWENTY minutes, a man entered the room and took a chair across from Ferris. Ferris stared for a very long while. He formed the words *My God!* on his lips, but no sound emerged. He wanted to speak, but even more, he wanted to understand.

It was Suleiman. His hair was lighter, his beard had been trimmed, but it was unmistakably the same man Ferris had seen so many times in briefings and mug books and photos pinned to office walls. In person, he looked even more intelligent than he had in the pictures. His eyes were pools that drew you in rather than giving off beads of reflected light. There were crow's-feet at the edges of the eyes, and a slight upward turn at the corners of the mouth, so that he seemed, oddly, to be smiling. There was a curiosity about this face and also a stone-cold hardness. Suleiman seemed to be waiting for Ferris to say something, as if he were a prize parrot that had been purchased in the souk. Perhaps he wanted to be flattered.

"I know you," said Ferris. "You are a famous man for me, but I did not think I would ever see your face except in a photograph. It must be an honor, that you have come to meet me."

"Oh, but I had to see you myself, Mr. Ferris. It would have been wrong to leave this meeting to anyone who did not have the knowledge."

Ferris didn't understand. "And why is that? You could have assigned any of your men to interrogate me."

"They would not be worthy. Because, sir, you are the first."

"The first," Ferris repeated. He did not want to give anything away, but he had no idea what Suleiman was talking about. The first CIA captive? The first American prisoner? He was speaking in riddles.

"Oh yes. You are our first defector." Suleiman smiled. There was almost a twinkle in those dark eyes. "The very first. And from the famous CIA! I had to meet you myself, so that I could decide if you are what you say. What you bring to us is so good, we think it must be bad. But I think it is a great day. And you see, we are ready for you. I have the video camera, to record this moment and send it to Al Jazeera for all our Muslim *umma*, so that they can rejoice with us. And with you. We are making a movie, you and me. A movie for the world."

Ferris narrowed his eyes but said nothing. Ferris had traded himself to save the life of Alice, that was true, but he was hardly a defector. If the video camera wasn't there to record his interrogation and beheading, what was its purpose? Instinct told him he should say as little as possible and let Suleiman establish the contours of their interaction.

"Thank you," said Ferris. "I am in your hands now."

"May God grant you good health. Would you like tea? Or coffee? Some water, perhaps?"

"Coffee," said Ferris. "And some mineral water."

Suleiman shouted out some orders to a coffee boy. Even in the terrorist safe house, they had minions. Then he turned back to Ferris.

"I have a first question for you. I am so curious. I cannot wait. When did you realize that you were a Muslim? When did you hear *al-dawa*—the call?"

"I'm sorry," said Ferris. He stuck a finger in his ear, as if he were clearing out a layer of wax. He wanted to hear the question again.

"When did you know that your grandfather had come from Lebanon into Bosnia before he came to America? Was it before you joined the agency? I wondered, you see, whether they would let a real Muslim into the CIA where he could learn the secrets of the Jews and the Crusaders."

Ferris tried to clear his head so that he could think—tried to see in his mind the pieces of this puzzle. Suleiman seemed to think he had volunteered to come into their lair because he was a Muslim. He wondered what was the right answer to his question, the one that would give him the most flexibility. He remembered his curiosity as a boy about his roots—never quite knowing what country it was that his grandfather had left, never understanding the secret that was buried under the grunts and mumbles. Could it be that his grandfather hadn't been a Catholic at all, as he claimed, but a Muslim? It was possible, certainly. He thought about his conversations with his mother only a few weeks ago, and that prompted him to make up an answer.

"It was later. After I joined the CIA. My mother found some family papers. That's when I knew."

"*Al hamdu l'Illah.* I think we have seen these papers. They are the ones you sent to us through your intermediary."

Ferris nodded, but his head was spinning faster. What papers? What intermediary? Who was the author of the elaborate game that was being played out? Into whose artifice of tradecraft had he fallen?

"We thought at first that the papers must be forgeries," Suleiman continued, "until we checked them ourselves in Lebanon, in the records of your vilayet of Tripoli. And they were real. They listed the birth of your grandfather. There was even a record in Tripoli of your father's birth in America. The others still thought you were a liar, but I began to wonder."

"Thank you," said Ferris.

"So I will call you by your real family name, Fares. That is right, now that you are with us and so near the land of your ancestors. Did you know that? The Sunnis of Tripoli are just a few dozen miles away, across the border. That is a gift for you, Fares. Perhaps we will let you go home, when we are finished with you. Would you like that? First, we will take you to Damascus, to give the tape of your testimony of faith to Al Jazeera, for all the *umma* to see. They are waiting for my word. And then we will go to Tripoli, to the home of your ancestors. Does that journey please you?"

"I would like that very much." A trace of a smile came across Ferris's face. He saw the contour of the legend, even though he still didn't understand who had constructed it or why. "I would like to go home. It has been a long voyage for me, to bring me here."

"I know. *Allah u akhbar.* God is the greatest. Thanks for the God."

"*Allah u akhbar,*" said Ferris. "*La ilaha ill-Allah, Muhammad-ur-rasool-ullah.*" He had just spoken the declaration of faith, the words that make a Muslim a Muslim: There is no god but God, and Muhammad is his prophet.

Now it was Suleiman's turn to smile. He placed his hand over his heart and then leaned toward Ferris and kissed him three times on the cheeks.

"Your information has been very good, Fares. The numbers of our telephones that were on your watch list. The Web sites that were not secure. The games you have played with us, to make us show ourselves. The fact you knew our codes, even the code name I use with my couriers, Raouf. At first many of us thought it was a trick, like all the other CIA tricks. It made no sense. Why would a CIA man give such information to Al Qaeda, except to trick us? But the information was so good. And then when you sent us word that you were really a Muslim and we checked the records of your family, we thought that perhaps it might be true. That was a reason we could understand. What is worse than to be a Muslim in the land of the *kufr* and the *jahil,* the unbelievers and the ignorant ones?" He stopped and looked at Ferris, studying him with those black eyes.

"I am alone," Ferris said. He was going to say more, but he stopped. He still didn't know what the right answers were, but that much certainly was true: He was alone.

"And then when you said through your intermediary that you wanted to come to us, here, and be part of us, we thought either this man is crazy, or it is true. He is what he says he is. The only test is to meet you and see what you have for us. Then we can know if this gold is real."

Ferris was quiet. He didn't want to put a foot wrong, and he thought the silence would work better for him than too much talk. "It is true," he said at last. "I am what I have told you."

"Oh yes," said Suleiman. "I am sure of it." But Ferris could tell from his voice that the Syrian-born man was in fact far from certain of his bona fides.

Ferris needed more information. He was still feeling his way in the dark. It was obvious that the pleasantries were ending and the real interrogation would begin soon. He tried to think how he could learn more without giving himself away. He needed to know how Suleiman's version of reality had been assembled. Now Ferris was only guessing. He needed to know more.

"I am glad that you listened to my intermediary," said Ferris. "That was an important part of my plan."

"Oh yes. We trusted Mr. Sadiki. We have known of him for a long time. He is the friend of our friends. And when he began giving us the messages from you, we were interested. And we understood the double game you had to play, so that your meetings with Hajj Omar would not be suspicious. Oh yes."

"And the bombing in Incirlik?" asked Ferris, still probing to see how much Suleiman knew.

"That was very good. The fake bombing. And making everyone think Hajj Omar had done that, to cover your tracks. Very good. It took us some days to understand that." His eyes narrowed down to slits, and his lips formed a thin, dubious smile. "I mean, I think that we understand. But we will find out later, yes? You are a friend, Fares. You are part of the *umma,* the *Dar al Islam.* You will help us."

Ferris sat back in his chair. He saw more pieces now. Someone had been giving Sadiki messages to pass to the Al Qaeda network after each of his meetings with Ferris. They had created the appearance that Ferris was using Sadiki as a secret channel to Al Qaeda—which was right, in a sense, but someone had turned it inside out. And it was obvious now that Omar Sadiki hadn't been kidnapped by Al Qaeda, as Ferris had believed, but by whoever was pulling the strings in this puppet show. But if Sadiki had never been kidnapped, why had they taken Alice? It was still too complicated for Ferris to understand. All he knew was that Alice was free. He came back to that centerline. She was alive. That was all that really mattered.

"Thank you for letting Alice Melville go," said Ferris. The words tumbled from his mouth. It was the one emotion that was not contrived, the only element of this puzzle he thought he understood. "She is not a Muslim, but I love her very much."

Suleiman cocked his head suddenly, like an animal that has heard a noise he doesn't like. "I am sorry. What are you saying? Who is Alice?"

"I am thanking you, that's all. For letting Alice Melville go free in Hama at the waterwheels. I was very grateful. That's all."

Suleiman stretched out his hands toward Ferris, palms up, in a gesture of innocence.

"But Fares, we did not release this person, Alice. How could we? Because we did not take her in the first place. In fact, I do not know who she is. Alice? Now you are worrying me. I wonder if you are playing a trick on me."

"My God," said Ferris. It was barely a whisper. He saw it now. It was obvious. There was only one man who knew enough about the CIA's most secret intelligence to send tantalizing bits of it to Suleiman. There was only one man who knew enough about Omar Sadiki to reprogram him—reverse his polarity so that he appeared to other eyes to be performing an entirely different secret mission. There was only one man who could know enough about Alice Melville to fake her kidnapping as a way of drawing Ferris in. It had to be Ed Hoffman. He had dangled Ferris like a shiny lure, a shimmering reflection in the hall of mirrors. Ferris hated Hoffman now in a way that he had never hated anyone.

"You are confused about something, Fares, and I am asking, why?" Suleiman said. He had been doing some thinking, too, in the moment of silence when the patterns had rearranged themselves in each man's mind. He moved his chair closer to Ferris and put a hand on his throat—not squeezing hard, but enough to remind Ferris that he had total power over him.

"Let me look in your eyes," the Syrian continued. "Look at me and tell me that what you say is the truth. This is my lie detector. To put my hand on your throat and look in your eyes. Say it."

"I am telling the truth," said Ferris. He tried to deaden his emotions down to nothing. And he almost succeeded. But there was a flutter in his eyelids, not quite a blink, but almost. He was trying too hard, and Suleiman could see that something was wrong.

"I think you lie, Fares. Something in you is false. Is it only a little? Is it everything? I do not know, and that makes me uncomfortable. But it is good that I am here with you, you see? Because soon I will know where the lies are. May God forgive me, but you are not my guest anymore. I am sending you away, in my heart."

"What am I, then?"

"You are my prisoner."

Suleiman shouted out a name, and the Egyptian man came running into the room, along with a second man who was wearing a black ski mask. Suleiman told the two in Arabic that it was time to question the CIA man. They would shoot the video for Al Jazeera later, when they knew what story it would tell. Then he stood, leaned over Ferris, spat in his face and walked out of the room.

THEY MADE Ferris sit down in a wooden chair, and across the arms of the chair they attached a big piece of plywood in which holes had been drilled. With thick duct tape and metal wire, they attached Ferris's arms and legs to the chair, and then they attached his two hands to the plywood, wiring down the fingers separately so that each one was exposed as a distinct target. When they had finished trussing him, the Egyptian brought a big metal hammer and laid it on the table between Ferris's immobile arms and fingers.

"Welcome to Guantánamo," he said.

They left Ferris there for twenty minutes. From the talk in the other room, the men seemed to be eating. Ferris felt his fingers throb in anticipation of the pain. Would he use his poison now, if he still had it? The suffering that lay ahead of him was pointless. He had come here to die, in the belief that by doing so he could save Alice. But she had never needed saving, because she had never been Al Qaeda's prisoner. Someone had tricked him out of his life for nothing. Ferris remembered a scene in a novel by André Malraux he had read in college. Two devout Communist partisans are facing torture, and one, in a *beau geste* of selfless heroism, decides to give the poison pill he has been hiding to the other man, who is weaker. He gives the capsule to his frail comrade—who drops it and lets it skitter away down a crack in the floor so that it is useless to both of them. For Ferris, that scene had been the measure of a meaningless death, until now.

SULEIMAN ENTERED the room, followed by the Egyptian and the man in the black mask. He sat in a chair across from Ferris, while the other two arrayed themselves on either side. Suleiman had put on a pair of gloves, to give him a better grip on the hammer and to spare his own smooth hands from the blood.

"We are not so good at this," said Suleiman, hefting the hammer in his gloved hand. "We do not have so many prisoners to practice on, but we learn from you. You teach us. Why do Americans not see, when you torture us, that someday we will use the same torture on you? You must be very stupid, not to know that when you break the rules of war, you will suffer the most. Maybe you lack imagination. I think that is it. You cannot imagine that it could be done to you, so you do not think about doing it to others."

He raised the metal hammer high, and then brought it down in a splintering crash onto the plywood, just beyond Ferris's right hand. Ferris screamed, even though the hammer did not hit him. The men on either side laughed, but not their leader.

"A practice swing," said Suleiman. "So this is what we will do. You have ten fingers. I will ask you ten questions, then ten more, then ten more. Each time you do not tell the truth, I will break one of your fingers. When we are done with the fingers, then we will start on your legs, and your eyes, and your tongue, and your teeth. When the hammer breaks from too much pounding, we will get another one."

"And if I tell the truth?" asked Ferris.

"But you are a liar," snorted Suleiman. He raised the hammer, held it poised in the air for a moment and then brought it down with hideous force on the little finger of Ferris's right hand. It hit at the middle joint, crushing the bone and skin almost flat against the wood. The pain was so searing that Ferris tore at his bonds in agony. But the only release was his scream.

"Too loud," said Suleiman. "Someone will hear." He turned and looked up to the Egyptian. He walked to the window and pulled back the thick curtain. "Who found this house? There are people in this neighborhood. I can see them, right there, out the window. This is a bad place. Before the next finger, you must put a gag on him, so that people will not hear." The Egyptian nodded.

Ferris was still moaning. He looked at the pancake of flesh that had been his little finger. Both hands would soon be destroyed, never again to hold anything, touch anything, feel anything.

"Shut up, please," said Suleiman. Ferris's moaning quieted down to a whimper. "Thank you. Now, I think, we begin. I ask question, you answer question. Each lie and I call my friend Mr. Hammer. Understand?"

Ferris croaked out an assent.

"Okay, first question. Who was the CIA man Harry Meeker? Why was he carrying those documents, please?"

"He didn't exist," said Ferris. As he spoke, Suleiman began to raise the hammer and Ferris screamed, "Stop! Please stop. It's true. Harry Meeker was fake. He was a dead body that we found. We put it together to look like he was a CIA man going to visit an agent in Al Qaeda."

"But he was carrying a message for me, this Harry Meeker."

"Yes, but it was fake, too. So that people in Al Qaeda would think you were working with us."

"W'Allah!" It was a raw, throaty cry of rage. Suleiman's face reddened, and in a reflex of anger, he raised the hammer again and brought it down on the finger next to the one that had been crushed. It wasn't as hard a blow; he seemed to pull back at the last moment, realizing that Ferris wasn't gagged yet. Ferris screamed, as much in fear as in pain. This time, he didn't stop screaming.

"Gag him," ordered Suleiman.

The Egyptian grabbed a rag and shoved it in Ferris's mouth. The man in the black mask was trying to attach a piece of duct tape when suddenly he heard a noise from outside the room and snapped his head around. They all did, and downstairs there was a sudden rip of automatic weapons fire, and all Ferris thought was: Maybe I will die quickly.

IT HAPPENED in one dense moment: The splintering sound of glass breaking, then the crack of an explosion, a sudden burst of light that blinded Ferris, the sounds of doors crashing in, and people shouting, and the fire of more automatic weapons. The room filled with smoke, and they were all gasping and choking. Ferris could hear men storming into the room. A blinded Suleiman was screaming curses and groping his way toward the window, but the men tackled him and the other two captors to the floor. The gunfire continued down below, but after fifteen seconds it stopped. All the guards were dead. The smoke began to clear, and Ferris's vision slowly came back. He saw Suleiman on the floor, bound and gagged. Men dressed in black uniforms were stuffing him into a large body bag and then carrying him out the door. Other black-clad men were doing the same to the other two, putting them in body bags and dragging them away.

A moment later, when the three Al Qaeda men had been hauled

off, someone came for Ferris. He was dressed in ninja black, too, but he appeared to be a medic. He gently cut Ferris's fingers free from the torture table and then began working on the crushed fingers.

"You will lose the little one," he said. "Maybe we can save the other." He spoke English with an Arab accent, Ferris noticed. He had an awful fear that he was going from one hell into another—exchanging captivity in an Al Qaeda safe house for the same thing in a Syrian prison. The medic swabbed Ferris's arm with an alcohol pad, then jabbed it with a hypodermic needle. After a few moments Ferris drifted into ethereal semiconsciousness, and then he was out.

35

FERRIS AWOKE IN AN INSTITUTIONAL bed, crisp white sheets, metal rails like a crib. He didn't know whether he was in a prison or a hospital. He looked down at his right hand and saw one finger in a splint. The little finger was gone; it had been amputated, evidently. He tried to move, but there was a leather belt tied across his chest as a restraint. He turned his head and saw an elaborate spray of flowers in a vase on his bedside table. He breathed in the fragrance and knew that it could not be a prison if there were flowers in his room.

Ferris had been awake ten minutes or so when a nurse came into the room. She was speaking in Arabic to a colleague standing in the hall. Ferris turned his head and saw, through the open door, that she had been talking to a dark soldier who was guarding his door; he knew then that wherever he was, he must still be in the Arab world. When she saw that he was awake, she removed the leather restraint from his chest and propped him up in bed. The nurse asked him if he was comfortable, and Ferris answered yes. She checked the dressing on the splintered finger, and the one on the stump, and said that he was healing well.

"Someone would like to see you, if you feel that you are well enough," she said. She helped Ferris to stand. Though he was weak from his ordeal, Ferris was able to walk about the room. The nurse handed Ferris some clothes. As he looked at them, he realized that they were his own, taken from the bedroom closet of his apartment in Amman. That was interesting, but he had no idea what it meant.

"Where am I?" Ferris asked.

"You are in Tripoli, sir," said the nurse. "In Lebanon."

Was he dreaming? The nurse told him to put on his clothes and said she would be back in five minutes to take him to see his visitor. She returned, as promised, and led Ferris down a long hall to a big oak door. She knocked once and called out, "Ya, Pasha." A voice answered in Arabic, and she pushed the door open.

HANI SALAAM was waiting for him in one of two big easy chairs at the far end of the room. He was smoking a cigar, and had on his face a look of immense satisfaction. Indeed, gazing at him, Ferris was not sure he had ever seen a man more content. The play was over. Before him was the Arab Prospero who had ordered up the sea and sky and wind, who had set the cast of players in motion, created monsters and fantasies—whose unseen hand had directed every instant of the drama that others imagined they were directing, who had turned white into black into white.

"My dear Roger," he said, rising and embracing Ferris. "You look quite satisfactory, considering what you have been through. Would you like a cigar? Please. You must have a cigar. You are a hero. You have saved more lives than you can imagine, perhaps more than we will ever know."

Ferris looked at Hani. For all the anger he was feeling, he could not help but smile as he watched the pasha: His moustache was finely trimmed. His hair was newly cut and freshly dyed, so that it had the sheen of a movie star's hair. He was wearing a new sport coat, blue cashmere with a thin yellow stripe, and he had on a gleaming new pair of shoes.

"Yes, I'll have a cigar," said Ferris. Hani handed him a Romeo y Julieta, in the long, fat size known as a Churchill. As Ferris put it to his lips, Hani lit a long-tipped match and held the flame to the end, so that it pulsed red-hot with each breath that Ferris drew.

Ferris puffed on his cigar and put his feet up on a padded stool that stood between them.

"You owe me a finger," he said.

"Yes, I do. That and a great deal more. But we will make it up to you, I assure you. I feel about you as if you were my own son. I always have. That has made this most painful for me, the necessity to deceive you. But as you Americans like to say, it was in a good cause. I console myself with that. But it will not bring back your lost finger. I am very sorry for that. I thought my men could get there in time. I did not think the interrogation would begin so soon. Not for the 'defector.' But as soon as we heard you cry out, we moved in."

"You did all of this," said Ferris, a touch of wonder in his voice mixed with the anger. "This was all your show. Hoffman didn't have a clue."

"Yes. It was my show." The Jordanian took a puff. "This is my world, you see. I understand it. You Americans are visitors. You try to comprehend, but it is really quite impossible. You only make mistakes. And you are arrogant, I am sorry to say. You don't know what you don't know. When I realized that, after that miserable business in Berlin, I knew I had to take over."

Ferris nodded. It was true, what he said. Ferris couldn't deny it. "And what was I?" he asked "Your pawn?"

"Not at all, my dear. You were my agent. My penetration of the CIA. I had my eye on you the moment you arrived. Except that I couldn't recruit you. You would never have agreed. So you were my virtual agent."

Ferris laughed out loud. "That's what Hoffman and I thought we were doing with Sadiki. We thought he could catch Suleiman by using Sadiki as a 'virtual agent.' I used the same words."

"But that was quite ridiculous, don't you think? I own Jordan. I can control everything and everyone in it. I have been using Sadiki myself for several years. Did Ed Hoffman really think he could play in my backyard like this without my knowing?"

"As you said, we Americans don't know as much as we think we do."

"Thank goodness you still have friends. Though I'm not sure why anyone still is willing to help you—other than the fact that you are so rich. But yes, I discovered that Ed Hoffman's men had been doing surveillance on Sadiki and his brother for some foolish new scheme. I decided then that things had gone far enough. And I had, in you, a perfect foil, Roger. A man I could dangle in front of Al Qaeda. A man who might pose as a CIA defector. A Muslim in the CIA, with the bona fides to prove it."

"How did you know that I was a Muslim? Assuming that's true, that you didn't have Sadiki feed them a bunch of forgeries."

"I knew it because I did my research. You Americans think you are the only people capable of meticulous work, but you are quite wrong. I had a hunch, and I did some checking. Quite a lot of checking, actually. I had people looking at census records in the United States, and the manifests of ships landing at Ellis Island. I had researchers in Bosnia visiting relatives you don't even know you have. I even sent one of my men to talk to your mother, to see if she had anything. And then I sent a team here to Tripoli, to consult the old Ottoman records. We needed documents, and we knew that Suleiman's men would come and check, too. They are not stupid, either, my friend. So it had to be real. And it was. Your grandfather's name at birth was Muhammad Fares. He kept it a great secret in America. But, my dear, this is the land where the secrets begin. We call it *taqiyya*."

"I borrowed that word from you," said Ferris. "I thought I understood it."

"But my dear, *taqiyya* is not something you can unpack from a box of tricks. For a Muslim, it is a means of survival. Your grandfather understood *taqiyya*. Because of *taqiyya*, you are here today. That is what we understand in the desert. What matters only is survival. We do not risk our treasure for anything else."

Ferris thought of all the effort he and Hoffman had put into their deception—the meetings in Abu Dhabi, Beirut and Ankara, the photos and tapes. They had worked so hard, and it had worked—to Hani's benefit. Ferris was angry at Hani, but he couldn't help smiling at how totally the Jordanian had deceived them.

"When we built the legend for Sadiki, that just made your job easier, didn't it?"

"Much easier. We could ride on your back. When you first put Sadiki into play, I did the same. I had him call his real contact on the fringes of Al Qaeda—oh yes, he had one—to say that an unhappy CIA officer was offering to give him secrets. They didn't believe it, but they were curious. After that first meeting with you, he brought them real intelligence, supplied by me, of course. Most of it was dead—old cell-phone numbers, operations that had gone cold. I gave them a lovely story about the Berlin recruitment and all your games with Amary. That was when they began to think you were a real traitor, to give them that information. Each time you summoned Sadiki to a meeting, I had more material for them. All the while, my dear, you were running your little show and locking my story in place. It was so convenient to have surveillance photographs of Sadiki floating around Abu Dhabi and Beirut and Istanbul, not to mention London and Paris. A bit of luck, that was."

"You played us for fools."

"Not really. I just played you. I followed in your draft. You are a superpower, and you create so much turbulence when you move, even when you think you are being quiet and clever, that sometimes if we are lucky we can slip in behind you and catch a ride."

"And the call we picked up from Suleiman? And the text message for me on his cell phone? You did that, too?"

"Yes, I am afraid so. We had to draw the string tight, to make sure we could pull you toward that final rendezvous. You had to believe that your silly game was working. We had an old intercept of

Suleiman saved in our databank. I am sorry, but it is not so hard to manipulate you."

Ferris put his hands together and gently clapped, as if the curtain were going down on a piece of theater.

"Very impressive. The only thing I can't forgive you for was manipulating Alice. She had a life in Jordan. She loved Amman. You've destroyed that. She can never go back now. They'll think she works for you."

"My dear Roger, everyone in Jordan works for me. Why should she be any different? But I must tell you honestly that you are deceiving yourself if you think that I was the one who put her in jeopardy. You did that. Al Qaeda might really have kidnapped her, if we had not taken her into, shall we say, 'protective custody.' You should not be angry with me. I had all the pieces in my hands." He took a big puff of his cigar and expelled a smooth round ring of smoke, but Ferris wasn't watching.

"I was so afraid for her, Hani. I was ready to die to save her. You used that. You counted on it. Without it, your plan wouldn't have worked. You turned my love for her into a weapon. How can I forgive that?"

Hani was silent. He looked toward the window of the hospital sunroom and the blue water of the Mediterranean, and then back toward Ferris. For the first time, there was a slight look of regret in his eyes, dimming his glow of contentment just a bit.

"I am sorry for that, Roger. I did count on your nobility, but really, you were doing what any man would do. I did not realize how much you loved her until you and I were together in her apartment. But I will tell you the truth: That just made me work harder to make sure everything went right. We were following you every minute. We put a powder on your shoes that had a signature we could follow; you had markers woven through the fibers of the jacket the driver gave you. We had the promise of help from the president of Syria himself, if anything went wrong."

Ferris nodded, but he was thinking of Alice. His cheeks reddened again with anger. "You beat her, when you kidnapped her from her apartment and took her to Hama. I saw the blood."

"First, my dear, she was not kidnapped. And we did not beat her, for goodness' sake. She had donated blood a month ago at the Palestinian Red Crescent, and it occurred to me that it might be useful later. We didn't even break into her place. She came with us willingly, for a simple reason, which is that she thought it would help you."

"You didn't have to force her?"

"Not at all. Alice is a more complicated woman than you seem to realize. She has a life that you do not understand. Do you think someone like that could work in Jordan, travel to and from the Palestinian camps, and not have contact with the Moukhabarat? I do not say this to upset you, but to please you. Like anything precious, she is veiled. She has been worried about you for a very long time, my dear. And for some perverse reason, she loves you as much as you love her."

Ferris blinked, and as he did so, his eyes grew moist. Had he understood anything? "I have to see her. Where is she?"

"She is nearby. She knows that you are fine. The flowers in your room are from her."

"Can I see her?"

"Of course, my dear. You are a free man. But first I think perhaps we need to talk about Ed Hoffman."

Ferris sat up with a start. It was a measure of how much he had been transformed by the cascade of events that he had barely thought of Hoffman since he awoke in his hospital bed. "Does he know what happened?"

"Oh yes, most of it. Some of it. He's in Amman. That's why I brought you here, actually. In addition to being your hometown, this is a place where you can be invisible until you decide what you want to do about Ed."

"He must be going crazy. This will ruin him."

"Not at all. This may be his finest hour. Or at least, his various bosses in Washington will perceive it as that. Together, we will exploit Suleiman's intelligence in Pakistan, Iraq, Syria, Europe. I do not think I am flattering myself to say that this is the greatest success we have had against Al Qaeda. Suleiman was the man at the center of everything. Now that we have destroyed him, it will take Al Qaeda years to recover."

"And the world will think it's Hoffman's operation that did it?"

"Of course. Real intelligence operations stay secret forever. You Americans cannot understand that. You are incapable of secrecy, because you are a democracy. But we do not have that problem. When it comes to the glory, *ahlan wa sahlan*, it is all yours. Or Ed's, I should say. You are a bit more of a problem."

"Why should I be a problem? I'm the person who made this happen. With your help, of course, Hani Pasha."

"You are not thinking, my dear. Ed Hoffman is going to believe that you were working for me all along. You may have been my virtual agent, but he will think it was real. There are inconvenient details. You are from a Muslim family and your grandfather came from the Sunni town of Tripoli, Lebanon, and you never told the CIA about that. I fear that may be awkward."

"But I didn't know myself. You're the one who discovered it."

"Yes. But, honestly, will Ed Hoffman believe you? And even if he does, will the CIA counterintelligence staff, and the inspector general, and the chairmen of the Senate and House Intelligence Committees? They will have so many questions. And those questions will make it difficult for you to remain at the CIA. People will think that you were my agent. And they will be right."

Ferris closed his eyes and put his good hand to his head to massage his temples. He needed to think. Where was he, really? Where did he want to go? He had come a great distance, but not to sit in this sunroom in Tripoli with the pasha.

Hani took a last puff on his Churchill and put it aside. The big cigar was almost down to its stub.

"In your own mind, you do not believe you were an agent of

Jordanian intelligence. But in objective terms, you were indeed my agent: I controlled you, targeted you, ran you. The fact that you were not consciously aware of it is a secondary point, I think. No matter what you say, no matter how many polygraph exams you pass, Hoffman and his friends will always have a suspicion. I am sorry, but that is the situation."

"That's crap, Hani. But assuming it were true, what do you think I should do?"

"The point is, you have won. You can do whatever you like."

FERRIS LOOKED at the light through the windows, clear and clean, illuminating so many dark places. What Hani said was true, at least part of it. Ferris had passed through a portal that he could not reenter. Yet he felt a sense of unfinished business. He had survived, but so many other people were dead, and too many of the killers were still at large. He felt like a hand puppet. He had been played skillfully, but the story wasn't over yet. He knew that better than anyone. He was the one who had first discovered Suleiman's existence, from an Iraqi agent in a dirty shack south of Tikrit. This was his case. He owned it, not Hoffman, not even Hani. And it wasn't finished. Hani was wrong: He hadn't won, yet.

Ferris closed his eyes and saw the face of his adversary. He let himself remember the room in Aleppo, the chair, the plywood to which his fingers had been attached, the video camera in the background, the diabolical certainty in Suleiman's eyes that he controlled the situation. They were making a movie; that was what he had said, a movie they would show on Al Jazeera. But what was Suleiman's movie? As he turned the question over in his mind, it was suddenly obvious to Ferris what he should do. He turned back to the Jordanian, so immaculate in his dress and deceit.

"Okay, Hani. Have it your way. I am your agent. 'Objectively speaking.' Nobody will ever believe I wasn't. But now that I'm your man, you must give me a final mission."

"What is that, my dear Roger?" Hani had a smile of deep completion. In his mind, the play was over. It hadn't occurred to him that
Ferris might want to write a final act.

"I want to destroy Suleiman's network," said Ferris.

Hani laughed. He thought Ferris must be teasing. "Do not be
greedy, my friend. That is another American failing. We have
Suleiman. Soon we will have many of his people. Isn't that enough?
What more do we need?"

"We need to destroy his idea. We've captured him and some of his
people, but they'll find others who are nearly as clever and angry. Hell,
they have most of Iraq as a recruiting ground. We're not finished yet.
When I was working with Hoffman, I wanted to create a poison that
would destroy everything Suleiman had touched. Contaminate him,
his ideas, his people. Make them radioactive for a hundred years.
That's still what we need: a poison pill. And I can be the poison."

"What are you talking about, Roger? You are bandaged and
infirm. You can barely walk."

"I can *think*. I can stop being so stupid and try to be smart. And
you can help me, Hani Pasha. That's what I am asking, in return for
what I've given you. I want to finish this."

Hani moved uneasily in his chair. It was clear now that Ferris was
serious. "And Alice?" he asked.

"She will never love me unless this is over. That's why I have to
end it."

"Very well. I am listening, my dear Roger. So long as you do not
undo the good we have accomplished."

"I need to ask you one question: Did you find a video camera in
Suleiman's safe house in Aleppo?"

"Yes, of course. It was in the room where you were interrogated,
if that is the right word for what they did to you. My men brought it
out of Aleppo, in case it had anything useful. It's in the other room, I
think."

"Good. Then we're in business. Now listen, *ustaaz* Hani. You are
the teacher, and I am the student. But I have an idea for you."

So Hani listened as Ferris talked. How could he not? Ferris thought out loud, stitching together a plan, gathering threads from Hoffman, from Hani, even from Suleiman himself, until he had something that sounded coherent. The Jordanian was wary. He wasn't a reckless gambler. He knew enough to pocket his winnings and walk away from the table. But in this casino, Ferris still had something big to play for. Hani didn't try to talk him out of his plan. He knew that Ferris would attempt it, no matter what Hani said. And in that sense, it was Ferris who had the power. He might be Hani's agent, "objectively speaking," but it was now Ferris's operation.

36

S ULEIMAN'S FACE WAS VISIBLE through the thick glass plate on the door of his cell. There were bags under his eyes and the imprint of stress and sleeplessness. But even in captivity, in the secret prison in Cyprus where Hani had stashed him after the raid, he still looked like a man who was in control. They had taken away his immaculate knitted prayer cap and the fastidious robe he had worn in Aleppo. He was dressed in prison garb now—not an orange jumpsuit, but the simple gray cotton of a Cypriot prisoner. He wore it with his own furious form of dignity. He would not be easy to break. They would have to torture him to blood and bones before he would talk, and even if Hani had been ready to do that, it would have eviscerated the part of the man who could actually tell them useful secrets. Hani was prepared to wait him out—long enough to find the psychological pins he could remove to produce the desired effect. But he would be a hard case.

"Let him break himself," Ferris had proposed back in Tripoli. In that moment, Hani realized that Ferris truly had become someone different. He understood that you cannot break a rock with another rock. It must crack along the fissures that are already there. Once you find them, you need apply only the gentlest pressure. Ferris in that respect had become a man of the East, using the tradecraft that was in his blood.

Hani and Ferris had come to Cyprus from Tripoli, taking the helicopter that first afternoon so they wouldn't lose any time. Hoffman was waiting in Amman, oblivious to what was happening, basking in his unearned credit. Alice was waiting in Lebanon. Ferris didn't want to see her until he was entirely hers and entirely free from his yoke of lies. It was just Ferris and Hani. They had come full circle from that dingy apartment in Berlin. Now they stood together outside their quarry's cell and outside his mind.

HANI LED Ferris to an empty cell down the hall. The American was dressed in the dirty clothes he had worn to Hama: the rough trousers, the shirt rank with his sweat. There were red welts on his face; he had insisted that Hani's men rough him up as if he were a street informant gone bad. They had taken the bandage off his finger, too, so the raw red stump was visible, still oozing pus. Ferris told Hani he was ready to start the interrogation. But for the moment, it wasn't Suleiman who would be questioned. It was Roger Ferris.

Ferris sat down in a rough wooden chair and waited while Hani's men bound his hands and feet. The interrogation room was cramped and dank; the walls were dripping with condensed moisture from the rot of the place. Across from Ferris was Suleiman's video camera, resting on the same tripod as in Aleppo. Hani sat across from Ferris, wearing a black ski mask.

"Roll it," said Ferris. There was a pause while Hani turned on the camera, and then Ferris began to speak in the halting, guttural cadence of a man who had been beaten into submission.

"My name is Roger Ferris." The words sounded rough and misshapen, as if they had been pulled out of his gut. "I work for the Central Intelligence Agency."

Ferris stared at the floor. He cradled the stump of his finger in his good hand as if he feared someone were about to chop off another.

Hani gruffly commanded Ferris to speak Arabic and finish with his story. Ferris started up again slowly in his weary, language-school Arabic.

"I am Roger Ferris. I work for the CIA. This is my confession. For many years, I have been part of an operation to penetrate Al Qaeda. We tried to trick the Muslim people into following our agent. We apologize to all the Muslim people."

Ferris stopped and looked fearfully away from the camera, toward Hani. At that, the Jordanian slapped Ferris hard on the cheek. Ferris groaned, and not simply for the camera. Hani had struck him with considerable force. His cheek was reddening from the stinging of the blow.

"Say the name," shouted Hani. "Who was your agent?"

Ferris struggled to find the words. His eyes darted back and forth. He put his mangled hand to his face.

"Our agent was a Syrian. His name is Karim al-Shams. He calls himself Suleiman the Magnificent. He pretended to be Al Qaeda's planner of operations. But all along, he was working for the CIA. We apologize to all the Muslim people. We do the work of the devil. We apologize to all the Muslim people."

The hand swept toward Ferris once more. This time, Hani hit him so hard he knocked Ferris from his chair to the floor. He lay there moaning until Hani turned off the video.

"Jesus," said Ferris, massaging the wound on his cheek after Hani had untied his wrists and sat him back in the chair. "That was pretty fucking good."

A CYPRIOT doctor was summoned to attend to Ferris. Hani insisted on it. He had understood the need for brutality on camera, but he was mortified that he had hit Ferris so hard he had drawn blood. He asked Ferris to take an hour to recover, and fed him kebabs and rice. He offered *arak*, too, but Ferris refused. The most important part of his plan was coming and he needed a clear head, however bruised.

Ferris changed into prison garb: simple gray trousers and tunic. He walked with Hani to a large interrogation room that had three chairs. Ferris sat down in one and waited while he was bound once again, hand and feet. Then he was left alone in the room. He couldn't see the video camera, but he knew it was there behind the two-way mirror, focused tight on the chair next to him.

Suleiman arrived ten minutes later, hobbling between two guards. He was cuffed and manacled, and the guards pushed him roughly into the chair next to Ferris. He didn't recognize the American at first, but when he saw who it was, he muttered an oath. Ferris looked up, his face far more battered than Suleiman's.

"You are Fares, the CIA man," said Suleiman. "What are you doing here, dog?"

Ferris stammered his words as if from the pain. He only needed to get a few sentences from Suleiman, just a few dozen phrases, and he would have it.

"You were wrong about me," he croaked. Then his head slumped down as if from exhaustion. He didn't speak, except for an occasional low moan, as he waited for Suleiman to draw him out. Thirty seconds passed, a minute. Ferris was beginning to worry that Suleiman wouldn't take the bait, but eventually he spoke again.

"Why are you here?" Suleiman repeated.

"They caught me," said Ferris. "They made me confess."

"So it is true? You are a Muslim? You were really working with us?"

"What?" Ferris strained, as if he could not hear, from the pain.

"You are a CIA man, but you were working with us?"

"Together?" Ferris groaned it as a question.

"Yes. Together. You were working with us, Fares?"

"Yes. All along."

"And all the CIA reports were true?"

"Yes, all true. You were inside the CIA."

"*W'Allah!*" said Suleiman with a smile. "I was inside the CIA. That is a satisfaction to me. Thanks be to God."

"Thanks be to God," repeated Ferris.

"We could have done great things together, for the *umma*. So many things."

Ferris groaned, and let his head slump back toward his chest. He had enough now. He didn't want to overplay his hand. Suleiman asked him another question, but he just moaned.

Ten minutes later, Hani entered the room in his mask and took the third chair and shouted to Ferris and Suleiman to pay attention. Hani spoke a rough Arabic dialect, not his usual elegant voice, but in the manner an Al Qaeda operative might use in interrogating a former chief who has betrayed the cause.

"Look at me, Karim al-Shams. The great 'Suleiman.' Were you getting information from the CIA man Roger Ferris?"

Suleiman laughed. It was a show of independence. Hani slapped him, far harder than he had done with Ferris. Then he kicked him hard in the shin, and the knee and the thigh. The hidden camera caught Hani's arm and leg, but not his face.

"Did you receive information from the CIA man Roger Ferris?" Hani repeated.

"Yes," groaned Suleiman. "And I am glad of it. Thanks be to God. This was our victory."

"Why did you do this terrible thing?" snarled Hani.

"We are proud of it. We are proud of this operation with the American."

"You insult the Muslim people. I put my shoe in your mouth. You have brought shame to the *umma*."

"I am not ashamed. I am proud. It is a great thing we did for the Muslim people, this operation with the American. It shows we can do anything."

Hani punched Suleiman full in the face, as if he couldn't control his rage. Blood spurted from his nose. Hani cursed him and got up and left. Behind the two-way mirror, the cameraman clicked off the video. They had all they needed now.

One of Hani's men came to untie Ferris. When his arms and legs were free, he stood over Suleiman and smiled down at him. That was all it took for Suleiman to realize what had just happened. There was a look of utter despair on his face. He knew, suddenly.

"You lose," said Ferris.

Suleiman cried out in anguish, the howl of a broken spirit. They had him. He had worked with a CIA man. He was worse than dead.

FERRIS HIRED a taxi in Beirut and told the driver he wanted to go to Damascus, three hours away over the crest of Mt. Lebanon. It was a Subaru, a comfortable enough car. He had wanted to take a *serveece* group taxi, but Hani had advised against it. It would seem odd for an American to be a passenger with Turkish laborers and Sudanese chambermaids. Ferris should find a good car and sit in the back, like a proper American. In truth, Hani hadn't wanted Ferris to go to Damascus at all. Let someone else deliver the tape to Al Jazeera. But Ferris had insisted. If there was trouble, he was the only one who could explain it. His presence certified the tape's provenance—he was the proof of its authenticity. Hani knew it was true, but still he protested. He offered to send a Special Forces team as bodyguards, but Ferris refused. That would make the trip more dangerous, not less. Hani agreed that Ferris was right, but he was unhappy. He did not want the bomb Ferris was carrying to explode in his hand.

The Subaru left the Beirut waterfront and began the steep climb through the hillside towns of Aley and Bhamdoun and up to the crest. There was deep snow atop Mt. Lebanon, and the roads near the summit were icy, even on this sunny day. They snaked up the highest ridge, past the Lebanese army checkpoints, and then rumbled down toward the town of Chtaura and the Bekaa Valley. Ferris began to feel a clutch of fear in his stomach as he neared the Syrian border. As long as he had been in the Middle East, he had dreaded this frontier. This was a point of no return. On the other side, you were at the mercy of hidden hands.

Hani had given him a Jordanian diplomatic passport. In theory, that should have made things easy. But the Syrians were curious. Why would this man "Fares" be traveling on behalf of Jordan? Their information systems were too primitive to do any serious search of another identity, but still, they were suspicious. They asked Ferris how long he would be in Syria, and Ferris answered that he expected it would be only a few hours. He had a delivery to make, and then he would be returning to Lebanon. That seemed to reassure the captain of the border police. Ferris might be trouble, but he wouldn't be trouble for long.

The car traversed the anti-Lebanon range along the Syrian border and in thirty minutes they were on the outskirts of Damascus. The city stretched for miles along the Syrian plain, a jewel of the East that had lost its sparkle. Ferris gave the driver the address of Al Jazeera's bureau in Abu Rummaneh, near the French Embassy. The office was in a bland, unadorned concrete building. Like most of Damascus it seemed to have fallen out of a time capsule from the 1960s. When they arrived, Ferris told the driver to wait; he would only be a few minutes and then they would return to Beirut.

Ferris clutched his little parcel with the original of the videocassette wrapped in brown paper. He had a copy in his coat pocket. He rang the bell marked "Al Jazeera," and when a secretary opened the office door, he asked for the office manager. A stocky man came out, wearing a George Raft double-breasted suit and a stained tie. The office manager scanned Ferris dubiously.

Ferris cleared his throat. He didn't want to seem nervous, but he couldn't help it. This was the end of a very long road.

"I have a tape for you, from Raouf," said Ferris.

"Who?" asked the station manager, backing away.

"From Raouf. That is the name he uses. He told me that you would be expecting a tape from him. A special tape that would be of great interest to your viewers."

The station manager looked ashen. He retreated quickly back into his office, and Ferris heard him talking on the telephone. His voice sounded submissive. Ferris heard him repeat the name "Raouf" several times, but he couldn't make out anything else. Eventually the manager returned. He looked relieved, and it was soon obvious why. He was getting rid of his troublesome guest. The manager handed Ferris a slip of paper, on which he had written an address in the Old City.

"You go see Hassan, if you have tape from Raouf," he said. "Not here. This address." He motioned with his hands, as if to shoo Ferris away from his door.

"Let me leave a copy for you," said Ferris, taking the cassette from his pocket and placing it on the table. "If anything happens to me and I cannot make my delivery, you will want to see it. It is very important, for all the Arabs. It is a special gift from Raouf."

The manager looked unhappy to be left with this worryingly important gift. But he didn't try to give it back.

THE ADDRESS was in Bab Touma, in the Christian quarter of the Old City, of all places. Perhaps that was another form of *taqiyya*. The driver navigated the weaving traffic and beeping horns along Baghdad Street until he got to the turn for Bab Touma. They inched down an old street, past remnants of the ancient city wall. They finally reached a cobbled lane that was too narrow for the taxi. The driver motioned with a flick of his wrist. The address was down there somewhere, amid the donkey carts and dark alleys. Ferris told the driver to wait; he would return in a few minutes.

Ferris set out on foot. His leg was throbbing from the shrapnel wounds, but he willed the pain to go away. There was a stream of Syrians in the narrow street, out doing their shopping. A butcher was chopping a raw hunk of lamb in the open air; a few doors down, two young men were looking at a Syrian girlie magazine in a barbershop while they waited to get their hair cut. A couple was shopping for a wedding ring in a jewelry store. Dark-eyed children were coming out of the playground of an Armenian school down the street. Ferris felt as if he were disappearing into the anonymous swarm of this Arab city, but he knew that wasn't so. He stuck out like scar tissue.

In every window Ferris saw a brooding icon of Jesus, a dark Eastern Jesus, one who truly knew what it was to suffer.

He saw the address just ahead. There was a little shop on the first floor, selling music and videocassettes under a colorful awning. Next to it was the entrance to a walkup apartment. There was a faint light upstairs, above the video shop. Ferris stopped and looked up and down the street. The bustling crowd seemed to have thinned. People were returning to their shops and homes. Perhaps they knew. That was the thing about a place like Damascus: It had a secret language. The moment something happened, or was about to happen, everyone knew it instantly. That was how people survived.

Ferris stuck his head in the door. It was dark inside, so he pushed the button for the hall light. A woman in a far doorway backed toward the darkness.

"Where does Hassan live?" asked Ferris.

The woman jerked her head, pointing her eyes upstairs, and then closed her door. Ferris mounted the creaky stairs. Each floorboard seemed loose underfoot, and the wooden banister wobbled. At the top of the stairs it was dark, and Ferris couldn't find the light. He fumbled about, his palm feeling along the wall for a switch, when a door opened. A man's bearded face was half illuminated by the light behind.

"Are you Hassan?" asked Ferris. "I have something for Hassan."

The bearded man didn't answer. He motioned for Ferris to follow him into the dimly lit room. Ferris didn't like anything about the scene, but he had no choice now. It had all come down to this. He had to make the delivery; that was all. The tape would do the rest. Behind him, he heard the click of the door lock.

Inside the apartment stood another man. Like the first, he had a thick beard. He was wearing a knitted prayer cap. From the cool intensity of his eyes, he might have been Suleiman's brother.

"I am Hassan," he said. "Who are you?"

"I have a tape for you, from Raouf," said Ferris. "Raouf told me to give it to you, for Al Jazeera. That was his last wish. He said that I should give it to you, and that you would be waiting for it."

"You are the American? The one Raouf was waiting for?"

"Yes," answered Ferris. He was being drawn in deeper, but it didn't matter. All that mattered was that they take the tape.

Hassan nodded. He knew who Ferris was—that was why he had opened the door—but he was unhappy. "We were waiting for this tape a few days ago. But then we lost contact. Where is Raouf? Why haven't we heard from him?"

"I don't know," answered Ferris. "I just know he wanted you to have this." He handed the brown paper parcel to his host. Hassan carefully unwrapped it and then looked at the cassette. He checked some markings that were written in Arabic on the side. They must have been code words. Hassan read them twice and then nodded.

"Thanks to the God," he said.

"Thanks God," repeated Ferris. "I will go now. Raouf said I should leave when I gave you the tape."

"No," said Hassan. "First we look at the tape."

A liquid heat flooded into Ferris. The dimensions of the room seemed to shrink. He had to push the room back somehow before it crushed him.

"I must leave," said Ferris, backing toward the door. "When you see the tape, you will understand. This must be shown on Al Jazeera."

"We will decide that," said Hassan. He handed the tape to the other man, who turned on the television set in the little living room. It had a built-in VCR player. In a few moments they would put the cassette in the player and the images would be on the screen. Ferris knew that he was running out of time.

"I have to leave," he repeated. "Now."

Hassan moved behind Ferris to block the door. This is it, thought Ferris. He stole a glance at the window and remembered the shop below. He thought he remembered that it had an awning.

"Play the tape," said Hassan. His assistant put it into the slot, and an image began to flicker on the screen.

Ferris moved instinctively, ignoring his bad leg, his bruised mus-

cles, the fear that was knotted in his limbs and joints. He turned so
that his back faced the window and hurled himself at full force
against the frame, shielding his head as best he could. He heard the
wood of the window frame splinter and crack against the force of his
body, and felt the shards of glass slicing his skin like a thousand
paper cuts. And then he was floating through the air, not sure if his
body would hit the sharp stone of the cobbled pavement or the soft
cloth of the awning. It took only an instant, but the next thing he felt
was a bounce against the awning frame, just enough to break his fall,
and then he was on the ground.

People in the streets were screaming, pointing at Ferris. He didn't
realize why until he put his hand to the back of his head and pulled
it back, covered in blood. He had only a few more seconds before
Hassan and his man would be down in the street after him. He tried
to stand and staggered for a moment before gaining his balance. And
then he began to run down the street, moving as fast as his bad leg
would allow. People were still screaming, but he didn't care. The best
thing that could happen to him was that the Syrian police would
arrest him. But they left him alone.

As Ferris neared the gate of Bab Touma, he realized that Hassan
and his man weren't following, either. Where were they? And then
it was obvious. They had started the tape just as Ferris had made his
leap. They had been transfixed by the image of Suleiman: shaken,
stunned, paralyzed. The poison pill had touched the first node. Now
it would continue and continue, passing up every nerve and synapse
until it reached the center of the center. And then the lights would
begin to go out, and the system would begin to recoil and wither, the
skin would peel back against itself.

FERRIS'S DRIVER was waiting just where he had left him. He had
a towel in the trunk, and Ferris used it to wipe away the blood.
Instinct told him to stay away from a Syrian hospital or the American
Embassy. He directed the driver to the French Embassy, the best and

most modern in the city. He explained to the French military officer at the front gate that he needed to see the DGSE station commander. Perhaps it was the blood, perhaps the look of absolute determination in Ferris's eye, but the French soldier invited him inside, behind the embassy's heavy door, while he made a call. The DGSE man arrived a minute later with a nurse who cleaned Ferris's wounds in the embassy clinic and called a doctor. He had broken two ribs in the fall, and he needed more than forty stitches to close all the cuts, but he had been lucky. Ferris explained a little of what he had done—not much, but enough that the DGSE man wouldn't look ridiculous when he filed his cable. When the Frenchman asked why he hadn't gone to the U.S. Embassy, Ferris answered, "I'm retired," and the Frenchman smiled sympathetically.

The French officer offered a diplomatic car and a driver for the return trip to Beirut, and Ferris happily accepted. It was over. He had only one purpose now, and that was to find Alice.

THE VIDEO ran on Al Jazeera twenty-four hours later. The announcer called it "a traitor's confession." It was like watching a public hanging. It might be appalling, but you couldn't take your eyes off it.

By the time the video ran, Ferris was back in Hani's care and protection. He didn't even bother to watch. He let Suleiman's "confession" do its work—let the shame and recrimination reverberate through the Muslim world, let the denials and countercharges percolate, let the spokesmen rant or gloat or simply duck for cover. It wasn't a story that would take days or weeks. It would require years before the network recovered from this toxin. For if the movement could not trust Suleiman, the sublime architect of the jihad, then it could not trust anything.

37

THE FIRST DAYS WERE AWKWARD. Neither of them wanted to say too much, for fear that would set loose a cascade of raw emotion that would destroy any chance of happiness. They were careful with each other, like a couple who have the good sense not to probe about past loves. Ferris had promised he would unravel all the lies and live only the truth, but that wasn't so easy. His was a life in which nearly everything turned out to be lies. It was more a question of starting over than of rewriting what had gone before, and Alice seemed to understand that. And there were secrets she had kept, as well—mysteries of her life in Jordan that she could not have explained fully to Ferris, or even to herself.

They met back at the hospital in Tripoli, where Alice had remained during Ferris's absence. When she first walked into the sunroom, Ferris wept. He hadn't meant to, but he couldn't help himself. He tried to tell Alice what had happened and then gave up, and she just held him close. She saw the bruises across his face and neck; she moved to take the bandaged hand in hers, but she realized with a start that he was missing a finger, and she could imagine the rest. Ferris didn't bother to tell her about his final struggle in Damascus. That could come later, if at all.

Hani gave them a car and driver, and they walked out the door of the hospital into the radiant winter sunshine of northern Lebanon. There was snow on the mountain behind them, and the purest blue in the sparkling waters. The purity of sun and sea seemed to take away some of the stain in the moment they set foot outdoors. Ferris went to the mosque in Tripoli where, according to Hani, his great-grandfather had been a sheik. He wanted to see it. He showed Alice the stone house where his grandfather had been born, and she just smiled, as if she, too, had always known he was a Muslim.

They drove south that afternoon along the coast to the tarnished emerald of Beirut. Hani had reserved a suite for them in the Phoenicia, overlooking the curve of the harbor and the snow of the mountain beyond. Alice hung out the "Do Not Disturb" sign and they undressed each other slowly, Alice being very careful of his wounds. She led him to bed, and they didn't make love for a long while; just touched and remembered and let love and desire return. He waited for her; it wasn't for him to initiate, now, but for her to take him. And she did.

They stayed in bed that night and all the next day, ordering up meals from room service and sitting out on the porch of their suite that looked onto the sea. They had infinite time now, nowhere to be, no lies to tell. Ferris was half asleep that afternoon when he heard Alice singing him a lullaby. She stopped when he awoke, and then started again, stroking the wiry black hair atop his head. Ferris let his mind amble back in time. He had lived the story backward, in a sense, but did he understand it forward? He thought so.

"You were part of it," he said.

"At the end, yes." She had stopped singing, but she kept stroking his hair. "I had been to Syria before. I knew what I was doing."

"For Hani?"

"Yes. He helped me stay in Jordan, so I helped him sometimes. But this last time, I did it for you. He said that you would be safe. And that otherwise you would never be free."

"Is there anything you need to tell me?"

She thought a long while. "No," she said. She touched his face and smiled, and after a time she fell asleep beside him.

THEY FLEW back to Amman in Hani's private jet. Hoffman was waiting, and though he may have been angry, he didn't show it. He was taking credit for everything, just as Hani had predicted, even the video on Al Jazeera. Hoffman wanted a full debriefing, and Ferris gave it to him. He left out nothing, and the story took nearly three hours in the bubble, start to finish.

"I want to resign from the agency," Ferris said when he had finished the story. Hoffman didn't try to talk him out of it. He mumbled something about how he understood entirely. Obviously he was relieved. Ferris was the only American who knew all the facts. In that respect, he was the last person Hoffman would have wanted to see at the CIA.

Hoffman offered Ferris a generous farewell package, not quite a golden handshake but at least silver-plated. There would be lifetime disability payments, plus a special early retirement deal because he had been wounded on duty, plus a special award from the director's unvouchered "Performance Fund," plus accumulated back pay for all the vacation hours Ferris had never used, and overtime and hazardous-duty pay he hadn't collected. It wasn't a fortune, but it was handsome. Hoffman said they wanted to give Ferris a medal, in secret, and asked if he would come back to Headquarters so the director could present it. But Ferris said no, they could keep the medal for him in a lockbox, next to the one from Iraq.

ROGER FARES and Alice Melville were married in Amman that June. He had disguised his appearance a bit, let his hair grow and worn a beard. Alice said he looked even handsomer. It was a simple ceremony. Ferris hadn't become a Muslim, but there was a Sunni sheik at the wedding, along with the Episcopal priest who said the vows. Alice's family flew out, along with Ferris's mother. He wasn't going to have a best man and then decided to ask Hani, who exulted in this confirmation that he had been forgiven for his manipulation. After the wedding, Alice continued her work with Palestinian refugee children. Ferris joined her, and the people in the camps were happy to have him. He spoke their language, and he listened to what they said. They worked happily through the fall, settling into Alice's apartment in the old quarter and teaching each other to cook.

One day in September, just over a year after they had met, they had a visit from Hani. He asked at first to talk to Ferris alone, but Ferris refused a private conversation, saying that was all over. So Hani told them both: He'd had an inquiry from a British journalist from the *Sunday Times* about a shoot-out in Aleppo involving a recently retired American diplomat based in Amman named Roger Ferris. Hani said he could turn the story off—he had enough friends in London, and in Beirut, Paris and Tel Aviv, too, for that matter, if that's where the leak had begun. But the word was out. That meant Ferris and Alice were no longer safe in Amman. Hani would protect them, but he wanted them to know.

They moved in early October to another city in the Arab world, where there was a relief agency that needed volunteers. They didn't tell even their friends where they were going. Before they left Amman, Alice learned that she was pregnant. The child was born in the Arab world, and in that sense, Roger and Alice had gone into the land itself, been penetrated by it, bled into its veins. They could not escape the enchanting, afflicted culture that had drawn them into its arms, and they did not want to. So they lived.